THE LOST

THE LOST

Simon Beckett

ORION

First published in Great Britain in 2021 by Orion Fiction,
an imprint of The Orion Publishing Group Ltd
Carmelite House, 50 Victoria Embankment
London EC4Y 0DZ

An Hachette UK Company

1 3 5 7 9 10 8 6 4 2

A CIP catalogue record for this book is
available from the British Library.

ISBN (Hardback) 978 1 3987 0690 3
ISBN (Export Trade Paperback) 978 1 4091 9277 0
ISBN (eBook) 978 1 4091 9279 4
ISBN (Audio) 978 1 4091 9280 0

Typeset by Born Group
Printed and bound in Great Britain by Clays Ltd, Elcograf S.p.A.

MIX
Paper from
responsible sources
FSC www.fsc.org FSC® C104740

www.orionbooks.co.uk

For Hilary

Chapter 1

It was when he smelled the blood that Jonah realised he was in trouble.

The quayside was pitch-black. None of the streetlights were working, leaving the crumbling warehouses in darkness, abandoned relics from a different era. In the old Saab's headlights, the scene resembled an industrial ghost town. Staring out through the windscreen, Jonah was reminded that, even though he'd lived in London most of his life, there were still corners of it he didn't know existed. And didn't want to know, if this place was anything to go by.

The quayside hadn't been easy to find. It was part of a desolate stretch of the Thames, an undeveloped area of riverbank that wasn't even shown on his phone's map. The directions he'd been given were vague, and several times he'd been forced to backtrack when some rutted road proved to be a dead end. Now he was parked on a patch of weed-choked wasteland, facing a long brick wall. Across the river, the sparkling lights of high-end apartments, bars and restaurants were strung out like jewels. Here, though, all was darkness. The sprawling redevelopment that had engulfed the rest of the docklands had, for some reason, bypassed this watery cul-de-sac. Although that wasn't surprising, given its name. Jonah had thought it must be a joke, but no. The proof was right there in front of him, a rusted street sign:

Slaughter Quay.

A couple of hours earlier, he'd been sitting outside a pub with a few others from his team, enjoying the late-summer evening after a handgun training session. His phone had rung while he was at the bar waiting to be served. He didn't recognise the number, and almost didn't bother taking it. But there were still people waiting their turn ahead of him, so after a moment he'd answered.

'Jonah? It's me.' And then, in case he might have forgotten: 'Gavin.'

Even though it had been the best part of a decade since he'd heard the voice, the years seemed to fall away in an instant. So did the pit of his stomach.

'You there?'

Jonah moved to a quieter part of the bar, the drinks forgotten. 'What do you want?'

'I need your help.'

No 'How's it going?' or 'Long time no see'. Jonah felt his jaw muscles clench.

'Why would you need my help?'

'Because you're the only one I can trust.'

Surprise momentarily silenced Jonah. 'You're going to have to give me more than that.'

There was a pause. 'I screwed up. I got it all wrong. Everything . . .'

'What are you talking about?'

'I'll explain when you get here.'

'Jesus, you can't just expect me to –'

'There's an old warehouse on the south bank, a place called Slaughter Quay,' Gavin went on in a rush. 'You won't find it on your satnav but I'll text you directions. It's the last warehouse on the quayside. I'll be waiting for you outside at midnight.'

'*Midnight?* Are you *serious?*'

'You'll understand when you get here.' And then Gavin had said a word Jonah had never heard in all the time they'd been friends. 'Please.'

The line went dead. *Shit.*

'You all right?'

It was Khan, another sergeant from SCO19, the Metropolitan Police's firearms unit. The big man's shoulders and neck were thick with muscle, and his arms and chest threatened to burst the white T-shirt. Jonah had once seen him kick a door, and the knifeman standing behind it, halfway across a room. But, off duty, he was a family man, the person anyone in the unit with a problem would go to.

Putting away his phone, Jonah nodded. 'Just someone I hadn't heard from in a while.'

'Problems?'

Jonah wasn't sure how to answer that. 'It's probably nothing. But he sounded –'

He broke off as someone gave him a push from behind. 'I thought you were going to the bar? Fuck's sake, I could brew them faster than you get served.'

Jonah looked round at the compact woman scowling up at him. Nolan did that a lot. The policewoman was several inches shorter than him and barely reached Khan's shoulder, but he wouldn't have given much for either of their chances if push came to shove. Even less if it was your turn to get a round in.

'We're having a conversation,' Khan told her, giving her his sergeant's look.

'Right.' She considered. 'Give me the money and I'll get them.'

Jonah had to laugh. 'It's OK, I'll go.'

'You sure?' Khan asked.

'Yeah, it's fine.' Jonah gave a shrug. 'Probably nothing anyway.'

He'd tried to convince himself of that as he'd gone to the bar. Whatever mess Gavin had got himself into, he could sort it out on his own. Jonah didn't owe him anything. Not one damn thing.

Yet the call had got under his skin. Even as he'd taken the drinks over to the table, he'd kept coming back to one thing Gavin had said.

You're the only one I can trust.

That might have held true once. Time was Jonah might have said the same thing. He'd known Gavin forever. Best friends at school, joined the Met and gone through training together and then been posted to the same borough. Gavin had always been more outgoing, with an easy attitude and ready grin that disguised a fiercely competitive nature. They'd shared a flat, even after Gavin passed his detective's exam and joined what was then the Specialist Crime Directorate, investigating human exploitation and organised crime. For a while Jonah had considered becoming a detective as well. He'd been told he had the aptitude by his superior officers, who'd urged him to sign up for the trainee detective programme. But for some reason – maybe because he didn't like to feel pushed – he'd chosen a different path. Surprising even himself, he'd taken the rigorous training required to be accepted onto SCO19, the Met's elite firearms unit. Gavin had mocked the decision, calling him an adrenaline junkie. Yet they'd stayed friends. And when Jonah started seeing Chrissie and Gavin hooked up with Marie, the four of them became a close-knit group. Nights out, holidays together. Good times.

But that had been years ago. Another life. So why was

Gavin crawling out of the woodwork now, asking for Jonah's help? Two things Gavin had never lacked were confidence and friends. He'd have to be desperate to call Jonah, and in the end that was what decided it. Because, no matter how much Jonah wanted to dismiss it, he kept coming back to the same thing.

Gavin had sounded *scared*.

So, making his excuses, Jonah had left the pub and gone back to his car.

Now here he was, at a derelict quayside in the middle of nowhere. Switching off the engine, he took a torch from the Saab's glove compartment and climbed out. An Audi he guessed must be Gavin's was parked nearby, but other than that there was no sign of life. An overgrown path led to the dark hulks of empty warehouses and industrial buildings, beyond which could be glimpsed the river, silvered by the sickle moon. Switching on his torch, Jonah set off towards them.

The path took him to a narrow lane that ran between boarded-up buildings. On one of them the ghost of ancient signage was still visible: Jolley's Tannery. Fine Hides and Skins. Others identified themselves as wholesale butchers or meat processing companies, while a huge, hangar-like structure declared itself to be an abattoir. Slaughter Quay had been aptly named.

It was an unsettling place to be at night. Jonah wasn't normally bothered by the dark, but he found himself listening for any footsteps beside his own as he walked down the narrow lane. He was glad when he reached the end of it and emerged onto the quayside. The lapping of water was louder here. Broken cobblestones showed through disintegrating asphalt, and the air was dank, smelling of salt water, rotting weeds and oil. A cluster of barges were moored together on the tar-black water, bobbing in unsynchronised rhythm. The quiet was broken by low bumps and creaks as they rubbed against each other. A larger boat was tethered slightly apart, and as Jonah walked past it there was a sudden hiss. Startled, he swung the torch, then relaxed as its beam caught a reflected glint of a cat's eyes. The dirty-looking creature was crouched in the shadow of a hatchway, hunched protectively over a part-eaten burger. One eye was half closed with injury or infection. The other glared malevolently as it gave a warning yowl.

'It's OK, it's all yours,' Jonah murmured, turning away. As he did, the torch beam fell on ornate lettering painted on the boat's bow: *The Oracle*. It was partly obscured by a rubber tyre tied to the side as a fender, but as Jonah shone the torch on it, another hiss from the cat reminded him he'd outstayed his welcome.

'I'm going, I'm going.'

The ground was muddy, squelching underfoot as he continued. Up ahead he could see where the quay ended at a lone warehouse that backed on to water on two sides. It was half hidden behind a framework of scaffolding, over which hung ragged sheets of translucent polythene. A sagging wire-mesh fence surrounded it, preventing Jonah from going any further.

There was no one else there.

Jonah swore and checked the time. Almost ten past midnight. He was late but not by much. He wondered if Gavin could have given up and left, but then he remembered the Audi parked by the quayside. He'd only assumed it was Gavin's, but it was hard to imagine anyone else being out there at that time of night.

So where was he?

He shone the torch around, but the quayside remained stubbornly dark and still. As the minutes passed, tension began to form a knot in Jonah's gut. When it got to twenty past, he called the number Gavin had called from. Pick up, Gavin, he thought, when the number began to ring. Then, as he listened, he became aware of another ringing, this one much fainter. Behind him.

Coming from the warehouse.

Jonah turned to stare through the mesh fencing. When his call went to voicemail, there was one last chime from the unlit building, followed by silence. The knot in his stomach grew tighter as Jonah redialled. The lonely ringing started again, and this time there was no doubting that it was inside the warehouse.

Oh, shit . . .

Ending the call, Jonah stared at the dark building through the cross-linked fencing. Underneath the scaffolding, the warehouse was an indistinct hulk, all hard angles and shadows. He debated calling it in, but if Gavin was injured it would take too long for any back-up to get there. And there was still a chance this could be a false alarm. It didn't feel that way, though, and Jonah realised he didn't have a choice.

He was going to have to go in.

'Jesus, Gavin . . .' he muttered.

There was a large metal gate set in the middle of the wire fence. It was secured by a sturdy-looking padlock, but further along Jonah found a gap in the fence big enough to squeeze through. Crossing the broken asphalt to the warehouse, he pushed through the polythene sheets to a pair of huge, hangar-like doors. They were locked but to one side of them was another door. When he tried it, it swung inwards with a creak of stiff hinges.

Jonah shone his torch through the open doorway. The light disappeared into a cavernous space, broken by girder-like iron pillars that disappeared up to a high ceiling.

'Gavin, you in there?'

His voice rang out before being swallowed. The air in the warehouse was cold and dank, heavy with a churchlike silence as he stepped inside. Taking out his phone, he called Gavin's number. The answering ring from the darkness seemed shockingly loud. It came from further inside the warehouse. Going towards it, he saw a faint glow behind one of the iron pillars. The phone was lying on the ground behind it, Jonah's name illuminated on the screen. It winked out when he rang off.

Christ, Gavin, what the hell have you got yourself into? And me?

He shone the torch around. Rough-cut timber, bags of lime and cement and rolls of translucent polythene were stacked haphazardly at one side, but there was no sign of Gavin. Then the torch beam caught something else lying on the floor. A police warrant card, lying face up to display a tiny photograph next to the owner's name and rank.

Gavin McKinney, Detective Sergeant.

There was a dark smudge on it, and Jonah felt something turn over in him as he realised what it was. It was then he noticed the dark splashes on the stone flags nearby. They glistened like oil, but Jonah knew it wasn't. He could smell it now, only faint but unmistakable.

The coppery tang of blood.

The black spatters formed a trail that vanished into the shadows. Heart thumping, he began to follow it. The splashes ended at a pair of double doors set in a bare brick wall. A sign reading *Loading Bay* was stencilled onto the peeling paintwork of one of them. It stood slightly open, a large, unfastened padlock hanging loosely from a hasp. Jonah hesitated. The smart thing to do would be to go back, to call for a blue-light response and let uniformed officers and paramedics find out what was on the other side of the door.

But by then Gavin could be dead.

He gave the door a soft push. It swung open with a groan, and he quickly stepped through, tensed for an attack as he fanned the beam around. None came. The light from his torch showed he was in a long, narrow room. Heavy chains hung down from a rusted winch fixed to a rail in the ceiling. Behind them was a huge, sliding door made from old timbers and black metal brackets. Jonah guessed it would open on to the quayside, where boats would have come to load or unload.

'Gavin?'

Water dripped somewhere in the darkness with a musical *plink*, but there was no answer. The smell of blood was stronger in here, mixed with something else. A cloying, animal reek. Jonah aimed the torch at the floor to see where the blood splashes led. Its beam passed over lengths of scaffolding poles and a pile of wadded-up polythene before coming to rest on something else.

A pair of legs.

Jonah rushed over, then stopped. In the torch beam, a man's body was lying face down on a large square of polythene sheeting. His arms had been fastened behind his back with a plastic tie, and another bound his feet at the ankles. Jonah couldn't see his face, but even after ten years he recognised the lean build and curly dark hair. Hair that was now matted with blood. Black in the torchlight, a viscous pool of it had spilled over the translucent sheet and onto the stone flags, fanning out like a dark halo.

Jonah found his voice. 'Gavin . . .?'

Nothing. Gavin's body had an eloquent stillness. Pale shards of bone and pulped tissue were visible in the dark hair, but Jonah could see that the blood was no longer flowing. It had begun to set on the polythene sheet and flagstones. Even so, he had to make sure. Careful to avoid the blood, he bent down and felt the side of Gavin's throat, below his jaw. The skin was cold and flaccid, bristly with a day or two's growth of whiskers but unmoved by any pulse.

9

Feeling numb, Jonah straightened and stepped away. A sound made him wheel round. There was no one there, and a moment later the *plink* of dripping water came again. He breathed out. There was no longer any question of what to do. This was a murder scene. He needed to get out of there and call it in without contaminating it any more than he had already.

Trying to close his mind to what was lying on the ground, he tried his phone. There was no reception. Gavin's phone had rung in the main warehouse, so the loading bay's thick internal wall must be blocking the signal. He'd started back for the door when another noise stopped him. It was too faint to place, but this time he was sure it wasn't dripping water. He stood, listening. At first all he could hear was the blood pulsing in his ears, then the sound came again. Clearer, this time.

A rustle of plastic.

The hairs on Jonah's arms rose as he turned towards the mound of wadded-up polythene sheeting lying a few yards away. It wasn't a single mound, he saw now, but three large, distinct bundles. They could have been building waste, but as the torch beam fell on them they reminded him of something else.

Cocoons.

As though hypnotised, Jonah felt himself drawn closer. The bundles were each five or six feet in length, bound up with black gaffer tape. They were dusty, coated with white powder that made it impossible to see inside, but now Jonah realised where the rank, animal odour he'd noticed earlier was coming from.

Gavin's body wasn't the only one down there.

Get out. Now! Jonah began to back away, but then the same noise came again. A silky, crinkling whisper. He saw that a corner of sheeting had come loose on the topmost polythene bundle. Reaching down, he eased the plastic aside. Below it, blurred beneath more polythene, was a face.

As Jonah stared, the mouth opened and the polythene was sucked tight.

He stumbled backwards. The urge to run overwhelmed him before reason asserted itself. At least one of these people was still alive.

But not for much longer.

'It's OK, I'm going to get you out,' Jonah said, fumbling at the polythene. There were multiple layers, wound round and round and held in place with long strips of gaffer. He wrenched and tore at both, trying to find an edge he could grip, but it was bound too tightly. The translucent covering made the blurred features look as though they were underwater, drawing in over them before slowly filling out again. But each time was weaker than the last. Pulling out his car keys, he tried to pierce the plastic with a sharp corner. It resisted, then gave way with a soft *pop*. Jonah tore at the hole with his fingers, until with a sibilant crackle, the polythene parted as though it had been unzipped.

Now the lower half of a face was revealed. The mouth was partly open but there was no movement or response. *Come on, please breathe*, Jonah willed, trying to tear more of the sheeting.

Suddenly, the mouth coughed and opened wider, spasming as it sucked in air. The polythene ripped, exposing a head topped with thick black curls. It was a young woman. Not much more than a girl, Jonah thought, although it was hard to be sure. Her skin was crusted with dried blood. In places it was livid and blistered, caked with the same white dust that coated the sheeting. Her face was contorted with pain and fear, but neither that nor the darkness could disguise a striking beauty that made the sight of her now all the more grotesque. Wishing he had some water to give her, Jonah continued ripping at the polythene, ignoring the human stench that came from the fouled plastic. He started talking as she coughed and fought for breath.

'You're safe now. I'm a police officer, I'm going to get you out, OK?'

She made a thin keening sound in her throat, then said something in a language Jonah didn't recognise. It sounded like it could be Arabic.

'I'm sorry, I don't understand. Just try to lie still so I can get you out.'

'. . . *hurts* . . .'

'I know, I'll be as fast as I can,' he told her. *Keep her talking.* 'What's your name?'

She murmured something he didn't catch. Christ, she was slipping away.

'Na . . . Nadine . . .'

'Hi, Nadine. I'm Jonah.'

He spoke with a calmness he didn't feel, but now another sensation was beginning to filter through the urgency. His hands had begun to burn, and he noticed how the skin was smeared with the powder from the polythene sheet. It looked blotched and angry, and remembering the bags of building supplies outside he realised what it was.

Quicklime.

Oh, Christ. Jonah tried to think. The caustic powder could eat away skin and flesh down to the bone, and the woman was covered in it. She must be in agony, and Jonah knew she needed more help than he could give her. He checked the signal bars on his phone and saw there was still no reception. Much as he hated it, he knew what he had to do.

'Nadine, I'm going to have to go outside to call for help,' he said, though he wasn't sure if she could understand. 'I'll be back as quick as I can, OK? I'll leave you the torch.'

He set it down on the floor; he couldn't leave the young

woman alone down here in the dark. She moaned again, becoming more agitated. Jonah wondered if she was delirious, but the reddened eyes were lucid and terrified as she stared up at him. No, not at him, he realised.

Behind him.

He heard the soft footstep as he spun around, bringing up his arms in a block. Too late. Something knocked them aside and smashed into his head. There was a burst of light and pain, followed by a weightlessness like falling.

And then nothing.

Chapter 2

There was the chink of rusted chains in the dark, like an unoiled child's swing. It had an irregular, ragged rhythm that beat at Jonah's head. He tried to retreat back into the blackness, away from the awful sound and the knowledge it carried with it. But that led to an empty tunnel, filled with dead leaves. *No, no, no.* Now he could feel someone else with him, a familiar presence. *Gavin.* His voice was a whisper from the darkness.

Once you lose something, you never find it again.

The rhythm of the chains was pounding in his head. Jonah felt dizzy and sick, as though he were spinning. Christ, why did his head hurt so much? Something sticky was in his eyes, gumming them shut. It took him several attempts to open them. When he did, he still couldn't see. Everything was black. The chains had stopped, but the hard surface he was lying on crackled when he moved. He tried to sit up. He couldn't. His arms were pinioned behind him, and his legs were tied together as well.

Panicking, Jonah began to struggle. It made his head throb even more and he slumped back as a wave of nausea rushed over him. He wondered if he'd gone blind. Gradually, other discomforts began to filter into his awareness. Thirst. Cold. His hands were burning and he was shivering, aching all over. There was a foul smell in the dank air, and now memory began to return. The warehouse. A young woman, coated with quicklime and half suffocated, wrapped in polythene along with two other bodies. And Gavin.

Gavin.

Realisation came to him then. Someone had knocked him unconscious and blood from the wound had stuck his eyes together. And now he was bound hand and foot, lying on – oh, Jesus – lying on a sheet of polythene.

He began to slow his breathing, focusing on his diaphragm as he took long, steadying breaths. Gradually, the panic receded. Opening his eyes, he realised that the dark wasn't as absolute as he'd thought. He was able to detect depth, maybe even shapes in the blackness. Turning his head – gingerly, every motion threatened to split it – he could make out a pale, vertical line of light. It was a partly open doorway, probably the way he'd come. And then he realised the light was growing stronger, accompanied by something else.

Footsteps.

Jonah shut his eyes as the door opened and the torch beam picked him out. He lay still, barely daring to breathe as the footsteps came closer. They halted next to him. Through his eyelids, the torch beam was filtered to a blood-red glow as it was shone directly onto his face.

Then it was gone, leaving miniature suns flaring behind his eyes. The footsteps continued past him before stopping again. There were more sounds: a grunt of exertion and the rustling of thick plastic. Opening his eyes to slits, Jonah saw the torch beam aimed at something on the ground. Silhouetted against it, little more than a shadow, was a bulky figure. It was stooping over something, but it was only when the crinkle of plastic came again that he understood what it was.

The figure was wrapping Gavin's body in the polythene sheet.

A helpless fury rose up in Jonah. He strained at the bonds fastening his hands and feet, then froze as the polythene he was lying on crackled. It was only soft, but the silhouette reacted. Jonah closed his eyes again as the torch beam swung back to him. He lay immobile, as though this were a nightmarish game of statues. *Don't come over. Please.*

Then the light went from his face.

He could feel himself shaking as the sounds of Gavin's body being wrapped up restarted. He tried to stay still, not daring to move in case the treacherous polythene gave him away again. Careful not to disturb it, he tested his bindings. Whatever was fastening his ankles was on top of his jeans and socks, but he could feel something smooth and thin digging into his wrists. A nylon tie, the same as Gavin had been tied with. Jonah tried to quash the despair he felt. The slender bands looked flimsy but were virtually unbreakable. Impossible to loosen, once they'd been ratcheted tight.

A noise came from where the shadowy figure was working. Through half-open eyes, Jonah saw it cut another length of polythene from a roll and spread it on the floor. Backlit by the torch beam, the shadow's broad back blocked his view as it heaved at the polythene-wrapped shape on the floor. There was the sound of tape being unpeeled from a roll, followed by more grunts of exertion.

Then the figure was standing. The moving torch beam allowed only glimpses as it began dragging Gavin's covered body, slithering it across the stone flags to the sliding door in the far wall. Letting it thump back onto the ground, the figure set the torch down beside it, then stepped into the shadows beyond its beam. There was the ratchet of chains being pulled, followed by a heavy metallic grating as the door slid open on its track.

From where he lay, Jonah could see a paler rectangle of night sky through the gap, and he heard the soft lapping of water. Then the figure was dragging Gavin's body outside. There was a heavy, hollow thump, as though it had been dropped into a boat, before the figure returned. Chains chinked and rasped as the sliding door was closed. The figure bent to retrieve the torch, and Jonah shut his eyes as the beam swung towards him.

The footsteps came over to where he was lying.

Heavy breathing came from above him. Even through closed eyelids, the torch was bright on his face. Something hard shoved against his shoulder. He allowed himself to flop loosely as a foot prodded him. *Don't move, don't breathe, don't think.*

The light was gone and the figure was walking away.

Jesus . . . Jonah opened his eyes a crack, in time to see the torch beam bobbing towards the door. Against it, he caught sight of a tall shadow before it stepped out through the doorway.

And then all was darkness again.

Jonah didn't know what had happened to his own torch, but that didn't matter. Only now daring to breathe, he began tugging at the tie binding his wrists. He tried to ignore the pain in his head, knowing that if he didn't break free now he never would. The tie resisted, and in frustration he gave his wrists an angry jerk.

He felt the tie give.

Jonah stopped, not trusting what he'd just felt. When he strained against the tie again nothing happened. But when he tried twisting his wrists, applying torque as well as tension . . .

The thin strip loosened another few millimetres.

He repeated the pressure and was rewarded with even more give. The tie was either damaged or faulty. Wrenching with the full strength of his arms, Jonah felt it sliding looser and looser.

Then, with a last twist, his hands came free.

His head was hammering as he pushed himself upright and reached for the tie binding his ankles. He felt a crushing disappointment when it didn't loosen in the same way. But whoever had bound him had been in a hurry. They'd rushed it, fastening the restraint over his jeans instead of around his bare ankles. Jonah tugged the denim out from under it but the slender noose was still too tight. Pulling off his trainers and socks, he tried again. The tie slid so far then jammed on the bone. *No, you bastard!* In desperation, listening for footsteps coming back, he tried to force it. It sliced into him like a potato peeler, but the blood acted as a lubricant. With a last effort that scraped away another layer of skin, he got it over his feet.

Jonah stood up, and almost collapsed as dizziness threatened to overwhelm him. He bent over, lowering his head as it throbbed in time with his heart. When he was sure he wasn't going to throw up or pass out, he straightened. The darkness was absolute. He tried to make out where the young woman, Nadine, and the other two polythene-wrapped victims were, but he couldn't see anything. And he didn't dare risk calling out. He hated the thought of what he had to do, but knew he'd no choice. If any of them was going to survive this, Jonah had to get out and get help.

Feeling around with his bare feet, he found his trainers and jammed them back on. He only had a vague idea where the door he'd come through was, but once he reached the wall he'd be able to find it. Arms outstretched, he began to edge forward and almost immediately kicked something.

He stopped dead as it skittered across the floor. But the noise hadn't been loud enough for anyone outside to hear, and Jonah felt a prickle of excitement. *Please. Please be what I think.* Kneeling down, he groped on the floor for the object.

A blue glow lit up the darkness.

Jonah could have wept. It was his phone, probably dropped when he was attacked. There was still no signal, and he dared not risk the flashlight being seen, but the backlit screen alone seemed like a beacon after so long in the dark. Jonah held it up and the room around him emerged dimly from the shadows. His euphoria died when he saw Gavin's blood pooled on the flag-stones, straight edges showing where it had overrun the polythene sheet. Just visible in the shadows beyond it were the cocoon-like shapes of the other victims, ghostly pale in the blackness. Now he had light, Jonah started over to check on the young woman, and as he did so he heard footsteps outside.

Someone was coming.

Shit, *shit*! Jonah looked around for something he could use as a weapon, but there was nothing. And he was already out of time. Hurrying to the doorway, he pressed himself flat against the wall next to it. As he reached it, his phone screen went out, plunging the room into blackness again. The footsteps were closer now. Jonah took a deep breath, trying to calm himself. *You can do this. It's just like an op.* Except that it wasn't. There was no team to watch his back, no one to call on for help. He was on his own. *Don't think about that. Go in hard and fast and forget everything else.* He took a deep breath, readying himself as the footsteps reached the doorway.

And stopped.

Jonah felt deafened by his own heartbeat. Each pulse threat-ened to split his head as he waited. There was a creak as the door swung further open. A wedge of light from a torch spread across the floor, outlining the edges of the door.

Adenoidal breathing came from outside. Jonah felt a feather-ing of disturbed air on his skin, then there was the sound of someone stepping over the threshold. But they didn't emerge from behind the open door. Jonah saw the torch beam begin to fan around the loading bay, and before it could show the empty sheet of polythene where he'd been tied, Jonah threw all his weight against the door.

Whoever was on the other side was big. The impact jolted Jonah's teeth and hurt his head, but there was a *whuf* of escaping breath. The torch clattered onto the floor, breaking the darkness with crazed swathes of light as it rolled back and forth. Flinging back the door, Jonah launched a kick at the figure but made only a glancing contact. Then the air was driven from his lungs as a shoulder rammed into him. He slammed into the wall, breathing in a sour, vinegary smell of old sweat. Heavy blows pummelled at him from the darkness. Jonah took most of them on his raised forearms, but something caught him on the side of his head. He managed to swing an elbow and felt it hit bone, bringing his knee up as the man in front of him jerked away. It thudded into a meaty thigh rather than groin, but caused his opponent to stumble back. Through blurred vision Jonah saw him double over, and for an instant thought he was falling. Then he heard the scrape of metal on stone as the shadowy figure snatched up a length of scaffolding pole from the ground. In desperation he kicked out before the other man could swing it and felt the flat of his foot sink into a heavy gut. There was a gasp of pain.

Then Jonah's kneecap exploded.

He cried out, but as he fell he grabbed the other man and dragged him down as well. They crashed onto the stone floor. His opponent was bigger and heavier, and there was a *thock* as his head struck the stone floor. Jonah clawed for a flailing arm and managed to lock it under him. He tried to clamp his legs around the man's middle but his left one refused to work. Gritting his teeth, Jonah used the pain as a goad, squirming around and partly pinning the bigger man. He bucked like a fish but Jonah clung to him. A fist clubbed at his head. He held on, close to passing out. The man's breath was coming in choked whistles now, his struggles becoming more frantic. *Hold on. Just a little longer. Hold on.* It became like a mantra, repeating again and again as Jonah rode out his captive's attempts to break free.

At some point he realised the thrashing had stopped.

For a while he didn't let go. Couldn't. His body felt locked, clenched in place. Even when he tried, his limbs wouldn't obey. Eventually, he forced them to loosen their hold. The man slumped and lay still. Jonah flopped over onto his back, muscles quivering as he sucked in air. Pain threatened to carry him away. There was a humming noise in his ears and a fluttering, like wings beating behind his eyes. The darkness seemed to take on depth. He felt himself sinking into it.

Come on! Move!

Jonah rolled over, and promptly threw up. Retching, he took a moment to recover, then he groped on the floor for the torch and shone it on his attacker. The man lay crumpled on his side, one arm draped over his face as though to shield his eyes from the light. His head was hidden by the dirty jacket that had rucked up around it during the struggle. Tensing, Jonah reached out and prodded him in the back.

The man lolled, but there was no other reaction.

Jonah sagged. He couldn't tell if the man was breathing or not, and the possibility that he might have killed him flitted through his mind before being drowned out by the need to get help. He started to push himself to his feet, only to cry out as his knee gave way and dumped him back on the floor. He lay gasping, then turned the torch onto his injured knee.

Oh, fuck . . .

His jeans were soaked with blood. The knee beneath them was misshapen and already starting to swell, and Jonah knew that he wouldn't be walking out of there. Pushing himself until he was sitting upright, he checked his phone. Still no signal. Stifling his anxiety and fear, he shone the torch across at the plastic-shrouded victims.

'Nadine, can you hear me?' he called, making his head throb even more. There was no answer. 'I'm going for help . . . Just hold on, OK?'

He held the light on the polythene bundles, hoping to see some sign of life. There was nothing, and Jonah knew he couldn't wait any longer. Gripping the torch in one hand, he pushed himself over to the wall and tried to climb to his feet. Dizziness and nausea washed over him. His knee wouldn't hold him up, and he slid back down the damp wall to the floor.

So much for that idea. He looked over at the door leading into the main warehouse. The fight had carried them back into the loading bay, but the doorway wasn't far away. Jonah told himself all he had to do was make it into the other side of the warehouse, away from these thick stone walls, and he'd be able to get a signal. A few metres, that was all. *Nothing to it.*

With the torch in one hand, he began crawling towards the doorway, trailing his injured leg behind him. Each movement sent a jolt of agony from his knee. It had swollen so much that it felt constricted by his jeans, and the throbbing in his head was almost blinding him. He felt crushed between the twin centres of pain, dwarfed by them. The few metres to the door seemed endless. He had to stop repeatedly, fighting not to throw up as he waited for the pounding to subside. His progress was agonisingly slow, and it was only when his hand struck something hard that he realised he'd reached the door. Pawing it open, he dragged himself through, then fumbled to try his phone again.

No signal.

Oh, come on . . . Jonah rested his head on the stone floor.

It was cold and soothing, smelling of dirt and mould. It wouldn't be such a bad thing to stay there, he thought, closing his eyes. *Just a few minutes. Just to rest . . .*

He jerked awake, convinced he'd heard a noise behind him. In a panic, he shone the torch back through the doorway, expecting to see the tall figure lurching towards him. There was no one there, and the loading bay was still and quiet. Turning away, Jonah started crawling again. He fixed his eyes on a pillar ahead of him, willing himself to reach it. *Only a few more metres, you can do that.*

But he couldn't. After a few more attempts he realised he couldn't go any further. He tried to think what he was supposed to do next. *Get help, that's right . . .* The phone screen swam in front of him, but his vision was too blurred to make out anything on it. He stabbed at it with dead fingers, mumbling in case anyone could hear. *Please. I need help.* He was losing it now, a rushing in his head drowning out everything else. As awareness slid away, only a sense of urgency remained.

Then blackness closed in around him.

Chapter 3

There was something wrong with the sky. It was a uniform, dirty white, in which the sun was a static glow directly overhead. It never changed, and there were shadows on it as well, darker areas in the corners. Gradually, the realisation came that there shouldn't be any corners. It wasn't like sky at all.

More like a ceiling.

Jonah blinked, moistening cracked lips. He was in a small room. Lying in a bed. His head and entire body ached but the pain felt muted, as though filtered through cotton wool.

Where . . .?

His memory was a blank. He raised his arm and saw tubes and wires emerging from flesh. He tried to push himself upright and gasped as pain ripped through his knee. Looking down, he saw his left leg was held in a raised metal structure, resting on what looked like sheepskin pads. It was covered in a white bandage from his foot to the top of his thigh, thick and constricting. Confusion fogged his thoughts. *What the fuck . . .?* Had he been injured on an op? Or a car accident? He tried sitting up again, but his leg refused to move. The attempt brought another spasm of pain.

'Hold on, love, don't do that.'

He hadn't noticed the nurse standing by the bed, half hidden behind a suspended drip and trolley of digital monitors. She finished making an adjustment to the drip flow and came to where he could see her more easily. She gave a cheerily professional smile.

'So we're awake, are we? How are we feeling?'

Jonah didn't know. He groped for some memory but found only panic and confusion.

'Where . . .?' His voice was a dry croak. He swallowed, trying to moisten his mouth. 'Why am I . . .?'

'It's OK, you're in hospital. You were injured. Just hang on and I'll go and fetch the doctor. She'll explain everything.'

No, wait . . . Jonah didn't want her to leave, but she was already going out. He lay there, clammy with anxiety. His mind was a hole, swallowing any thoughts as soon as they arrived. Clenching his fists, he tried to slow his breathing and focus on the small, clean pain as his fingernails dug into the flesh of his palms.

The door opened again. The nurse came in, accompanied by a stern-faced woman in blue scrubs. She came to stand by the bed while the nurse took a clipboard from its foot and began making notes.

'Hi, there. Good to see you awake,' the newcomer said. She had a strong Irish accent. 'I'm Dr Mangham, one of the consultants who've been looking after you. How are you feeling?'

Jonah's heart was still racing. 'Confused,' he managed.

'That's perfectly understandable. I know you'll have a lot of questions, but would you mind answering a few of mine, first? To start with, can you tell me your name?'

For a bad second or two there was nothing, then the answer presented itself. 'Jonah. Jonah Colley.'

She nodded, as though he'd passed a test. 'Can you tell me what your job is, Jonah?'

'I'm . . . I'm a police officer.' His confidence began to return as he found himself able to remember. 'A sergeant.'

'Good. And do you know where you are?'

Jonah looked around the room. There was no accompanying memory, but the location was obvious enough.

'In hospital . . .'

'Can you remember why you're here?'

Scraps of memory began to filter through, bringing the onset of panic. Jonah looked down at his hands. The skin was reddened and sore.

'I was in a warehouse. At a quayside . . . I was attacked.' It was coming back to him now, a cascade of nightmare images. Gavin and the young woman. The fight. He put his hand to his head, felt stitches and shaved stubble. 'Jesus, what . . .?'

He gasped as he shifted, sending pain lancing through his knee.

'Try to take it easy,' the doctor told him. 'We had to operate on your knee, so it's best not to make any sudden movements for the time being. Now, I expect there's a lot you want to ask, so I'll try and answer any medical questions while we do a quick examination. Is that OK?'

The nurse was already bustling around, strapping a blood pressure cuff around Jonah's arm.

'How long have I been here . . .?' he asked.

'Two days. Keep your eyes on my finger,' she said, raising it in front of his face and moving it from side to side. 'Can you remember being awake before this?'

'No.' He felt anxiety bubbling up again as he explored the holes where memories should be. 'I can't recall anything since . . . since before I was brought in.'

'That's not uncommon. You had a head injury that required stitches and left you with a hairline fracture of the skull. It caused swelling on your brain so we thought we might have to operate, but fortunately the pressure reduced without intervention. OK, I want you to squeeze my fingers. Good. Now the other hand.'

Jonah obeyed dumbly, struggling to grasp any of this. 'Is there any long-term damage?'

'That's what we're trying to find out. But the scans are reassuring, and from what I've seen so far I'm not too worried. You came in with other injuries as well – cuts and contusions, and chemical burns on your hands – but they're mostly superficial. Can you push with your right foot against my hand? Hard as you can. That's it.' She straightened. 'Well, there doesn't seem to be any muscle weakness or motor impairment. We'll have to run more tests, but I think you can be optimistic. Your coordination and muscle strength seem fine, which, frankly, is better than we'd hoped, and the skull fracture should heal on its own over time. You are likely to suffer the effects of concussion for a while, though. Headaches, light sensitivity, perhaps a little confusion. You might find your thoughts are a bit muzzy, but that should only be temporary.'

'Should?'

'Brain injuries are difficult to predict. Some people recover very quickly, with others it can take longer. But try not to worry. We're very happy with how you've responded.'

Try not to worry. Yeah, that'll work. Jonah lifted his hand to touch the stitches on his head again, then decided he didn't want to. 'What about my knee?'

'Yes, I was coming to that.' The doctor pursed her lips as she looked down at the pinioned limb. 'It sustained a lot of damage. Your kneecap was . . . Well, there are multiple fractures, and some bone fragments were displaced. Plus there are ruptures to the tendons and ligaments. But the good news is the initial operation went well.'

Jonah stared down at his leg. 'Initial operation? You mean there'll be more?'

'You'd best ask the orthopaedic surgeon about that. He'll be along later to discuss options. But you're obviously very fit, and the muscles around your knee are well developed. That'll help when it comes to rehab.'

Options. Rehab. Words that didn't seem to have any connection to him. 'How long before I can get back to work?'

The doctor smiled. But it was a professional one, meant to deflect. 'I don't think you should be worrying about that for the time being.'

If she was hoping to reassure him, it had the opposite effect. 'I need to make my report . . .'

'I'm sure you do, and there's a detective inspector who's very keen to talk to you. But that can wait till tomorrow.'

'I'd rather not wait.' Jonah was desperate to fill in the blanks of the past two days, to find out what the hell had been going on in that warehouse.

The doctor's smile had a definite edge. 'So would he, but I'm afraid that's my decision. The best thing you can do now is rest.'

Jonah wanted to argue. Questions were jostling to be asked, about Gavin, about the young woman and the other victims, about the unknown man he'd fought with. But all at once he felt drained. And then, as the doctor and nurse left, he saw something that momentarily took everything else from his mind. Before they closed the door, Jonah caught a glimpse of a uniformed police officer in the corridor outside. Jesus, they'd put a *guard* on his room? It made no sense. But then none of this did.

As Jonah's eyes closed, Gavin's voice seemed to chase him down a dark tunnel.

I screwed up. I got it all wrong. Everything . . .

Chapter 4

Ten years ago

'Daddy, are you awake?'

He tried to burrow his head into the duvet but it was tugged away from him. He blinked as sunlight jabbed at his eyes.

'Dad*dy*, wake up!'

A small hand took hold of his cheek. 'Ow,' said Jonah.

'Are you *awake*?'

'No.'

There was a cackling laugh. 'You are!'

I am now. Lack of sleep dragged on him. He'd worked late and hadn't got in till after dawn. He closed his eyes. 'No, I'm asleep. I'm dreaming a hideous monster's sitting on me.'

More laughter. 'That's not a monster. It's me!'

'Who's me?'

'Theo!'

'No, this is too big to be Theo. It's definitely a monster. And you know what happens to monsters, don't you? They get EATEN!'

Theo squealed as Jonah grabbed him and pretended to bite his arm. As the small arms and legs flailed delightedly, the bedroom door opened.

'You'll make him sick, he's just had his breakfast,' Chrissie said, heading to the wardrobe. She was wearing a short bathrobe, and Jonah took a moment to admire her legs. He enjoyed watching her, and a flicker of interest crossed his mind. But she'd already done her hair, which in Chrissie's language was a clear 'hands off' signal. And even if there wasn't an excitable four-year-old to consider, it had been a long time since daytime sex had figured in their marriage.

'OK, champ, you heard your mum.' Jonah swung Theo off the bed and set him down.

'I want to go to the funfair!'

'What funfair?'

'The one with the castle! By the seaside!'

Not being aware of any fortifications or seafront in North London, Jonah took that to mean it wasn't an actual funfair. But Theo rarely let reality cramp his imagination, and Jonah didn't want to either. That would happen soon enough.

'Tell you what, let's skip the funfair today. How about the park instead?'

Theo considered. 'Will there be dragons?'

'Absolutely no dragons.'

'What about magic carpets?'

'No magic carpets, either. But there will be some rusty swings, and a creaky roundabout. And if you're *really* lucky, I might let you skin your knees on the slide again.'

More outraged laughter. 'No!'

'Oh, you mean you don't want to go to the park?'

Theo bounced his head in a vigorous nod. 'Yes!'

'OK, then. And if you like, we can –'

'Theo, Mummy needs to get ready for work. Go and watch TV,' Chrissie cut in.

'But *Mummy* . . .'

'Now, please.'

Theo looked at his father. Hoping. Jonah gave a rueful smile. 'Better do as your mum says.'

Dragging his feet, the image of desolation, his son trudged to the door. Jonah waited until he'd left the room.

'You're going into work? I thought this was your day off?'

Chrissie was rooting through drawers. 'Neil asked me to go in.'

Neil Waverly was senior partner in the law firm where Chrissie worked part-time. She'd started off as a pool secretary, but two months ago had been appointed as Waverly's PA. The lawyer was a few years older than Jonah, and a lot more successful. His cashmere suits were tailored to camouflage an expense account paunch, and he arranged his hair to hide a bald patch. Neither dented his ego. Jonah had started visualising the man's face when he worked out on the punchbag.

'Well, if Neil wants you to go in, there's no more to be said, is there?' he said. So much for him getting any more sleep today.

'Don't start.'

He hadn't meant to. Couldn't help it. 'Can't somebody else go?'

'No, that's what they pay me for. You're glad enough of the extra money.' She pulled on a pair of pants under her bathrobe before taking it off. Jonah tried to stifle the suspicion that they were new. 'Anyway, I don't complain about *you* working late shifts, like last night.'

And here we go. But Jonah was too tired to face the same old argument. One he knew he wouldn't win. 'I thought we were having a family afternoon,' he said. Knowing it was capitulation.

'So did I, but it'll have to wait. I'll be late finishing, so I'll have to meet you at the restaurant later. The babysitter should be here at seven.'

Jonah had forgotten they were seeing Marie and Gavin that evening. 'Theo's going to be disappointed you won't be home when he goes to bed.'

'It's only for tonight. You'll have a better time without me anyway.' Chrissie reached behind her back to fasten her bra. It had lace insets. Jonah couldn't remember seeing it before either. 'Don't pretend you won't.'

'Maybe you should try coming with us sometime.'

'Maybe you should get off my back,' she said, turning away.

Which was how most of their conversations ended these days.

Jonah pushed Theo on a rusted swing until his laughter turned to hiccups, spun the creaking roundabout until he felt dizzy himself, and was waiting to catch his son's small body before he could skin his knee again on the slide. The play area didn't have much else in the way of equipment: a jungle gym that predated any recent health and safety laws, a lopsided hobby horse that threatened to dislodge its riders, and a crawl-through length of bendy pipe that would have looked more at home in roadworks. But Theo never minded any of that. As far as he was concerned, the play area was a magical place of excitement and laughter, regardless of the cracked tarmac on the park paths, the over-grown rhododendron bushes choking the trees, and the uncut grass that doubled as a minefield of dog waste.

Jonah felt his tension from the scene with Chrissie fall away as he watched his son's simple joy. He wondered how long it would be before the world ground that away. Not yet, he hoped.

There weren't many other people in the park. It was an overcast weekday. The morning dog walkers had left, and the only other occupant of the play area was a young mother with a pushchair, busy fussing with her baby's blankets. It would have been nice if there'd been a potential playmate there for

Theo, although he didn't seem to mind. Most of his friends were at school, but because his birthday fell just outside the cut-off point, he wouldn't be starting till autumn. Even so, he seemed perfectly content, humming to himself in the bright blue anorak and red bobble hat. Jonah was glad Theo could be happy in his own company. Chrissie said he was like his father, easily satisfied.

She didn't mean it as a compliment.

Jonah yawned. A short distance from the play area, a man in a grubby combat jacket was sitting on a park bench. His head was shaved and he looked like a rough sleeper, nursing a jumbo-sized bottle of something that probably wasn't Pepsi. Jonah had clocked him straight away, wary as a police officer and parent for anyone hanging around a children's play area.

But the man seemed oblivious to anything except the contents of the bottle. Yawning again, Jonah smiled as he watched Theo. His cheeks were pink from the crisp air, matching the colour of his knitted hat as he tried to turn the slow-moving roundabout faster. Jonah stopped himself from warning his son to be careful. *You can't wrap him in cotton wool.*

'Come on, time to go.'

'Aww . . .'

'Don't you want some lunch?' There was a park café on the other side of the trees they usually went to, a painted wooden hut that smelled of stewed tea and chips.

Theo considered. 'One more go on the roundabout.'

'Just one.'

'And then the Snake.'

That was Theo's name for the crawl-pipe. Jonah had already checked it was clear of anything more sinister than dead leaves. Junkies used the park at night, and it wouldn't be the first time he'd found discarded needles lying about.

Jonah caved, as he always did. 'OK. Only five minutes, though.'

Lifting his son firmly onto the roundabout, Jonah spun it to the requisite speed and then sat back down. Theo's face grinned at him as he went past in a blur of blue and red. Smiling to himself, Jonah yawned again. He would have happily stayed at home and had an early night instead of going out. But it would be good to see Marie and Gavin. It had been a while since they'd gone out as a foursome, and Gavin seemed to be having a tough time of it at work. He didn't go into many details, but from what he'd confided to Jonah he was part of an operation involving a particularly brutal gang of traffickers and drug smugglers from Eastern Europe. Romanian or possibly Russian, because, according to Gavin, trying to gather evidence on them was like grasping smoke. His frustration made Jonah glad he'd chosen firearms. It was no less stressful, but at least in his line of work he generally knew who he was up against.

Jonah rubbed his eyes. Some food would help wake him up. Soup or a sandwich in the park café, and then a quick trip to the duck pond before heading home. Find something on TV to keep Theo entertained and maybe see if he could grab an hour's sleep before the babysitter arrived. That reminded him that Chrissie had said she'd be late, and from there it was only a small step to Neil bloody Waverly. Was there anything going on there, or was he just being paranoid? His instincts said otherwise. And his instincts were usually pretty good.

He hoped they were wrong this time.

We'll work it out. We're both adults. Another yawn overtook him. Christ, he was tired. The roundabout creaked rhythmically as it spun, a mechanical counterpoint to a blackbird singing in the trees nearby. Jonah listened to the gaps between the off-key notes grow longer as it slowed . . .

The creaking had stopped. So had the blackbird. Jonah's head suddenly jerked up. Shit, had he fallen asleep? He blinked, realising that the roundabout was stationary and silent.

There was no one on it.

'Theo?'

A noise came from the crawl-pipe. Jonah breathed out in relief, the sudden fear vanishing before it had time to fully form.

'Oh, no, Theo's disappeared. I'd better go to the café and have ice cream without him.' Jonah got up and went to the pipe. Grinning, he bent down to look in its mouth. 'I don't suppose he's going to be hiding in –'

A blackbird erupted from the pipe, startling him as it broke into panicked flight. Jonah stared into the empty tube, where a circle of daylight stared back from the far end. He straightened.

'Theo?'

The play area was empty. Theo wasn't on the swings. Not on the roundabout or see-saw. Jonah could see he wasn't in the small cage at the top of the slide either, but he hurried over to check anyway.

'This isn't funny, Theo, come out now.'

A screen of rhododendrons and leafless trees framed the play area, but there was no blue anorak among them.

'Theo? Theo!'

The fear was turning into panic. He looked in the pipe again, as though his son might have somehow materialised inside it. Only dried leaves occupied its hollow length. *Keep calm, he's got to be here somewhere. You weren't asleep that long.*

Was he?

'*Theo!*'

The impossibility of the small figure not being there was too vast to accept. It couldn't be. Jonah turned in a circle, looking for anyone who might have seen him. There was no one in sight. The young mother with the pushchair was gone and so was—

Oh, Jesus.

Jonah's heart was pounding now, really pounding. The bench where the man with the shaved head and combat jacket had been sitting was empty.

'*THEO!*'

He ran to the surrounding trees and bushes, searching for some sign, a glimpse of blue. Then as he turned away to call again, he glimpsed something on the ground. A small patch of colour at the fringe of the trees. Not blue. Red.

Jonah ran over.

Lying in the mud and leaves was Theo's bobble hat.

Chapter 5

Jonah had just finished breakfast when the detective inspector arrived the next morning. It was still early, and when the door opened he expected it to be a nurse or orderly to collect his plate. Instead, a cadaverously thin man in plain clothes came in, and the sight of him momentarily took Jonah aback. Beneath a thick mop of brown hair, the man's face resembled a plastic mask that had been melted. Burn scars had alternately drawn the skin to an unnatural smoothness, or else puckered it like dripped candle wax.

His trousers flapped around skinny legs as he breezed in, indifferent to Jonah's stare or so accustomed to the reaction that he ignored it.

'Glad you're back with us, Sergeant Colley. I'm DI Jack Fletcher.' He cursorily flashed a warrant card before pulling over a plastic chair without asking. 'The doctor says you're well enough to be interviewed, and I'm sure you can appreciate there are a few questions we'd like answered.'

'Yes, sir.'

'Wonderful. But you're off the clock, so let's drop the "sir", shall we?' The DI settled himself on the chair, fidgeting to get comfortable on the hard plastic. 'How much can you remember?'

'Up to trying to phone for help. Nothing after that.' Jonah paused, for a second transported back to the warehouse's cold stone floor. 'How did you find me?'

'You were lucky.' It was so blunt as to sound accusing. 'You managed to call in before you blacked out. Although it took a while to locate you, because you didn't make much sense.'

Jonah searched his memory, but there was no recollection of any of that. 'How's the girl? Nadine?'

Fletcher leaned forward, suddenly intent. 'How do you know her name?'

'She told me when I tried to get her out. Is she OK?'

'Did she say anything else? A second name?'

'No, she was too weak.' Jonah didn't like this. 'Haven't you spoken to her yet?'

Fletcher sat back again. 'None of the victims survived.'

The news hit Jonah hard. He thought of the young woman he'd struggled to save. Jesus, for her to have gone through all that . . .

'Do you know who they are?' he asked.

Fletcher paused before apparently deciding to answer. 'Not yet. The other two were males in their twenties or early thirties. One was black, the other probably Eastern European, going on his dental work. But we're still trying to identify them.'

'What was –'

Jonah was going to ask him about Gavin, but then the door opened again and a woman in black jeans and a leather jacket came in. She looked a year or two shy of Jonah's own age, dark-skinned and slim, her black curls cropped close to her head. A leather shoulder bag, like a satchel, was slung over one shoulder and she carried two disposable cups with lids.

'Coffee with,' she said, handing one cup to Fletcher.

Peeling off the lid, the DI sniffed at the steam rising from it and took a sip. He grimaced.

'Christ, where'd you find this?'

'All there was, sir.'

She seemed unconcerned by his disapproval. Without saying anything to Jonah, she went to stand at the foot of the bed.

'This is DS Bennet,' Fletcher said, setting down his cup with an expression of distaste. 'Sergeant Colley was just telling me he spoke to the female victim. Apparently, he tried to get her out. She told him her first name was Nadine.'

The policewoman gave Jonah a speculative look. 'You uncovered her from the plastic?'

'Only her face, then I was hit from behind and knocked out.' He noticed Fletcher and Bennet exchange a look. 'Wasn't she uncovered when you found her?'

Fletcher seemed to debate for a moment whether to answer. 'No.'

Jonah felt sickened. The man he'd fought must have put the plastic back over the young woman's face while Jonah was unconscious. Making sure she was dead this time.

'What about the suspect?' He was almost afraid to ask. Since waking the day before, Jonah had been trying to come to terms with the possibility that he might have killed someone who'd attacked him. He'd known when he became a firearms officer that he might have to take a life during an operation: that was an accepted part of the job. But this was different. He'd been off duty, blundered into a situation he knew nothing about. Self-defence or not, if the man who'd attacked him had died, there'd have to be an inquest. Maybe even charges.

The DI ignored the question. 'We're going to record the interview, so let's get started. Bennet?'

The DS took a digital recorder from her bag. After she'd set it going and they'd gone through the formality of identifying themselves for the recording, Fletcher turned to Jonah.

'Why don't you start at the beginning?'

Neither of them interrupted as Jonah told them about Gavin's call, and how he'd gone out to the quayside. He was faltering at first, but habit and discipline soon clicked in. He'd made countless verbal reports during his career, and as he spoke, the familiar pattern and cadences took over, insulating him from the worst of the memories.

Even so, some threatened to overwhelm him. Describing finding Gavin, then having to watch while his body was wrapped in polythene and dragged away brought it all vividly back. And his breath caught as he relayed the fight and his nightmare crawl to try and call for help.

When he'd finished there was a silence. Jonah felt exhausted, his nervousness mounting as he waited for one of them to speak.

'I just want to get this straight,' Fletcher said after a moment. 'You say you hadn't had any contact with Gavin McKinney for years, yet you claim he phoned and asked for your help completely out of the blue. He wouldn't say why, yet you went to meet him at an abandoned warehouse at a place called, God help us, "Slaughter Quay". At midnight. Have I got that right?'

A headache had started to form, throbbing in time with Jonah's pulse. 'Yes.'

'And when McKinney didn't show up, you tried calling him and heard a phone ringing from inside the warehouse. So you went to investigate. On private property.' Fletcher let that hang. 'Leaving aside the fact that you're supposed to be a police officer, I'm curious why you'd go running to help someone you claim you hadn't spoken to in a decade?'

Jonah didn't like that *you claim*. 'I didn't "go running". But it sounded like he was in trouble.'

'What sort of trouble?'

'Like I told you, he didn't say.' Jonah shrugged, uncomfortably aware of the gaps in his story. 'I'm guessing he must have been working undercover, but why he'd call me, I don't know.'

'What makes you think he was undercover?'

'Why else would he have been there on his own?' Fletcher's attitude was sounding a warning bell for Jonah. 'The language the girl spoke sounded Middle Eastern, and last I heard, Gavin was working trafficking and organised crime. The only thing I can think is that he was following up some lead on an investigation that got out of hand.'

'So he called an off-duty firearms officer for help instead of requesting emergency back-up?' One of Fletcher's eyes had started watering. Taking out a tissue, he began to dab at it unhurriedly. 'Trust me, Colley, whatever McKinney was doing in that warehouse, he wasn't undercover. And it wasn't part of any investigation.'

Jonah was more confused than ever. 'Then what was he doing there?'

'That's the question, isn't it? Which reminds me . . .' Fletcher folded the tissue and put it away. 'Bennet, will you do the honours?'

The policewoman reached into her satchel again and handed Jonah a small evidence bag. His phone was inside, scuffed and scratched beneath the plastic. He flashed back to it skittering across the warehouse floor when he'd accidentally kicked it. The memory left him clammy.

'Is that your phone?' Fletcher asked.

'Yes. Thanks.'

'Oh, I'm not returning it,' the DI said before Jonah could open the bag. 'I just wanted to confirm it's yours. And I'll need your passcode and permission to examine it.'

Jonah felt as though the temperature in the room had dropped ten degrees. 'Why?'

'I'd like to check the call data to see when McKinney called you.' Fletcher's smile was predatory. 'We found his phone at the warehouse, but we're still trying to unlock it. I'm sure you'll want us to corroborate your story.'

As much as Jonah hated the idea of his private life being pored over, he knew if he refused it would look like he'd something to hide.

'Have you got something for me to sign?'

Bennet handed him a form and a pen. He made a show of reading it, but the words might as well have been a foreign language for all he could take in. His fingers felt wooden and reluctant as he filled in the form, hesitating over entering the pin number, before finally signing. Bennet took the form and his phone, putting them both back in her satchel.

'Let's talk about you and Gavin McKinney,' Fletcher said. 'You met at school, didn't you? Both of you came through the fostering system. He got put in care as a kid, you never knew your parents. Must have given you a shared bond, wouldn't you say?'

Jonah couldn't see where this was going. 'I suppose.'

'More than "suppose". McKinney's wife said the pair of you were thick as thieves at one time. Joined the Force together, best man at each other's wedding. He was even your son's godfather.'

There was something about the way Fletcher looked at him that kindled Jonah's unease. He said nothing.

'Then about ten years ago the pair of you suddenly lost touch,' Fletcher went on. 'McKinney's wife couldn't say why, but something must have changed. You'd been best mates for most of your lives and suddenly you stop talking. What happened?'

Jonah didn't want to talk about this. 'We'd got families, commitments. We just drifted apart.'

'Just drifted apart.' Fletcher nodded, as though that was

perfectly reasonable. 'A pretty abrupt "drift", if his wife's to be believed. And it happened not long after you lost your son.'

The question felt like a punch to Jonah's heart. 'A lot of things changed after that. I got divorced, I lost touch with people. It wasn't a good time.'

'I'm sorry if it's painful for you,' Fletcher said, not sounding it. 'I'm just trying to establish why McKinney would call *you* for help after a gap of ten years. Not one of his colleagues, not someone he was still in touch with. You. There has to be a reason, and a good starting point would be understanding why the pair of you went your separate ways in the first place.'

'It wasn't because of Theo.' Jonah was trying to stay calm but he could hear the emotion in his own voice. 'If you want to ask me about the warehouse, go ahead. I'll tell you everything I know. But leave my son out of it.'

The DI's jaw moved, as though he were chewing something. 'So there was no falling-out between you and McKinney? You didn't hold any sort of grudge against him?'

'If I had, why would I have gone to help him?' But a cold feeling had begun to grow in Jonah. 'You think I'm *lying*? Jesus Christ, you don't think *I* killed him, do you?'

'We're just trying to establish the facts,' Fletcher said.

Which wasn't the same as a *no*. Jonah felt he'd slipped into a nightmare.

'Is that why there's a police guard outside the door? Because I'm a *suspect*?'

Fletcher gave a shrug. 'The guard's a precaution. The press have been all over this. We've been keeping a tight lid on details, including your name, but it's only a matter of time before something leaks out. I'm sure you wouldn't want a reporter waltzing in here any more than we would.'

'So I'm not a suspect?'

'What you are is the only witness from a multiple homicide,' Fletcher snapped with sudden heat. 'We've only your account of what happened, and frankly I'm finding some of that hard to believe. So you'll have to excuse me if you don't like some of my questions.'

Jonah felt the nightmare worsen as the implications of the DI's words sank in. If his was the only account, it meant that they hadn't been able to question the suspect. He remembered the man's unresponsive body after the fight, the *thock* of his head hitting the stone floor. *Oh, Christ . . .*

'You didn't answer before when I asked about the man who attacked me.' Jonah hesitated before going on, afraid of what he'd hear. 'Is he dead?'

Fletcher sat back and crossed his legs, showing a band of livid scar tissue above his sock. 'Let's talk about him, shall we? You watched him bundle up your mate's body and drag it outside to what you think was a boat, and then had a knock-down fight with him, yet you didn't get a good look. You can't say how old he was, or if he was black, white or whatever. Only that he was a big, heavily built man who was taller than you.'

Jonah's mouth had dried. He didn't know what game the DI was playing, but he'd no choice except to go along with it.

'I told you, it was dark. And I'd got a cracked skull by then. Ask the doctors, if you don't believe me.'

'Oh, I'm not disputing your injuries. That'd be stupid, wouldn't it? It's just that we've only your word for how you came by them.'

Even through his anxiety and confusion, Jonah realised that something about this wasn't right. He was missing something.

But before he could say anything there was a brisk rap on the door. A nurse poked her head around it, the same one who'd been on duty when Jonah woke the day before. She gave the detectives a smile, tapping her watch.

'Sorry, but I'll have to ask you to –'

'Jesus Christ, do you mind?' Fletcher snapped, the taut skin of his face an angry red. 'I'm in the middle of an interview!'

The nurse's smile vanished. 'You've already run over the time you agreed with the doctor. If you want to arrange another –'

'I tell you what, don't tell me how to do my job and I won't tell you how to clean bedpans, all right? Or is that too –'

'Sir,' Bennet said quickly.

She didn't say anything else, but didn't flinch as the DI turned his glare on her. He was the one who looked away first.

'Fine, OK, we're done.'

Bennet gave the nurse a tight smile. 'Five minutes to wrap things up, then we'll be out of your way.'

'Five minutes, that's all.' The nurse shot Fletcher a last angry look before she went out.

'We'll pick this up next time,' Fletcher said, climbing to his feet as Bennet switched off the recorder and put it back in her bag.

'Wait, I don't understand what's going on.' Jonah was relieved they were going but more confused than ever. 'At least tell me if he's dead or not.'

The DI paused by the door. He and Bennet exchanged another look.

'That's a good question. There was blood on the warehouse floor we were able to identify as McKinney's. It looked as though it had run off whatever he was lying on, so that supports your story about the plastic sheet at least. There was a smaller amount belonging to you, as well as from another individual we haven't been able to identify.'

'I told you, the man I fought hit his head when we fell. That'll be his.'

'So you say. The thing is, the only fingerprints we found were yours, and the only bodies there belonged to the three victims wrapped in plastic. We found McKinney's car parked near yours, but there was no sign of his body or any boat moored outside the warehouse. And this mysterious attacker you claim you fought and left unconscious?' Fletcher spread his hands, a magician demonstrating they were empty. 'Well, it looks like he got up and walked away.'

Chapter 6

Ten years ago

In the weeks after Theo vanished, Jonah's life entered a new dimension. The days were a nightmarish, sleepless blur. On that first afternoon he'd stood by, dazed and numb, as police cars and vans arrived and the park was cordoned off. Jonah felt he was trapped in a bad dream as the quiet green space began to fill with figures in yellow hi-vis jackets and white coveralls. He'd lost count of the number of times he'd related what had happened, forcing himself to answer questions when he wanted to scream with impatience. You need to check shops and CCTV around the park, he repeatedly told the officers who questioned him. They'd given him assurances, employing the same calm and measured manners he'd used in interviews himself.

Then they'd asked more questions.

The worst of it was that Jonah *knew*. Knew what they were thinking. Knew what went on in cases like this. But the possibility that it could relate to Theo, to his *son*, who'd been laughing with him only hours before, was too enormous to grasp. He'd insisted on staying in the park, as though leaving that place without Theo would somehow be an acceptance of what had happened, making it irreversible.

Calling Chrissie to break the news had been the second-worst moment of Jonah's life. There had been times when he'd wondered if she'd actually loved their son, so cold could she seem towards him. But she'd become hysterical on the phone, screaming into it until the connection abruptly went dead. When she arrived in the park with her mother, he held out his arms, as much out of a need for comfort for himself as to offer it. She knocked them aside and begun flailing at him.

'*How could you? How could you have fucking let him go?*'

He stood there mutely, making no attempt to defend himself from either her attack or her accusations until two PCs intervened, easing her away and leading her sobbing back to her mother. Jonah had almost welcomed the sting of her blows on his face.

He blamed himself as well.

When he saw Gavin crossing the cordon, he could have wept with grateful relief. Come on, let's go somewhere private, Gavin said, steering him like a zombie to the police trailer that had been set up inside the park entrance. There were chairs, desks and a whiteboard arranged inside, but no one was using it. Gavin shut the door behind them and took a flat bottle of vodka from his jacket.

'Here,' he said, holding it out. Jonah shook his head but Gavin pressed it on him. 'Go on. You're no use to anyone like this.'

The alcohol burned a track down Jonah's throat to his stomach. He realised he was shaking.

'I fell asleep, Gav. I fell *asleep* . . .'

If Gavin had offered any sympathy, Jonah would have lost it. But instead he told him to get a grip, snapped that a guilt trip wouldn't help. When Jonah raised the vodka to take another drink, Gavin had taken it away from him. We need you functioning, not pissed, he'd said.

He listened without comment as Jonah described what had happened and described the man he'd seen on the bench. He'd always been a good observer, and the image felt seared on his brain. Tall and in his thirties, the impression of a gaunt, rangy build given even while seated. Pale skin with a bony skull closely shaved but a shadow of stubble on the lantern jaw. Frayed, dirty blue jeans and a greasy olive-coloured combat jacket. Gavin listened in silence, then said something that would echo in Jonah's mind for years to come.

'We'll find him,' he'd said, looking Jonah in the eye. 'I promise, I'll do whatever it takes.'

Jonah had desperately wanted to believe him. But when he went back outside and saw the police tape cordoning off the play area, the CSIs in coveralls searching the bushes where he'd found Theo's hat, the reality of it threatened to crush him.

The next two days were torture. Each minute was an eternity, a limbo of waiting for the doorbell or phone to ring. Chrissie wouldn't speak to him, or if she did, the conversation would quickly descend into shrill accusations. They were more strangers to each other than the family liaison officer who waited with them. The televised appeal they made was a disaster, a surreal nightmare of bright lights, cameras and microphones. As they took their seats Jonah rested his hand on Chrissie's shoulder, as much to bolster himself as her. When she'd shrugged him off, it had been caught for all to see, and things went downhill from there. Chrissie was sullen and cold, leaving him to answer most of the questions. He tried, but his mind refused to engage, leaving him tongue-tied and lost in front of the judgemental lenses. When a journalist asked if it was true he'd fallen asleep, a tsunami of guilt left him unable to speak.

'Yes, he did,' Chrissie hissed into the silence.

That was the sound bite that made the news.

Being in the small terrace was torture for both of them. The familiar surroundings now seemed alien, utterly changed by Theo's absence. It seemed impossible that he wasn't there. Each room still held his presence, echoes of his voice and laughter. When it became unbearable, Jonah would go out, walking quickly but with no destination in mind. Fantasies about finding Theo, or getting his hands on the man from the park, would play through his mind. He tried not to think what might have happened to his son. Could still be happening now. He kept checking his phone for missed calls or texts, the fear he might be missing something building up until he'd be driven back to the purgatory of the empty house.

And the waiting would go on.

Gavin was a frequent visitor. He tried to hide it, but Jonah could see the same terrible knowledge he felt himself reflected in his friend's eyes. Although he'd never worked a missing child case himself, he was only too aware of how they unfolded. Statistics that had been cold numbers before took on a hideous new significance now he was on the other side. He was all too familiar with the 'golden hours' concept, that the odds of finding a missing child alive shrank vanishingly the longer it went on. He was unable to stop checking the time, agonisingly aware of how quickly it was slipping away.

Then, out of the blue, there was a suspect.

It was the early morning of the third day that Gavin turned up at the house. Chrissie was still sleeping, seeking temporary oblivion in prescription tranquillisers that left her drugged and drowsy. Gavin told him not to disturb her, but Jonah could tell by his face that something had happened.

'We picked up the down-and-out from the park,' Gavin told him.

The man's name was Owen Stokes, a thirty-four-year-old Liverpudlian with a criminal record ranging from burglary to aggravated assault. Many of the offences were alcohol- and drug-related, and he'd only been released from prison two months before. But he'd skipped his last appointment with the probation officer, disappearing from the halfway house where he'd been staying after robbing two of the other residents. He'd been arrested the night before, drunkenly urinating in a shop doorway, and fitted Jonah's description so perfectly that the connection was made straight away. Still drunk, he'd brazenly admitted being in the park on the morning Theo disappeared, Gavin had said, taking out his phone. He'd hesitated.

'You shouldn't be seeing this. I shouldn't even have it myself.'

'Just show me,' Jonah said.

It was footage from Stokes's interview. Jonah immediately recognised the man from the park. Big and raw-boned in a greasy, olive-green combat jacket. Head shaven smooth, and a mocking sneer on thin lips. When he twisted around to look behind him at the door, Jonah saw the radiating lines of a black spider web tattooed on the back of his neck.

He'd slouched in the chair, seeming bored by the questioning. The smirk never left his face, and at one point he'd even yawned.

'You got it all wrong, pal,' he'd drawled at the interviewing detectives, his accent heavy enough to be a parody. 'I'm not into kiddies, 'specially little boys. Now if he'd got a sixteen-year-old sister, I might be interested.'

He'd laughed, and Jonah had wanted to reach into the screen and tear the man's throat out. He never even heard Chrissie enter the room, or realised she was there until she spoke.

'Is that him?'

She was standing behind them, looking at the phone screen over their shoulders. Gavin had tried to put it away, and then dissuade her from watching, but she was having none of it.

'Theo's mine as well. I want to see.'

She watched the footage in silence, all the way to the end. When it had finished, she'd turned to Jonah with an expression of utter contempt.

'You let *that* take my son?'

She'd walked out without another word.

Late that night, the doorbell had rung. It was DCI Wells, the SIO in charge of the search. He'd already spoken to Jonah once that afternoon, when he'd confirmed that Owen Stokes was in custody and being questioned. When Jonah saw him on the doorstep with the family liaison officer, both of them grave-faced, he'd known he was about to hear what he'd dreaded.

But it wasn't the confession from Stokes he'd been expecting. He and Chrissie had sat side by side but apart on the sofa as Wells told them about an overgrown culvert hidden in the thicket of rhododendrons by the play area. The culvert had already been checked and had been found to have a cover of iron bars. What had been overlooked was how rusted the bars were, or that the hinges had broken, leaving a narrow gap at one side. It was difficult to see and difficult to get to, Wells said, apologetically, at least for an adult.

Though not for a four-year-old boy.

Then Wells had shown them a photograph. It was of a small shoe, a miniature trainer, dirty and water-stained. The same brand, size and colour as Theo had been wearing the morning he'd disappeared.

It had been recovered from inside the culvert, Wells had told them. The search hadn't been able to go very far in, because the dank stone tunnel quickly narrowed, descending to a network of subterranean waterways too small for an adult to fit inside. But, again, not the smaller body of a child.

'I don't understand,' Jonah had said. 'What about Stokes?'

Wells had shaken his head, as though that was already old news. He'd been released, he told them. CCTV cameras outside the park entrance had showed the man leaving on his own. Not only that, but a couple walking their dog in the park had confirmed that Stokes had approached them asking for money. It had turned out they were Salvation Army officers, not in uniform, who'd tried to persuade him to go to the hostel. He'd eventually become abusive before walking off, but by the time-scale Jonah himself had provided, it wouldn't have been possible for Stokes to have anything to do with Theo's disappearance.

Jonah felt like he was suffocating. 'No, that can't be right,' he'd said. 'Theo wouldn't just wander off like that. Someone must have taken him.'

'How would you know?' Chrissie had said in a flat voice. 'You were asleep.'

She'd been led out by the liaison officer, leaving Jonah and the DCI alone in the living room. Jonah had stared down at the photograph of his son's shoe, still held in his hand.

'So what does this mean?' he'd asked, unwilling to comprehend it even now.

Wells had looked as though he'd rather be anywhere else but there. 'We'll do our best to find him,' he'd said, 'but you have to understand the difficulties. The stream feeds into a network of underground watercourses that run for miles. Even with fibre-optic probes, we can only go so far. I'm sorry, but you have to be realistic.'

And then, with a sigh, the DCI had said the words that finally brought it home to Jonah, that stabbed home the realisation that he was never going to see his son again.

'I'm sorry . . .'

Next day, Jonah had gone back to the park for the first time. At the play area, high-pitched voices and laughter rang from the children who played there, watched over by bored-looking parents. Seeing them, Jonah felt an envy so sharp it hurt. The crime scene tape had been taken away, except for a small area cordoned off within the rhododendrons. Here the leathery-leaved bushes had been cut back, exposing a low archway whose stone blocks were wet and green with algae. It straddled the same stream where he and Theo had played Poohsticks, a dark cave into which the fast-flowing water disappeared. Rusted iron stumps protruded from the stonework, but a new gate of galvanised steel had been fixed over its mouth like the bars of a cage.

Jonah's eyes blurred as he stared into the darkness beyond, with a sense of bleakness and loss so great it had neither beginning nor end.

On his way out, he stopped by the bench where Owen Stokes had sat. Ordinary slats of weathered wood, stained white with bird droppings. A pressure built up in him at the sight of it. He wanted to lash out, to stamp it into splinters, and it took all his willpower for him to turn and walk away. DCI Wells had got it wrong. Something like this, something so monumental, couldn't just happen. Theo, his laughing boy, couldn't have just ceased to be. Something had to be to blame.

Someone.

Chapter 7

'Come on, you can do it.'

I can't. I really can't. He squeezed his eyes shut and gritted his teeth. Doing his best.

'You're doing great. Just a bit more.'

You call this great?

Sunni eased his leg fractionally more.

'Jesus!' Jonah slapped the padded bench, tears leaking from his eyes.

'OK. I think we've done enough for one day.'

Jonah nodded weakly.

'I know it might not seem like it, but you're doing really well,' Sunni said.

He wiped the sweat from his forehead. 'Yeah, feels like it.'

'You've had a bad injury, so it's going to take time,' she told him. 'That's normal. But take it from me, we are making progress.'

Progress. Having someone manipulate his leg, trying to bend it a few millimetres at a time, while he broke out in a clammy sweat and tried not to yell out loud at the pain. He'd been shocked the first time he'd seen his knee without its dressings. It was purple and swollen to twice its normal size, with stitched wounds criss-crossing its misshapen surface. It looked like an offcut from a butcher's shop, something a dog had been chewing on, rather than part of him.

The orthopaedic surgeon had been briskly realistic. Jonah's knee had suffered the sort of trauma seen in motorbike accidents. The patella had shattered, and there was also damage to the ligaments and tendons. The surgeon sounded pleased with himself as he'd described rebuilding the patella, securing the displaced bone fragments with titanium screws and wire. But the damage was extensive. Further operations might be required, though that would be assessed in a few months' time, when the joint had had time to heal. Either way, Jonah should be prepared for recovery to be a long and painful haul.

Jonah had been trying not to think about his future, but that was becoming harder. There was talk of him being discharged in another day or two, but even the most optimistic prognosis made it clear he wouldn't be returning to his team any time soon. Perhaps at all.

The prospect of that scared him.

'The battle's in here.' Sunni tapped a finger against Jonah's temple as he pushed himself upright on the bench. 'Pain's just your body's way of telling you something's wrong. It's how you deal with it that matters.'

It was just hard to believe that when it hurt so much.

Still, at least he was mobile again. To start with he'd been pushed to his physio sessions in a wheelchair, but now he could make it there and back on elbow crutches. This was his second week in hospital, and as he swung himself along the familiar corridor to his room, he thought how quickly he'd adapted to its routines and rhythms. It helped that he was allowed visitors now. There had been formal visits from his bosses, right up to the Chief Superintendent, and from a Police Federation representative checking on his welfare. And it had been good to see some of his team again, especially Khan and Nolan. It was a reminder that the normal world outside the hospital still existed.

They'd also been able to tell him more about the larger fallout following the events at the quayside. The murders at Slaughter Quay had made national headlines, accompanied by the predictable media glee over the quayside's name. The general assumption was that it was part of an undercover op that had gone tragically wrong, something the enquiry team's PR machine had evidently done nothing to deny.

But there were precious few details in the news stories Jonah read. The formal police statements were little more than platitudes, vowing to bring those responsible to justice. That even extended to Gavin. His death was now officially regarded as a 'no body' murder, and much had been made in the press of the fact that his killers hadn't been found. Yet while the media coverage portrayed him as a hero who'd died trying to save others, the police tributes to him seemed oddly low-key. There were no off-the-record theories as to the killer's identity or motives; no unattributed quotes from anonymous sources. With so many question marks hanging over the case, the official policy seemed to be to say as little as possible rather than admit ignorance. Starve the story of oxygen and let the press fill the vacuum with speculation.

At least Jonah's own involvement had been largely overlooked. There were references to 'an unnamed police officer' who'd been injured, but little else. And the three unidentified warehouse victims received even less attention. According to rumours passed on by Khan and Nolan, each of them had been clubbed, then wrapped up in polythene sheeting while they were still alive. Cause of death had been asphyxiation, aggravated in the young woman's case by dehydration and organ failure.

The polythene hadn't only been to conceal the bodies prior to their disposal. It had been the means of execution.

But Khan and Nolan had been unable to tell him any more than that. Although the three victims hadn't been identified, that didn't prevent the media from concluding they must be illegal migrants, probably killed by the same traffickers who'd smuggled them into the country. Nadine's first name and possible Middle Eastern ancestry had been made public, but without a photograph to humanise her, she and the two other victims became little more than a footnote. Their deaths had prompted press calls to crack down on organised crime gangs, and predictable criticism of UK borders and immigration policy. Yet the outrage somehow overlooked the fact that three individuals had died brutal, senseless deaths.

Fletcher and Bennet had been back to interview Jonah on two more occasions, neither any more pleasant than the first. The DI clearly thought he knew more than he was saying, and Jonah couldn't blame him. There might not be any actual evidence against him – he was thankful he'd taken care not to get any of Gavin's blood on him when he'd checked for a pulse. But the man he'd fought with still hadn't been found, and apart from the single call from Gavin on his phone log, there wasn't anything to corroborate Jonah's version of events. It left him in limbo, uncertain if he was a suspect or not.

So far Fletcher wasn't saying.

The walk from the physio suite was a long one. But, tired as he was, a heaviness descended on him when he came into view of his room. Although there was no longer a PC outside – the guard been quietly removed several days ago, which Jonah took as a good sign – the small windowless space felt like a cell. It was bad enough during the day, when the harsh fluorescent light showed every scuff mark and gave the room a timeless, purgatorial feel. It was even worse at night. Jonah hadn't slept well in years, but since being in hospital he'd have welcomed his old insomnia. Closing his eyes now meant the cinema of his subconscious would start. He couldn't recall much about the nightmares, except that he'd wake, terrified and gulping for air, convinced there was someone in there with him.

There never was.

By the time he reached his room, he was out of breath and sweating as though he'd been for a run. Wanting nothing more than to collapse onto his bed, he opened the door and then stopped.

A woman stood at the foot of the bed reading his medical charts. She was in her thirties, dressed in ordinary clothes rather than a nurse's uniform or scrubs. She looked startled when he walked in but then smiled.

'Hi. You must be Jonah. I'm Corinne Daly,' she said, hooking the chart back on the bed rail.

From the way she'd said it, she seemed to think he'd recognise the name. He didn't but tried to hide his ignorance as he went into the room.

'I'm not scheduled for anything else today, am I? I've only just been for physio.'

'No, but I was passing. And now you're back I thought this might be a convenient time to talk.'

Jonah's heart sank. He could guess now why she was there. 'Are you a counsellor?'

He'd been offered counselling to help him deal with what had happened, and while he hadn't taken it up he hadn't actually declined, either. Although it was supposed to be voluntary, he'd been worried that refusal might count against any eventual return to work. He didn't want to make it any more difficult than it already promised to be.

But he'd thought he'd have weeks to decide. He hadn't expected to have it dropped on him like this.

The woman seemed to hesitate fractionally, though her smile never faltered. 'I don't call myself a *counsellor*, as such . . .'

Jonah didn't care what she called herself. 'Look, I'm really tired. Can't it wait?'

'Well, I suppose it could, but now I'm here . . .'

Jonah hesitated. The physio and long walk back had really taken it out of him, and the last thing he felt like was fielding questions about his state of mind. But it might be better to get it out of the way, at that. And who knew? It might even help him sleep better.

'It's not going to take too long, is it?' he asked, going to sit on the bed.

'Just as long as you want,' she said, her smile brightening as she moved out of his way. 'Do you want a hand?'

'No thanks, I can manage.' He leaned his crutches by the bed and lowered himself onto it, leg outstretched. He mustered a smile of his own. 'So, how's this work?'

'Well, how about we start with you telling me how you're feeling? And please, call me Corinne,' she said, rummaging in her handbag for her phone. She held it up. 'Mind if I record this?'

'Uh, no, I suppose not.'

Sitting down in the chair next to the bed, she took off her jacket. She wasn't how Jonah expected a counsellor to look. Her clothes would have looked more at home on a night out than a therapy session.

'Sorry, still working out how to use it . . . There.' She looked up from the phone's screen. 'Before I start, is it OK to call you Jonah or would you prefer Sergeant Colley?'

'Jonah's fine.'

'And you're sure you don't mind me recording this?'

'No, go ahead.'

'Thanks, that's brilliant.' She had a nice smile, he realised. 'So, you were telling me how you were feeling?'

'OK. You know.' He shrugged. 'The knee hurts a bit.'

'It must have been a very traumatic experience.' She was looking at him with an expression of sympathy. 'What was your first thought? When you went into the warehouse and saw the bodies?'

'I, uh, I don't know. It's hard to describe.'

'Can you try?'

Jonah rubbed the back of his neck, hating having to put it into words. 'Shocked, I suppose.'

'Can you describe it?'

Jonah had already done that more than enough times already. He could still feel the warehouse's chill, smell the dank air as his footsteps echoed on the stone floor.

'Can we come back to that later?'

Something that could have been disappointment flitted across her face, then passed. 'Of course. But could you tell me how you felt? Were you scared?'

Jesus, what sort of a question was that? 'It was an unknown situation,' Jonah said, falling back on jargon.

'Is that a yes?'

He searched for a way out, then shrugged. 'If you like.'

'Did you fear for your life?'

It was a clumsy thing for a counsellor to ask, but Jonah could guess now what this was leading up to. She was fishing for signs of PTSD. Trouble sleeping, mood swings. Flashbacks.

'There wasn't much time to think about it,' he said, wishing he'd not agreed to this.

She nodded, as if he was finally telling her what she

wanted to hear. 'No, of course. I expect you just did what you had to?'

'Uh, well . . .'

'I realise your training would have helped in that sort of situation, but . . . Well, it must have been hard to deal with. I understand you knew the police officer who died, DS Gavin McKinney. In fact, he was best man at your wedding.'

Here we go again. 'We knew each other years ago, but I hadn't seen him in a long time.'

'I see.' Again, there was a hint of disappointment. 'And the other victims. Can you tell me a little about them?'

'No, sorry,' Jonah said, kneading his eyes. He really wanted to lie down and sleep. 'The only one I actually saw was the girl.'

'The girl. Right.' Daly quickly leafed through her notes. 'This would be . . . Nadine, is that right?'

'That's what she told me.'

Daly blinked. 'She was alive when you found her?'

Jonah was beginning to feel uncomfortable about this. 'I don't think I should be going into details like that.'

'No, of course not,' she said quickly. 'But that must make it worse, finding one of the victims alive. And then being unable to save her. How does that make you feel?'

Suddenly Jonah found it hard to talk. He looked away. 'Not great.'

'Did she tell you anything else apart from her name?'

'What's that got to do with it?'

It came out sharper than he'd intended, but even if he'd felt comfortable discussing that, he didn't see how it was relevant now.

'I was . . . I'm just trying to get an idea of how it might have affected you.' Daly's cheeks had reddened. She seemed flustered. 'It must have been devastating. Especially after everything else you've been through.'

He thought he must have misunderstood. A counsellor couldn't be this ham-fisted. 'Everything else?'

'Well, you're no stranger to tragedy, are you? I mean, not after what happened to –'

'I know what you mean.' Jonah felt like he'd been clubbed. 'That was completely different.'

'Yes, of course.' Daly was nodding earnestly. 'But as a parent myself I can't begin to imagine what that must have been like. Do you think you can ever get over something like that?'

'What *is* this?' Jonah's growing anger and incredulity was giving way to a growing unease. All at once it hit him. 'You're not a counsellor, are you?'

The bright smile held for a moment longer, then she let it go. 'I never said I was.'

Oh, shit. 'You're a reporter.'

'I prefer journalist, but –'

'Get out.'

'Listen, Jonah, I'm sorry we got off on the wrong –'

'Get out. Now, or I'll call security.'

Daly's face hardened. 'And how would that look? "Firearms officer calls for hospital rent-a-cop to evict female journalist". How do you think that'll play out on social media?'

'I don't care.' Without thinking, Jonah pushed himself off the bed, and pain lanced through his knee. His leg buckled, and he clutched at the bedside cabinet for support. *'Fuck!'*

'Oh, God, are you all right?' Daly made to help him but stopped when Jonah raised a warning hand.

'Just . . . go, all right?'

She gave him one last worried look, then took a business card from her bag. She set it on the bed.

'In case you want to get in touch. It'll be worth your –'

'Out. Now.'

Jonah braced his arms on the cabinet, trying to ride out the pain. He didn't look up as he heard Daly go to the door, or when she went out. Only after it closed behind her did he raise his head. The empty room still smelled of her spiced perfume. He breathed it in, then let it out again as the extent of his blunder sank in.

Shit.

Chapter 8

Ten years ago

The drizzle hazed the yellow glow of the streetlight. It trickled down Jonah's turned-up collar and down the back of his neck. He ignored it. He was aware of it on some distant level, just as he was aware of the cold that numbed his hands and feet and pierced through the too-thin jacket he wore. But the physical discomfort seemed apart from him. All his attention was fixed on the building across the road, on the light coming from a single lit window and the doorway to the street below it. His whole world had shrunk down, narrowing to exclude everything except that view. He'd never once taken his eyes from it as he stood in the shadowed mouth of the alleyway opposite.

Waiting.

He'd been there now for hours. Seen the short winter day come and go, the dirty afternoon sinking first into a muddy dusk and then concealing night. He'd watched the light come on in the window, seen a silhouetted figure moving in a shadow-play behind the grubby curtains. And he'd waited.

It wouldn't be much longer.

Somewhere inside him was a sense of disbelief that he was actually going through with this. But, like his awareness of the cold and drizzle, it was buried so deeply it barely registered. Jonah was a raw nerve, so accustomed to the all-encompassing pain that it had become the norm, blanketing out everything else.

The *snick* of a door opening came from across the road. He stood motionless as someone emerged. Even in the dark, Jonah could recognise the shambling figure of Owen Stokes.

He'd spent long enough studying the man.

He couldn't remember when he made the decision. He wasn't sure if he actually did: somehow it was just there, a necessity that he accepted without question. The first thing he did was move out of the house. Chrissie was glad to see him go, and he couldn't bear staying there any longer. He booked into a budget hotel apartment, a studio with cheap furnishings and mouldy bathroom, where the hallways smelled of last night's takeaways and burnt toast. Gavin had offered him the settee at his and Marie's, but Jonah knew that would have been putting pressure on all of them. They had a young son, Dylan, and problems of their own. Besides, Jonah didn't want Gavin breathing down his neck. Not for what he had in mind.

Not that there was anything he could do straight away. Owen Stokes had been recalled to prison for skipping out on his probation officer and it would be another twenty-eight days before he was released. The thought that this was the man's only punishment made Jonah feel sick. But it was also a motivation. It gave him something to aim for, a reason to get out of bed each morning and face each interminable day.

No matter what Wells had said about proof, Jonah knew Stokes was guilty. *Knew* it. He could see it in the arrogant smirk, the sneering unconcern the man had shown for the disappearance of a four-year-old boy. Of his *son*. It was an affront to the universe to accept that Theo had squeezed through a rusting iron gate into that watery darkness. Not voluntarily. Witnesses made mistakes and timings could be wrong, but Jonah was his father.

He didn't need any more proof than that.

On the twenty-eighth day, he'd parked his car on the road close to the probation office a half-hour before it opened. Close enough to give himself a good view of the entrance, far enough away not to be noticed. It was almost two o'clock when he saw the despised figure in its combat jacket approaching. Jonah sat upright, almost giving in to the impulse to confront him there and then. Restraining himself, he sat in the car for another interminable hour until Stokes re-emerged from the building. Jonah waited until he'd gone past the car, then he got out and followed. He trailed behind, feeling the blood pulsing behind his eyes as he stared at the black spider-web tattoo on the thick neck. He knew he had to be patient for a little longer. An open street in broad daylight wasn't the place or time for what he had in mind. It had to be somewhere dark. And private.

So Jonah had hung back, though he'd made no attempt to conceal himself. Stokes didn't know him, and there was no reason for him to think he was being followed. And even if he did, Jonah didn't care. But Stokes seemed oblivious, not so much as glancing round as Jonah boarded a bus after him. When the other man got off, Jonah did as well. He slowed while Stokes paused to light a cigarette, then carried on following him. Reaching an austere brick building, Stokes threw his cigarette onto the pavement and went inside. It was a men's hostel, Jonah saw as he walked on past.

Crossing the road, he went to the alleyway a little further along the street. Just inside was a recessed doorway. It was half hidden by the rusting steps of a fire escape, and the fire door was padlocked, a drift of litter banked up against it. Moving into its shelter, Jonah fixed his eyes on the entrance across the road, oblivious to the stink of piss and refuse.

Then, hunching himself against the cold, he waited for night to fall.

Now he was all but invisible, another shadow in the dark alleyway. He stiffened as the sound of the entrance door opening came from across the road. Light spilled out, then a familiar silhouette emerged. Jonah stared from the alley as Stokes set off down the street.

Then he followed him.

The muscles of his neck and shoulders were rigid, and his hands were clenched into tight fists. His rubber-soled boots made little noise, but with all his attention focused on the man ahead he didn't see the empty can until he'd sent it clattering across the pavement. It made enough noise to raise the dead, and Jonah kept his head down as Stokes glanced back. There was no one else on the street but it was too well-lit and public, car headlights streaming past on the road. Jonah forced himself to carry on walking, keeping his eyes downcast as Stokes stopped ahead of him.

'Got a light, pal?'

The voice was hoarser than it sounded on the interview video, the Liverpool accent even more pronounced. Allowing himself to glance over, Jonah saw Stokes had an unlit cigarette held in one hand. The deep-set eyes that gazed back seemed mocking, and the urge to lash out at them was almost overpowering. Resisting it took all his self-control.

'No.'

Jonah walked on past, his fists balled so tightly that his cropped fingernails cut into his palms. As he left Stokes behind, he listened for any rapid footfalls, ready to swing round and face him. None came, and now Jonah began to worry that he might lose him if he got too far ahead. He risked a glance back.

The pavement where Stokes had stood was empty.

Jonah swore. He quickly scanned the street, but there was no sign of the man. Backtracking, he saw a narrow side street a short distance from where Stokes had been. Hurrying to the corner, he looked down. There was no one in sight. The only light came from the small neon sign of a bar further down, but Jonah didn't think Stokes would have had the chance to make it that far.

Christ, where *was* he?

Abandoning any attempt at stealth, he set off down the dark street. A noisy air vent protruded from the wall of a building, belching steam like bad breath. The air thickened with the smell of fried onions and charred meat, but there was still no sign of Stokes. *Come on, where are you?* There was no pavement and the brick walls of buildings crowded in at either side, blocking out the night sky. It was like being at the bottom of a man-made canyon, where doorways and passageways formed deeper areas of blackness in the shadow.

Jonah swore again under his breath, furious at himself as he headed for the bar. It was the only place Stokes could be. The neon sign said *The Full House* and as Jonah drew near to its glow, he heard a scuffed footstep behind him. He spun round, heart pumping as he brought up his hands. A tall figure was behind him. Dark as it was, Jonah recognised him straight away.

'What the *fuck* are you doing, Jonah?' Gavin hissed, stepping into the light cast by the bar sign.

Jonah's relief was followed by anger. 'Keep out of this.'

'Forget it. I'm not going to let you do anything stupid.'

'I don't know what you mean.'

Gavin grabbed his arm as he started to turn away. 'Come on, Jonah, I know what you're doing. You think you're the only one who knew Stokes was out today?'

Jonah pulled his arm free. 'You've been following me?'

'I knew you'd try something like this so I was waiting by the hostel. Christ, what were you *thinking*? I know you're hurting, but what good do you think this is going to do?'

'What *good*?' Pure rage put a quaver in Jonah's voice. 'I'm going to find out what that bastard did to my *son*, that's what *good*!'

'For Christ's sake, what happened to Theo was nothing to do with Stokes! You *know* that! If you don't believe Wells, at least believe me!'

'Fine, I believe you. Now fuck off.'

'Don't be stupid. It's not worth getting yourself killed or sent down over a piece of shit like Stokes. I can't let you do that.'

'I'm not asking for your permission.'

'Come on, Jonah . . .'

'Are you going to stop me?'

'Yes, if I –'

Gavin staggered back as the punch caught him on his cheek. All Jonah's grief and fury, all the guilt, suddenly erupted. He swung wildly at the target in front of him, no longer caring who it was. Gavin brought his arms up to protect himself but didn't fight back.

'Fuck's sake, Jonah, don't be a –'

He grunted as another punch hooked into his ribs. Then light exploded in Jonah's vision as something crashed into his face. He shook his head to clear it, stepping in to swing again. But Gavin moved forward as well, and Jonah doubled up as a knee smacked into his groin.

The pain was intense. He dropped to the ground, and suddenly the madness in him broke. He was dimly aware of Gavin crouching beside him, an arm round his shoulders as sobs tore through Jonah.

'I'm sorry, I am,' Gavin said. 'I know it's fucked up, but what happened wasn't anyone's fault. It was a shitty, awful accident, but that's what it was. An *accident*. Stokes had nothing to do with it. Christ, you think I wouldn't be helping you if I thought he did? I'd crucify the bastard myself, but that's not what happened. And doing something stupid won't bring Theo back.'

Jonah couldn't speak. He stayed slumped on the ground as the sobs continued to rack him. Only when they'd run their course did he find his voice.

'I don't know what to *do*, Gav! Oh, Christ, I-I look round and he's just *gone*! I can't bear to think of him alone in that . . . that fucking dark hole. If I hadn't –'

'If you hadn't been pulling shifts, if Chrissie hadn't gone into work, if the fucking council had repaired the culvert.' Gavin gave a heavy sigh. 'It's all ifs and bollocks. Sometimes life turns to shit, and there's nothing you can do about it. You can't predict some things, so you need to stop torturing yourself. Theo was a beautiful little boy, and he loved you. He loved his dad. That's what you need to remember.'

Jonah cried again, but without the violence now. The insanity that had possessed him for the past few weeks had gone. He felt weak but clear-headed, as though he'd come through a fever. He sat up, wiping his eyes.

'Sorry I went for you.'

Gavin touched his cheek and winced. 'Don't worry about it. You always did fight like a girl. How are the balls?'

A laugh burst from Jonah, though it sounded more like sob. 'How do you think?'

Gingerly, he began getting to his feet. Gavin helped him up. 'Come on, mate, let's get a drink.'

Chapter 9

'Congratulations! You're famous!'

Fletcher spun the newspaper through the open doorway of Jonah's flat. Standing in the hallway, Jonah fumbled the catch on his crutches. The newspaper slapped against his chest, spilling pages as he grabbed for it.

'You got a full-page spread,' the DI sneered. 'There's a nice photo of you in your uniform. Very heroic. You'll want souvenir copies to frame on your wall.'

As soon as he'd opened the door to see Fletcher and Bennet in the corridor outside, Jonah had known why they were there. He'd already seen the article online. Daly's business card identified her as a staff writer for one of the more lurid nationals, and every day since his discharge from hospital he'd checked the newspaper's website, waiting for something to appear. After nearly two weeks he'd begun to hope he might have got away with it.

Until that morning.

'Well? Aren't you going to invite us in?' Fletcher demanded.

Jonah reluctantly stood back. 'Will it take long? I've got somewhere to be this afternoon.'

'It'll take as long as it takes.' Fletcher strode past him, trousers flapping around stalklike legs and bony hips as he went to the nearest chair. 'Don't worry, you won't be late for your mate's send-off.'

A memorial service was being held for Gavin later. It promised to be a grim enough affair, without Jonah having to rush to get there on time. But he knew he'd be wasting his breath asking if this could wait until later. He wouldn't give Fletcher the satisfaction of saying no.

Bennet stepped inside then motioned for Jonah to go ahead of her. 'I'll get the door.'

By the time Jonah reached the living room, Fletcher was already flopping down into one of the armchairs, bony knees sticking up like spikes. Jonah dropped the newspaper on the coffee table as he went to the other chair.

'I know it looks bad, but I thought she was a counsellor,' he said, easing himself down into the chair. Bennet followed him in and sat on the sofa near the DI.

'Oh, a *counsellor*.' Fletcher's burnt face was flushed and angry. 'Show you her credentials, did she? Offer to let you cry on her shoulder?'

'OK, I made a mistake –'

'A *mistake*?' The DI snatched up the newspaper and tore through its pages before reading from one. '"*I'll never forget the scene in that warehouse,*" says hero police firearms officer Jonah Colley. Hero, did you hear that? "*Obviously, I was scared but I don't think of myself as brave. I just did what I had to do.*" Was that a *mistake*?'

Jonah's own face was burning. 'That isn't what I –'

'I haven't finished. *Sergeant Colley is still recovering from the injuries he received in what police sources refuse to confirm or deny was part of an undercover human trafficking operation gone tragically wrong. Four people lost their lives in the abandoned warehouse on the aptly named Slaughter Quay. One of them was*

Detective Sergeant Gavin McKinney, the whereabouts of whose body remains unknown. A highly respected Metropolitan Police officer, he was a close personal friend of Sergeant Colley. "Gavin was best man at my wedding, and a great cop. I'm devastated by his death," says Colley.'

'I didn't say any of that,' Jonah cut in.

'OK, this is where it gets really good,' the DI said, ignoring him. *'None of the three victims have been identified, but it's now known that at least one, a young woman believed to be Middle Eastern and known to the police only as "Nadine", was still alive when she was found. Colley becomes visibly emotional at the memory. "I just wish I could have done more to save her".'*

Fletcher lowered the newspaper. 'Not exactly cutting-edge journalism, but full marks for colour, don't you think?'

'I told you, I didn't tell her any of that,' Jonah said, his own face burning. 'As soon as I realised what was going on I threw her out. Fine, I mentioned that the girl told me her name, which was stupid. But that's all. She already knew all that stuff about Gavin, so she'd obviously been talking to someone else.'

'That's *all*?' The DI's blue eyes were icy in the flushed scar tissue of his face. 'You discussed an ongoing murder investigation with a fucking reporter!'

'I didn't "discuss" anything! Christ, do you seriously think I'd want plastering all over the papers like this?'

Fletcher's face held naked disdain. 'That's what I've been trying to work out.'

'What's that supposed to mean?'

Instead of answering, Fletcher opened the newspaper and held it up. Theo's laughing face stared out at him from the page. Jonah had seen the photograph earlier online, but the sight of it still winded him. He could remember taking the photograph on Theo's fourth birthday, only a few weeks before he'd disappeared.

Could still hear his son's delighted chuckle.

'*Big smile, Theo! Say supercalifragilisticexpialidocious.*'

'*No! That's silly!*'

'*You've got to say it when you have your picture taken on your birthday.*'

'*No, I haven't!*'

'*Come on, just try it.*'

'*Supercala . . . friji . . . biscuit . . .*' his son had managed before dissolving into laughter.

Click.

Fletcher tossed the newspaper back onto the coffee table. 'Nice bit of publicity, if you're wanting to get the story back out there. Was that the plan? Use the warehouse investigation to remind people what happened to your boy, see if you can't shake a few apples from the tree? Who knows, with a bit of luck you might even get the case reopened.'

'Case? You mean Theo's case?' Jonah felt like he'd just walked off a step. 'What are you talking about?'

'I think it's time we were honest,' Fletcher said. 'You never accepted your son drowned, did you?'

Jonah's mouth had dried. He opened it to speak but found he'd no idea what to say.

'What's that got to do with anything?' he managed.

'Bear with me,' Fletcher said. 'I'm curious to know if you believe he died in that culvert. Because that'd mean it was all on you.'

'It *is* all on me,' Jonah grated. 'I fell asleep and let him wander off. I've had to live with that ever since.'

'But they only found a shoe, not his body. At the back of your mind there must have been doubts. Maybe it wasn't his, maybe the inquest got it wrong. Maybe something else happened. Something you could blame someone else for.'

'I don't need anyone to tell me my son's dead. Or that it was my fault.' Jonah felt rattled and confused, unable to understand why Fletcher was pushing this.

'So you're telling me you never wondered?' the DI went on. 'That you just accepted it, thought, "fair enough, now I know what happened I'll move on"?'

Jonah looked away. He hated this, hated laying himself bare. Especially to Fletcher. But he knew the DI wasn't going to let it go.

'Of course I didn't. If he drowned, I wanted *proof*. All I got was a shoe.' Jonah stopped, struggling to compose himself. Just talking about it brought back the desperation of that time: that terrible, yawning *absence*. It was still with him, even now, waiting below the everyday surface. He cleared his throat. 'It didn't matter what I wanted, though. That was all there was, so I'd no choice but to accept it.'

Fletcher folded his hands as he considered him. 'Did you, though?'

'I don't follow.'

'You're a firearms officer. You'd know which boxes you'd have to tick to convince everyone you were safe to return to duty. And admitting you didn't accept the coroner's findings wouldn't have been one of them.'

Jonah could feel his hold on his temper beginning to slip. 'I didn't pretend, if that's what you mean. Everything else had been ruled out. It was the only thing that could have happened.'

There was something faintly reptilian about the way Fletcher considered him, like a lizard contemplating a fly.

'That's not strictly true, is it?'

Something cold raised its head in Jonah. 'What's that supposed to mean?'

'Just that everyone assumed your son had been abducted at

first. There was even a suspect.'

'Not for long,' Jonah said, his confusion and disquiet growing. 'He had a solid alibi. The enquiry cleared him.'

'But did *you* believe that? Even if someone was only suspected of taking your boy, there'd always be that lingering doubt. I'd think you'd be desperate to get your hands on him. Wring the truth out of the bastard.'

Jonah's chest had tightened. 'Where's this going?'

The DI gave a nod to Bennet. Without a word, the police-woman took out a photograph from her bag and reached across to place it on the coffee table in front of Jonah. He picked it up. It was a police photo, showing the shaven head and coarse features of the man Jonah had seen near the play area the morning Theo disappeared.

'Recognise him?' Fletcher asked.

'He was the suspect. Owen Stokes.' Jonah's heart was racing. 'Why are you showing me this?'

'We found photographs of Stokes on McKinney's laptop. Recent ones. By the look of it, McKinney had been keeping him under surveillance. Following him, staking out where he was staying.' He raised his eyebrows. 'You wouldn't happen to know anything about that, would you?'

Jonah felt like the world had tilted. 'No, of course not!'

'So you've no idea why McKinney was so interested in Owen Stokes?'

'No, I've told you! You've examined my phone, for God's sake, you've seen I wasn't in contact with Gavin.' Jonah put the photograph back on the table, suddenly loath to touch it. 'Was Stokes part of an investigation he was working on?'

But Fletcher was shaking his head even before he'd finished.

Stokes wasn't on our radar at all. He's kept his nose clean for the past couple of years. No cautions, no arrests. And he doesn't have any gang affiliations we're aware of. He's a loner, keeps himself to himself. There was no official reason to keep him under surveillance any more than there was for McKinney to be at that warehouse. In fact, the only connection we can find between McKinney and Owen Stokes is what happened ten years ago.' Fletcher regarded him through lidded eyes. 'You, in other words.'

'No.' It was Jonah's turn to shake his head. He tasted bile in his throat. 'No, that doesn't make any sense. Why would Gavin be following Stokes now?'

'That's the question, isn't it? But it might go some way to explaining why McKinney called you that night rather than anyone else. And why he wanted you to go to the warehouse.'

Jonah's mind baulked at where this was heading. 'I don't understand.'

Fletcher drummed his fingers on his leg before continuing. 'The blood we found at the warehouse that we couldn't identify. We've got a DNA match. It belongs to Owen Stokes.'

All the air felt sucked out of Jonah's lungs. 'That's not possible . . .'

'Oh, I assure you it is. DNA doesn't make mistakes like that.'

'Owen *Stokes* . . .?' The room swam. 'Jesus Christ, you're trying to tell me *that's* who was at the warehouse? *Owen Stokes?*'

'I know, I'm finding it hard to believe as well,' Fletcher said. 'Especially the part where you claim you fought the suspect in your son's abduction without realising.'

Jonah felt close to passing out. There was a rushing in his ears, and his vision seemed to be pulsing.

'Are you all right?' Bennet asked as he leaned forward. 'Shall I get you some water?'

He shook his head. *Christ, this couldn't be happening.* 'That's why you think Gavin was following him? Why he wanted me to go out to the warehouse? Because of what happened to *Theo*?'

Fletcher spread his hands. 'If you have a better theory, I'm all ears.'

'*Why*, though? It was ten years ago, why would Gavin start following Stokes *now*?' Something like panic was replacing disbelief. 'Jesus Christ, are you saying the fucking enquiry got it *wrong*? They insisted Stokes didn't have anything to do with it, they said it was impossible! And now you sit there and tell me *he's* the one who killed Gavin and three other people at the warehouse? Who nearly killed *me*?'

Fletcher looked taken aback. 'No, that's not what I said. McKinney's judgement was hardly sound at the best of times, and with his track record we shouldn't jump to any conclusions. And you need to calm down –'

'Calm *down*? You drop something like this on me and expect me to be *calm*? Gavin had Stokes under fucking *surveillance*! Why would he have done that, or called me unless he'd found something out about Theo?'

Bennet stepped in smoothly, giving Fletcher a quick glance, as though asking him to back off.

'At this stage we're still trying to find out what happened,' she said. 'The point to remember is that even if McKinney thought Owen Stokes was somehow involved in your son's disappearance, that doesn't mean he actually was. DCI Wells, the SIO of the original investigation, died a few years ago but we've spoken to his deputy, DI Conway. We're satisfied there's nothing to suggest anything was overlooked or any mistakes were made in the search for Theo. We made sure of that before we broached this with you, so –'

'So Owen Stokes wasn't responsible for what happened to your son, OK?' Fletcher interrupted, his face still flushed. 'Regardless of whatever else he might or might not have done, the inquest's findings still stand. Nothing's changed in that respect.'

Jonah's jaw was so tightly clenched it hurt. Nothing had *changed*? *Everything* had changed. Again. Owen Stokes wasn't some hapless down-and-out, he was a killer. He'd fooled the investigation about his true nature ten years ago, fooled everyone. That undermined every shaky foundation Jonah had rebuilt his life on.

But he kept that to himself as Fletcher continued.

'That said, McKinney was obviously following him for a reason. Given your history with Owen Stokes, the fact he chose to call you rather than anyone else makes me think he might have been on some sort of half-baked vendetta. So you can see why I'm struggling to believe you didn't know anything about it.'

Jonah took a few seconds, making sure he was in control of himself before he spoke. 'A while ago you thought I'd killed Gavin. Now it sounds like you're accusing me of going after Stokes with him. Do I need a lawyer?'

It was a bluff, but Fletcher shrugged. 'I don't know. Do you?'

They stared at each other. Jonah's heart was pounding, with anger but also dismay at the direction this was taking.

'What about Owen Stokes?' he asked, trying for a calm he didn't feel. 'Are you doing anything to catch him, or just going for the easy target?'

'You need to watch your attitude, Colley,' Fletcher said, the putty-like skin of his face darkening again.

I need to watch a lot of things. Jonah's anger seemed to have expanded beyond himself now, allowing him to feel detached from it. But he couldn't keep the scorn from his voice.

'Yes, sir.'

Fletcher seemed on the point of responding but Bennet

shifted slightly, quietly clearing her throat. As though some signal had passed between them, Fletcher clamped his mouth shut. He rose to his feet.

'We'll leave it there for now.' Retrieving the photograph of Owen Stokes, he made a contemptuous gesture at the newspaper. 'You should frame that. It's the only good press you'll get.'

Leaving Bennet to follow, he strode out.

After they'd gone, Jonah couldn't sit still. His crutches made muted thumps on the carpet as he paced around the small flat, going aimlessly from room to room. His mind was boiling, churning over what he'd heard. In the space of a few minutes the framework by which he'd rebuilt his life after Theo's disappearance had been undermined. For years he'd willed himself to believe the official explanation. He'd tortured himself over it, imagining Theo giggling as he'd crept away from his sleeping father to hide in the cave-like culvert. As though watching a film, he could visualise his son toppling into the cold, fast-running water. See the small body, buoyed up by its blue anorak as it drifted alone in the subterranean dark.

The thought of it had haunted him every day since. But as awful as it had been, at least he'd *known*. Or thought he had.

Now all that had been torn apart.

The news that it had been Owen Stokes he'd fought with in the darkness of the warehouse, that the man cleared of abducting Theo had murdered Gavin and three other people, was incomprehensible. Christ, how could everyone have got it so wrong? Including him. The thought that he'd literally – *literally* – had his hands around his neck was too much to bear. Going into the bedroom, he went to the punchbag hanging in the corner and threw his crutches to one side. Balancing himself with his weight braced on his good leg, he began thumping punch after punch into the heavy leather bag, imagining the hated face smirking in the photograph. He swung faster and faster, grunting with the impact until one wild punch made him twist and come down on his bad knee.

'Ah, fuck! *Fuck!*'

He collapsed onto the bed as pain shafted through the joint. He sucked air through his teeth as tears of rage and frustration ran down his face.

Owen Stokes. Owen fucking Stokes.

After a while, he sat up, massaging his knee before hobbling to retrieve his crutches from the floor. Going into the kitchen, he ran a glass of cold water, but set it down when he saw the age-yellowed painting stuck to the fridge door. It could have been a blue giraffe or a teapot, messy and beautiful. *Daddy, look what I made!* Chrissie had been going to box it up, so Jonah had claimed it. He hadn't planned to keep it there so long, but once he'd put it up he couldn't bring himself to take it down.

Going into the living room, he stopped by the window. His flat was a characterless space on the ninth floor of a tower block in East London. He'd moved there after the divorce. Partly because it was cheap and close to the tube and bus routes, mainly because he didn't have the inclination to hunt around. He picked up a framed photograph from the windowsill. Theo beamed out at him from it, frozen in time. Another captured moment hung on the wall, this one of Jonah and Theo laughing, their hair wet after a swimming lesson.

Oh, Christ . . .

He slumped down on the sofa. Whatever Gavin had found out about Stokes – and that was the only explanation that made any sense, no matter what Fletcher and Bennet said – Jonah bitterly regretted the flawed reasoning that had led to him keeping it to himself. At least, until it was too late. That decision had cost him his life, and probably that of the young woman Jonah had failed to save. Maybe the other two victims as well. And it had robbed Jonah of the chance to learn what had really happened to Theo ten years ago.

Jesus, Gavin, you had to go it alone, didn't you?

But the thought was without heat. After a while, Jonah stirred. He looked at his watch and saw more time had passed than he'd realised. He'd have to leave for the memorial soon. The prospect still depressed him, but now there was an incentive for him to go. There would be people there who would have known Gavin, worked with him. Somebody might know something, and while Fletcher would already have spoken to anyone who might have information, Jonah knew how a few drinks could loosen tongues.

It was a place to start.

He showered, then dried off and went into the bedroom. Opening the wardrobe, Jonah took out his uniform and laid it on top of the duvet. He put a clean white shirt next to it, and then sat down to pull on his uniform trousers. It was awkward, but they were looser than the jeans he normally wore, so went over his knee brace more easily.

Standing up, he balanced on one leg, steadying himself against the wall as he buttoned his shirt and knotted his tie. Tunic next, tugging it down as he studied his reflection in the mirror inside the wardrobe door. The stitches on his scalp had been taken out but the wound was still visible. For the time being he'd kept his hair shaved to a stubble, and from time to time it still felt like someone else was looking back at him. The uniform hung loose on him as well. He'd lost muscle bulk since he'd been injured, though not so much that anyone would notice.

Tightening his belt another notch, he closed the wardrobe door. As the mirror swung past, he caught a glimpse of a figure behind him.

Jesus! Jonah almost fell as he spun around. There was no one there. Heart thumping, he hobbled over to check the hallway. Empty. *What did you expect? The front door's locked.* His leather jacket was hanging up behind the bedroom door, swinging on a coat hanger. He looked in the mirror again, saw his own pale face looking back at him. *There, you see?*

Straightening his shoulders, Jonah swung himself down the hallway. Tying his shoes was as much fun as always with a leg that wouldn't bend, but at last he was ready. Setting his uniform cap on his head, he took a deep breath.

Then he went to say goodbye to Gavin.

Chapter 10

The collar chafed Jonah's neck. He started to ease it with his fingers again, thought better of it and put his hands down by his side. *Stop fidgeting. It won't make this go any faster.*

The wooden pew was hard and uncomfortable. The memorial service was being held in an old, austere church that smelled of cold stone and beeswax. A large, framed photograph of Gavin was propped on an easel at the front. It showed a decade-older version of the man Jonah had known. More lines on the face, but the crinkled eyes and reckless grin were the same.

Jonah was still in a turmoil over Fletcher's news about Owen Stokes. But he'd managed to calm himself during the taxi ride over there, and in the hushed atmosphere of the church he'd realised he needed a better strategy than steaming in with a host of questions. He wasn't sure who'd have answers anyway. He'd spoken to Marie on the phone shortly after leaving hospital. The conversation had been as difficult as he'd expected, but it had been clear she didn't know much either. If anything, even less than Jonah, although the way she'd been slurring made it hard to understand what she'd been saying. She'd sounded either drunk or on something. Or both. Although with her husband murdered and his body still not found, Jonah couldn't blame her.

The church wasn't as full as he'd thought it would be. There were a few police uniforms present, though not as many as he'd expected. He'd wondered if Chrissie would be there, but he couldn't see her. Not that he was surprised. Or sorry, as it saved him having to decide whether or not to tell her about Owen Stokes. It might come to that, but Jonah didn't want to involve his ex-wife yet, not until he knew more himself. Chrissie had been quicker to accept their son's death than Jonah, had even remarried the last he'd heard. She wouldn't welcome him lobbing a hand grenade into her new life any more than Fletcher would thank him for telling her.

For now, it was better to stay quiet.

The minister was winding down. The service had been mercifully short, with only a brief and relatively vague eulogy delivered by a detective superintendent. There was a final, intoned prayer, a few more words, and then the final piece of music was played. It was 'Ave Maria', which Jonah felt certain wouldn't have been high on Gavin's list of favourites. It was only a recording, but in the echoing church the plaintive melody was surprisingly powerful. The moment was broken by the bass rumble of a stifled belch from the end of the pew. Jonah glanced over as the thick-set man sitting there bumped the end of his fist against his chest.

'Pardon,' he muttered.

Nice.

Then the music ended, and the service was over. Jonah stayed seated as the front pews began to file out. Marie came first, sobbing as she was propped up by an older man who, he guessed, was her father, and a teenage boy with Gavin's lankiness and dark curly hair. Jonah felt a pang as he realised it must be Dylan. Jesus, when did he get so big? The last time he'd seen Gavin's son, he could only have been, what? Six? Seven? *Ten years ago. Do the maths.*

Behind them were two women whose resemblance to Marie identified them as her sisters. The other pews followed them out, but it didn't take long until it was Jonah's turn. He waited for the heavy-set man at the end to leave first, then edged out on his crutches.

The people from inside the church had gathered outside, but they were quickly dispersing, most of the uniformed police officers heading for the church gate and their waiting cars. Relieved to see the cameras and press were also packing up and leaving, Jonah joined a short queue of people waiting to pay their respects to the widow. His nervousness grew as the line shortened. As the self-conscious handshakes and condolences continued in front of him, he saw DC Bennet standing apart from the mourners, her black leather jacket and jeans a natural camouflage in that setting. There was no sign of Fletcher, and Bennet's face registered no emotion as she looked across. He gave her a stiff nod anyway as the queue moved closer.

In front of him, the heavy-set man from inside the church was speaking to Marie. Jonah couldn't hear what was said, but then the man was moving away and it was his turn to pay his respects. Marie was wearing a black dress and heavy make-up that was losing its battle with the tears. From a distance she looked much the same as he remembered. A different hair style and perhaps a little heavier, but otherwise not much had changed. As Jonah stepped into range of her perfume, though, he saw the lines and puffiness that the make-up failed to disguise.

He took a deep breath. 'Marie, I'm so sorry . . .'

He didn't get any further. She stepped towards him, wrapping both arms around his neck so suddenly he tottered on his crutches.

'Oh, Jonah . . .!'

He returned the hug as best he could. A cloying smell of perfume engulfed him, but it wasn't strong enough to mask the stale alcohol on her breath. As she sobbed against him, he became aware of the stares he was receiving. He felt himself flush, imagining the whispers. *That's him. The one who found Gavin.* Standing beside Marie was her teenage son. The boy held himself stiffly, clenched against whatever emotion he was trying to keep in check. The physical resemblance to his father was striking, although there was a sullen, resentful look that Gavin never had.

Marie straightened, stepping back without letting go as she took in Jonah's crutches. 'Oh, God! Look at the state of you . . .'

'It's not that bad.'

She wasn't listening. 'I still can't believe he's gone . . .'

She bowed her head as one of her sisters – an older, fleshier woman cast from the same mould – rubbed her shoulders. Jonah felt acutely self-conscious, but she was still holding on to him, preventing him from moving away.

She sniffed, 'Dylan, do you remember Jonah? He's a friend of your dad's.'

The teenager raised his eyes long enough to glower at Jonah. 'So what?'

'*Dylan!*' Marie's face tightened. 'What did I tell you? That's no way to –'

'I'm going to the car.'

Turning on his heel, the boy walked away. Marie glared after him before composing her face back into its tragic smile.

'I'm sorry, Jonah. It's been a difficult time for him . . .'

'I know, it's OK.'

'You are coming to the reception, aren't you? There's a buffet and drinks, so . . . oh, Jesus . . .'

Her sister put her arm around her. 'Shh, don't, Marie. Of

course he's coming.'

She gave Jonah a look that dared him to refuse. He mustered a smile.

'I'll see you there.'

His crutches scraped on the stone flags as he limped away. Poor Marie, he thought, and poor Dylan. The memorial service had been a timely reminder that he wasn't the only one wanting answers. Bad enough for Gavin's wife and son to have to deal with the raw grief of Gavin's death without the pain and confusion of not having a body to mourn. Jonah knew all too well how that felt.

What burned in him now was the possibility that the same man could be responsible.

The news about Owen Stokes had thrown him into a turmoil, but he was beginning to think more clearly again now. Enough to wonder what Fletcher had meant earlier, when he'd made the disparaging crack about Gavin's track record, and said his judgement wasn't 'sound'. The DI had been flustered and irate, but Jonah thought he might have let slip more than he'd intended. By the sound of it there had been more going on with Gavin than Jonah was aware of.

He needed to find out what.

Following the path until he was a discreet distance from the huddle of mourners, he stopped underneath a large stained-glass window. It was protected by a scuffed plastic screen, and without the sun to give them life the colours were muted. Pasty-faced saints and angels stared out blankly onto a world they wouldn't recognise. Jonah knew the feeling.

Opening the taxi app on his phone – it had eventually been returned without comment by Fletcher – he ordered a cab. The estimated arrival time was twenty minutes. He was still on his phone when someone spoke from behind him.

'Jonah?'

The voice was female and familiar, though he couldn't immediately place it. Not until he turned around and recognised the reporter from his hospital room. She was wearing black for the occasion, although the short black dress under the open jacket would have been more suited to a dinner party.

'Hi, Corinne Daly. We spoke at –'

'I know who you are,' he told her, turning away.

She fell into step alongside him as he headed for a side gate. 'I appreciate how hard this must be, but I'd just like a few words.'

'I've got nothing say.'

'Look, I'm sorry we got off on the wrong foot at the hospital –'

'*Wrong foot?*' Jonah stopped, partly from anger but also because there were steps down from the church path to the pavement. He wasn't going to attempt them with the journalist there. 'You sneaked into my room and pretended to be a therapist.'

'I walked into an untended room, I didn't sneak,' she said, the smile vanishing. 'And I didn't pretend to be anything. It's not my fault you jumped to the wrong conclusion.'

'And what about the garbage you wrote? I saw your piece this morning. I didn't say any of that.'

'That wasn't *garbage*,' she snapped. 'It was factually accurate and reflected the tone of our conversation. And it was actually very sympathetic. More sympathetic than I could have been.'

'Meaning what?'

She smiled, friendly again. 'Believe it or not, I'm not an enemy. I can understand why you don't trust me, but I'm not some ogre. I know what it's like to lose friends. And I'm a parent myself. My daughter Maddie's six. I don't know what I'd do if anything happened to her.'

'I'm sure she'd be proud of you.'

The barb had been thrown casually but he saw it had stung.

'She is, actually,' she said, colouring. 'She knows her mother tries to expose bad people and liars.'

And sneaks into hospital rooms pretending to be a therapist. Jonah checked his phone, wishing the taxi would hurry up. The app told him it was delayed. *Shit.*

'Then what are you doing here?' He looked towards the road, as though that might make his cab materialise sooner.

'I came to pay my respects. And I hoped I could have another word with you.'

'I've already told you, I've nothing to say.'

'You don't know what I want to talk about yet.' She gestured towards the church. 'I'm sorry about Gavin McKinney, but he isn't the only victim, is he? What about the other three? No one's holding memorial services for any of them.'

'They haven't been identified yet.'

He was annoyed with himself straight away for responding. Daly cocked her head at him.

'No? Supposing I told you I'd heard one of them has been? And that they weren't an illegal migrant.'

He knew he shouldn't take the bait, but he couldn't help himself. 'Was it the girl?'

Daly's smile was engaging. 'Why don't we meet up somewhere we can discuss it properly? A pub or coffee bar, I don't mind. Or we could talk over dinner, if you like.'

Is she serious? 'Look –'

'What's going on?'

Jonah hadn't heard Bennet approaching. From her startled expression neither had Daly. She took in the leather jacket and jeans. Her smile was politely disdainful as the policewoman came to stand by them.

'We're having a private conversation. And you are . . .?'

'DS Bennet. This is a private ceremony. The church is off

limits to press, so I'll have to ask you to leave.'

'Actually, I think you'll find the ceremony's over. And I'm outside the church anyway.'

'Actually, I'm not arguing. You need to go.'

Daly's smile became edged. 'Do you really want to make a scene at a memorial service? In front of all the family?'

Bennet gave a shrug. 'I don't mind.'

If it was a bluff, it was convincing. She seemed relaxed, but there was poised physicality about her. Jonah decided he wouldn't like to cross DC Bennet himself, even with two good knees.

Evidently Daly felt the same way. She made a show of turning to Jonah in an attempt to pretend she wasn't backing down.

'Good to see you again, Jonah. Remember what I said. Any time you want to talk . . .'

She started to walk away, then turned back to Bennet with a smile that was all spite.

'Love the goth look, by the way.'

Daly's high heels clicked triumphantly on the flagstones as she strode down the path to the gate. Bennet stared after the journalist with the lazy consideration of a cat watching a bird.

'What did she want?'

'She was asking about the other victims. And before you ask, I didn't tell her anything.'

'I hope not.'

'She told me one of the victims had been identified,' Jonah said, before she could walk away. 'She didn't say who, but she'd heard they weren't an illegal migrant.'

Bennet turned her dark eyes on him. He felt they were somehow judgemental. 'What else did she say?'

'Nothing, that was all. She wanted to find out what I knew.'

'And you didn't tell her anything?'

'How could I? I don't know anything.'

She studied him for a moment, then gave a nod. 'OK.'

'Is it true?' he asked as she started to go. 'Have you identified one of them?'

'You shouldn't listen to rumours,' Bennet said, walking away.

Chapter 11

The reception was in the private room of a pub. It was a large space with French windows and a curtained-off stage at one end. Tables and chairs had been set out and a long, white cloth-covered buffet table was laden with sandwiches, quiches and stainless-steel warming dishes for hot food. No more than a dozen people had turned up, the small number making the big room seem even emptier.

From what Jonah could see, hardly any of them except him wore police uniforms.

Sitting at a table, surrounded by her family and glasses of beer and wine, Marie looked shell-shocked. Teenage nieces and nephews had congregated nearby, where Dylan sat pale-faced and silent. Jonah went over and was once again pulled into Marie's tearful embrace. She smelled of make-up and red wine.

'Jonah, I'm so glad you came! Where is everyone?' she fretted. 'Why aren't there more people here? All his workmates, all those people from the church, where *are* they? I don't understand!'

Neither did Jonah. 'They're probably on their way,' he said, but he'd been one of the last to leave. Anyone planning to attend the reception should have been there by now.

Marie looked around the empty room, as though seeing it for the first time.

'It's like a nightmare. I keep thinking I'm going to wake up, but I can't. God, I can't bear to think of Gav lying in that place on his own, all . . .' She wiped at her eyes and took a gulp of wine. 'I'm glad it was you who found him. You were always such good friends, I never could understand why you lost touch.'

Jonah had already been through this when they'd spoken over the phone. 'It was just one of those things.'

But she wasn't really listening. 'I still can't take it in. You always know there's a risk, but you never think anything bad'll actually happen. Not to Gav. And for someone to take his body . . . who'd *do* that?'

He was relieved when she didn't wait for him to answer.

'That DI . . . Fletcher, the one with the face. He came round again last night, asking if Gav ever talked about someone called Owen Stone or Stokes. But he wouldn't say why.'

Jonah's heart rate had jumped at the name. 'Did he? Say anything, I mean?'

'No, you know what Gav was like. He never talked about work.' Her eyes searched his face, pleading and scared. 'Is that . . . is that who they think did it?'

'I'm not sure what they think, Marie. They aren't telling me anything either.'

It was true as far as it went, and he wouldn't be helping Marie by opening up even more uncertainty for her. He doubted she'd have any reason to connect Owen Stokes with Theo's disappearance. He hadn't been a suspect for very long, and even if Gavin had mentioned his name it was unlikely she'd remember after so long.

But Jonah still hated himself for the evasion. He felt even worse when she clutched at his hand.

'I'm so glad you're here. I can talk to you, you know what it's like. How could you *stand* it?'

'Just try to take it one day at a time,' he told her, wishing he had a better answer.

'I do, but it's that . . . that not *knowing*. I just wish someone would tell me who did it or why, or what he did with . . . with . . . Oh, God!'

The older man Jonah took to be her father came over and gently prised her away.

'Now, Marie, come on. Gavin wouldn't want you to get upset. Think of Dylan.'

That prompted more tears. Her father stayed by Jonah as one of her sisters led her back to her seat.

'This is the first time she's left the house in weeks. I'm her dad, I'm supposed to be there to support her, but I've no idea what to say. What am I supposed to tell her? Or Dylan?'

'Haven't the police said anything at all?' Jonah asked.

'Not really, just that they're following leads. But what does that mean? They say they can't give away details of an ongoing investigation. Not even to his *wife*. Where's the compassion in that?'

The man seemed to collect himself, blinking at him as though he'd forgotten anyone was there.

'Anyway, it's a free bar.' He made an attempt at a smile but his eyes were far away. 'Please order whatever you like.'

Jonah moved off with a sense of guilty relief. Going to the bar, he ordered a beer, opting for a bottle rather than a glass on the theory that it would be easier to carry. Taking a pull from it, he regarded the almost-empty room. So much for his big hopes of learning more. Where the hell *was* everyone? The place should have been packed with Gavin's colleagues and senior officers, but it looked like they'd all left as soon as the church service was over. As though they couldn't wait to get away. Jonah didn't think even the awkward questions surrounding Gavin's death could explain a snub on that scale.

So what was going on?

'Nice to see somebody in a uniform decided to turn up.'

Jonah looked round and recognised the thick-set man who'd been on the same pew at the church. He was standing at the buffet table, an overladen plate in one hand and a half-eaten sausage roll in the other. Rather than a suit and tie for the occasion, he wore a black polo-neck sweater and navy chinos under a tan leather jacket, the front of which was speckled with flakes of pastry. He was munching as he looked at Jonah, the small eyes above the bunched cheeks shrewd and watchful. Not exactly hostile, but not friendly either.

'Not much of a turnout, is it?' The man's voice was gruff and slightly hoarse, as though he was getting over a cold. 'Look at it. It's a fucking insult.'

Jonah made his way over. 'You a friend of Gavin's?'

'I am.' The big man drew himself up. 'I worked with him for eight years, up till I took early retirement last year.'

'I'm Jonah –'

'I know who you are.' He popped the rest of the sausage roll into his mouth and spoke around it. 'I recognise you from the paper this morning.'

'That was a stitch-up.'

'Yeah, I thought it might be. Fucking reporters.' Brushing the crumbs of pastry from his mouth, the other man stuck out his hand. 'Jim Wilkes. Detective Constable as was.'

He was looking expectant, as though his name might mean something. It didn't. Jonah took the offered hand. It was fat and leathery, still greasy from the sausage roll. Wilkes gripped hard enough to hurt if he hadn't been ready for it. Letting go, the other man set down his plate and picked up a pint of lager.

'Jesus, what a fucking business. I still can't believe it. I mean, *Gavin*? Doesn't seem possible.' He considered Jonah's crutches. 'Looks like you've been in the wars yourself. So what happened in there?'

'What have you heard?' Jonah countered.

'Fuck all. I've been asking around but nobody's talking. I was a detective for twenty-five years, I can understand some details not being made public. But apart from PR bollocks fed to the press, I've not heard anything. No word on any suspects, or what Gav was doing there. Nothing.' Wilkes rolled his shoulders, like a boxer squaring up. 'I'm not an idiot, I can tell when something's being hushed up. But Gav was a good mate. I'd like to know what's going on.'

Jonah thought for a moment, weighing up risks against opportunity. After having his fingers burnt once with Daly, he wasn't about to take anyone at face value. But the big man had the look of an ex-copper, and Marie clearly knew him. If he wasn't a friend of Gavin's, he wouldn't be there.

Besides, Jonah had been hoping to find someone who could fill in some of the blanks from the last ten years. Retired or not, if Wilkes had worked with Gavin, he'd know a side of his life that Marie never would. If Jonah wanted to hear about that, he'd have to give something in return.

So, leaving out any mention of Owen Stokes, he quietly gave the ex-detective an edited account of the events at the warehouse. Wilkes listened grimly, his expression darkening even more as he heard how Gavin's body had been bundled up and dragged away. When Jonah finished, he was surprised to see the big man had teared up. Taking out a handkerchief, he blew his nose.

'Pity you didn't kill the fucker.' He cleared his throat,

stuffing the handkerchief back in his pocket. 'And you never got a proper look at him? Even when you were watching all that time?'

'It was pitch-black,' Jonah said, nettled. 'You should try getting knocked out and tied up, see how you get on.'

'I was just saying, no need to get humpty.' Wilkes frowned into his glass. 'So it was just one man?'

'That's all I saw.'

'Doesn't sound like an organised gang were involved, then. The papers made it sound like it was migrants who'd been killed by traffickers, but what you've said sounds more like a lone psycho to me.' His frown deepened. 'I still don't get what Gav was doing there, though. Or why he phoned you. No offence, but I can't recall him ever mentioning your name. If he was in a bind, then how come he called you instead of . . . instead of someone else?'

'I'm still trying to work that out myself.' Jonah didn't want quizzing too closely about that, not with Fletcher's revelation about Owen Stokes still so fresh. He nodded at the big man's nearly empty glass. 'Get you another?'

'Won't say no.' By the look of him, he rarely did. 'Let me get some more grub and I'll come with you.'

Jonah waited while he loaded his plate, then they headed to the bar. Wilkes favoured one hip as he walked.

'Been waiting months for a bloody op,' he grumbled. When his lager arrived, he raised it at Jonah. 'Here's to Gav.'

Jonah tilted his own bottle – he was still on his first – to acknowledge the toast but he didn't echo it. 'When did you last see him?'

The ex-detective's pouched eyes slid away. 'Not recently, as such. You know how it is after you've left.'

Jonah did. He'd met up with his team for a drink shortly

after he came out of hospital. Although it had been good to see them, he'd already felt like an outsider.

'But you kept in contact?'

'Yeah, 'course.' Wilkes sounded defensive. 'We'd meet up for a beer or a curry, that sort of thing. Though not so much after he moved out.'

'Moved out?'

'Didn't you know?' The small eyes were shrewd and triumphant. 'Him and his missus were separated. He was renting a flat in Ealing.'

That was news to Jonah. Marie hadn't said anything, but then she probably wouldn't have wanted to dwell on it. Not when any chance of a reconciliation had died along with Gavin.

'What happened?'

'It's not my place to say,' Wilkes said, looking down at his beer.

'No, of course.'

Jonah occupied himself with his own beer, letting the silence work for him.

'Between you and me, things had been rocky between them for a while,' Wilkes said, leaning in. 'You know Gav, he was no saint. He liked to play hard, but that's all it was. He'd never had to move out before.'

Jonah took a moment to make sure his face didn't give anything away. 'Was he seeing anyone else?'

'Christ, no, not after . . .' Wilkes seemed to catch himself. 'I mean, it was never anything serious, he wasn't that stupid. I suppose you can't blame his wife for getting upset, but you've got to blow off steam in this job. Specially with the pressure he'd been under, what with the suspension and all.'

'Suspension?'

Wilkes gave him an incredulous look, enjoying Jonah's shock.

'Jesus, you really are out of touch. He'd been suspended without pay, although no one's going to want to admit that now. Wouldn't look good in the press if it came out the DPS had been on his back for months, would it? Bastards.'

Suddenly, a lot of things became clearer for Jonah. The Directorate of Professional Standards investigated allegations of misconduct against the Met's officers. If Gavin had been in their sights, that wasn't good.

But it explained the muted official reaction to his death, as well as the empty room Jonah was standing in now. A low turnout at the church, with the media waiting outside, was one thing. That would have raised too many eyebrows, but a private reception afterwards was something else. Whatever Gavin was being investigated for, it was bad enough for his colleagues not to want tarnishing by association.

Except for Wilkes.

'What was he supposed to have done?' Jonah asked.

The ex-detective took another drink, scowling. 'Some trumped-up bullshit. You know how it is, sometimes you've got to bend the rules to get things done. Doesn't matter now, does it?'

It did if it was something to do with Gavin's presence at the warehouse, Jonah thought. Because that could potentially tarnish him as well. Jesus, no wonder Fletcher was so suspicious.

'Was he accused of being on the take?'

He could see from the hunted expression that flitted across Wilkes's face that he'd hit home. The big man hid it behind bluster.

'You want to talk about that, ask someone else. I'm not going to bad-mouth him when he can't defend himself. And I don't care what anyone says, Gav was a good man. He deserved better than *this*.' Lager sloshed in his glass as he waved it at the almost-deserted room. 'A half-arsed eulogy and pork pie in the back room of a pub. And the two-faced bastards can't even be bothered to come!'

Wilkes's face was flushed and angry. Jonah didn't want to upset him more than he already was, but he had to know.

'Whatever it was he was suspended for,' he asked, 'Do you think it could be connected to what happened at the warehouse?'

It took Wilkes a moment or two to come down from his high horse. 'I can't see how it could. Like I say, it doesn't even sound like he had any business being there. Not unless . . .'

'Unless what?'

Wilkes rubbed his nose, looking discomfited at the direction his thoughts had taken.

'Well, it's not like he'd got much left to lose, is it? He'd got the DPS after him, his wife had kicked him out and he was suspended without pay. He was shafted, however you look at it. So if he got wind of something in that warehouse he might have just thought 'fuck it' and gone steaming in. If it worked out, he'd end up smelling of roses, and if it didn't . . .'

He didn't finish. But there was a certain kind of sense to it, Jonah thought. Gavin always had a reckless streak, a gambler's mentality that sometimes led to stupid risks. More often than not they'd work out, bolstering Gavin's belief that it was the natural order of things. But not always, and sometimes it was other people who got hurt.

It was all too easy to see a similar pattern playing out here.

Jonah fell silent as the big man threw back the last of his drink and banged down his glass.

'Let's get a proper drink.' He motioned the barman over. 'Two brandies. Large ones.'

The drinks had only just arrived when there was a commotion

from Marie's table. She was on the phone, agitated and shaking her head. One of her sisters took it off her and spoke into it as the other comforted her. The other people around her were talking among themselves, upset and angry.

'Hello, now what?' Wilkes said.

The sister ended the phone conversation and said something to Marie, who started crying again. Her father was helping her up, and others around her were standing as well.

Wilkes knocked back his brandy. 'Better see what's going on.'

He set off over without waiting for Jonah to arrange himself on his crutches. The whole family were milling about now, preparing to leave. Two of them broke off to speak to Wilkes. Whatever had happened, it didn't look good. After a moment Wilkes came back, carrying himself with an air of self-importance.

'Better get your coat. The party's over,' he told Jonah. 'Some bastard's broken into their house.'

Since the last time Jonah had visited, Gavin and Marie had traded up their cramped, two-bedroom maisonette to a detached house in a modern development. The sales brochure probably would have described it as 'executive', skirting over the mean dimensions and the way the houses had been squeezed close together. Large cars were parked in driveways barely big enough to hold them, the front gardens reduced to token patches of turf edging concrete block paving. It wasn't the sort of place Jonah would have wanted to live, but then he wouldn't have been able to afford it anyway. Mean or not, the mortgage repayments would have been a stretch on a detective's salary.

Especially one who'd been suspended without pay.

Climbing out of Wilkes's car, Jonah followed the big man up the drive to the front door. It was open, a wood-effect PVC with a frosted panel set in its top half. It didn't appear to have been forced, so whoever had broken in must have found another way. But the house was a mess. Most of the rooms had been ransacked, drawers and cupboards emptied and the contents scattered on the floor. That would make it harder to determine what had been taken, but the signs suggested that it had been a rushed job. The house had a burglar alarm, and it seemed the thieves had torn through the house grabbing whatever valuable items they could carry before anyone responded. In the living room, a large, expensive TV and speaker had been left untouched, probably too big to move.

Marie wandered from room to room, propped up as she'd tearfully surveyed the damage. 'Who'd do something like this?' she kept repeating. 'Today of all days? How can anyone be so heartless?'

Jonah picked his way through the house. The worst-hit room was Dylan's bedroom. All his computer equipment had gone, along with a gaming console and headphones. The teenager seemed especially aggrieved that a pair of still-boxed trainers was missing as well.

'Shit! *Shit!*' he yelled, punching the wall. 'What's the point of having an alarm?'

'Don't swear,' his mother pleaded. 'It could have been worse –'

'That's all right for you to say, it's not your stuff that's gone! I didn't want to go in the first place, I said it was a waste of time!'

'Oh, don't say that, Dylan! You know you don't mean it!'

'Spoilt as shite,' Wilkes said under his breath as they turned away. 'That's his mother to thank for that. Gav wouldn't have let him get away with it.'

At the back of the house, a panel in the rear porch had been smashed and the timber door frame inside was splintered.

Wilkes crouched down to examine it, looking like a polo-necked Buddha as he nodded sagely.

'Opportunists,' he grunted. 'Bastards keep an eye out for funeral notices, when they know everyone's going to be out. Kicked the panel in, then crawled through and forced the lock on the door. Went for the computer stuff they knew they could flog and then legged it. They'd have been in and out in a few minutes.'

'They must have been small,' Jonah said, looking at the size of the broken panel.

'Probably kids. Send the smallest through first to open up and let the rest in. Like a chimney sweep.'

Wilkes gave a wheezing laugh at his joke, but Jonah wasn't convinced. 'Look how jagged the edges of the wood are. Even a kid would risk getting snagged on that.'

'So what? I've seen the bastards get through places you wouldn't believe.' His knees cracked as he heaved himself to his feet. 'You've got forced access right here. Don't overcomplicate it.'

Jonah still felt doubtful, but burglaries weren't his field. By contrast, the ex-detective was in his element. He strutted around the house, bossing the two patrol officers there as though he were the SIO instead of a retired DC. After demanding to know when the SOCOs – scenes of crime officers – would arrive to dust for fingerprints and what follow-up enquiries would be carried out, Wilkes had seemed satisfied that he'd made enough of an impression.

'Don't worry, I'll make it my personal business to get this sorted,' he assured Marie.

She'd found an untouched glass and a bottle of wine and seemed to be picking up from where she'd left off at the wake. Her sisters were staying with her, and one of her brothers-in-law was going to secure the back door and porch, so once the police officers had left, Jonah couldn't see any reason to stay. As he took his leave, Marie gave him a wine-scented hug that had him teetering on his crutches again.

'Stay in touch, won't you?' she sniffed.

Jonah hugged her back. Sorry as he felt for her, it was still a relief to leave. Outside, it was cold, a chill in the air giving a foretaste of winter to the late-autumn twilight. But at least the burglary had put Wilkes in a better mood.

'Rough day,' he said, pulling on brown leather gloves as they walked down the path. His bad hip didn't seem to be troubling him anymore, and he sounded more energised than he had all afternoon. 'I thought Marie looked well, considering. Wouldn't say no to her sisters, either.'

Jonah gave him a look, but Wilkes was too buoyed up to notice.

'I'd offer you a lift but I'm not going your way,' the big man said as they reached his car.

Jonah hadn't told him where he lived, but he didn't want a lift anyway. He was in no rush to spend any more time in the ex-detective's company. It had been a long day, and he still hadn't had a chance to process what he'd learned about Gavin, let alone Fletcher's bombshell about Owen Stokes. He was tired, his knee was aching, and he'd not eaten since breakfast. All he wanted was to go back to his flat so he could try to order his thoughts.

But then he might be missing an opportunity.

'Got any plans for tonight?' he asked.

Wilkes paused by his car, jangling his keys. 'Why?'

He sounded wary but also cautiously hopeful. Jonah had noticed Wilkes didn't wear a wedding ring, and there had been no mention of any family. That didn't got necessarily mean he hadn't got one, but there was something about the ex-detective that made Jonah think he was on his own.

So was he, if it came to that. He allowed himself a moment to imagine walking into his flat, sinking onto the sofa with a beer and some food. Then he pushed it away from him.

'We never finished that drink,' he said.

Chapter 12

'I *know*, all right? I'm not a complete –' Daly broke off, raising her eyes skyward as the voice from her phone droned on. 'Of *course* I realise how much time I'm spending on it, Giles, but . . . No, I didn't get much from the memorial service, but I'm meeting a contact later who . . . I understand that, but – yes. Yes, fine, if that's what you want.'

She stabbed at her phone to end the call before tossing it onto her desk.

'Fucking prick!'

She glowered through the darkened window, unable to see past the ghost of her own reflection. Then she picked up the phone to check the call wasn't still connected.

'Prick,' she muttered, putting it down again.

She slumped back in her chair and stared at the words on the glowing laptop screen in front of her:

Questions still surround the events at Slaughter Quay, in which four people including a Metropolitan police officer were brutally murdered. No explanation has yet been given . . .

The cursor blinked at the end of the hanging sentence. Daly glared at it, then held her finger down on the backspace key to delete what she'd written. The words vanished in reverse order, until the page on the screen was blank. Leaning back, she pushed her hands through her hair and glared up at the ceiling.

'Fuck . . .'

She wrinkled her nose as she caught a whiff of sweat from her armpits. She was still wearing the black dress from the memorial, but now it was rumpled and creased. Worse, it was marked from where it had been spattered by a loose lid from a takeaway latte. It was her best one, her little black number she reserved for special occasions. She'd intended to change out of it after the service, but she'd left the house in a rush that morning and hadn't realised she'd forgotten her everyday clothes until it was too late to go back. She didn't even wear it for funerals as a rule, but she'd guessed Colley would be there. And, let's face it, her legs looked pretty good in the short black number. Much better than her normal frumpy funeral dress. She'd caught Colley checking them out – you're welcome – before the hard-faced police bitch had turned up to spoil things. Now the bloody dress would need dry cleaning. Which was another cost she could do without, because there was no way bloody Giles would approve *that* on expenses.

'Fuck,' she said again. Just because.

It was infuriating. She *knew* there was more to the warehouse murders. Four people murdered, one of them a detective sergeant, yet no one wanted to talk about it. No media blitz, no on- or off-the-record briefings. And no suspect or suspects, at least that anyone was admitting.

Something was seriously off.

Even the memorial service that afternoon had been weirdly underwhelming. There had been none of the fuss she'd have expected for a murdered officer. OK, so maybe they were cagey about saying too much when his body still hadn't been found. But that in itself should have sparked a massive response.

So where was the public appeal for information? It was like they didn't *want* to keep the story in the news.

Like they were embarrassed.

She still hadn't been able to get any official comment on what Colley and McKinney had been doing at the warehouse. At the time everyone had assumed it was some kind of op, which would explain all the secrecy. But why would a firearms officer be involved in something like that? Colley seemed like a straight arrow, but she'd begun to hear rumours about McKinney. Rumours that he hadn't been exactly squeaky clean, that he'd been under some sort of cloud when he'd been killed.

And then there were the victims.

Daly was sure they held the key. To a large extent they'd been overlooked, reduced to faceless ciphers, unidentified and apparently unmissed. Daly knew she'd been guilty of that herself, too busy focusing on McKinney and Colley at first. And when she'd tried to follow it up, Giles, her editor, had lectured her about how 'more dead migrants' didn't sell newspapers or attract advertisers, and told her not to waste any more time on it. As far as he was concerned, Slaughter Quay was old news.

But Daly didn't see it like that. It had been the look on Colley's face in the hospital when he'd talked about trying to save the young woman called 'Nadine' that had brought it home to her. OK, he'd thrown Daly out soon afterwards, but even so. There was a real human tragedy here that was being over-looked. And if it turned out that any of the three anonymous victims *weren't* more of Giles's 'dead migrants', then it would blow the whole trafficking theory out of the water.

Bloody Giles would have to let her run with the story, then.

So Daly had started digging. There hadn't been much to go on, but she'd started sifting through missing persons websites, looking for anyone reported missing around the same time who matched the victims' admittedly vague descriptions.

She'd surprised herself when she'd found someone.

The police refused to confirm it when she'd approached them, but they hadn't denied it either. She took that to mean they wanted to verify the ID with DNA, or whatever, before making it public. Which gave her a narrow window of opportunity to beat them to the punch and get the name out there first.

But to do that, she needed something more concrete than she had at the moment. That was why she'd gone to McKinney's memorial service. She hadn't exactly misled Colley when she'd told him one of the victims wasn't an illegal migrant. If she was right, she'd only be pre-empting the official announcement, and she'd wanted to see how he'd react. His surprise had seemed genuine, and for a second or two Daly had thought he was finally going to open up.

Then that bitch of a policewoman had interrupted.

Sighing, Daly checked her watch. She'd spent all afternoon trying to track down acquaintances of the missing person who might – *might* – be one of the three warehouse victims. But they'd all refused to talk to a journalist. There was only one left to try, and they'd finally agreed to meet her that evening. *So screw you, Giles.* The downside was it would mean another late night, and another phone call she really didn't want to have to make.

One she'd been making all too often recently.

As the ringtone sounded, she kneaded her eyes with a thumb and forefinger. She stopped when it was answered, giving a smile that was as forced as it was unconscious.

'Hi, Mum, it's me.' Her shoulder slumped along with the smile. 'I know I did, but I've been held up at work. No, I don't know how much longer I'll be. Has she been OK? Yes,

I'm sure you have, but . . . Well, is she there? I know it's late, that's why I'm –'

She closed her eyes at the accusing voice, as unrelenting as a dental drill.

'I do realise that, yes. And I'm really grateful to you and Dad. No, I know you didn't but it was different then. For a start, Dad wasn't a – Look, can we not do this now? Just put Maddie on. She isn't in bed yet, I can hear her . . . She's my daughter and I want to speak to her. No, I wasn't snapping, but it's been a long day, so . . . Yes. Thank you.'

She bowed her head, closing her eyes again as she waited. Then a new voice came on, younger and higher-pitched. Daly's face split in a smile that was as heartfelt as the other had been strained.

'Hey, sweetheart, how are you? Have you had a nice day? No, Mummy isn't coming home just yet, so you get to spend another night at Nanna and Grandpops'.' Her smile broadened as she listened. 'Wow, that's fantastic! A zebra! I tell you what, you keep it safe, and then we can find a nice place for it to go tomorrow. How does that sound?'

The fatigue had dropped from Daly's face, but then the first voice chimed in again in the background. Daly's smile began to fade.

'Yes, I can hear her. OK, put Nanna on again. Yes, I love you too, sweetie. Goodnight. Yes, you be a good . . .' The smile vanished altogether as the first voice returned. 'I was still . . . No . . . yes, but – OK, I'll call you in the morning.'

Ending the call, Daly seemed to deflate. She stared at nothing in particular, then put away her phone and picked up her jacket from where it hung over her chair. *Time to go.* She wasn't the only one working late in the open-plan office but she was one of the last. Jamal was still there, slumped in front of his monitor and oblivious as ever as he tapped away at his keyboard, while Lauren was hunched over hers. The red-haired woman gave Daly a snake-eyed glance as she went past but, as usual these days, they ignored each other. *Bitch.*

She took the lift down to the sub-basement car park. Normally, she took the stairs, but her bloody shoes were killing her. They did wonders for her legs but, God, they made her feet and lower back pay for it. Her mind went to Jonah Colley again as the doors slid shut and the old lift began to drop. There was something about him she'd warmed to. He was fit, she'd seen that even beneath the baggy T-shirt and jogging bottoms in hospital. Not bad-looking, either. God knows, she'd dated worse. A *lot* worse.

But there was something else. A wounded quality that made her want to – well, maybe that needed to wait until after she'd got the story, she thought, smiling.

Daly hoisted her bag further onto her shoulder as the lift reached the car park. The subterranean smell of damp, rubber and exhaust fumes greeted her as the doors slid open. Her heels clicked on the concrete floor as she made her way to the bay where she'd left her car. It was at the far end, the low ceiling and dim lighting making it seem even further away. There were still a few other cars there as well, though not so many. Other firms rented floors in the building, insurance or financial companies whose staff were pulling even later shifts than she was. There seemed something forlorn about the lonely vehicles left there, an air of semi-permanence that probably had more to do with Daly's tired state at that time of night.

She was halfway across the concourse when she heard the cough.

It was muffled, as though someone had tried to stifle it. The empty space amplified it, bouncing it off the hard walls so it was impossible to pinpoint. Even then Daly would have thought nothing of it . . . except that it seemed to have come from ahead of her. Where there were more spaces than cars.

Except for hers.

The prickling began at the nape of her neck, stirring the fine hairs like a breeze. But the air in the man-made cavern was stale and still. Daly slowed, a faint perturbation breaking through her thoughts. The car park was badly lit at the best of times, but normally she barely noticed. Now, though, she became aware of the deeply shadowed recesses and corners where the light didn't reach. One of them was by her car.

'Hello?'

Her own voice startled her, ringing out before quickly dying. *Oh, this is stupid.* But someone was obviously down here. So where were they? Daly had visited sink estates, wandered alone through riots and interviewed gang members. None of them had fazed her, yet now her usual assurance wavered.

'If there's somebody there, say something.'

She let her voice echo to silence before reaching into her bag. Grabbing up the phone with one hand, with the other she gripped the small bottle of spray perfume she always carried. From a distance it could pass as a pepper spray, and it would do a similar job if she sprayed it in the fucker's face.

'I'm warning you, I've got mace,' she said, fumbling to start the video recorder on her phone. 'And I'm live-streaming this. If you try anything, you're going to be all over social media! Your call.'

She brandished her phone at the darkness. The only response was the slow drip of water from some drain. *OK, fine.* Holding the phone out in front of her, Daly went to her car. She was starting to feel self-conscious, aware of how she must look. But she'd stood behind police tape at too many crime scenes, reported on too many murders and assaults to think it could never happen to her. She'd take stupid over dead any day.

As she neared her car, she relinquished the perfume and grabbed her car keys. The VW beeped, lights flashing as she unlocked it from yards away. The silent car park mocked her with its shadows and dark corners. No one jumped out. And then she was opening the door, sliding inside and pulling it shut behind her. The locks engaged with a reassuring *thunk*.

'Shit . . .'

She let out a long breath, feeling limp as the tension left her. Her hand was cramped from holding the phone so tightly, but only now did she lower it. On a sudden impulse she turned to check the back seat, then relaxed again when she saw it was empty. *God, you really are jumpy, aren't you?* Daly gave a rueful smile at the thought of how she must have looked, striding towards her car with her phone outstretched. Like a priest in a horror film warding off vampires with a crucifix. *Jesus, I hope no one checks the CCTV.* The thought set her off giggling as she started the engine and pulled away. The fear that had gripped her moments before was forgotten, the idea that someone had been watching from the darkness now seeming ludicrous. As she presented her fob at the barrier, her thoughts had already moved to the meeting she was about to go to, and how she should play it.

The sound of the car's engine faded, leaving the car park quiet once more. One of the light fittings in the ceiling flickered and buzzed. Water dripped again, a solitary fluid note in the darkness. As the haze from the car's exhaust settled, a figure stepped out from the blackness of a doorway.

Keeping to the shadows away from the CCTV cameras, it slipped past the barrier and was gone.

Chapter 13

Jonah groaned, covering his eyes with an arm. Christ, how much had he had to drink? It was a long time since he could remember feeling this hung-over. His mouth was so dry it hurt. But then so did everything else. *It won't get any better lying here.* Gingerly sitting up, he paused to let the throbbing in his head subside, then swung his legs from the bed. He sat there on its edge for a while, putting off the moment when he'd have to stand. When he reached out for his crutches, he realised they weren't in their normal place. He looked around until he saw them lying on the floor near the doorway. The sight brought no corresponding memory of leaving them there.

Pushing himself up by the bedside table, he hopped over to retrieve the crutches. He went into the bathroom, took a couple of paracetamol and drank two glasses of water. His body was crying out for a bacon sandwich, but Jonah tightened his resolve and worked out for the best part of an hour: physio routine first, before running through the limited exercises he could manage with his bad knee. It made his head hurt even more, but gradually that began to ease as he warmed up. Hangover or not, he could feel how much more he was able to do even than the week before as his strength and stamina returned.

The workout left him sweating and breathless but more like

himself. He felt better still after a hot shower. He'd nowhere to
be that morning, so after drinking a glass of orange juice straight
off, he indulged his hangover with grilled bacon, poached eggs
on toast and black coffee.

Nursing a second coffee, he reflected that the only thing
he'd gained from an evening in Wilkes's company was that
crutches and alcohol were an even worse combination than
he'd thought. He'd learned nothing more about Gavin. Wilkes
had spent most of the night reminiscing over war stories from
his time in the force. But Jonah had the feeling that there
was still something he'd been holding back, something that
cut deeper even than the suspension. And talking to Wilkes
had painted a compelling picture of the pressure Gavin must
have been under in his last days and weeks. At least now he
better understood Fletcher's cracks about his track record and
judgement. He just had to decide what it meant.

And what to do about it.

A chime from his phone announced a text, pulling him from
his thoughts.

Just checking all's well. No need to reply. M.

He felt a twinge of guilt. Miles and his wife Penny ran an
informal support group for parents who had lost a child. Their
definition of 'lost' was wide-ranging, encompassing anything
from bereavement and disappearance to estrangement. Their
own daughter, an only child, had died twenty-odd years before,
and helping others had been their way of coping. Jonah's
attendance had petered out as the years went by, but Miles had
always been on the end of a phone, prepared to talk or – more
often – just listen.

Jonah's guilt grew as he realised how long it had been since
he'd last called them. It must be over a year. *Nearer two, be*

honest. He didn't even know if the support group was still active. They'd both be pushing seventy now, perhaps older. And Miles was a voracious devourer of news, so he'd have seen Jonah's name mentioned in reports and would have known he was injured. *You should have let them know you were all right, not made them have to ask. They deserve better than that.*

Resolving to set that straight now, he started to call Miles. The harsh *driing* of the doorbell interrupted him before he could. He quickly texted I'm fine. Will call, then reached for his crutches. The doorbell rang again.

'All *right*, I'm coming!' he called.

He thumped irritably down the hallway and put his eye to the spyhole. Distorted by the convex lens, a gargoyle face stared back at him. Jonah rested his head against the door. *Great.* Straightening, he opened it.

Fletcher and Bennet stood in the corridor, coats damp from the rain.

'Can we come in?'

Jonah moved back to let them inside. He could barely wait to close the door behind them before he asked.

'Have you found Stokes?'

'Love a cup, thanks,' Fletcher said, going without invitation into the kitchen. By the time Jonah followed them in he was already pulling out a chair at the table, his mac hanging on him like a loose sail. 'Two sugars in mine.'

Bennet's face remained impassive. She took the chair next to the DI.

'Just tell me, have you found him?'

'Not exactly.'

'What does that mean?'

The DI sat down and made himself comfortable. 'Talking'll be a lot easier if you stick the kettle on.'

Jonah stayed where he was. 'Just tell me why you're here.'

Fletcher nodded to Bennet. 'Show him.'

The policewoman produced a thin folder and took out several large, glossy photographs. She leafed through them, removing two and setting them on the table so Jonah could see.

'This is one of the surveillance photos we found on McKinney's computer, with part of it enlarged,' she said, sitting back. 'It was taken two weeks before he died, according to the date on the file. There were a lot more like it, but you get the gist.'

The main photograph was full colour. It showed the bar of a pub, glasses and bottles lined up behind it against a long, ornate mirror. Several people stood or sat on tall stools at the bar, but only one of them jumped out at Jonah. A tall, broad-shouldered man with a shaved skull, wearing a denim jacket. He was hunched over the bar, his back to the camera, apparently staring into his drink. Visible above his jacket collar, the black lines of a spider-web tattoo covered the back of his neck. The enlargement was of the mirror behind the bar, in which the reflection of the man's face was clearly visible. Sullen and heavy-boned, with a thin-lipped gash of a mouth and deep-set eyes.

Owen Stokes.

Jonah gave a start as Bennet's phone suddenly rang. She glanced at it, then turned to Fletcher.

'I should get this.'

She went out into the hallway, pulling the door shut behind her. Fletcher regarded Jonah sourly.

'If you're not going to make a drink then for God's sake sit down, Colley. You're getting on my nerves standing there.'

Jonah considered standing anyway, decided that would be childish, and sat down. 'Why are you showing me this?'

'Let's call it context. Your friend McKinney was following Stokes prior to your little party at Slaughter Quay.' Fletcher paused to give him a questioning look. 'I don't suppose you've anything else to share about that?'

'I've already told you what I know.'

Fletcher nodded, as though that was what he'd expected. Taking two more photographs from the folder, he slid them across the table and sat back without comment. These were black-and-white stills from street CCTV footage. Both appeared to have been taken at night on the same stretch of empty road, though the vantage points suggested they were from different cameras. The quality was poor, the images grained and blurry, but Jonah recognised the figure in them as Owen Stokes. He was wearing what looked like the same denim jacket and jeans as before, this time with a dark baseball cap jammed down onto the shaved skull. One of the stills had caught him heading towards a camera, while in the other shot he was striding away. His shoulders were hunched and he walked with his head down, so the cap's peak obscured his face. But in trying to shield his features he'd exposed the back of his neck. Above the turned-up jacket collar, the radiating lines of the spider-web tattoo were clearly visible.

'OK, it's Stokes again.' Jonah set the photographs down and shrugged. 'I don't understand what I'm supposed to be looking at.'

Fletcher reached across and tapped the date and time stamp on one of the photographs. 'They were taken in Ealing around eleven-thirty p.m., give or take, the night before McKinney died. Not far from his flat.'

Jonah felt his flesh crawl. 'Stokes knew where he lived?'

'Looks that way, doesn't it?' Fletcher's eye had started watering. He took a tissue from his pocket and began to dry it. 'You know he wasn't living at home anymore, then?'

'Only since yesterday.' Jonah was still trying to take in this new revelation. 'So Stokes knew Gavin was watching him?'

'Either that or he was making a social call. Popping round for a cup of sugar, like mates do.'

Jonah looked up from the photograph. 'You're not serious.'

'Stranger things have happened.' Fletcher gestured at the photographs. 'These only show that McKinney and Stokes were aware of each other before that night at the warehouse. How and why is open to debate.'

'No. There's no way Gavin was working with Stokes. No way.' Jonah shook his head, wanting to dislodge the thought before it took root. 'Stokes must have realised he was being watched and followed Gavin back to his flat. If this shows anything it's that the warehouse was probably a set-up. Stokes could have led him there deliberately.'

'That's one possibility.'

Something in Fletcher's voice stifled Jonah's protest. He watched as the DI took another photograph from the folder. It was from a street camera again, also taken at night. Stokes was the only subject in this as well, carrying a large holdall slung over one shoulder. But it was a different location, and Jonah stiffened when he recognised the modern houses in the middle-class street.

'This is the road where Marie and Gavin live, but I don't . . .'

He trailed off, a cold shock running through him when he saw the time and date stamp.

The previous afternoon.

'It was taken around the same time as the house was burgled.' Fletcher said. 'Which probably explains the holdall he's carrying. Although somehow I can't see him going all that way just to nick a teenager's laptop and games console.'

Jonah felt as though his mind had stalled. 'Then what was he after?'

'You tell me.' Fletcher rocked his chair backwards, balancing it on two legs as he regarded Jonah.

'How am I supposed to know?'

The chair banged down onto all four feet as Fletcher suddenly leaned forward. 'Because you're holding something back, Colley, it's written all over you. Whatever McKinney was doing at that warehouse, whatever was going on with him and Owen Stokes, I don't believe he'd have left you out of it until the last minute. Something happened you're not telling me about.'

'You've examined my phone, if I'd been in contact with –'

'Stop pissing me about. First off we find out Owen Stokes was at the warehouse, and now it turns out he broke into McKinney's house yesterday, looking for God knows what. And then there's you, batting your eyes and pleading ignorance. So I'll ask you one last time. What aren't you telling me?'

The kitchen door opened as Bennet came back from her call. She glanced at them, registering the tension, but gave no other sign. Giving a minute shake of her head in answer to Fletcher's questioning look, she resumed her place. The DI's almost lipless mouth tightened, making Jonah think that whatever message had just passed between them, it couldn't have been good news.

'You've come just in time,' Fletcher said to her. 'I was explaining to Sergeant Colley how last chances work. And he was about to tell me what it is he's been withholding from us all this time.'

'Whatever it is, you need to ask yourself if it's worse than multiple homicide,' Bennet said, surprising him. 'Because that's what you're implicated in. Your call, but if you don't cooperate, you can say goodbye to your career. And that's the best you can hope for.'

'Then maybe I should get a lawyer,' Jonah shot back, trying not to show the alarm he felt at her words. 'And I'm sure the

Police Federation would love to know one of their members was being threatened.'

'No one's threatening you, we're just pointing out the alternatives. But I think you already know that.'

The policewoman's relaxed assurance was more unsettling than her superior's hostility, but Fletcher didn't give Jonah a chance to respond.

'You want to hide behind someone's skirts, fine.' The DI's grin was hard, stretching the taut skin of his face. 'Make a complaint, see where it gets you. Get someone to sit in and hold your hand if you like. You're hiding something, Colley, so you can either tell us what it is voluntarily, or carry on like you are doing. And you've been on the job long enough that I shouldn't have to spell out how that's going to end.'

He didn't. And although the DI's attitude rankled, Jonah knew Fletcher was right. He *was* hiding something.

Just not what they thought.

'OK, I didn't just lose touch with Gavin McKinney,' he told them, forcing out the words. 'There's a reason I hadn't spoken to him for so long, but it's nothing to do with any of this.'

Fletcher crossed his arms. 'Go on.'

Even after ten years, Jonah still felt the old reluctance. Not that it mattered anymore, even to him. But silence could become a habit. *Say it.*

'He slept with my wife.'

Chapter 14

Ten years ago

The house looked the same as ever as Jonah walked up the path to the front door. That seemed wrong somehow. It should be ramshackle and falling down, not untouched by what had happened. Keys in hand, he looked at the step where Theo had once fallen, the tears from a grazed knee replaced by laughter as Jonah had picked him up and swung him round. *You've broken the path! Theo's harder than concrete!*

Tearing his eyes away, he unlocked the door and went in.

He'd phoned Chrissie to tell her he was going to collect the last of his things, but it had gone straight to voicemail. They'd had hardly any contact with each other in weeks. At some point Jonah knew they'd have to sit down and talk about the divorce, but he didn't have any appetite for that. He hadn't even got around to consulting a solicitor yet, even though he was sure Chrissie wouldn't have wasted any time. One of the advantages of being a PA to the senior partner at a law firm instead of a police officer on compassionate leave. No doubt Neil Waverly would have been there to offer advice and a sympathetic shoulder. And the rest. Jonah had always suspected they'd been sleeping together even before . . . Well, *before*. But it didn't seem to matter now. *Good luck to her*, Jonah thought. *And God help the poor bastard.* Now it didn't seem to matter.

The empty hallway greeted him; no toys littering the floor, no small shoes or clothes on the coat hooks. It hit him afresh, robbing him of breath and weakening his legs, so that it was a few seconds before he became aware of hearing the shower running upstairs.

Oh great, Jonah thought. Chrissie must be home. He contemplated turning around and leaving. But then he'd only have to come back again later. Squaring his shoulders, he started up the stairs.

'Chrissie?' he called, pushing open the bedroom door. 'I left you a message, I've come for –'

He stopped. Gavin was by the bed, caught in the process of fastening his jeans. He was shirtless. Behind him the quilt lay in a rumpled heap.

The smell of sex thickened the air, subtly different to the scent Jonah associated with the room. With him and Chrissie.

'Fuck,' Gavin said. He straightened. 'I know how this –'

Jonah hit him in the mouth. Gavin stumbled and toppled backwards as his legs struck the edge of the bed. Jonah threw himself on top of him, straddling his chest and swinging punches. Gavin was yelling, trying to block the blows with his forearms and struggle free, but then one caught him flush on the jaw. It sent a shock all the way up to Jonah's shoulder and Gavin's eyes blanked. Barely noticing the pain from his knuckles, Jonah raised his arm to hit him again, and there was a burst of light as something crashed against the back of his head.

Dazed, he could hear angry voices through the ringing in his skull, and then Gavin was pushing free from under him. The room lurched dizzyingly as Jonah tried to get up, but there was no strength in his arms. Gavin was on top now, pinioning his arms with his knees as he pounded Jonah's unprotected face. Jonah felt his nose burst, then everything seemed to tilt as he fell off the bed onto the floor.

He became aware of shouting above him.

'. . . nearly fucking killed him! Jesus, you didn't have to hit him as well! What's *wrong* with you?'

'Just shut up, OK? Just shut the fuck up!'

With an effort, Jonah tried to push himself upright. He got part way and then slumped back, half sitting up against the side of the bed. He swallowed, tasting the coppery tang of blood. He lifted his hand – when had it got so heavy? – to touch his head. His fingers came away slick and wet.

Gavin was still shirtless, one eye swollen shut. Chrissie wore an untied bathrobe, the fabric clinging and damp, her hair straggly and wet. The remains of a hairdryer were scattered like shrapnel on the carpet around her. Jonah tentatively touched his head again. *Jesus, she hit me with a hairdryer?*

'You OK?'

That was from Gavin. Jonah felt something break inside him. 'Ge' away from me.'

Turning on his side, Jonah got one knee under him and tried to stand up.

'Here, let me –' Gavin said, starting forward. Jonah threw off his hand.

'*Fuck off!*'

Using the bed for support, Jonah pushed himself to his feet. The floor felt like it was moving, but after a second he was able to stand unaided. As though they hadn't seen each other naked before, Chrissie seemed to realise her bathrobe was hanging open. She wrapped it around her, her mouth tightening as she hurriedly fastened the belt.

'What are you doing here?' she demanded.

'I came for my things.'

'So what? You can't just come barging in, you don't live here anymore!'

'I called, I left you a message.' Jonah was shaking. 'Maybe if you hadn't been busy fucking my best mate, you'd have heard it!'

'Look –' Gavin began, but Jonah turned on him.

'Don't! Not a fucking word!'

Chrissie had folded her arms, chin coming up as she glared at him. He knew the expression from countless other arguments. This time there were tears in her eyes, but Jonah chose to ignore them.

'What I do isn't any of your business!' she spat. 'You're the one who walked out, what did you expect?'

'Nothing from you,' he shot back. But he was looking at Gavin as he said it.

Chrissie had worked up a head of steam. 'So now you're the victim? God, that's rich!'

'What's that supposed to mean?'

'I'm not the one who fell asleep and let my son drown, am I? If you want to blame someone, look in a fucking mirror!'

'Jesus Christ, Chrissie,' Gavin said.

'What, you're on *his* side now?' She dashed the tears from her eyes. 'God, you're as pathetic as him! Where are you going?'

This last question was aimed at Jonah, who was heading unsteadily for the door. His anger had died. Now he only wanted to get out of there. He had to hold onto the banister as he went downstairs. The thump of footsteps came from behind him.

'Jonah, wait!'

Gavin was trying to drag on his shirt as he hurried along the hallway. 'Just give me a chance to explain! This was a mistake, OK? She was upset and lonely, and . . . things happened! I'm sorry.'

Yeah, me too. Jonah stopped at the front door as a wave of dizziness passed over him.

Gavin seemed to misinterpret it.

'Can we at least talk it through? Go for a drink or something. Please.'

Jonah felt a sense of dislocation as he looked at the man in front of him. It was like looking at a stranger. Turning away, he opened the door and walked down the path to the street.

He made it halfway to his car before he threw up.

Chapter 15

There was silence when Jonah finished. Fletcher's face was the usual mask, showing no hint of judgement or sympathy. Bennet's was equally unreadable. Jonah knew they'd have heard far worse, but that didn't make it any easier. This was the first time he'd told anyone what had happened, and while the memory had lost most of its power to hurt, it didn't feel any less sordid.

Fletcher let him sweat for a few moments before he spoke. 'Why didn't you tell us before?'

'It's ancient history. I didn't think it was relevant.'

'Not *relevant*? You forgot to mention that a murder victim slept with your wife? That's not just relevant, that's a motive.'

'Not much of one, if I waited ten years. My marriage was over by then anyway, it's not as though that's why we broke up.'

'Things like that fester. And ten years is plenty of time to build a grudge.'

'We've already been through this,' Jonah said wearily. 'I didn't kill him, you know that.'

'Do I? Because right now I'm starting to wonder what else you might be hiding.'

'I'm not hiding anything. That's it, that's my big secret. I fell out with my best friend because he slept with my wife, OK?'

Fletcher gave him a considering look. 'Were you surprised?'

'You mean when I found my best friend in bed with my wife? What do you think?'

'Let me put it another way. Was it out of character?'

That was harder to answer. Jonah had known Gavin was unfaithful to Marie long before he'd found him with Chrissie. He'd liked to 'play hard', as Wilkes had put it, but it had always been a casual thing for him. Jonah had called him on it more than once, but Gavin just shrugged it off.

We can't all be plaster saints, he'd said.

'I didn't think he'd do that,' Jonah admitted.

'That's not what I asked.'

'Look, I trusted him. I don't know what else I can say.'

'You could start by explaining why you'd want to help the man who got into your wife's pants?'

There were times when Jonah asked himself the same thing. 'He used to be a friend. Like I told you before, he sounded like he was in trouble.'

'And I suppose you're such a soft touch you just went along with it. Even after he'd slipped it to your wife behind your back.'

Jonah noticed Bennet glance in disapproval at the DI. He knew the man was trying to provoke him, but the wound was too old for that to work. So he said nothing, and had the small satisfaction of seeing Fletcher's mouth tighten in irritation.

'I'm assuming you know that McKinney had been suspended.'

'I only found out after the service yesterday. Why didn't you tell me?'

'Are you serious?' The DI's incredulity wasn't feigned. 'You're an unreliable witness in a murder enquiry, I don't have to tell you –'

He broke off, a hand going to his throat.

'Sir?' Bennet said, stepping towards him.

'I need a drink of water.'

His voice sounded weak and hoarse, and he seemed to be having trouble swallowing. Jonah started to push himself up from the chair.

'I'll get it,' Bennet told him.

She crossed quickly to the sink, took a clean glass from the drainer and filled it from the tap. Fletcher said nothing as he took it from her. His hand seemed to have developed a tremor as he raised the glass to his mouth. Bennet's face gave nothing away, but she watched the DI closely as he drank.

'Do you want a tea or coffee?' Jonah asked, regretting his earlier stubbornness.

'No.' Fletcher's manner was even more brusque than usual. He put the glass down, as though disowning it. 'Let's talk about McKinney's suspension. Do you know what the allegations against him were?'

Wilkes had edged around that. 'Not really.'

'He was on the take. Accepting bribes from the gangs he was supposed to be investigating in return for information. Raids he was involved with had a habit of drawing a blank, suspects would magically skip out just before they were due to be arrested. He denied it, claimed he was being stitched up. But he'd been going off the rails for a while. Skipped shifts, turned up drunk or so hung-over he could barely function. Punched out a colleague who criticised him. Oh, and he failed a drugs test.' The DI raised his eyebrows at Jonah. 'Any of that surprise you?'

Even though he'd known it would be bad, it was still a shock to hear what Gavin had been accused of. Jonah didn't know what to say.

'He wasn't like that when I knew him.'

'No, he just slept with your wife. Maybe you should reflect on that next time you're deciding where your loyalty lies.' Fletcher got to his feet. 'Will she corroborate what you've told us?'

'She won't be happy. She's remarried.'

'Her happiness isn't high on my list of priorities. Neither's yours. Do you have her phone number and address?'

'Nothing recent. We aren't exactly on each other's Christmas card lists.'

'There's a surprise.'

Fletcher headed to the door, leaving Bennet to gather up the photographs from the table. Jonah had one last glimpse of Stokes's hunched figure hurrying along the dark street, the spider-web tattoo an inked tracery on the back of his neck. Then she'd put them back in the folder.

'We'll be in touch,' Fletcher told him as they went out.

Jonah's car was an automatic, which meant he didn't need to use his left foot to operate a clutch. He'd already checked with the surgeon and his insurers, who'd insisted on an additional premium before clearing him to drive. Even so, he hadn't planned to drive for a few more weeks, to give his knee more of a chance to heal.

But then he hadn't planned a lot of things.

The Saab was in a rented lock-up a half-kilometre away, part of a row of garages on a small cul-de-sac. The walk seemed a lot further on crutches. As Jonah drew near, he recognised the BMW that was parked outside. The car was a beauty; a red saloon over twenty years old. It belonged to Stan, the garage owner who he'd originally bought the Saab from. An old-school mechanic, as well as owning an engine and body repair shop, Stan had a sideline renovating and selling old cars. He maintained the Saab for Jonah and still had a proprietary interest, grumbling at each annual service if he felt it hadn't been treated with the respect it deserved.

'You're late,' he told Jonah. He was barrel-chested with sinewy arms corded with muscle, a battered Harris tweed jacket worn on top of his overalls.

'Sorry, it took longer to get here than I thought.'

Stan gave his crutches a jaundiced look but made no comment. He held out the Saab and garage keys.

'I changed the oil and brake fluid when I brought it back, but you'll need to check the tyre pressures. It won't have liked standing all this time.'

It wasn't the only one, Jonah thought, unlocking the heavy-duty padlock. The dark blue Saab almost filled the small garage, and what space was left was taken up by clutter. A selection of old power tools and half-used tins of paint covered the shelves on the back wall, while boxes of papers Jonah hadn't got around to sorting were stacked in the corners.

'You want me to bring it out for you?' Stan asked. He sounded irritable, but Jonah had known him long enough not to take any notice.

'How much do I owe you?'

'I'll put it on your next bill.' Stan levelled a finger and fixed him with a baleful glare. 'Check the tyre pressures, OK?'

Getting back behind the wheel of a car was trickier than he'd expected with his bad knee, but at last he managed it. He sat there for a moment, enjoying the feeling. It wasn't much of an achievement, but it meant a return to something like normality. Jonah hadn't realised how much he'd missed that.

He just wasn't looking forward to where he was going.

He'd avoided giving Fletcher a straight answer when he'd asked for Chrissie's address. They hadn't been in contact with each other for years, but he knew where she'd last been living. She'd married Neil fucking Waverly six months after their divorce came through, and it hadn't taken long on social media to check that they were still at the same address. He knew he was risking antagonising the DI even more, but Jonah rationalised that he hadn't exactly lied. He just wanted a chance to talk to Chrissie before they did.

It was better if she heard about Owen Stokes from him rather than them.

The house was part of an elegant Georgian terrace, tucked away behind a beech hedge and mature lime trees near Primrose Hill. A stainless-steel intercom was set into a stone gatepost next to the ornate wrought-iron gate. Pausing to rub his knee, which was stiff and sore from the drive, Jonah pressed the buzzer and waited.

'Hello?'

The woman's voice was distorted by the intercom, making it hard to identify. Jonah leaned closer to the grill.

'Chrissie?'

There was a pause before the voice came back. 'No, I'm sorry. Mrs Waverly isn't at home.'

He could hear what sounded like a Spanish accent. *Since when did Chrissie have staff?* Thanking her, he started back towards his car on his crutches. He intended to wait, but he hadn't gone very far when a white Range Rover went past. He caught a glimpse of a blonde woman before it pulled into one of the residents-only parking spaces outside the house he'd just left. The rear doors opened, disgorging two young children in school uniforms. A boy and girl of six or seven, alike enough to be twins, noisily continuing whatever argument they'd been having inside the car.

When the woman climbed out after them, Jonah's first thought was that it must be a neighbour. The blonde hair had subtle highlights, and she had sunglasses pushed onto the top of her head. She was slimmer than Chrissie had been, and her clothes were the sort of expensively overstated style a woman who lived on this street and drove a new Range Rover would wear. The little boy was tussling with the little girl as they waited by the gate.

'Mum, tell her!'

'It's not me, I haven't done anything!'

'Oh, for God's sake, Abigail, be quiet! You too, Harry! I won't tell the pair of you again.'

As she went to the electric gate, Chrissie gave a cursory glance in his direction, automatically threat-assessing the stranger with the stubbled head and crutches. She turned away, then slowed as she looked again.

'Hi, Chrissie,' he said.

He saw her face harden, the middle-class mother replaced by the ex-wife he remembered.

'Mummy needs to fetch something from the car,' she told the boy and girl, unlocking the gate with a fob. 'Tell Rosa you can go on PlayStation.'

They forgot their argument and ran excitedly down the path. He'd known she had kids – he'd seen that much on her social media – but the reality of it hadn't sunk in until he saw her with them. Chrissie had a new family. One that had nothing to do with Theo.

'I didn't recognise you,' she said. Her voice was neutral. Wary.

'Same here. You look good.'

He meant it. Now he was closer he could see there were a few more lines around her eyes and mouth, but she looked tanned and fit in a tailored white jacket and skin-tight jeans that showed off her figure. The heavy gold chain around her neck probably cost more than his car. Even her perfume was different, smelling of sandalwood and money.

'What do you want, Jonah?'

Yep. It's Chrissie, all right. 'We need to talk.'

She stood by the open gate, one hand still on it as though ready to either escape inside or bar Jonah entry. 'Why?'

'I don't want to go into it in the street. Can we go inside?'

'Not until you tell me why you're here.'

'It's about Gavin.'

'I heard what happened. I'm sorry, but –'

'I wouldn't be here if it wasn't important.'

She looked back towards the house, then gave a sigh. She held open the gate.

'You'd better come in.'

Chapter 16

The kitchen was open-plan, with a double-size range cooker and gleaming appliances. There were no pictures fixed to the door of the huge fridge, but on one wall was a large, framed photo montage of the two children laughing and smiling. On beaches, in the garden, blowing out birthday candles: a compendium of happy memories. With a pang, Jonah looked away.

A young woman with dark hair was by a vast granite-topped island. She gave a professionally polite smile as they entered, a flicker of surprise registering when she saw Jonah.

'Harry and Abigail said it was OK for them to have an hour on PlayStation,' she said to Chrissie, opting to pretend he wasn't there. Jonah recognised the voice and accent as the woman he'd spoken to earlier.

'They can have half an hour before homework,' Chrissie told her, hanging her handbag over the back of a bar stool at the island. The young woman allowed herself another glance at Jonah, unsuccessfully trying to hide her curiosity.

'Would you like me to make a coffee . . .?'

'No, thank you, Rosa. You'd better go and see what the twins are doing.'

The young woman bobbed her head and left. Jonah watched her go.

'Before you start, she just helps out,' Chrissie snapped. 'Loads of people have nannies these days.'

'I wasn't going to say anything.' Jonah had more sense than to pass comment. 'So how old are the twins?'

Chrissie's smile was reflexive, softening her face. 'Six. Abigail's the oldest. Only by two minutes, but you'd think it was two years.'

'Congratulations.'

'You wouldn't say that if they were yours,' she said, but her smile vanished as she realised what she'd said. 'I didn't mean –'

'I know.' He found himself feeling sorry for her. He nodded at the framed family montage on the wall. 'They look like great kids.'

'Thanks.' The strain was back. Turning away, she took a jar of ground coffee from a cupboard. 'You might as well sit down.'

Jonah took one of the bar stools at the granite island. He noticed that she hadn't asked what he wanted. Old habits.

'I'm sorry about Gavin,' she said, without looking at him. 'Have they caught who did it?'

'Not yet.'

She began spooning coffee into a cafetière. 'How's Marie?'

'About as you'd expect. It was the memorial service yesterday.'

'I heard. I thought about going, but after all this time . . . You know.'

He did. He doubted Marie knew what had happened between her friend and her husband, but it would still be difficult for Chrissie to face her again.

'I hadn't realised you'd kept in contact.'

She didn't add *with Gavin* but she didn't need to.

'Actually, that's sort of why I'm here. The police might want to talk to you.'

'To *me*?'

He took a breath. 'I had to tell them about you and Gavin.'

She stopped and stared at him. 'Why the *fuck* would you do that?'

'They wanted to know why I stopped talking to him.'

'Jesus *Christ*! That's just fucking *great*!'

'Look, it wasn't much fun for me either, but I didn't have any choice. They just want you to corroborate what happened.'

'Oh, is that all? And what if I don't want to *corroborate* anything?'

'Then they'll keep coming back until you do.'

'God, I don't believe this! It was *years* ago, why does it even matter anymore?'

'Oh, I don't know, maybe because Gavin was murdered? Someone beat him to death and took away his body, so I'm sorry if any of this *inconveniences* you!'

Silence. They were both red in the face, breathing heavily. A movement in the doorway caught his eye. The young nanny was looking at them anxiously from the hallway.

'Is everything OK, Mrs Waverly?'

Chrissie composed herself. 'Everything's fine, thank you, Rosa.'

Chrissie closed the door behind her.

'That's going to be all around the snobby mummy brigade this time tomorrow.'

Jonah rubbed the back of his neck, where the muscles had started to knot. 'Sorry.'

'That makes two of us.' She put her head back and closed her eyes. 'I knew, I *knew* I shouldn't have let you in.'

But there was no heat in the statement, or any hostility in her face now. Only weariness. Chrissie seemed to have aged ten years from the confident woman he'd seen outside.

'There's more,' he told her.

'Of course there is. No, just wait,' she said, before he could go on. 'I want to be sitting down before I hear it.'

Jonah remained silent while she poured two coffees into bone china mugs. 'Still no milk or sugar?'

'No thanks.'

She set the mug in front of him and sat down across the island. 'All right, let's hear it.'

'There's a suspect. It's Owen Stokes.'

He watched her face change. 'You mean the man they thought took Theo? I don't understand . . .'

She wasn't alone in that. Sparingly, leaving out anything that wasn't strictly relevant, Jonah told her what he knew. It felt strange. He'd never discussed cases with Chrissie when they'd been married. Even if he'd wanted to take his work home with him, she wouldn't have wanted to hear about it.

Chrissie's expression grew more strained as she listened. She crossed her arms even tighter, as though to ward off what he was saying.

'Nobody's mentioned this before. How come this is the first I've heard about it?'

'They didn't know it was Stokes until they got the DNA results. And now I think a lot of people are worried how it looks. No one is clear about what happened, so now it's about damage limitation until they've a better idea what they're dealing with.'

'But why was Gavin even *at* the warehouse unless –' Her face had paled. 'Oh, Jesus.'

'We don't know anything for sure,' Jonah said gently, knowing what was going through her mind.

She wasn't listening. 'The inquest said no one else was involved, it was an accident! Now, after ten years, it turns out this – this Stokes actually took my *son*?'

'We don't know that for sure,' Jonah said, aware he'd somehow stepped into the role Fletcher had occupied. 'Everyone insists the enquiry's findings still stand. Gavin was . . . he was going through a bad time, so maybe when he came across Stokes again he just jumped to conclusions.'

'Is that what you think?'

He started to say *I don't know*, but the words stuck in his throat. He shook his head.

'No.'

'I can't believe this is happening.' Chrissie closed her eyes. 'God, I feel sick.'

'Are you OK . . .?' He began to get up.

But she shook her head, hand raised to stop him. He sat back down again, knowing there was nothing he could say that would help. She looked down at the granite island top.

'It never ends, does it? You try to move on, but . . .' Her eyes were brimming. 'I still miss him, you know. I know you thought I didn't care, but I did.'

'I didn't –'

'Yes, you did. It was always you he wanted. It didn't matter if I was there or not. But I was his mum. He was mine as well as yours. There's not a day goes by when I don't think about him. And what happened.' She shook her head, as though dispelling whatever images had been conjured up. 'I hated you, you know.'

'Chrissie –'

'It's all right, I'm past that now. But I did. It felt like you'd come between us while he was alive, and then you let this . . . this fucking unbelievable, awful *thing* happen. You, the one he idolised! I couldn't bear it, I just . . . I just wanted to hurt you, any way I could.'

'Is that why you slept with Gavin?'

She gave him another look, but she'd no appetite for a fight either.

'I felt worthless. I'd lost my little boy, my marriage was a wreck. I just wanted the whole nightmare to *stop*. Just for a few minutes. So when Gavin came round again, I just thought . . . why not? I knew I'd hate myself even more afterwards, but that was the point. I did it to spite myself as much as you.'

Jonah felt raw. Although he'd not gone there to have this conversation, it was a long time coming.

'You said when Gavin came round "again"? What did you mean?'

She gave him a pitying look. 'You seriously think that was the only time he tried it on?'

'Why didn't you say something?'

'And how would that have gone down? If I'd tried telling you your precious best buddy was wanting to get into my pants, you'd have said I was just causing trouble. You'd have believed him rather than me any day.'

'That's not true.'

'No? Admit it, you still don't want to believe it even now, do you?'

She was right: he didn't. Chrissie shook her head.

'See? You always did have a blind spot where he was concerned. And don't think he didn't use that. He always put himself first, but you never could see it.'

Oh, believe me, I did, he thought, but let it pass. With an almost imperceptible sigh, Chrissie straightened.

'So what happens now?'

'I don't know,' he admitted, then broke off as the kitchen door burst open. Two small whirlwinds swept in.

'Mummy, Harry won't let me have my go!'

'I will, you're just rubbish!'

'I'm not, you're cheating! Tell him he can't –'

They stopped when they saw Jonah, identical expressions of

surprise on not quite identical faces.

'Abigail, Harry, this is Jonah. He's a friend of Mummy's,' Chrissie told them. 'What do you say?'

There were shy smiles and 'Hello's. Jonah found himself looking for any echoes of his son in the upturned features.

He wondered if they knew about their half-brother.

'Mummy, tell Harry I can have a turn!' the little girl said, turning away from Jonah now the novelty had worn off.

'No, that's not *fair!*'

'OK, enough,' Chrissie declared. 'Where's Rosa?'

On cue the young woman hurried into the kitchen, looking harried. 'Sorry, Mrs Waverly, I only stepped out to take a phone call –'

'Never mind, just get them started on their homework, I'll be along in a minute.'

Jonah waited until the young woman had ushered her charges out. 'I should go,' he said.

Chrissie didn't argue. She glanced back down the hallway, making sure no one could hear.

'Should I be worried?'

'You mean about Owen Stokes? I can't see why you should be.'

'You've just told me he killed Gavin and three other people, and he broke into Marie's house yesterday. After Theo . . .' She stopped, unable to say it.

'That was different,' Jonah told her, putting as much conviction as he could into it. 'Gavin put himself in Stokes's crosshairs when he started following him. Stokes doesn't know anything about you, and there's no reason for him to care if he did.'

She nodded, but still looked unconvinced as she opened the door. Jonah went out, pausing to turn when he'd negotiated the step.

'Good to see you again, Chrissie.'

From the look on her face, he wasn't sure she felt the same way.

'Watch yourself, Jonah,' she told him, closing the door.

Chapter 17

Dusk was settling by the time he reached Slaughter Quay. He pulled onto the same patch of weed-choked tarmac as before, at the last minute giving in to some superstitious urge and parking in a different spot to last time.

His was the only car there. He looked over to where Gavin's Audi had been, then climbed out. A cold wind was coming off the water, bringing a dank smell of oil and mud. Balanced on his crutches, Jonah shivered and wondered what he was doing there. After leaving Chrissie's, he'd felt at a loss. He didn't want to go back to his flat, so he'd set off driving without any clear destination. But, as though the idea had only been waiting to present itself, before he'd got to the end of the road he'd already made up his mind.

Even now he couldn't say why, except the compulsion had been growing since he'd left the hospital. He wasn't fooling himself that coming back would bring any sort of revelation or help him understand what had happened here.

He just needed to see it again.

In which case, he thought, maybe he should have gone earlier. The light was fading fast as he set off along the path towards the quay. He followed the same route as before, crossing the narrow side street by the old tannery building, where cobblestones showed beneath the broken tarmac like scabbed wounds. The only sound was the metronome click of his crutches, but as he neared the quayside he could hear the slosh of the river against the pilings. The moored barges announced themselves with the protesting squeal of rubber fenders. The large one still bobbed a little away from the rest, like an unwelcome guest at a party. The paintwork on its bows spelling out *The Oracle* was flaked and faded, and Jonah noticed a sun-bleached *For Sale* sign propped in a window.

No sign of the cat this time.

It was colder as he neared the end of the quayside. The wind cut in directly from the water, bringing a front of piercing cold and damp that made his knee ache. Up ahead he could see the last warehouse. The damaged fencing had been replaced but otherwise it looked as he remembered. A derelict shell with boarded-up doors and broken windows.

He'd wondered how he'd feel being there again, but the truth was he felt nothing. There was no emotional shock, no catharsis. No answers. He looked at it for a while, then turned away and started back for his car.

But it was a long walk, and as the light fell the lonely quayside seemed to take on a more sinister aspect. The deepening shadows brought an uncomfortable sense of déjà vu. He did his best to ignore it, until he heard a metallic chink, like swinging chains. All at once he was back in the loading bay, with the smell of blood and Gavin's body on the plastic sheet. He faltered, his heart seeming to stutter.

Then it had passed, leaving him clammy and shaken. There were no chains, only a section of wire fencing rocking in the wind. *Jesus* . . . Letting out an unsteady breath, Jonah set off along the quayside again. All he wanted now was to be back in the warmth of his car. Cutting away from the waterside, he went back down the narrow lane by the old tannery. It was even darker down there, and he had to watch his footing on the cobbles.

He wasn't sure when he realised he wasn't alone. The awareness came gradually, a subliminal unease that became impossible to ignore. Without knowing why, Jonah felt the hairs prickle upright on the back of his neck.

Looking up, he saw someone at the far end of the lane.

It was a woman. In the gathering dark it was hard to make her out, her face a pale oval above the long dark coat. But Jonah knew she was watching him. His mouth had dried. *No. Not possible . . .* He took a faltering step and stumbled as one of his crutches caught on a cobblestone.

When he looked up she'd gone.

The lane was empty, as though she'd never been there. And maybe she hadn't. Jonah was already beginning to doubt what he thought he'd seen. He hurried down the lane as quickly as he dared, looking all around as he emerged from it. Night had almost fully fallen, the distant lights on the far bank of the river twinkling in the growing dark. But it wasn't so dark that Jonah wasn't able to see there was no one there.

The Saab was an indistinct shadow, standing alone on the waste ground. He unlocked it and climbed in, sitting in darkness while his heartbeat returned to normal. He realised he was trembling. Going back to the quayside had shaken him more than he'd realised. He'd tried to convince himself that what happened at the warehouse hadn't affected him, that apart from his knee, there were no lingering effects.

Yeah, right.

He held up a hand. It was still trembling, but not so much. He felt OK to drive, and the sooner he left that place the better. Going there had been a stupid idea, especially when it was getting dark. It was just that and an overactive imagination, he told himself, starting the Saab. It couldn't be anything else.

Because the figure in the lane had looked like the young woman who'd died at the warehouse.

A rat scurried out from behind an overflowing bin. It paused to consider the intruder, bead-like eyes glinting in the streetlight as it scented the air. Then, unafraid, it continued on its business.

Jonah gave the bins a wide berth as he went down the alleyway at the side of the ornate Victorian building. This part of Hammersmith was mainly commercial: shops and small businesses with a few flats above them. It was bustling during the day, but now everything was closed or in the process of shutting. When he'd left the quayside, he'd automatically started heading to his flat, but he'd felt too restless and on edge to go back there yet. His entire body was a knot of tension. He'd felt pummelled and off-balance ever since Fletcher and Bennet's news that Stokes was behind the break-in at Marie's. Then there'd been the humiliation of having to tell the detectives about Chrissie and Gavin, followed by visiting Chrissie herself. Although he was pleased for her, seeing his ex-wife with her new family had been emotionally hard. For him to cap the day off with a trip to Slaughter Quay had been inviting trouble. No wonder he was having flashbacks and jumping at shadows.

But, despite his rationalisations, the memory of what – *who* – he'd thought he'd seen in the lane remained an unsettling thorn at the back of his mind. Not so long ago he'd have called Khan or someone else from his team. Arranged to meet up for a beer and either talked it through or, more likely, banished the dark mood with company and a few drinks.

He didn't feel able to do that now, though. Not with Fletcher prowling around, and not for this. It was too personal, too tied up with his past. It was then that Jonah had remembered the text he'd received from Miles that morning.

If there was anyone he could talk to about this, it was him.

Today was a Thursday, which meant there should be a support group meeting later. With a sense of relief, Jonah had pulled over and called Miles to check. It had gone to voicemail, so he'd left a message saying he'd be coming to the meeting and hoped that was OK, then rang off.

He'd felt better after that, as though the thought alone was enough to settle his nerves. There had been some time to kill, so he'd stopped off at a café for a sandwich. The meeting house shared premises with a snooker and pool club, which occupied the bulk of the building. Jonah went around the back. Tucked away by the air vents was a small doorway. A small sign above it said, *Friendship House. All Welcome.*

He tried the door. It was unlocked, so it seemed he'd been right about there being a meeting. Opening it, he went into a large, echoing room that smelled of cold plaster and stewed tea. The floor was unvarnished boards, splintered but worn smooth by wear. Plastic chairs and folded trestle tables were stacked against the walls, and a faded poster was pinned to a cork noticeboard. Printed on it in bold red letters was a forlorn looking promise: *You're not alone.*

Jonah closed the door behind him. There was no one about, but someone must be there for the door to be unlocked and the lights left on. He drew a breath to call when the lights went out.

Darkness engulfed him. Panicking, he spun round, stumbling backwards as he half raised a crutch to fend off an attack. Something struck the backs of his legs, and there was a metallic clatter as he toppled over an unseen stack of chairs. He fell to the floor, hurting his knee and flailing around as they crashed down around him.

The lights came back on.

Jonah blinked, dazzled by the sudden brightness. A man wearing an unbuttoned overcoat was standing in the doorway at the far end of the hall, one hand still on the light switch. He was tall and slightly stooped, his thinning grey hair neatly brushed. The wire-rimmed glasses magnified his eyes, which right now were widened in an almost comical expression of surprise.

'Jonah?' He looked even more horrified when he noticed the crutches. 'Good God, are you all right?'

'Fine. I just, uh . . .' There was really nowhere to go with that, so Jonah abandoned the sentence. 'Hi, Miles.'

The older man hurried forward. 'Here, let me help.'

'It's all right, I'm fine. Really.'

The panic had subsided, leaving embarrassment in its wake. Favouring his bad leg, Jonah found one of his crutches and began clambering to his feet. That made yet more noise among the fallen chairs. Miles moved them aside to give him more room.

'If I'd known you were coming, I'd have left the lights on. I was just shutting up shop.'

'Didn't you get my message?' Jonah asked, stooping to retrieve the other crutch.

Miles paused in the act of righting a chair. He looked mortified. 'No, I'm sorry. I'm afraid I haven't been paying much attention to my phone.'

'It's OK, don't worry about it.' Setting the last chair back on its feet, Jonah took in the empty hall. 'Isn't there a meeting tonight?'

Miles adjusted his glasses, his discomfort evident. 'Look,

why don't you take a seat while I pop the kettle on? We can chat over a cup of tea.'

Jonah watched him go into the kitchen with concern. Something wasn't right, but Miles would tell him in his own time. Pulling up a chair, he sat at a trestle table, listening to the sounds coming from the kitchen. As ever, being there filled him with conflicting emotions. It took him back to a painful time, the worst of his life. Yet there was also a reassuring sense of calm, a comforting familiarity that tempered the emotional impact. Just like it always had.

He'd first heard about the support group when a flier dropped through his letterbox. There'd been no accompanying note and he didn't recognise the handwriting on the envelope. Inside was only a small, cheaply printed sheet of A5, and the block capitals at the top had hit Jonah like a punch: *HAVE YOU LOST SOMEONE?* Underneath, in smaller text, were a few more lines:

Loss takes many forms. You needn't suffer through it on your own. Come and meet others who understand how you feel. Share or stay silent, it's your choice. Tuesdays and Thursdays, 7 p.m., Friendship House.

There had been a Hammersmith address and a mobile number. Jonah never did find out who'd sent it. He'd guessed it came from someone on his team, who'd wanted to help but was too embarrassed to do it openly. Jonah hadn't been interested anyway. Screwing the flier into a ball, he'd thrown it in the bin.

But he'd gone back later and fished it out again. Smoothed it out and stuck it in a drawer. It was another few weeks before he finally gave in and went to Hammersmith for the first time. The hidden-away entrance behind the snooker club had been hard to find, and its location hadn't inspired confidence. There was nothing for him there, he'd thought.

He'd been wrong.

For two years, the twice-weekly meetings had been a lifeline, helping him get through each awful, empty week. The small hall became a sanctuary. Often there were only a few people there, sometimes only himself, Miles and Penny. On those occasions, talk would generally be about something else entirely rather than the defining tragedies that had brought them together.

Gradually, Jonah's attendance had dropped off. But even when he no longer went to the meeting himself, he'd kept in touch with Miles. Or had, until recently. Now, looking around the empty hall, Jonah felt his conscience prick at how he'd allowed contact to lapse.

Miles came out of the kitchen bearing a tray. He'd taken off the overcoat, revealing his usual uniform of an open cardigan over a worn but crisply ironed white shirt. Some things, at least, never changed.

'Here you go,' he said, setting down the tray. On it were two mugs of tea and a plate of biscuits. Custard creams, Jonah saw. They'd always been Miles's favourite. 'Say if you'd like more milk.'

'This is fine, thanks.'

Jonah never took milk or sugar anywhere else. Here, though, it somehow seemed natural. Miles sat down, moving a little stiffly, Jonah noticed. With another pang, he saw how his scalp showed through the thinning grey hair, and how the large but finely boned hands were mottled with liver spots he couldn't remember seeing before.

But the smile was the same, and so was the warmth in the brown eyes. 'It's good to see you again, Jonah.'

'I've been meaning to get in touch before now, but . . .'

'Good grief, there's no need to apologise. I'm just glad you're all right. After I saw that newspaper article yesterday

152

and realised you'd been at that awful place . . .' He shook his head. 'How are you?'

'I'm OK.' Jonah shrugged. 'I won't be doing ballet any time soon.'

'A great loss to the world of dance, I'm sure.' The soft brown eyes were searching. 'But that isn't what I meant. How *are* you?'

Jonah looked down at his mug. He'd gone there to talk, but that didn't make it any easier.

'I went to see my ex-wife earlier. She's remarried, with twins. They're nice kids.'

'Ah.' Miles nodded, considering his own mug. 'I'm glad for her, of course. But that can't have been easy. And I read that the police officer who died along with those other poor souls was a friend of yours. A close friend?'

From anyone else it might have felt like prying. 'He used to be.'

'I'm sorry. I'm sure he was a good man.'

A good man. Jonah had no idea if that described Gavin or not. 'I don't know. But he was a friend for a long time. I don't like thinking of him as a bad one.'

'A little of both, then. Like the rest of us.' Miles sighed. 'I'm not going to ask what went on in that place, but from the fact that you're here I suspect you're finding it hard to deal with. Which is perfectly understandable.'

Jonah started to speak, but his throat threatened to close up. He cleared it before trying again.

'Let's say it's brought the past back in a way I wasn't expecting.' Much as he might want to, he couldn't tell Miles about Owen Stokes. Chrissie had a right to know, but Jonah had taken enough of a chance telling her. 'There's a lot of things I don't understand. I need to find answers, but I don't know how.'

'But you're intending to find out?'

The simple clarity of the question cut through the fog that had surrounded Jonah. 'Yes.'

Miles considered him for a while before speaking.

'I remember the first time you came here. You sat at the back of the room, looking like you wanted to lash out at the world. I knew how you felt. I think most people who pass through that door would. Angry, confused, looking for someone to blame. And above all *hurting*. You were like a clenched *fist*.'

He held up his own to demonstrate.

'I can't tell you how heart-warming it was to see you gradually open up. For Pen as well as me. That's why I was concerned when I realised you were involved in this dreadful business. Of course, I hoped you weren't too badly hurt physically, but I was more worried about the emotional impact it might have. New trauma has a habit of unearthing old, and you've already experienced something most people never have to endure. I'd hate to see you clench into a fist again, Jonah.'

'I won't,' Jonah said.

'I do hope not. And I know you aren't stupid enough to take the law into your own hands.'

It was said pointedly, but then Miles's eyes crinkled in a smile. He reached for the plate and held it out.

'Have a biscuit.'

Jonah took one, deciding it was time to move the conversation away from himself. 'How's Penny?'

'Oh, she's . . . well, not too good, actually. That's why I haven't been coming here so often. I only called in tonight to make sure everything was OK and collect the post.' Miles was suddenly preoccupied with his tea. 'Pen has cancer.'

'Christ, Miles . . .' The news jolted Jonah out of his own problems, making him feel selfish for putting them first. 'Where?'

'Pretty much everywhere, really. At least, by the time they caught it. She's not having any treatment. She felt . . . well, we'd rather make the most of the time that's left. I won't say we're reconciled, but we've both accepted it. Some days are better than others, but by and large she's in good spirits.'

'I'm so sorry . . .'

'I know.' The smile was back. 'She'd love to see you. You must come round again. Soon.'

'I will,' Jonah promised.

It was after nine by the time Jonah got back to the flats. His knee was aching, so he parked on the road outside rather than contend with the long trudge back from the garage. The black sky was smudged with smoke-like clouds, only the brightest stars visible through the city lights as he made his way across the concrete concourse to the entrance. Hearing about Penny had left him sobered and saddened, yet in an odd way had also cleared his head. His own problems were no more comprehensible, but now at least he could view them with more perspective.

A group of youths was standing under a covered walkway off to one side. Jonah looked them over with the ingrained habit of a police officer, though not enough for it to be read as a challenge. They watched in silence as he went into the foyer and pressed the call button for a lift. One of the overhead lights was out, and it struck him yet again how dismal the place was. The wall tiles were cracked and filthy, while the glass panels in the entrance were misted where decades of graffiti had been scoured off.

Not for the first time, he wondered why he was still there. It wasn't as though he had any reason to stay, and there was nothing keeping him from moving.

But as usual the thought didn't gain any traction. Willing the lift to hurry up, he stooped to rub his aching knee, flexing the sore joint. A wave of cold air swept over him as two youths came in from outside. When the lift doors opened they followed Jonah in. Both had their hoods up, one of them wearing his over a black baseball cap. The other had a savage case of acne. They looked seventeen or eighteen, and there was a wired quality about them both. A sweetish chemical odour clung to their clothes. They weren't looking at Jonah directly, but he caught one of them darting a glance towards the other as the doors slid shut.

Neither of them pressed a button to select a floor.

Oh, great. Jonah didn't recognise them, but he guessed they were there to either buy or sell, and had decided a lone invalid was an easy target. Keeping his eyes on the illuminated floor numbers above the doors, he shifted his stance to distribute his weight on his crutches and bad leg.

'I'm police.'

They stirred, looking from him to each other and back again. 'You what?'

It was the smaller of the two, greasy blond hair peeping out from under the hood. Jonah kept his gaze on the floor indicator.

'You heard.'

The indicator flickered as the lift passed another floor. Jonah continued to gaze above their heads, his face stone. He could feel the tension building, knew it could go either way. Crutches or not, after the day he'd had, he didn't care.

The lift stopped. The doors chimed open.

Jonah could feel them watching him as he got out and unhurriedly went down the corridor. He listened for any sound that they were coming after him, but there was only a squeaking glide as the lift doors shut again. When he heard it start to descend, Jonah stopped and turned. A strip light flickered and buzzed on the corridor behind him, but otherwise it was empty.

Not sure if he was relieved or disappointed, he continued to his flat and let himself in. Taking off his jacket, he went to the fridge and took out a beer. He drank straight from the can, then took out his phone and ordered a pizza. Normally, he tried to limit his junk food, but it was late and he was too tired to cook anything.

Again, that sort of a day.

He'd finished the can and was contemplating having another when the doorbell rang. Just using one crutch, he limped into the hallway and looked through the spyhole. He half expected to see the dickheads from the lift, but it wasn't them. The person standing outside was even less welcome.

Jonah leaned his head against the door. *Perfect. That's just perfect.* The doorbell buzzed again, followed this time by a brisk knock. Straightening, he opened the door.

Corinne Daly gave a bright smile as she held out a pizza delivery box. 'I hope you didn't order anchovy.'

Chapter 18

Jonah didn't take the box. 'What do you want?'

'Well, a drink wouldn't go amiss, if you're offering.' Her grin faded when Jonah didn't respond. She offered the pizza box again. 'Can you at least take this? I'm getting greasy fingers.'

He still didn't move. Daly sighed.

'I came up in the lift with the delivery guy and said I'd give it to you, OK? I even tipped him. I haven't poisoned it, honest.'

Jonah took the box and started to shut the door.

'No, wait!' Daly leaned into the closing gap. 'I'm not working now, this is my own time. I came to apologise.'

'I don't want to hear it.'

'Please, just listen! I've found out some things you might want to hear.'

Jonah stopped, still holding the door part shut. 'What things?'

'Let me come in and I'll tell you. Look, in case you're worried . . .' She rummaged in her shoulder bag and took out her phone. 'I'm turning it off. There.'

Daly held it up, showing him the screen as the phone shut down.

'See? It's off, it's not recording. And you'll want to hear what I've got to say.'

Jonah hesitated, but curiosity won out. He opened the door to let her in.

'I'll give you five minutes.'

That earned him a smile. 'Thank you.'

He let her go into the living room first. She put her shoulder bag onto the coffee table and sank onto the sofa with a sigh. She stayed like that, long legs stretched out in front of her, slender throat upturned. Jonah was suddenly aware of how attractive she was. Pushing away the thought, he sat down in the armchair so the coffee table was in between them.

'So, what is it you want to tell me?'

'I'll come to that in a minute. There's something I want to get off my chest first.' Daly sat up, suddenly uncertain. 'I kept thinking about what I did, at the hospital and the memorial service, and . . . I wanted to apologise for the way I behaved. That's not me, OK? I don't like to think of myself as that sort of person. Sometimes I just don't much like what I have to do, or myself for doing it. And this has been one of those times.'

Jonah wasn't convinced this wasn't another attempt to play him. But she looked tired and vulnerable sitting there, not the confident journalist who'd ambushed him in his hospital room or confronted him outside the church. And her apology seemed genuine.

'So why keep on doing it?'

'Believe it or not, I still like being a journalist. Somebody's got to hold people to account, and on a good day that's how I see what I do. But mainly it's because I'm a single parent with a mortgage and a six-year-old daughter. I need the money.' She gave him a rueful smile. 'I'm not looking for sympathy, I just wanted to . . . I don't know. Explain, I suppose. So you don't think I'm a complete cow.'

'OK.' This wasn't what Jonah had expected, but he wasn't ready to roll over yet. 'You said you'd found out some things I should hear.'

She looked down, acknowledging his suspicion. But when she met his eyes again there was no mistaking the gleam in them.

'I know who one of the victims is.'

That got his interest. 'Which one?'

Daly smiled. She sat back, knowing she'd set her hook.

'I think that deserves a slice of pizza.'

'His name's Daniel Kimani.'

Daly wiped her fingers on a piece of kitchen roll. The last piece of pizza was congealing in the open box, a half-empty can of beer next to it. That was her second. Jonah was on his third, having had one before she arrived. He'd told himself it would be his last.

Daly had insisted on waiting until they'd eaten before telling him anything else. He'd been impatient at first, but had decided it was better to go with it. So far, she hadn't given him any cause to regret letting her in. She'd done most of the talking, at least when she wasn't eating pizza and drinking beer, but she'd avoided the subject of Slaughter Quay. Although part of him remained guarded, Jonah actually found he was enjoying her company.

Now, though, she was ready to get down to business.

'He was a post-grad student from Kenya,' she continued, dropping the screwed-up kitchen roll on the coffee table. 'Twenty-six, came here on a student visa two years ago to take a PhD in politics and sociology. Well thought of, by all accounts, but not much for socialising. Only had a few friends and even then kept himself to himself, but he was a keen human rights campaigner. He was reported missing two days before you found his body at Slaughter Quay. Didn't show for meetings at the university and wasn't answering his phone. His flatmate said he hadn't been home since going out in a rush one morning. But he didn't tell anyone where he was going or who he was meeting.'

Jonah's mind had been racing as he listened. If this Kimani was in the country on a student visa, then that put a massive hole in the theory that the three warehouse victims were illegal migrants, or the victims of a trafficking gang.

'How do you know all this?' He hadn't seen any mention of it in the news, so either it had only just been released or Daly had a well-placed police contact.

'It didn't come from the enquiry team, if that's what you're thinking. They aren't saying anything, so I did some digging of my own.' She tried not to look pleased with herself, but her pride leaked through. 'I checked through all the missing persons announcements around that time matching the description the police put out – and believe me, there were a lot – and whittled them down. Daniel Kimani ticked all the boxes. Some of his friends from the university had put up a small reward for information, so I contacted them and asked to meet. They filled me in with the rest.'

Jonah felt anti-climax set in. 'So this isn't an official ID? It's coming from you?'

'Yes, but it's only a matter of time before it's confirmed,' she said, colouring. 'If I can work it out, I'm sure the enquiry already has.'

And perhaps discounted it, Jonah thought. He tried not to let his disappointment show. 'Like you say, there are probably a lot of missing people matching the same description.'

'But how many of them also know a young woman called Nadine?'

The name sent a shock through Jonah. Daly grinned, enjoying springing the surprise.

'Apparently, Kimani had been seeing someone called Nadine for a few weeks beforehand. None of his friends knew her surname or anything about her, but his flatmate saw her briefly when she visited the house. Early twenties, curly black hair, looked Mediterranean or Middle Eastern. Very attractive. Sound familiar?'

It did. An image of Nadine's terrified face, filthy and scalded with quicklime burns, flashed into his head. He swallowed, trying to push it back into its box.

'So they were in a relationship?'

It would be even worse if it was her boyfriend's body she'd been lying on, maybe even seen killed. But Daly shook her head.

'That was my first thought, but Daniel Kimani was gay. None of his friends could say why he'd been seeing her, but they were pretty sure it wasn't a sexual relationship.'

'Have they told the police?'

'Of course. They were thanked for the information and told they'd be informed of any developments.'

So Fletcher must know already. The enquiry would surely have DNA and fingerprint confirmation by now if the body really did belong to Kimani. Which meant either it wasn't his . . .

Or they'd decided not to release his identity.

Jonah felt buoyed by the news, but also annoyed. Daly had done what he should have thought of himself. He'd been sitting back and letting the enquiry do all the work, as though Fletcher was ever going to tell him anything he didn't have to.

Call yourself a police officer . . .

'What were these friends' names?' he asked.

Daly gave a wry smile. 'You don't really expect me to reveal my sources, do you?'

He didn't but it was worth a try. 'What about the other two victims? Have you found out anything about them?'

'Not yet.' Daly paused, looking down at her beer. 'So you hadn't heard of Daniel Kimani? The name doesn't mean anything to you?'

But Jonah wasn't about to give anything away. 'Why are you telling me any of this?'

It was Daly's turn to look surprised. 'I thought you'd want to know. Look, I don't want to be rude, but are you having that last slice of pizza?'

The change of tack threw him. 'No, help yourself.'

'I'm not normally such a pig, but I skipped lunch,' she said, reaching for it and taking a bite. She gave a groan of pleasure. 'God, I'm such a hypocrite. I'm always lecturing Maddie about junk food, and now look at me.'

'Maddie's your daughter?' he asked, remembering the conversation they'd had outside the church.

'Yeah. I love her to bits, but she can be a complete monster when she wants to be. Winds my parents round her little finger. You know how it is.' She screwed up her face as she realised. 'Shit. Sorry, I didn't . . .'

'It's OK.' Jonah had learned long ago not to react to unintentional barbs. That wasn't the same as being immune to them. 'You said you were a single parent?'

Daly was eager to move past her gaffe. 'It's no big story. Her father didn't run off or die or anything, he was just a shit. Let's just say it's another episode in my life I'm not especially proud of. And there have been a few, believe me. But it got me Maddie, so I owe him that much.'

'Does he ever see her?'

'No. That was never going to happen, I knew that from the start. But it's his loss. He wasn't the sort to bring much joy into her life even if he'd stuck around. So, you know, good riddance. I'm sorry for Maddie, but she's a happy little girl, she's got a loving family. I just wish . . .'

'What?' Jonah asked when she stopped. Daly shrugged a shoulder, studying her beer.

'That I could be around more for her. I mean, I've got to work, and I try to make the most of the time we spend together. I try to be a good mum, I really do. But it's hard, sometimes.' She stopped, shaking her head. 'Sorry. I shouldn't be moaning to you about my problems. Not after what you've been through.'

Jonah shrugged, uncomfortable with the direction this had taken. 'I'm OK.'

'Yeah, 'course you are.' Daly smiled. She tucked her legs under her on the sofa, twisting to face him more directly. 'I'm sorry about Gavin McKinney. Were you very close?'

Jonah felt a cloud pass over him. 'We used to be.'

'I know you don't want to talk about it, but when I –' She stopped. 'Never mind.'

'What?'

Daly shook her head. 'It doesn't matter.'

Jonah looked at her, trying to scent a trap. She had her head down, hair falling across her face. 'Go on.'

'I was going to say I lost my best friend a few years ago, so I've got some idea what you're going through. Completely different circumstances, she took an accidental overdose. At least everyone *said* it was accidental, but I always wondered, you know? I kept thinking I should have done more, that I let her down.'

She paused, as though giving Jonah the opportunity to say something. But his feelings for Gavin were too complex to walk into that minefield. When he didn't respond, Daly bit her lip.

'I've got a question, but I don't like to ask,' she said.

Jonah smiled, but he felt some tension creeping back. *Here it comes.* 'Then maybe you shouldn't.'

Her own smile soon flickered out. Somehow she'd moved nearer on the sofa, legs still curled under her but now leaning towards him.

'I've heard rumours about your friend. That he was in trouble. And he shouldn't even have been at that warehouse because he'd been suspended. Is that true?'

Shit. Jonah set his beer down. 'Where'd you hear that?'

'It's OK, I don't expect you to confirm anything, but . . . Well, you can't deny it, can you?'

Jonah was sobering fast. 'Jesus Christ,' he said, marvelling at his own stupidity.

'OK, I'm sorry, forget I said anything,' Daly said, as he started to get up. 'Please don't –'

But Jonah had already jumped to his feet, momentarily forgetting about his knee. He gave a gasp as his full weight came down on it, sending a burst of pain lancing through the joint. His leg buckled under him, and as he grabbed for the armchair his shin caught the edge of the coffee table. It tipped over, spilling the beer cans and Daly's handbag onto the floor. Jonah flopped back into the chair, gritting his teeth against the throbbing in his knee as she hurried over.

'Oh, God, not again! Are you OK?'

'Yeah, just . . . stupid.'

And embarrassed. His knee was still throbbing but less so now. Enough for him to be aware of how close Daly was. She had one hand on his shoulder, the other resting on his chest. When he opened his eyes, her face was only inches from his. He could smell her perfume, and the heat from her hands burned through his T-shirt. Neither spoke. Daly leaned closer, or maybe it was the other way around.

Then Jonah's phone rang.

They both jumped like guilty teenagers. Daly retreated back to the sofa as the phone clamoured again. It had fallen from the coffee table onto the floor, so Jonah had to bend awkwardly to reach it. As he picked it up he saw the name on the illuminated display.

Marie.

'I need to take this,' he said.

He didn't, but it was an excuse to put some distance between them. Still rattled and angry at himself, he took the phone into the hallway. He pulled the door shut behind him, leaving enough of a gap so he could see Daly as he answered.

'Hi. Are you OK?' he asked, keeping his voice down and avoiding saying Marie's name.

'Oh, Jonah, Jonah . . .' The sound of crying came down the phone. 'I wanted to . . . You were his best friend, you know he wasn't . . . Can you come round?'

She sounded slurred, almost unintelligible. He glanced through the doorway. Daly was still on the sofa, looking for something in her handbag. 'Why, what's happened?'

'. . . it was just there, right there, all the time . . .'

'What was?' God, how much had she had?

'. . . like he's talking to me from the grave . . .'

Jonah kneaded his eyes, unable to make any sense out of what she was saying. 'Listen, I'll call you in the morning, OK?'

'I miss him so much . . . they don't understand, no one understands . . .'

'In the morning,' he repeated. 'You go to bed and try to get some sleep.'

There was sniffling, another incoherent comment and then the line went dead. Jesus, Jonah thought. Marie had every reason to be in a state, but she'd sounded far gone even by her standards. And 'talking to her from the grave'? What was that about?

Pushing the door open, he went back into the living room. Daly still looked flustered, the flush on her cheeks extending down her throat and into the open neck of her shirt.

'I should be going,' she said, not meeting his eyes.

He nodded. They went to the front door. Jonah unlocked and opened it. Daly gave an awkward smile.

'Well . . . thanks for the pizza.'

'You're welcome.' Something occurred to him. 'Hang on, I'd better come down with you.'

She paused, a guardedness about her. 'Why?'

'There were some teenagers hanging around outside earlier. I'll walk you to your car.'

She gave a startled laugh. 'Seriously? Thanks, but I can take care of myself.'

Face burning, Jonah watched her go. Her footsteps clipping a rapid beat that bounced off the corridor's walls as she headed for the lifts. He closed and locked the door, then rested his head against it.

'Oh, you fucking idiot!'

Daly heard the door close behind her. She carried on down the empty corridor to the lifts, jabbing the call button repeatedly when the doors didn't open straight away.

'Come *on* . . .'

The lift pinged and its doors opened. There was no one inside. Daly stepped in and pressed the button for the ground floor. Her shoulders relaxed minimally when the doors slid shut and she felt the weightless drop as the lift began to descend.

'Shit, shit, *shit*!'

She'd blown it. She shook her head, grimacing. What the hell had she been *thinking*, quizzing him like that? But it was late and she was tired, and – surprise, surprise – it turned out Colley was a nice guy. There was definitely something about him, and she'd been unprepared for how readily she responded to it. She'd actually started to forget why she was there. She'd let herself get carried away, and then tried to make up for it by blurting out that question about McKinney. OK, so the beers hadn't helped, but she couldn't just blame it on that. If his phone hadn't rung when it did . . .

But it had. Nothing happened. *So get over it.*

She rummaged inside her shoulder bag. Her phone was in there, still switched off. Ignoring it, she took out the digital voice recorder. The small red light was on to show it was running. She rewound it for a few seconds, then pressed play. Colley's voice came from the tiny speaker, reedy and thin but recognisable.

'*. . . because he'd been suspended. Is that true?*'

'*Where'd you hear that?*'

'*. . . You can't deny it, can you?*'

Daly stopped the playback. At least the recording was clear enough. Even though she'd been careful to leave her bag open, she'd been worried that the microphone wouldn't have picked up their voices from inside. But it had, at least until it had fallen onto the floor when the coffee table had been knocked over. Not that there had been much to hear after that anyway.

More's the pity.

Still, maybe she'd got enough at that. Colley had obviously never heard of Daniel Kimani, but the way he'd clammed up when she'd asked him about McKinney told her what she needed to know. She'd only been fishing, making out the rumours she'd heard were more solid than they actually were.

But he hadn't been shocked or surprised. Or refuted it, which was as good as a confirmation as far as she was concerned. And he'd been reticent about McKinney even before then. She frowned, remembering Colley's answer when she'd asked if they'd been close. He'd said they *used to be*.

As in, they weren't any longer.

Daly felt a slow spread of excitement. God, what if there was some sort of history between McKinney and Colley? What if they hadn't been at the warehouse on some sort of undercover operation? That could cast a whole new light on whatever had happened. Shit, it might even mean Colley was a *suspect* . . .

Her excitement died as she remembered when they'd talked about her daughter. He'd tried to hide it, but she'd seen the sadness on his face. And offering to walk her back to her car might have been patronising, but there'd been something . . . well, *sweet* about it. He'd been concerned for her, and when was the last time she could say that about anyone?

And in return she'd stitched him up.

Daly put the recorder back into her bag. Her reflection was framed in the glass panel set in the lift doors. It was scuffed and smeared, throwing back a distorted image of a no longer young woman with a sharp face. It didn't look like her. *Get used to it. It's going to look less like you every year.*

Her reflection gazed back, cynical and knowing.

The lift bumped as it reached the ground floor. The doors squealed open, revealing the fluorescent-lit foyer. It smelled of piss, stale alcohol and the sickly sweet smell of resin and hope-lessness. She hurried out through the grubby glass entrance. It was cold outside, the concrete bridges and overhead walkways deserted. At least the gang Colley had warned her about had gone. There'd been some teenagers hanging around outside when she'd arrived, so perhaps that was who he'd meant. She'd made a show of ignoring their stares and sniggers. If anything, she'd walked more slowly. That was one thing she'd learned from her job: no matter how scared you were, never let it show. Daly had interviewed rapists and murderers, thrust her recorder in the faces of rioters and brazened her way through situations she'd have been terrified of any other time. It was all about attitude. And what had started out as an act had soon become ingrained, as though her laminated press card granted actual invulnerability.

She reminded herself of that now, as her footsteps rang out in the darkness. It seemed like every other streetlight was broken, creating pools of darkness she had to cross before the next patch of light. The only parking space she'd found was a couple of hundred yards away, and as she walked away from the flats, she hoped her car was still there and in one piece. Neither was a given, not in a neighbourhood like this.

She shivered as a gust of wind blew a faint spray of rain against the back of her neck. The shame she'd felt in the lift was already forgotten. She was on the trail of something, she could sense it. And even though she hadn't got as much as she'd have liked from Colley, on top of what she'd learned about Daniel Kimani, there was enough to make Giles sit up and take notice. Daly gave a little grin to herself, beginning to edit her memory of the evening into a more palatable shape.

She was still grinning when someone whistled behind her.

It wasn't loud. Not a wolf whistle, or a fingers-in-the-mouth shrill. Just two soft notes; one high, one low. Daly tensed but didn't look back. She continued walking, even though all her senses were focused behind her now. Probably just someone out walking a dog, she told herself. Except she couldn't hear the scratch of dog claws on the pavement, or any footsteps other than her own. She continued at the same measured, unhurried pace. What had she just been telling herself? *Don't let them see you're scared.* A serious attacker wouldn't advertise his presence, which meant it was just some tosser wanting to feel big. Get himself off by frightening a lone woman on a dark street. *Well, think again, prick.*

The whistle came a second time.

It was closer, and now Daly felt a flutter of alarm. She couldn't pretend anymore that the whistle wasn't meant for her. And while she didn't want to give this creep the satisfaction of thinking he'd spooked her, if she didn't react at all it would give the same message. *OK, then. Let's call this wanker's bluff.*

Pulling out the bottle of spray perfume, she turned around. The empty street mocked her. There were closed shops and waste ground on both sides of the road, tall slabs of dirty brick interspersed with patches of scrub and wire fencing. There was no one in sight but the broken streetlights left swathes of blackness where anyone could be concealed. Daly held the bottle of perfume poised, putting on her best fuck-you glare.

'This is mace, arsehole! I've had a really shitty day, and if you want to try and make it worse, go ahead!'

Nothing. No movement, no sign of life. Daly tried not to acknowledge the fear that wanted to bubble up. She gave a start as the edge of her vision registered a movement at the other side of the road. But it was only a cat. No, an urban fox, she realised, seeing its size. Jesus, here? The dark shape picked its way silently across the road, then abruptly stopped. It stared into what looked like the dark mouth of an alleyway a few yards from where Daly stood, eyes glinting bright in the streetlight's glow. Then it turned and slunk away.

Daly stared into the shadows where the fox had been staring. Had it seen something there? Suddenly she remembered the incident in the underground car park a few nights before.

How she'd been convinced there was someone hiding down there, waiting. *Oh, stop it! You're just scaring yourself!* Whatever the fox had or hadn't seen, no one was showing themselves now. *Because there's no one there. Pull yourself together.* With a last glare down the dark street, she turned away – deliberately slowly – and carried on walking.

She'd barely taken half a dozen steps when the whistle came again.

Oh, fuck! Fucking hell! Daly told herself to stay calm, but it took a huge effort of will not to glance behind her or speed up. *Don't let him see he's scared you. That's what the pathetic bastard wants.* Christ, where had she left the fucking *car*? Gripping the bottle of perfume like a talisman, she groped in her bag again, this time for her phone. It was only when she pulled it out that she realised it was still turned off. *Shit, shit, shit!* Her hand shook as she fumbled to switch it on, fingers suddenly clumsy. The bloody thing always took an age to start, but the creep behind her didn't know that. Putting it to her ear, she began to talk loudly into the dead phone.

'Police, please. I'd like to report an attempted assault. Yes, right now. It's on . . .' She blanked as she tried to think where she was, then she saw a street sign up ahead. '. . . Ashton Way. I'm being followed, so please send a car. Yes, straight away. Thanks.'

The phone chimed as she finished speaking, its screen lighting up as it came on. *About bloody time.* She brought up the keypad before realising she couldn't call the police now without giving herself away. As she hesitated, she saw her car up ahead. *Thank God!* Relieved, she realised it was a while since she'd last heard the whistle. She turned and looked back down the street. It was still empty, but now it also *felt* empty. The streetlights here were working, forming a well-lit patch of road through which anyone following her would have to cross. She'd not only see them coming, she'd easily be able to reach her car before they could catch up.

So fuck you, you sad bastard! Exultant, she gave the empty street the finger, just in case, and turned to hurry the last few yards to where she was parked.

Someone stepped out of a dark passageway in front of her.

Daly jumped, startled. Yet logic told her that whoever had been whistling couldn't have overtaken her. No way, not without her seeing them. This couldn't be the same person, and the realisation gave fuel to her anger.

'Why don't you watch where you're –' she began.

But she didn't finish, or hear the perfume bottle smash when it hit the ground.

Chapter 19

'Oh, Jonah, thank God!' Marie practically pulled him inside when she opened the front door. She looked distraught and dishevelled. 'The police have just left! Oh, Jesus . . .!'

'OK, calm down, Marie.' He'd seen Fletcher and Bennet leaving as he'd pulled up outside. He wasn't sure if they'd seen him or not, but he'd hung back until they'd gone anyway. There was no reason he shouldn't visit Marie, but the less he had to explain himself to Fletcher the better. 'Come on, let's go and sit down.'

She'd sounded hung-over when he'd called her that morning. She hadn't wanted to get into why she'd phoned the previous night, saying she'd rather explain in person. Knowing Marie, that could either mean she'd forgotten the drunken call or had just wanted company. After Daly's visit the evening before, Jonah had been planning to do some digging of his own, trying to verify what she'd told him about Daniel Kimani. Marie had been insistent, though. And there was always the chance it actually was something important.

They went into the kitchen. All the visible signs of the break-in had been cleared away, except for the back door. The broken panel in the porch was still boarded up with plywood, and fresh, unpainted wood showed where the splintered frame had been replaced.

Dylan was sitting at the kitchen table, his head bowed. He looked up as Jonah walked in. His face was pinched and pale, but it clouded when he saw Jonah.

'What's he doing here?'

'I asked him to come, Dylan. He's here to help –'

'Yeah? What's he going to do? Bring Dad back?' The chair clattered over behind him as he stood up. 'This is fucking shit!'

'Dylan!'

Marie clutched at her son's sleeve as he went past but he shrugged her off. He looked on the verge of tears as he barged past Jonah and rushed out. His footsteps thumped upstairs, then a door slammed, shaking the walls.

Jonah steered Marie to the kitchen table and pulled out a chair for her to sit down. A half-empty bottle of wine stood on the table next to an empty, lipstick-stained glass.

She reached for the bottle of wine and slopped it into her glass, filling it almost to the top. Jonah held a brief debate with himself, then decided he ought to say something.

'Maybe you should go easy on that,' he said, sitting down as well.

'I know, but I need something to steady my nerves.'

She took a long drink, swallowing as though it was water. Jonah waited until she lowered her glass.

'Why don't you tell me what's happened? Why were the police here?'

He could guess but he needed to hear it from her. Marie gave a shudder.

'It was that DI Fletcher again. He said it was that . . . that Owen Stokes who broke in here.' She looked at Jonah, wide-eyed and tremulous. 'That's who he was asking about before! He wouldn't say why, but that's who they think must have killed Gav, or he wouldn't keep on about him. And now he's broken in here! I don't understand, why would he *do* that?'

She sounded terrified, and Jonah couldn't blame her. 'I don't know, Marie. What else did Fletcher say?'

'Nothing! He just kept asking if I'd any idea what this Stokes was looking for, but why would I? What could be here that he'd want?'

Jonah didn't know that either. 'Did he say anything else?'

'Just that there was nothing to worry about. Jesus Christ, nothing to *worry* about? Easy for him to say!' Her hand was shaking as she reached for her glass again. 'He told me we should go and stay with my sister for a few days. Just to be on the safe side. Why would he say that unless he thought this Stokes might come back?'

'It's probably just a precaution, but it's not a bad idea.' For once Jonah was in agreement with Fletcher. If Stokes had found whatever he'd been searching for, then he'd have no reason to return. But if he hadn't, then he might decide to try again. Next time when Marie or Dylan were home. 'Have you asked your sister about it?'

'Not yet. God, I don't know what to do, it's just too much! And that DI took the letter as well!'

'Letter?'

'That's what I called you about last night. I found it in my bedroom when I was clearing up. It was on the floor, in with all the mess where the drawers had been tipped out. Like Gav was reaching out to me, you know? He must have hidden it last time he came over.'

Now Jonah understood what she'd meant by *'from the grave'* the night before. 'You don't have a copy of it, do you?'

'No, I didn't think there was any need. I didn't know that bloody Fletcher was going to take it, did I?'

Jonah gritted his teeth in frustration. There might be

something in the letter to explain why Gavin had acted as he had. It was even possible that was what Stokes had been looking for, and Jonah had missed his chance of seeing it. Christ, if he'd only gone there a little earlier . . .

Marie was reaching for the bottle of wine again. Jonah beat her to it.

'Here, let me.' He poured her a small amount, setting down the bottle out of her reach. 'What did it say?'

'It broke my heart when I saw his handwriting.' Marie wiped her eyes. 'We'd been going through a bit of a rough patch. We'd have got over it, I know we would, but this past year everything just seemed to go *wrong*. Gav was under a lot of pressure at work, and we'd got a few money problems. That's why he moved out, and then he got suspended. He wouldn't talk about it. He just brushed it off and said not to worry. But the letter was . . . I don't know, different.'

'How different?'

'More like how he used to be, you know? Years ago. He said he was sorry he hadn't been a better husband and father. He knew he'd let me and Dylan down, let *everyone* down. He said he wanted to make amends and although he couldn't undo the past, he'd been given a chance to make things right.'

Jonah found himself sitting up straighter. 'Did he say how?'

'No, just that he wanted us to be proud of him. And that if things didn't work out, a lot of people were going to say bad things about him, but that we shouldn't believe them. And if . . . if anything happened to him, to remember he loved us both. Oh, God!'

She broke off, her face creasing as she covered her eyes. Jonah put a hand on her shoulder. He badly wanted to ask if the letter had made any mention of Theo, if that was what Gavin had meant by *setting things right*. But Marie would surely have said if it had, and she'd want to know why he was asking. Fletcher obviously hadn't mentioned Jonah's connection to Owen Stokes to her. And, though he didn't like keeping it from her, Marie had enough to deal with at the moment without him adding to it.

'Did Gavin say what he was planning to do?' he asked gently.

She shook her head, wiping her eyes on a tissue. 'No, but it's obvious, isn't it? He was going to try and save those poor sods at the warehouse. That's the sort of person he was. He said you'd explain.'

Jonah thought he must have misheard. 'He said what?'

'That you'd explain. He mentioned you in the letter as well, right at the end. He said I shouldn't trust anyone else, no matter who they were. Except you, and to tell you he was sorry. And that you'd explain.' She blinked at him over the tissue. 'What did he mean?'

Jonah shook his head, but a cold chill ran through him. Gavin must have known he was in danger to have written the letter, but he'd obviously thought he'd have the chance to explain to Jonah first. Something had happened to upset his plans, but the fact that he'd mentioned Jonah at all meant he hadn't phoned him that night on the spur of the moment. Gavin had intended for him to be involved all along.

The only reason Jonah could think of for that was that it had something to do with Theo.

'What else did it say?' he asked.

'I-I can't remember. Not much. I didn't want them to take it, but that DI said it was evidence. He told me I'd get it back, but how long will that take? It's not right.'

'It's just procedure,' Jonah said, but he felt in a turmoil. Fletcher would seize on the letter as proof that he knew more than he was saying. And there was no way he could explain it.

Jesus, Gavin . . . Even dead he was managing to foul things up.

'I just wish Gav had *said* something, that we'd had a chance to talk!' Marie took another unsteady drink of wine. 'I should've known something was wrong that last time he came here. Him and Dylan had a big row over something stupid. Dylan wanted money for new trainers and when Gav wouldn't give him it, he had a fit. I left them to it, but afterwards Gav seemed . . . subdued. Sad. Like he knew he wouldn't see us again.'

Perhaps he did, Jonah thought. 'When was this?'

'The same day he went to that . . . that fucking warehouse! He must have hidden the letter then, as well. I'd had a tidy-out a few weeks before, sorting stuff out to give to a charity shop. Some of mine as well, it wasn't all his. But if the letter had been in any of the drawers then, I'd have found it. It was heartbreaking, seeing it lying there.'

She stopped off at the sound of thumping footsteps on the stairs. Through the hall doorway, Jonah saw Dylan run down the stairs and hurry to the front door.

'Dylan? Where're you going?' Marie called.

The teenager grabbed a jacket from a coat hook in the hallway. In the dim light his face looked like a ghost's.

'Out.'

'Now? Out where?'

'Just *out*, all right?'

'You can't, you heard what the inspector said! We've got to go to Aunt Karen's for a few –'

The house reverberated as the front door slammed. As the echoes died to silence Marie gave Jonah a weak smile.

'He's a bit highly strung at the moment. Finding out it wasn't just an ordinary burglary shook him more than losing his things. Something like that coming on top of everything else, he's bound to be upset.'

Jonah nodded, thinking about the teenager's white face. 'Do you know where he's gone?'

'No, he's always taking himself off somewhere, but he never tells me where. Well, he's at that age, isn't he? Nowhere nearby, because he keeps getting taxis. I don't think he's going to friends, and when I asked if he was seeing a girl, he bit my head off. God, I hope he's not getting drugs from somewhere.' She looked hopefully at Jonah. 'Could you have a word with him? He might listen to a friend of his dad's.'

Jonah doubted that, but he wanted to speak to Dylan anyway. Ideally before his taxi came.

'I should go. Call me any time, if you need anything.'

Marie was already leaning across the table for the bottle of wine as he went out.

There was no sign of Dylan when he went outside, but going down the path he saw the teenager standing further along the street, where he'd be out of sight of the house. He seemed impatient and preoccupied, checking his watch as he stared off down the road. When Jonah's crutch scuffed on the pavement, he flinched and spun around. For a moment he looked young and scared, then he saw who it was and his expression hardened. With deliberate nonchalance, he turned away.

Jonah limped over. 'You OK?'

Dylan continued staring down the road, as though Jonah might disappear if he didn't make eye contact. 'Yeah.'

'Waiting for something?'

'No.' He shrugged, realising the flaw in his answer. 'A taxi.'

'Can I give you a lift?'

'No.'

The teenager wouldn't look at him. 'Your mum's pretty upset. I know it's a bad time, but –'

'Just leave me alone, all right?'

He glared at Jonah, close to tears. Jonah nodded.

'OK. See you later.'

Dylan didn't respond. Leaving him there Jonah went back to his car. Climbing in, he adjusted the mirror so he could watch the teenager on the street. Even at that distance, he looked wound so tight he was ready to snap. It could be that Marie was right about the drugs, yet Jonah didn't think this was about rushing off to buy a fix. He seemed in a barely contained panic. That might be understandable after the trauma of the past few weeks, but he hadn't been in a state like this at his dad's memorial service. Even when the house had been burgled, his reaction had been to throw a king-sized strop. OK, Fletcher's news about the break-in was scary, but that didn't explain why he suddenly had to rush out.

Or where he was getting the money from for taxis.

A silver Vauxhall with a taxi sign on its door went past. Jonah started the Saab's engine as Dylan waved it down and hurriedly climbed into the back. He waited until it drove away, letting it draw slightly ahead before setting off after it.

Busy watching the car in front, he didn't notice the one that pulled out behind him.

Chapter 20

Jonah stayed a couple of cars back. The silver Vauxhall continued to head north through the outer boroughs of London with no sign of stopping. He wondered where the hell Dylan was going. Apart from anything else, the taxi fare would be costing a small fortune.

After a few more miles, the Vauxhall turned off into a street of large but run-down Victorian and Edwardian villas. A hundred years ago it would have been an affluent, professional neighbourhood. Now the once-grand houses were dilapidated and subdivided into cramped bedsits and flats. If Dylan was intending to buy drugs, this looked the right place to do it. Up ahead, Jonah saw the taxi indicate and pull in to the kerb. He drove past, then pulled in and parked a little further along. Angling the rear-view mirror so he could see the street behind him, Jonah watched as the Vauxhall's passenger door opened and Dylan got out. The teenager looked around furtively, then turned onto the path of a large house, disappearing behind its overgrown privet hedge.

Jonah climbed out – awkwardly, because his knee had stiffened up – and retrieved his crutches. There was no gate on the path Dylan had taken, but wrought-iron gateposts stood at either side, rusted and crooked. The garden was long, overhung with old sycamores and horse chestnuts that had shed most of their leaves. The path's uneven paving led past overflowing wheelie bins to a tall, four-storey house that still bore signs of its former grandeur. There were elaborately carved wainscoting and cornices, their timbers now rotting and hanging loose. Bay windows stood either side of the front door, one of them obscured on the inside by a pinned-up sheet in place of a curtain.

He made his way to the scuffed plastic intercom panel, its double row of buttons testament to how many people now lived there. There were no names, only flat numbers running from one to twelve, some of them barely legible. He was about to press one at random, hoping to bluff someone into buzzing him in, when the door abruptly opened.

'Sorry,' Jonah said, shuffling aside as a woman came out. She barely gave him a glance as she brushed past, trailing an odour of cigarettes and soup. Catching the door before it could close, he went inside.

The hallway was gloomy. At some long-ago point it had been decorated in various shades of green. Pea-green walls, dark green paintwork, and a swirl-patterned green carpet. With the only light coming from a small window on the stairway, it felt like being at the bottom of a stagnant pond. There were several doors on the ground floor, all of them painted the same dark green and all of them closed. The house was quiet, but as Jonah debated what to do, he heard a distant door open and close from somewhere above him.

It came from one of the higher floors. He considered the steep stairs without enthusiasm, then started up. The threadbare carpet threatened to snag his crutches with every step. On each landing he paused to check for any sign of Dylan. From behind some of the doors came the muted sounds of TVs or music, but all remained resolutely shut. Then, on the third floor, he heard the squeal of hinges behind him. Turning, he saw a single eye peering out at him through a narrow gap in one doorway. It stared at him for a moment, then the door was slowly closed.

He thought the next floor would be the last, but when he reached it there was another, narrower stairwell disappearing up to the attic. There was no guarantee Dylan was up there, but the door Jonah had heard closing had sounded high up, as though it came from the very top of the house.

With a sigh, he started to climb.

There was only a single door here, old and solid. It opened outwards, onto the landing rather than into the room, and two extra locks had been fitted. One above and one below the original mortice, stainless steel and expensive. The door frame had been reinforced as well, he saw, fresh drill holes every few inches showing where it had been screwed into the bricks on either side.

Pausing to catch his breath, he noticed there were black smudges on the door by the lowest lock. Footprints, and large ones at that, as though someone had tried to kick the door in. An attempt had been made to wipe them off, leaving the general shape still distinguishable but no identifiable tread pattern.

Jonah stood outside the door, listening. Soft sounds of movement came from the other side, but no voices. There was no spyhole for anyone inside to look out onto the landing, but he still moved to one side before he knocked. The sounds from inside abruptly stopped. Jonah knocked again.

'Who is it?'

The voice was Dylan's. It sounded high-pitched and panicked.

'Landlord,' Jonah said.

There was a pause. 'What do you want?'

'I need to check the meter.'

Jonah had no idea if there even was a meter in the room, but he guessed Dylan wouldn't either.

'Can't you – can't you come back later?'

There was a note of desperation now. Jonah almost felt sorry for him.

'It won't take long.' He took his flat keys out and jangled them so Dylan could hear. 'If you don't open the door, I'll let myself in.'

'No! Wait, just . . . just give me a minute.'

The sound of hurried movement came from inside, the click of something being closed followed by the heavy scrape of furniture. Jonah knocked again.

'Come on, hurry up.'

'All right, I'm coming!'

A key turned first in the middle lock then the ones top and bottom. When the door swung open Jonah quickly moved into the gap, blocking it with his body so it couldn't be slammed. The teenager was alone. Confusion warred with shock as he saw who it was. Jonah stepped inside and gave him a smile.

'How you doing, Dylan?'

The room was a small studio, a little better than a bedsit, though not much. The only natural light came from a small and grubby roof window. There was an ancient nylon carpet, ridged and stained, and a grease-caked mini-oven on top of a fridge. A sagging two-seater sofa faced a small gas fire and behind that was a straight-backed chair and a single bed with rumpled sheets. On a chipped wooden coffee table in front of the sofa was a twist of tin foil and a packet of cigarette papers. A half-smoked joint had been mashed out in a cracked saucer, a filigree tail of smoke still rising from it.

The teenager stared at him, white-faced. 'What do you want?'

'Believe it or not, I'm trying to help you,' he said, going to a small wardrobe by the bed. It was barely big enough for anyone to be hiding in, but he checked anyway. A few shirts and jeans were hung up inside, though not the sort of thing a teenager would wear.

'What are you doing?' Dylan asked.

'Making sure you haven't got any friends hidden away.'

'I haven't!'

'Then you won't mind me taking a look.'

There was only one other door, at the other side of the room. It was a cramped cubicle containing a stained toilet and washbasin, and a shower behind a mildewed plastic curtain. The curled husks of dead spiders lay in the dry shower tray.

Dylan was getting over his shock, blustering to bolster his confidence. 'I told you, there's no one here! And it's none of your business anyway.'

'Maybe not. But I'm a police officer and I'm betting you aren't the legal tenant, so there's that.' Jonah let the curtain drop back and turned to face Dylan. 'And I'm pretty sure that roll-up over there isn't just tobacco.'

Dylan's face fell as he saw what was on the coffee table. He started to lunge towards it.

'Leave it,' Jonah told him. 'Why don't you tell me what you're doing here?'

'Nothing.'

He wouldn't look Jonah in the eye.

'Whose flat is this?'

'It's a friend's. He lets me use it.'

'What's his name?'

Dylan's eyes darted around the room, as though for inspiration. 'Why should I tell you?'

Jonah sighed. 'It's your dad's, isn't it?'

The teenager seemed to consider denying it, then gave a grudging nod. When Jonah had seen the bedsit door's extra locks and reinforced frame, for a second or two he'd thought he might have been wrong about Dylan rushing off to buy drugs. But a drug dealer would have installed a spyhole as well, to see who was outside. The bedsit didn't have one, which suggested its tenant didn't expect many callers. And even though Dylan had a key, the clothes in the wardrobe obviously weren't his. They looked like they belonged to someone older.

According to both Fletcher and Wilkes, Gavin had moved into a flat in Ealing after he'd split up with Marie. There had been no mention of anywhere else, and Jonah was sure the DI would have quizzed him if he'd known about it.

So why had Gavin rented this place and then kept it secret?

'You need to tell me what you're doing here,' he said.

'Nothing.' The shrug was forced. 'I just come here sometimes. To get away, smoke a bit of blow.'

The posturing rang hollow. The teenager was scared but trying hard not to show it.

'Did your dad know?'

'No, 'course not.' His expression became guilty. 'I only started coming . . . you know. After.'

'Then how do you know about this place?'

The teenager hitched a shoulder in a gesture that was painfully reminiscent of his father. 'I saw Dad come here one night. I was on my way to see a mate and he got out of a car in front of me. He didn't see me, but I saw him let himself in downstairs, then after a bit the light came on in the attic window. I hung around waiting for him to come out again, but he didn't.'

'Do you know what he was doing?'

'Why would I?' There was an evasiveness now. Dylan began to fidget as Jonah stared at him, saying nothing. 'I thought he might be coming to see someone, OK?'

'You mean a woman?'

'No, Father Christmas, who do you think I mean?' Dylan coloured again, realising he was pushing it. He went on, grudgingly. 'Wouldn't have been the first time. And I knew he'd got the other flat, so it wasn't as though he was living here.'

Except, apparently, he was. Or at least he was spending enough time here to merit having a change of clothes.

'How did you get the keys?'

'Does it matter?'

'Yes. How did you get them?'

'How do you think? I took them, all right?' He seemed close to tears. 'We fell out the last time he was home, and I was pissed off with him and went through his coat pockets.'

Marie had said her son had argued with Gavin over money to buy new trainers. Yet Dylan had complained that a pair he'd just bought had been stolen in the break-in, and he'd obviously been able to replace those. The ones he wore now looked both new and expensive.

'Why did you take the keys?' he asked.

'Because I wanted to get back at him!' Dylan was shouting, tears flowing freely. 'He'd fucked off and left us, and I thought he was shagging someone else, so I thought it'd serve him right to get locked out of his – his *fuck flat*! I didn't know that he wouldn't . . . that he'd get . . .'

That he'd get murdered that same day. Jonah felt sorry for him, but he couldn't ease up just yet.

'What about rent?'

Angrily, Dylan brushed at his eyes. 'What about it?'

'Who's been paying it?'

'How do I know?'

Gavin could either have paid in advance or set up a regular payment that was continuing, but that was one for Fletcher. Jonah nodded down at the new-looking trainers Dylan was wearing.

'Where'd you get the money for those?'

'What?'

'Your mum said you fell out with your dad because he wouldn't buy you any trainers. But you had a new pair stolen the other day, and the ones you're wearing now look pretty new as well. Where'd you get the money from?'

'Mum gave it me.'

He was a bad liar. 'Try again. What did you sell?'

'Who says I sold anything?'

'You got money from somewhere, so don't piss me about. What did you find here?'

'Nothing!' The teenager suddenly seemed nervous. 'OK, there was a laptop. I didn't know the password, so I-I sold it.'

That was bad. There was no telling what information might have been on the laptop Gavin had kept here. And no way of finding out, unless it could be recovered.

'Who did you sell it to?'

'I can't remember.'

'You're going to have to, because the police are going to want to know. Who was it?'

'A mate.'

'What's his name? And don't give me some made-up bollocks this time.'

'Barry.'

'Barry who?'

'I don't *know*, he's the friend of a mate! I get my gear from him, OK?'

Shit. Jonah could try and get the laptop back himself, but even if it hadn't already been sold on, he didn't have the resources to crack the password himself. Much as he wanted to know what was on it, that was better left to Fletcher as well.

'What else did you sell?'

'Nothing.'

'Look at me.' Jonah waited until the teenager raised his head to give him a sullen stare. 'You didn't only buy the trainers, there was all the computer and game stuff that was stolen from your room. You said it was new and a laptop couldn't pay for it all. Or the taxi over here, so where did you get the money from?'

'Look around, does it *look* like there was anything worth selling?'

'Then why did you rush over here?'

'I didn't.'

'I was there, I saw you. Were you worried that whoever broke into your house might come here as well?'

'No.' The denial was unconvincing. Dylan gave another Gavin-like shrug. 'I just wanted to get out, that's all.'

Fine, Jonah thought, resigned. If Dylan didn't want to tell him then he'd have to see how well his attitude went down with Fletcher.

'Where are the keys?' he asked.

'Why?'

'Just give them to me, OK?'

'Fuck that, I don't have to!'

'Yes, you do. Either that or I'll have to take you in.'

It was a bluff, but Jonah hoped the teenager wouldn't realise that. Dylan glared at him, his face red and his fists clenched, but then looked away. He shoved his hand into his pocket for the keys.

'This is shit,' Dylan muttered.

'Leave them on the bed and go home,' Jonah told him.

The teenager tossed them onto the mattress, then went to pick up the twist of foil and cigarette papers from the coffee table. Jonah shook his head.

'That stays here.'

'Oh, *what* . . .?'

'*If* that's yours, then you could be looking at up to five years for possession.' It would be more likely a fine or reprimand. On the scale of things, Dylan could have been doing a lot worse than smoking resin. But Jonah had promised Marie, and a scare might do the teenager good. 'And do you really want your mother to know what you've been doing here?'

'What . . . what are you going to tell her?'

Jonah sighed. 'Just go home, Dylan.'

He waited on the landing until the sound of the front door slamming came from downstairs, then went back into the bedsit. There would have to be an awkward conversation with Marie, and an even more uncomfortable one with Fletcher. But they'd have to wait. Closing the door behind him, he made sure it was locked.

Then he went to search for whatever Dylan hadn't wanted him to find.

Chapter 21

The room didn't seem big enough to conceal anything. There weren't any obvious hiding places except for a few kitchen cupboards and the wardrobe. But Dylan had rushed over there in a panic when he'd thought there was a chance the bedsit might be broken into as well. And whatever he'd wanted to check, it was more important than his stash of dope.

So what was it?

Jonah knew he was entering dangerous territory. The bedsit was part of a murder enquiry, and he was still a police officer. The sensible thing would be to lock up, go back to his car and phone Fletcher.

Yet once he did that he'd be cut out of the loop, told only what the DI felt he needed to know. Gavin had to have had a reason for keeping the bedsit's existence a secret, and this was Jonah's only chance to find out what it was. Stokes had been looking for something when he'd broken into Marie's, and from the kick marks on the door someone had tried to break in here as well.

If there was even a small chance Gavin had hidden something in here that concerned Theo, then Jonah had to know what it was.

Wishing he'd brought gloves, he used the cuffs of his jacket to avoid handling anything and began to search. It didn't take long. Whatever Gavin had used this place for, he hadn't bothered with many home comforts. The shelves inside the wardrobe held only a few pairs of socks and underwear, and all he found on top of it was a broken button and a thick layer of dust. The bedside cabinet yielded a spare set of keys but nothing else, while there was nothing inside the grease-clogged oven or under the sink but a collection of crusted pans. The small bathroom cubicle was equally disappointing, with nothing inside the toilet cistern except limescale and water. Next Jonah looked under the mattress before lowering himself awkwardly to the floor to see under the bed. After that he checked outside the roof window, standing on a chair to make sure there was nothing on the slates or in the gutter.

There wasn't. Climbing down, he considered what to do next. Dylan had hidden *something* before he'd let opened the door, and he hadn't had long to do it. So where was it?

Jonah looked at the keys Dylan had left. There were five of them on a simple ring. One for the external door downstairs, one for the central lock on the bedsit door, and one for each of the two additional locks.

So what was the fifth one for?

The extra key was smaller than the others, more like one that fitted a padlock. Maybe it fitted a garage somewhere, Jonah thought. It couldn't be for anything in the room or he'd have –

He stopped, looking at the bed. He'd checked underneath, but now he noticed how the headboard was pushed up against the wall, covering the area immediately behind it. He didn't have to move the bed far before he could see there was something behind it.

A rectangular hatch set in the wall.

There were hinges on one side, while the other was held in place by a padlock hooked through a steel hasp. But although the padlock had been looped into place, it hadn't been locked. In his hurry, Dylan hadn't fastened it when he'd pushed the bed back.

Gotcha.

Unhooking the padlock from the hasp, he opened the hatch cover. Cold air wafted from the black hole cut in the plasterboard wall. Easing himself to the floor, Jonah peered inside. The hatch opened into the loft space under the eaves. It was dark and the smell of dust and damp brickwork tickled his nose. There were little chinks of light in the darkness where daylight leaked through cracks between the roof slates, though not enough to see by. Taking out his phone, Jonah switched on the flashlight and aimed it inside.

A white skull stared back at him.

'*Fuck!*'

He recoiled, dropping his phone as he banged the back of his head against the hatch. The phone had fallen onto the rafters below the hatch, but its flashlight had stayed on. A blizzard of dust motes whirled in its beam, which was canted to shine almost directly onto the pale oval shape that had startled him. It was wedged in the angle of a sloping timber roof beam, and Jonah gave a sour laugh as he saw what it was.

A wasp's nest.

It was the size and shape of a misshapen rugby ball, with hollows and concavities in its papery surface that gave the vague appearance of a face. The striped husks of dead wasps were littered all around it, and Jonah couldn't hear any buzzing coming from inside. It looked old, and even if it wasn't, he didn't think wasps would be active so late in the year. Even so, he still waited to make sure there was no sign of life before leaning through the hatch to retrieve his phone. The flashlight's beam dazzled him. It had landed just out of reach, forcing him to lean in further as he groped for it at full stretch.

His hand touched something that crinkled.

He snatched it back. *OK, so there's something down there . . .* Squinting against the brightness, he tried to see what it was. But the torch beam rendered everything else pitch-black. Blinking away the blotches of light in his vision, Jonah reached down again. This time he was careful not to touch anything except the phone's hard case as he picked it up. Making sure he had a firm hold, he turned it to aim the beam downwards.

The light gleamed dully on a black vinyl holdall. It sat against the wall directly under the hatch. It was open, exposing the neck of a black plastic bin liner. An effort had been made to bundle it up, but it had been half-hearted. Inside Jonah could see stacks of twenty-pound notes, some bound with rubber bands, others loose and peeping from the open mouths of envelopes.

Jesus Christ, he thought, stunned. Chrissie had been right. In spite of everything, he hadn't wanted to believe Gavin was crooked. Jonah had convinced himself he'd acted as he did because of something he'd discovered about Theo and Owen Stokes, that he'd been trying to right a ten-year-old injustice.

But the holdall in the roof space told a different story. Maybe this was what he'd meant in the letter by 'putting things right', Jonah thought bitterly. By the time Gavin had died he'd fallen so far he thought he could make up for his sins by leaving his family a bagful of dirty money.

No wonder Dylan hadn't wanted to give up the keys.

Disappointment was an acid taste in Jonah's mouth. There was no point him staying there any longer. He considered leaving the hatch open: he'd disturbed the scene enough as it was. But even though the bedsit's door seemed secure, that would be making it too easy if anyone managed to get in.

Replacing the hatch cover, he fastened it with the padlock and then picked up the keys. Dylan's half-smoked joint was still on the coffee table with the cigarette papers and twist of foil. If that was found there it would mean more trouble for Dylan and Marie, and they had enough to contend with already. And stroppy or not, Dylan was still only a kid. Not much older than Theo would have been, and that thought was enough to make up Jonah's mind.

Going to the coffee table, he made sure the joint was out before putting it in his jacket pocket along with the foil and papers. Then, with one last look around, he turned to leave.

A floorboard creaked on the landing outside.

His first thought was that it was Dylan, but he immediately discounted it. If the teenager had intended to sneak back in, he'd have waited until he'd seen Jonah leave.

This was someone else.

As quietly as he could, Jonah edged closer to the door. No other noise came from outside, but he was certain whoever was on the landing hadn't gone. He could *feel* them out there, just on the other side of the door. Listening, just as he was.

Carefully, he reached for the handle. But it began to move before he could take hold of it, slowly revolving as though of its own accord. There was the faintest of creaks as pressure was applied, but Jonah had locked the door after Dylan left. As the handle swung back to its original position, he readied himself with the keys. Crutches or not, he had to see who it was. Taking hold of the handle in one hand, he gently fitted the key into the lock.

Click.

It was as though a bubble had burst, releasing the tension that had been building. Jonah heard a floorboard creak again on the landing, then another. *Shit!* Abandoning any attempt at silence, he unlocked the door as heavy footsteps began pounding down the stairs. Flinging it open, he rushed to the stairwell and started down. Too fast: his crutches skidded off a stair edge and suddenly he was falling. He grabbed for the banister, jarring his knee and hurting his arm and ribs, but managed to keep from tumbling down the stairs. Breathless, he hauled himself upright and listened.

The stairwell was quiet. Whoever it was had gone.

Jonah banged the side of his fist against the wall in frustration. *Jesus Christ, was that him? Was that Stokes?* The anti-climax was crushing. Snatching out his phone, he started to call Fletcher. If they could get people around there straight away, they might have a chance of catching the bastard before he got too far.

But he stopped. What was he going to say? Fletcher wasn't going to believe it was Owen Stokes just on his say-so, and Jonah was beginning to have doubts himself. When it came down to it, he hadn't actually seen who it was on the landing. It could have been anyone. He'd already been jumping at shadows the day before, when he thought he'd seen the young woman from the warehouse again at Slaughter Quay. What if this was more of the same?

None of the other residents had come out to see what the commotion was, so at least Jonah was saved from having to explain. Feeling tired and flat, he went back to the bedsit to lock up before making his way downstairs. More carefully, this time. It was harder than climbing up, and he almost fell again when one of his crutches caught on the worn carpet, pulling the rubber ferrule off the end. He had to tamp it back into place, jaw set against the pain from his protesting knee, before continuing.

He saw no one on the way down, although on the third floor the hushed creak and click of one of the doors being closed announced the presence of the same silent watcher as before. Maybe that was who he'd heard creeping around outside the bedsit, he thought wearily. Some neighbour wanting to see what was going on.

Right then, that seemed more likely than Owen Stokes.

By the time Jonah reached the ground floor, he was exhausted. His arms ached from the crutches and his knee was throbbing constantly. The prospect of having to phone Fletcher when he got back to his car depressed his spirits even further. Opening the front door, he started lowering himself down the steps before he realised there was someone on the path.

'Going somewhere?' Bennet asked.

Chapter 22

If the intention was to crush the resistance of those inside, then the interview room was a triumph of design. Overhead, a strip light cast a harsh glow that leached life and emitted a hum like a tireless insect trapped in the ceiling. The walls were a cold grey and the metal legs of the scuffed table were bolted to the floor. The chair Jonah sat on was moulded plastic but seemed to have been engineered for a different shape to the human body. After the first twenty minutes, his thighs had gone numb, and a dull ache had begun in his lower back. He stretched from time to time as he waited, but otherwise tried to shut his mind to the discomfort. He was hardly a stranger to rooms like this. He'd been in dozens like it over the course of his career.

Just not on this side of the table.

He'd been driven to the station by two uniformed PCs who'd arrived as the street outside the bedsit filled with police vehicles. They'd ignored him, chatting desultorily to each other in the front of the car while he sat alone behind them. He'd hated that, hated the sense of being on the wrong side of the procedural machine. At the station he'd been taken to an interview room, and then left. Time had slowed to a crawl and it was almost a relief when Fletcher eventually walked in. The DI looked tired, his baggy clothes creased and the usually taut, livid skin on his face was slack and pale. Bennet came in afterwards, closing the door behind them. They took the two chairs on the other side of the table. After the rigmarole of identification for the benefit of the records, the DI stared at Jonah without speaking, letting the silence stretch before he spoke.

'How long have you been a police officer?'

'You know how long.'

'Remind me.'

'Sixteen years.'

'Sixteen years,' Fletcher echoed. 'Long enough to know you don't trample over a crime scene. Although you've a habit of doing that, haven't you?'

'I didn't know it was a crime scene until I got there. And I was careful not to touch anything with my bare hands.'

'You shouldn't have touched anything at all.'

There was nothing Jonah could say to that. Worst of all was knowing that he'd brought this on himself. He'd hoped that Fletcher and Bennet hadn't seen him arriving at Marie's as they'd left, but of course they had. The DI had told her to drop him at the nearest tube station, and then double back to wait outside Marie's. When Jonah had set off after Dylan, he'd been so intent on keeping the silver Vauxhall in sight it never occurred to him that someone might be following him as well.

The shock of finding Bennet outside had been replaced by the realisation of how much trouble he was in. And anger at his own stupidity. He'd been hoping that his news about Gavin's bedsit and the hidden money would offset any censure over the fact that he shouldn't have been there in the first place. Now, instead of him offering up the information voluntarily, he'd been caught apparently sneaking out. That placed him in a very different position.

Fletcher studied Jonah across the interview room table. 'The flat was rented by someone calling himself Richard King. Does the name mean anything to you?'

Jonah shook his head. 'No. I told you, I knew nothing about it.'

'The landlord told us King paid six months' rent in advance,' Fletcher went on as though he hadn't heard. 'Cash up front, plus a chunky deposit. The landlord didn't ask for an ID or references on account of having a wad of cash waved in front of him, but the description he gave us matches McKinney, and he identified him from a photo. McKinney's son has admitted stealing his dad's keys and selling a laptop from the bedsit. That was before he found the money and started helping himself to that.'

'What about the laptop? Have you recovered it?' Jonah asked.

'That comes under "none of your business". But no, we haven't. I think we can safely say it's gone for good.'

That was no surprise, but its loss was still bitterly disappointing. If Gavin had kept any additional information on Stokes, the chances were that it would have been on the second laptop he'd kept in the bedsit.

'There was a whisker under seven hundred and forty thousand pounds hidden in the roof space,' Fletcher continued. 'Whisker in this case being around five grand filched by the boy. Nearly three quarters of a million in used notes. Any suggestions how McKinney got his hands on that much cash?'

'I've no idea.'

'OK, then let's put it this way. Do you think he came by it honestly? A bank loan, maybe? Or perhaps he was just a thrifty saver.'

Jonah started to say he didn't know, but the words lodged in his throat. 'No.'

'At least we agree on that. I think this pretty much puts a bow on the question of whether McKinney was corrupt. Which leaves me, yet again, wondering how you fit into all this.'

'I keep telling you, Dylan's mother asked me to keep an eye on him because he'd been acting strangely. I didn't know the money or bedsit even existed until I followed him there. And I was on my way back to the car to call you when I saw DS Bennet.'

'Of course you were. And here's me thinking you only told us because you got caught coming out.'

'I know how it looks, but that was just bad timing.'

'You seem to have a lot of that.'

There was nothing Jonah could say to that either. The DI waited to see if his sarcasm would provoke a response before going on.

'What about the letter McKinney left for his wife? He told her if anything happened to him she should trust you. That you'd *explain*. How were you supposed to do that if you didn't know anything?'

'I've no idea.' Jonah was painfully aware how unconvincing he sounded. 'He must have planned to tell me when he saw me.'

Fletcher rocked his chair back, contemplating him.

'For the sake of argument, let's assume you really were as stupid as you claim and didn't know about any of it,' he said. 'The bedsit, the money, oh my goodness, what a surprise. The thing I'm having difficulty with is why a police officer of sixteen years' standing would decide the best course of action wasn't to, I don't know, maybe *report* evidence pertaining to a murder investigation rather than search the place himself? And I'm not talking about a quick shufti. You moved the *bed* to get to a concealed loft hatch! You were looking for something, so if it wasn't the money, what was it?'

Jonah knew there was no point in denial. 'I thought Gavin might have information about Theo.'

'And why would you think that?'

'You said yourself he must have had a reason for following Stokes and wanting me to meet him that night. The only thing I can think of is that he found out something about what happened ten years ago.'

'I've already told you, there's no –'

'I know what you said, but this is my *son* we're talking about. If there's any chance Gavin knew something different, then of course I'm going to want to know about it!'

Fletcher said nothing for a while, studying him through lidded eyes.

'OK, let's talk about this mystery visitor you claim you heard outside,' the DI said, abruptly changing the subject. 'You told Bennet whoever it was ran off before you saw them. But you knew Owen Stokes had broken into McKinney's house looking for something, and you'd just discovered a bagful of hidden cash. If you could find the bedsit, so could he. Are you telling me it never even crossed your mind it could have been him?'

All the arguments that had run through Jonah's mind in the bedsit came back. He remembered standing by the door, separated from whoever was outside by a few inches of timber. He'd convinced himself it couldn't have been Owen Stokes, but now he felt new doubts forming.

'I didn't see who it was. It could have been anyone,' he said, trying to believe it himself. 'I didn't think you'd thank me for pressing the panic button because some tenant was poking around outside. Anyway, Stokes wouldn't have run off like that. Not if he was after the money.'

'That's your reasoning, is it? There's a possibility the man who killed your mate and put you in hospital, who you *still* aren't convinced wasn't somehow involved in your son's disappearance, was *right there* and you didn't bother to *tell* anyone?'

'DS Bennet was outside watching the house,' Jonah said, the doubts growing. 'If it was Stokes, she'd have seen him leave.'

Bennet's voice was as inflectionless as her expression. 'There was a back door.'

Christ. Jonah could feel a panic sweat break out at the thought that he might have been wrong. 'Are you saying it *was* him? Did somebody in one of the flats see him?'

'We're still interviewing the residents,' Fletcher said. 'Right now, I'm more interested in why you might have decided to keep something like that to yourself when you're supposedly so keen on catching Owen Stokes.'

Because I didn't trust myself. Because I thought I saw a dead woman at Slaughter Quay.

'You can't seriously think I'd have kept quiet if I'd thought it was him? Why the hell would I do that?'

'Oh, I don't know. Maybe the three quarters of a million pounds you'd just found in the loft had something to do with it.'

'If that was all I was after, why did I leave it up there? I'd have taken it with me,' Jonah shot back. 'I don't care about the *money*, I want to know what happened to my son! And if there had been anything about him in there, I didn't trust you to tell me about it!'

'This is a *murder* enquiry, Colley, I don't have to tell you anything!'

'Then don't be surprised when I try to find out on my own!'

There was a silence. Fletcher remained impassive, but the tight skin of his face looked flushed and feverish.

'You know your trouble, Colley? You think the world owes you a free pass. But you don't have any special *rights* because you're a police officer or your son died. I thought at first you and McKinney might have been on some sort of vendetta against Owen Stokes, but now I'm inclined to think it was just thieves falling out. We already know McKinney was crooked, so maybe him and Stokes stole the money from a gang and then fell out over it. And nothing I've heard so far convinces me you aren't in it up to your neck as well.'

Jonah was struggling to remain calm. 'Then why don't you charge me?'

'Oh, don't worry, I will when I'm ready. I'll look forward to it.'

They glared at each other. The atmosphere in the small interview room fairly crackled. Bennet glanced at Fletcher and cleared her throat.

'Sir, perhaps we should . . .'

'All right, Bennet, I don't need reminding,' he snapped. He seemed on the point of getting up, then he stopped. 'One other thing. There was a strong smell of dope in McKinney's bedsit. I don't suppose you'd know anything about that, would you?'

'I didn't see Dylan smoking anything, if that's what you mean,' Jonah said. Strictly speaking, he hadn't: the joint had been quietly smouldering on the coffee table.

'No?' Fletcher's smile was predatory. 'Well, he didn't return the favour. He swore blind if anyone was smoking dope there it must have been you.'

Oh, Dylan, you little bastard . . . 'It wasn't.'

'Then you won't mind emptying your pockets, will you?'

'Are you serious?'

'Don't I look it?'

Jonah considered objecting, just on principle. But there was no point. The chair scraped against the floor as he pushed it back. He rose to his feet, leaning on the table for balance. One by one, he went through all his pockets, dropping the contents on the table. Wallet, car keys, flat key. Coins, an unused tissue, a packet of chewing gum.

'Jacket as well,' Fletcher instructed. 'The inside ones.'

Reaching inside his jacket, Jonah unzipped both inside pockets. He took his phone from one and put it on the table, then pulled out the pocket linings to show they were empty.

'Satisfied?' he asked.

'Not yet. Don't have any objection to a quick pat-down, do you?'

Jonah started to object, then gave in. He balanced as best he could, then held out his arms and waited.

'Do the honours, Bennet,' Fletcher said.

'Don't you think a male officer should do that, sir?'

He gave her a look, then shook his head. 'Fine, I'll do it myself.'

Moving Jonah's crutches out of the way, the DI quickly ran his hands over Jonah's chest and arms, then crouched to pat down his legs.

'Are we done, or do you want me to strip off as well?' Jonah said, lowering his arms.

'We're done. For now.' Fletcher started towards the door, then stopped. 'On second thoughts, your car's still at the bedsit. DC Bennet's heading back over there soon. She can give you a lift.'

The policewoman's face showed a rare reaction. 'But sir –'

'I'm sorry, is there a problem?'

It was a petty payback. Bennet composed her features back into the usual mask.

'No, sir.'

'Thought not.' Fletcher turned a malevolent glare to Jonah. 'I'll look forward to speaking again, Sergeant Colley.'

*

Bennet wasn't happy. She marched in silence through the corridors to a fenced-off car park at the back of the police station, leaving Jonah to keep up on his crutches. By the time he caught up with her she'd already yanked open the Polo's door and climbed in. Not convinced she'd wait long enough for him to put his crutches in the back, Jonah wrestled them into the passenger seat with him.

'This wasn't my idea,' he said, struggling to fasten his seat belt as she pulled up to the exit barrier and wound down the window to present a pass.

'Never said it was.'

Resigning himself to a silent journey, Jonah stared out of the window as she pulled into the evening traffic. It was cold inside the car, the chill from the seat striking through his jeans. Without comment, Bennet put the heater on, filling the cabin with a noisy blast of cool air that gradually began to warm.

Even more gradually, the atmosphere in the car began to thaw as well.

'What's going to happen to Dylan?' Jonah asked after a while. 'Will he be charged?'

'Not my call.'

'He's just a kid.'

'He's seventeen. Old enough to know you don't help yourself to a bagful of money you've found stashed in a loft.'

'He thought it belonged to his dad.'

'Right. Because every police detective can salt away three quarters of a million. Nothing wrong with that at all.'

Bennet's profile was stern and unforgiving in the glow from the passing streetlights. But after a moment or two she shrugged.

'He'll probably be let off with a warning. But that's only a guess. Like I say, it's not my call.'

Jonah badly wanted to ask how the search was progressing for Owen Stokes, but he knew she wouldn't tell him. There was one thing he needed to say, though.

'Is it true one of the male victims has been identified?'

'I thought I told you not to listen to rumours.'

'This was more than a rumour. I was told his name was Daniel Kimani.'

Bennet's momentary silence was confirmation enough. 'Who told you that? The journalist again?'

Jonah hesitated. But Daly hadn't said anything about the information being confidential. In any case, if she was going to publish it, the enquiry team had a right to know.

He nodded. 'Is it true?'

'What else did she say?'

'That he was Kenyan and here on a student visa.'

'Did she tell you anything else?'

'No, that was all. But she's still digging for a story.'

'She's a reporter, of course she is.' The only outward sign of any agitation was the tapping of Bennet's index finger on the steering wheel. 'Are you helping her?'

'No, of course not.'

'Why was she confiding in you?'

'She was hoping I'd give up something in return. Don't worry, I didn't.'

But even as he said it he wondered if that was true. The memory of Daly's visit was still an uncomfortable one.

'Why didn't you mention this to DI Fletcher earlier?' Bennet asked.

'It slipped my mind.'

It had, though only at first. But by then Jonah had only wanted to get out of that interview room. He didn't want to give Fletcher any more excuses for holding him.

'I wouldn't let anything else slip, if I were you,' Bennet said.

She dropped him off by his car. It was only when he was back in the familiar seclusion of the old Saab's cabin that he realised how tired he was. It had been another long day, so he parked on the road near his flat again rather than walk back from his garage. As he approached the lighted entrance to the flats, his thoughts were already on sitting down with something to eat, watching a game or something non-demanding on TV.

The first he realised he wasn't alone was when the bottle exploded at his feet.

Jonah was spattered with beer and shards of glass. Startled and furious, he looked in the direction it had come from. A short distance away, a group of shadowy figures stood under a concrete awning. It was too dark to make them out properly, but he thought he recognised the two youths who'd got into the lift with him the night before.

Jonah stared at them, waiting for them to do something else. When they didn't, he turned away, making a show of not hurrying as he continued to the entrance. Part of him wanted to confront them, to vent his frustration with himself and Fletcher, but he'd got into enough trouble for one day. Teenagers or not, there were more of them than him, and he was on crutches. And if they had knives, all bets were off.

No footsteps sounded behind him as he limped into the foyer. As he waited for the lift, he kept an eye on the entrance, half expecting the gang to appear. But the glass doors showed only the floodlit concourse outside. Getting into the lift, Jonah watched the indicator tick off the floors as it ascended. With everything else that had happened, he'd forgotten all about the would-be muggers. They obviously hadn't forgotten him, though, and now they had friends. *Great.* He didn't kid himself that being a police officer would put them off for long. Even if they believed it, he was too obviously on his own, and his crutches marked him as vulnerable. Sooner or later they'd try something.

But that was a problem for another day. Back in his flat, Jonah locked the door then went into the kitchen and sat down at the table. Leaning one of his crutches against it, he reversed the other. It was the one he'd snagged on the worn stair carpet as he'd left the bedsit, pulling loose the rubber ferrule. Taking hold of it, Jonah pulled and twisted until it slid off the aluminium tube with a soft *pop*. He held the hollow end of the crutch over the kitchen table and gave it a gentle shake.

Dylan's half-smoked joint, cigarette papers and twist of foil fell out.

After the day he'd had, Jonah was almost tempted to smoke the joint himself. Instead, he threw the papers, foil and joint into the bin. He'd hidden them in the crutch when Bennet had gone upstairs to the bedsit. Just as well, because Fletcher would have loved to charge him with possession of a Class B drug. He'd probably have searched him even if Dylan hadn't pointed the finger.

Like father, like son, Jonah thought, replacing the ferrule on his crutch. Gavin might not have intended to drop him in the shit, but that's what he'd managed to do. First with his phone call, then the letter to Marie. And now with a secret bedsit and three quarters of a million from God knew where. Even dead Gavin was still causing him grief.

Opening a beer, Jonah hoped he hadn't left behind any more surprises.

Chapter 23

'You fucking shit!'

Jonah involuntarily stepped back, almost teetering off the edge of Marie's doorstep. Her face was contorted as she confronted him through the open doorway.

'Look, Marie –'

'Three quarters of a million pounds! *Three fucking quarters of a million*, and I won't see a penny of it, thanks to you.'

He'd tried calling her that morning, feeling he ought to explain about the bedsit. In hindsight, he should have known when she didn't pick up or respond to his message. From what Fletcher had said, the police had already interviewed Dylan, so Marie would know what had happened. But he'd felt obligated to explain to her in person. When she didn't call him back, he'd driven over to her house, hoping she hadn't already left for her sister's.

Bad idea.

'It's obvious Gav wanted us to have it, but oh, no! You had to stick your nose in, didn't you?' she yelled. 'And now the police are asking all sorts of questions. They're even acting like Dylan did something wrong! He was only going to that place to be close to his dad. He didn't want to upset me, that's why he'd not said anything. He swears he didn't even know the money was there, and my son's no liar!'

Jonah wondered if Dylan had mentioned the dope he'd been smoking, or if that had slipped his mind as well. He tried to get a word in again.

'Marie, if you'd just let me –'

'Everything OK, Mum?'

Dylan had appeared in the hallway behind her. He dropped a packed bag onto the floor next to the two suitcases that already stood there, looking out at Jonah with an expression of smug spite.

'It's fine, sweetheart, you go and finish packing,' Marie told him. She turned back to Jonah with renewed venom.

'Christ, I wish I'd never asked you to help. No wonder Gav stopped talking to you, he knew what a fucking disaster you were! Jonah by name, Jonah by fucking nature. Just stay away from us in future. I don't want to set eyes on you again. Ever!'

The door slammed in his face.

'Always a pleasure, Marie,' he said to the closed door.

Turning away, he went back to his car. He couldn't blame Marie for being angry. From her perspective all he'd done was bring even more trouble down on them. The fact that he hadn't had any choice, that his actions had been dictated by events, wouldn't cut any ice with her any more than it had with Fletcher.

Or with himself either, come to that.

Jonah had lain awake half the night, second-guessing every-thing he'd done. But most of his self-flagellation rested on the possibility that it really *had* been Stokes outside the bedsit, that he'd made the wrong call and let him get away. If that were true, then he deserved Fletcher's contempt. Yet Jonah still couldn't bring himself to believe that. There had only been Jonah standing between whoever was outside and three quarters of a million in used notes.

If that had been Stokes, surely he'd have tried to take it?

Discovering the money had changed everything. It seemed to settle once and for all the question of whether or not Gavin had been corrupt. And as Jonah had watched dawn break outside his flat window, another disquieting thought had occurred to him. Regardless of who'd been at the bedsit, Stokes had been looking for something when he'd broken into Marie's house. The obvious conclusion was that it was the money, yet how could Stokes have known about that?

Unless Gavin had told him.

Jonah still didn't want to believe that Gavin and Stokes could have been working together, but there was a queasy logic to Fletcher's suggestion. For one thing, there were still the three warehouse victims to factor in. Nadine, Daniel Kimani and the second, as yet unidentified, man. At first glance, Kimani's presence seemed to undermine the theory that the murders were trafficking-related. That had always seemed strained, especially since Fletcher had said Stokes had no known gang affiliations.

But Gavin did. And three quarters of a million pounds was a motive all by itself. People had been killed for a lot less, which raised all sorts of new and unsettling possibilities about the victims. And if – *if* – Gavin had been working with Owen Stokes, was it too big a stretch to think that might have led to him stumbling across something to make him re-evaluate what happened ten years ago?

Something about Theo?

Which brought Jonah full circle. All the way back to why Gavin had phoned him that night. Gavin's motives might be more complex than anyone knew. Maybe the money and the idea of trying to make amends for past mistakes weren't mutually exclusive, at least in his mind. Maybe one led to the other, and Owen Stokes, the warehouse victims and all the rest of it were inextricably linked together.

Or maybe Jonah was just clutching at straws.

Starting the car, he drove away from Marie's. He hadn't felt this adrift or helpless since Theo had disappeared, and he was still no closer to making sense of any of it. But there was one place he might find answers.

Although he'd have to stop off first.

Wilkes's house was a 1960s semi-detached set in a small dead-end street. It was the last house forgoing the PVC doors and windows of its neighbours in favour of the timber originals, peeling paint and all. There was a thumbnail version of a garden, in which a few straggly rose bushes were being slowly choked by weeds.

Jonah walked up the short path to the front door and pressed the bell. It made a rusty crunching noise, so he rapped on the wooden door as well. There was the sound of a bolt being shot, then the door opened.

The big man was unshaven and unkempt. He wore a stained white T-shirt and had a towel draped around his neck. A sour odour of alcohol and old perspiration came from him, and the eyes above the broken-veined cheeks were yellowed and bloodshot. He peered at Jonah with hung-over resentment.

'What do you want?'

'I wondered if we could have a talk.'

Wilkes gave a hacking cough, sounding as though he was dislodging something wet from his lungs. 'What about?'

'I'll tell you inside.' Jonah raised the carrier bag he'd had hooked over one wrist. 'I brought this.'

It was a bottle of Jameson's whiskey, the brand Wilkes had been drinking in the pub. The ex-detective's mood brightened.

'Nice one.' He stepped back, holding the door open. 'Go on through.'

The house smelled of cigarettes, fried food and unwashed laundry. The carpet felt gritty underfoot as Jonah went down the dim and narrow hallway to the living room. It was dominated by an old but huge wall-mounted TV, in front of which was a well-worn leather recliner, its cushions split and flattened. On a low coffee table, a dirty plate and mug sat on scattered car magazines.

'Take a pew,' Wilkes called. 'Be with you in a minute.'

The only option other than the recliner was a token armchair, which spoke volumes for the ex-detective's social life. Jonah moved the magazines that covered its seat, looking around for a clear space before putting them on the floor. Leaning his crutches against the chair, he sat down.

Wilkes came in, wearing what looked like the same black polo neck as he'd worn at the memorial service and holding two cans of Stella.

'We can start off on these and open the Jameson's later,' he said, handing one to Jonah. 'How'd you know where I lived?'

'You mentioned it the other night.'

Wilkes hadn't told him the street or house number, but there was only one person by his name in that area. The recliner creaked under the big man's weight as he lowered himself into it and cracked open the beer.

'Cheers,' he said, raising his can before taking a long swallow.

Jonah contented himself with a token drink. Even if he hadn't been driving, he didn't want to get into another drinking session, but Wilkes would take it as a slight if he abstained altogether. The big man lowered the can and stifled a belch.

'So. What did you want to talk about?'

'Did you know Gavin had another flat?'

He was watching the other man carefully to see how he reacted. The ex-detective frowned.

'He what?'

'He had a bedsit, as well as the flat in Ealing.'

Wilkes's bewilderment seemed genuine. 'Why would he have that?'

'I only found out about it yesterday,' Jonah hedged. 'His son stole the keys and was going there to smoke dope.'

'Yeah?' Wilkes gave a phlegmy chuckle. 'Sounds like his old man.'

'So Gavin didn't mention it?'

'Not to me.' He sounded unhappy about that.

'Any idea why he might have needed two flats?'

'If he'd still been living with his missus, I'd have said he wanted somewhere to take women back to. But he wouldn't need that when he'd moved out. Who else knows about this place apart from you and his kid?'

'Just his wife and the enquiry team.' Jonah tried to nudge the questioning away from this. 'So you can't think of any reason why he'd have it?'

The ex-detective gave him a jaundiced look. 'I've already said, haven't I?'

Jonah let it go. Wilkes considered him over the can as he took another drink.

'I've got a question for you. If you and Gav were such good buddies, how come you weren't talking?'

'I told you, we lost touch years ago.'

'Bollocks. His wife said the two of you ran around like a pair of dogs, then *boom*. Nothing. That doesn't happen for no reason.'

Jonah took a drink of beer, debating how much to tell him. But the ex-detective would know if he was holding back.

'I found him in bed with my wife.'

Wilkes threw back his head and laughed. 'Oh, fuck me! I knew it! I *knew* there was something!'

'Glad you find it funny,' Jonah said.

The big man's shoulders were shaking. He had to put his can of beer down to wipe his eyes.

'Sorry, I shouldn't laugh but . . . oh, Christ, that's priceless! His best mate's wife. That's Gav for you, never could keep it zipped. That's what started it.'

'Started what?' Jonah asked, his annoyance falling away.

Wilkes drained his can and crushed it in a meaty fist. 'Let me get another one of these and I'll tell you.'

Her name was Eliana Salim.

She'd been smuggled into the UK from Syria with a dozen other young women, crammed inside a container of stuffed toys. Her parents had been killed in the war and her plan was to work as a nanny until she could afford to bring over her younger sister, who was living with relatives.

It didn't happen.

'She was a real looker,' Wilkes said, taking a drink from his can. 'Like a model. Good job for her, because instead of putting her in a backstreet brothel with the rest, it meant the gang who brought her over put her to work as an escort. Same job, but she got to dress up and smile at some rich bastard before she got fucked.'

Guarded night and day with three other young women, the only time she was allowed out of the small flat they shared was to work. One night while she was being driven to a private party in Mayfair, her driver was flashed by a patrol car.

'He was carrying a knife and cocaine, so the stupid bastard panicked and put his foot down,' Wilkes continued. 'When he realised he couldn't get away, he pulled onto a side street, shoved them at Salim and kicked her out of the car. Told her to make her own way back to the flat or else, and then took off.

She wasn't stupid, though, so she went to the nearest police station and asked for help. It was just bad luck for everyone it was Gav who got the call to interview her.'

By the time Gavin arrived at the station, the driver was in custody as well. He was Armenian, part of a local gang known to be involved in widespread human trafficking and prostitution. Wilkes frowned at his beer can as he remembered.

'They were only small time, but we knew they were facilitators for a big international OCG from Eastern Europe. That's organised crime gang,' he added, with a glance at Jonah. 'We'd been working with Interpol and the National Crime Agency, trying to get a handle on these bastards for years, but it was like wrestling snakes. They were fucking brutal. They didn't just kill anyone who talked, they tortured and killed their family as well. So when Gav saw Salim sitting in an interview room, he knew it was an opportunity to get someone on the inside.'

'As an informer, you mean?' Jonah couldn't believe what he was hearing. 'He made her go *back*?'

Wilkes looked away, rubbing the back of his neck. 'He didn't *make* her, he just said there might be a way to get her sister over here if she cooperated. And if she didn't . . . well, she could be looking at months or years in a detention centre before being deported. Which, given the sort of people we were dealing with, she probably wouldn't want.'

Jesus . . . Even by Gavin's recent standards this was a new low. 'Could he even *do* that?'

'Fuck, no. He shouldn't have, anyway. Informers are supposed to be registered, and that's after you've jumped through all the safety hoops and red tape, but Gav knew there wasn't time for any of that. If it was going to work, she had to get back before her minders started to wonder why it took her so long. If they thought she'd returned of her own accord, they might start letting their guard down around her. I mean, it was a fantastic opportunity. We might never get another chance like that to get inside intelligence on the bastards. Not just them either, it was the people they were pimping her out to as well. And believe me, there were some big names. Politicians, businessmen, bankers. Gav knew he was taking a gamble, but he thought it was worth the risk.'

'What about the risk to *her*?' Jonah said, appalled. 'For Christ's sake, he was sending her back to be prostituted!'

Wilkes had the decency to look embarrassed. 'Yeah, well. It looks bad when you put it like that, but she knew what she was getting into. Nobody forced her. And it was a risk for Gav as well. There was a real shitstorm when it came out. Looked for a while like he was going to get sacked.'

He should have been, Jonah thought.

'Why wasn't he?'

Wilkes gave a shrug. 'Stable door, and all that. The damage was done, and it'd have been stupid not to use an asset that was in place and willing.'

'*Asset?*' Jonah said, before he could help himself.

'What else would you call her?' Wilkes's stare was as hard as his tone. 'You needn't look like that, either. It's easy to judge when it's not you getting your hands dirty.'

Jonah knew he couldn't afford to antagonise Wilkes, not if he wanted to hear the rest. He raised his hands, making a show of backing off.

'OK. What happened?'

Giving him a last sour look, Wilkes took another drink before continuing.

'I'm not sure even now how he swung it, but they agreed to let him be her handler. The excuse was that he'd already established a rapport, but if you ask me, it was so they could limit the fallout if shit hit the fan. He roped me into it as well, which I wasn't thrilled about. Not to start off, anyway, because it looked like he'd fucked up. We couldn't risk trying to get in touch while she was being watched twenty-four seven, so we had to wait for her to contact us. Gav had slipped her his phone number, but we didn't hear anything for weeks. Then he got a text out of the blue asking to meet. Turned out he'd been right about her minders easing up. They stopped watching her all the time, started letting her go out by herself, so Gav's gamble had paid off. Christ, he was cock-a-hoop. I was supposed to go with him to meet her, but he said it was better if he went on his own. Unofficial, like.'

Wilkes stared down broodingly at his beer, the broad forehead furrowing.

'With hindsight, maybe that wasn't such a good idea. But at the time . . . Anyway, that became the routine. Gav would drop me off in a pub while he went to meet her somewhere they'd prearranged, then he'd pick me up afterwards and brief me on what she'd said.'

Gavin obviously hadn't wanted Wilkes getting in the way. 'Did he tell you he was sleeping with her or did you guess?'

'Well, Gav being Gav, I guessed.' Wilkes didn't meet Jonah's eyes. 'But I didn't see the harm. I mean, Salim was giving us good stuff. Names, times and places, bits of information she'd overheard. All low-level but it was gold compared to what we'd been getting before. Suddenly Gav was the blue-eyed boy. Didn't do me any harm, either, if I'm honest.'

What about Salim? This time Jonah kept the thought to himself. 'So what went wrong?'

Wilkes's face clouded. 'He got too close. I thought he was just getting his leg over, I didn't think it was *serious*. But he started acting distracted, like his mind was somewhere else. He was on a short fuse as well, and I mean *short*. He was under a shitload of pressure, so no one thought much of it at first. Then someone on the team made a crack about Salim, and Gav lost it. He'd have taken the poor bastard's head off if I hadn't pulled him away. After that it was obvious he'd got it bad. He started pushing to bring Salim out, saying she'd done enough. Trouble was, she was doing too good a job. After all the kicking and screaming the brass did, now we were starting to get information they didn't want to turn off the tap. Just a bit longer, they said. Another couple of months and then she'd be pulled out.'

Wilkes drained the can and crumpled it, letting it drop to the carpet.

'And then we lost contact with her. No phone calls, no messages, nothing. We'd had the flat she was living in under surveillance but suddenly there was no activity there either. Knowing the sort of bastards we were dealing with, that wasn't good. Gav was beside himself. I was worried if we didn't do something soon he'd go in there on his own.'

Jonah stiffened at that, thinking about the warehouse.

'Did he?'

'He didn't have to.'

The flat was raided at dawn. The operation had been meticulously set up and planned so as to give as little warning as possible. The front door was broken in and armed officers surged in first, shouting warnings as they went from room to room.

But the flat was empty. It had been cleaned out, leaving behind bare mattresses on the beds and the bathroom stripped of any sign of human habitation. Eliana Salim and the other young women, as well as their guards, were nowhere to be seen.

'The whole place stank of bleach,' Wilkes said. 'Every surface had been wiped down, all the drawers and cupboards emptied.

I thought, thank fuck, because I'd been expecting to find a body and blood everywhere. It was starting to look like they'd just upped sticks and taken Salim and the other girls somewhere else. Gav was going spare, and I was about to say we should get out and leave it to forensics. Then there was this shout from the kitchen.'

Jonah waited while Wilkes reached down and picked up another can from beside the recliner. He opened it and drank half straight off.

'There were people standing around the fridge, just staring inside. I can remember looking in and wondering what all the fuss was about, because there was just this white dinner plate with a lump of bloody offal on it. Then I realised what it was. The evil bastards must have found out Salim was an informer. So they'd cut out her tongue and left it for us to find.'

'Jesus . . .' Jonah had known it would be bad, but he was still shocked.

'We found the rest of her in the bins behind the house,' Wilkes continued, after another drink. 'They'd dismembered her and wrapped the body parts in cling film. Put them in plastic bags and dumped them, like they were rubbish. Fucking animals. I tell you, I've seen some things in my time but never anything like that. She must have been killed a few days before and rats had . . . well, Salim's fingerprints or DNA weren't on the database, so the only way we could identify her was by her head.'

'God, Gavin had to . . .?' Even though there was no excusing what he'd done, Jonah wouldn't have wished that on him. But Wilkes shook his head.

'Christ, no, I couldn't let him do that. I'd been her handler as well, so I volunteered. Gav was in a bad enough state as it was without that. I thought he'd get sacked or reprimanded at least, but that would have caused too much of a fuss. No one wanted to draw attention to a fuck-up like that, and Salim didn't have any family here to cause trouble. So they swept it under the rug and Gav was put on paid leave for a few weeks. He came back when things had quietened down, but he wasn't the same.'

The broad forehead creased as Wilkes struggled to articulate his thoughts.

'He seemed . . . I don't know. Sort of hollow. Like he was pretending to be who everyone expected, but he didn't give a fuck anymore. That's when he started hitting the booze. I mean, he'd always liked a good time, that was just Gav. But not like this.'

'Was that when he started taking bribes?' Jonah asked.

Wilkes stopped mid-drink. 'What sort of a fucking question's that? I told you, Gav got things done, even if it meant bending a few rules.'

'Like sending Eliana Salim back to be killed?'

'I thought you were his fucking mate?' Wilkes's face was flushed and angry. 'Is this about putting the boot in because he fucked your missus?'

Jonah stopped himself from responding. *Take a breath.*

'There has to be a reason for what happened in that warehouse. Why he was there, why he called me. I just want to find out what it was. I think . . .' He hesitated, unsure how much to say. 'I think it could involve something that happened years ago. I – my son disappeared. The inquest said he'd drowned, but I think Gavin might have found out something. Something to make him think they'd got it wrong.'

He couldn't tell Wilkes too much, certainly not about Owen Stokes, not when his identity hadn't been made public. But the ex-detective was the only person who could tell him about Gavin. Jonah wanted to keep him onside if he could.

'Yeah, I'd heard about your son. Sorry about that,' Wilkes said, gruffly. 'But I don't see what that's got to do with any of this.'

'It might not. I just need to know for sure.'

The big man's colour was returning to normal, but he still looked far from happy.

'Yeah, well, I don't see how I can help you. But if you want to know if I was surprised when he got suspended, no, I wasn't. What happened to Gav was a crying fucking shame, but if you ask me, a big part of him died before then, when he saw what was in that flat. And that's all you're getting. End of fucking story.'

He tilted his head back and drained the can. Crumpling it in his fist, he dropped it on the floor next to the others and stood up.

'You can see yourself out.'

Chapter 24

Jonah was hardly aware of the journey back to his flat. He drove without conscious thought, body and brain functioning automatically while his mind sifted through what he'd heard. Part of the picture, at least, was becoming clearer. What had happened with Eliana Salim must have affected Gavin deeply. It had been his decision, his actions, that had led to the young woman's death, and the knowledge must have eaten away at him. And Jonah knew how poisonous the combination of loss and guilt could be. In the early days after Theo disappeared, it had been Gavin who'd counterbalanced those darker impulses in him, pulling him back from the brink. And later, after their fight, Miles had done the same. There had been no one to pull Gavin back, though.

And it had claimed him in the end.

Parking on the street near his flat, Jonah wondered if Fletcher was aware of the disastrous operation. Possibly not. Although it would be a matter of record, it had been years ago. It might not be thought relevant unless the enquiry team knew about Gavin's emotional involvement with Eliana Salim. And who would have told them about that? According to Wilkes, not many people realised even at the time.

But Jonah didn't think the impact of Salim's murder on Gavin could be underestimated. If nothing else it provided a context for his later actions. Her death had been a turning point, setting him on a self-destructive path that ultimately ended at the warehouse. It was even possible there was a link between the organised crime gang who'd murdered Salim and the warehouse killings as well. That might be stretching things too far, since Fletcher had said Owen Stokes had no known OCG associations.

Even so, there was no knowing what had been going through Gavin's mind at the time. Maybe he'd found out about the victims inside the warehouse and it had brought back what had happened to Eliana Salim. Maybe the memory of how he'd failed her had goaded him to act on his own, to go rushing in regardless of consequences.

Walking back to the flats, for the first time Jonah felt he was finally beginning to get a sense of what had gone on that night. Not all of it, not by a long shot. He was still no closer to fathoming Owen Stokes's involvement, or his relationship with Gavin. Still, it felt good to have found out *something*. It might even be enough to convince Fletcher he actually was telling the truth.

Don't get carried away. You shouldn't expect miracles. But as he reached the flats he felt more positive than he had in weeks, and his good mood lasted the rest of the evening.

Until Stan phoned to say his garage had been broken into.

The row of garages was deserted when Jonah got there just after midnight, a low, featureless block in the darkness. There was no sign of Stan. The BMW's cabin light wasn't on, preventing Jonah from seeing if anyone was inside. Switching on the Maglite he'd taken with him, he went over and peered through the driver's window.

'You took your time.'

Jonah spun around, almost overbalancing as a figure emerged from the shadows behind him. Stan raised an arm, squinting against the dazzling beam.

'Get that bloody light out of my eyes!'

Jonah lowered the torch. 'Jesus, Stan . . .'

'Can't see a fucking thing,' the old man grumbled, blinking. He held a heavy wrench in one hand.

'I thought you were waiting in the car.'

'You thought wrong.' He set off past Jonah towards the darkened row of garages. 'Come on, bring that searchlight over here.'

Jonah shone the torch around them as he followed Stan, driving back the shadows to reveal run-down brickwork and shuttered doors. He pointed to the bottom of the garage door.

'I saw it when I was putting my own car away. Look what the bastards did!'

The padlock lay in pieces on the ground, its U-shaped locking bar smashed out with enough force to leave broken metal scattered all around. It looked like someone had taken a lump hammer to it, and the door was little better. Where it had been secured by the padlock, the sheet metal was buckled from repeated blows.

So much for this being a random break-in, Jonah thought. He turned to shine the torch behind them again, making sure no one was there. Some of the locks on the neighbouring garages were little more than window dressing, easily snapped off. Yet instead of going for one of them, someone had been to a lot of trouble to get into his. Remembering the bottle smashing at his feet the night before, and his feeling that the teenage thugs were building up to something, Jonah thought he could guess who. Either they'd seen him going to his garage or somehow they'd found out it was his.

Bastards.

'You going to call your mates?' Stan asked.

He meant the police. But the only thing of any real value Jonah kept in the garage was the Saab, and, fortunately, he'd parked that on the road. The damage was too minor to be an insurance claim, and there was no point wasting police time for a dented door and broken padlock.

'Let's take a look first,' he said. 'Give me a bit of room.'

He didn't expect anyone would still be inside, but if his work had taught him one thing, it was not to take anything for granted. As the old man moved away, Jonah went to one side of the door and leaned both crutches against the brick column separating it from the next garage. Bracing himself on his good leg, he took hold of the door's bottom edge and tried to lift it. The door resisted, warped from the hammering it had taken. Then, with a screech of twisted metal, it slid up.

Stan tutted. 'Just look at that. Bastards made a right mess.'

It looked as though every box had been upended and its contents scattered over the oil-stained floor. And while there might not have been much there to steal, the thieves had helped themselves to what there was. Jonah saw that the power tools he'd kept on a shelf fixed to the back wall were missing. A drill, a small band saw, an angle-grinder. None of them worth very much, but they'd taken them anyway.

'Looks like they busted into your locker, as well,' Stan said.

Jonah shone the torch onto the old metal cabinet that stood in the far corner. Its doors had been forced and now stood slightly ajar. There hadn't been much inside, mainly boxes of old papers that he hadn't got around to sorting but wasn't ready to throw out. They'd been unceremoniously dumped in front of the locker, spilling papers across the concrete.

'Hope you hadn't got anything important in there,' Stan said from behind him.

Jonah gave one of the part-open doors a listless push with the end of his crutch. The door started to swing shut, then met resistance. With a faint squeak of dry hinges, it slowly swung open again.

Shockingly white in the torchlight, a hand slipped out through the gap.

'Jesus God Almighty!'

Jonah barely heard. The hand was resting palm up with its fingers curled, as though in supplication. It was small and smooth, and lay with an awful, heavy limpness. Using his crutch, he eased the door further open. There was another oath from behind him. Jonah put his crutch back onto the floor, suddenly needing its support.

The body had been loosely wrapped in polythene. The sheet had come unfastened at the top, revealing a lolling head encased inside a transparent plastic bag. Black gaffer tape had been wound around the neck to seal the bag shut, and the plastic lay slack and still over the nose and open mouth. The inside of the bag was beaded with condensation, and the hair compressed inside the bag further obscured the face. But not so much that Jonah couldn't recognise the woman wedged like a broken doll inside his cabinet.

It was Corinne Daly.

Chapter 25

'I didn't kill her.'

It wasn't the same interview room as before, but it might as well have been. Same utilitarian chic, same scuffed walls, same bolted-down table. And, sitting at the opposite side of the table from Fletcher, Jonah had been repeating the same thing for hours.

The DI gave a sigh. It wasn't for effect: the detective looked gaunt and tired, the taut skin on his face the colour of putty.

'Then what was her body doing in your garage?'

'I keep telling you, I don't know. But I didn't put it there.'

Jonah was all too aware of how weak that sounded. Technically, this was only a voluntary interview, but he had no illusions about what that meant. If he'd been arrested, the police could only hold him for twenty-four hours, although that could be extended to four days if there was need. As it was, because he was there 'voluntarily', the questioning could drag on indefinitely. The clock would only start ticking once he was arrested.

When he'd first been brought in, he'd felt confident that wouldn't happen. Confident enough not to demand a lawyer, in fact. Despite everything, he was reluctant to accept that he might actually need one, trusting to the fact he'd done nothing wrong.

Now it was starting to look like a bad move.

'So, you admit Daly came to your flat two nights ago,' Fletcher continued. 'To "apologise", I think you said.'

'That's right. She said she felt bad about how she'd treated me.'

'And you believed her? After she'd tricked you in the hospital and ambushed you at McKinney's memorial service?'

'I know how it sounds, but yes. She told me she was having doubts about her job.'

'So you offered her a shoulder to cry on, is that it?'

'No, we just talked,' Jonah said. He was more thankful than ever now that Marie's phone call had come when it did. Maybe nothing would have happened between him and Daly anyway, but if it had, he might have found himself with even more to explain.

'What time was this?' Fletcher asked.

'She got there about half-nine. You can check because I ordered a pizza. She arrived at the same time and brought it up.'

'She delivered your pizza?'

'It was sort of a joke. I think she was worried I wouldn't let her in.'

'So, she arrived around nine-thirty. What then?'

'She said she wanted to apologise. We got talking and ended up sharing the pizza and having a drink.'

'Very forgiving of you.' Fletcher took out a carefully folded tissue and dabbed his watering eye. 'What did she have to drink?'

'Beer.'

'How many?'

'A couple, I think. Small cans.'

'And you?'

'The same. I'd started one before she arrived so . . . one more than her.'

'That would be three, then.' It was hard not to think that Fletcher was enjoying this. 'You say you got talking. What about?'

'General stuff. She told me about her daughter. And she said one of the victims had been identified.' He glanced at Bennet, who stared back without a flicker of emotion. 'She told me he was a Kenyan student called Daniel Kimani.'

From Fletcher's lack of surprise it was evident he already knew. 'Anything else?'

'She knew about Gavin's suspension, but wouldn't say who'd told her.'

'And what about you? What did *you* tell her?'

'Nothing about Gavin or the case, if that's what you're worried about.'

'Oh, I'm not the one who should be worried. But, just to be clear, you had beer and pizza and civilised conversation with a journalist who'd made you look stupid. And then she said goodnight and left. Is that it?'

'Pretty much, yes.'

'And what time was that?'

'About eleven. Maybe half past.'

'She was there for *two hours*? My, you did have a lot to talk about. Did I mention we'd found her car? Parked not far from your flat. So we know she didn't make it back there. She didn't turn up for work the next day either. Or call her parents like she was supposed to. In fact, nobody saw or heard anything from her after she came to see you.'

'She was fine when she left my flat. Check the CCTV cameras, if you don't believe me.'

'Oh, we are doing. But all the ones nearby seem to have been smashed. Funny that, eh?'

Jonah felt too wretched to care about the jibe. 'Do you know yet how was she killed?'

Fletcher looked at him for a moment. 'You're priceless, Colley, you know that? You seriously think I'm here to *discuss* it with you?'

'She'd been wrapped in polythene like the warehouse victims,' Jonah pressed on. He wanted this on the record. 'From what I saw she was fully clothed and I didn't see any blood, so I'm guessing she was knocked unconscious and then left to suffocate. Again, the same as the three victims at the quay-side. The plastic bag was new, but I expect he'd learned from what happened before with the girl. Nadine. He wasn't taking chances on Corinne Daly surviving.'

'And by "he" you mean . . .?'

'You know who I mean. It had to be Owen Stokes. He must have been waiting outside the flats and jumped her when she came out.'

'Ah, of course.' Even Fletcher's nod seemed sarcastic. 'Seems like Owen Stokes is to blame for a lot of stuff that happens around you.'

He stopped as the interview room door opened and Bennet came in. She was carrying a small evidence box, which she set down on the table. Looking at it, Jonah felt a feathering of apprehension.

Fletcher continued. 'You're claiming that Owen Stokes killed Corinne Daly after she left your flat, and then broke into your garage to leave her body? Why? To frame you for her murder?'

'Yes, that's exactly what I'm saying.'

'And this happened when? Tonight, when the break-in was reported? Or two nights ago when she actually disappeared?'

'I don't *know*. I've told you, tonight was the first time I'd been back to the garage since I took my car out. That was the morning before Corinne Daly came round. Stokes could have broken in there any time after that.'

Fletcher pursed his lips, rubbing the backs of his fingers under his chin as you would a cat. 'Well, I suppose that would fit the pathologist's preliminary findings. She says Daly probably died around forty-eight hours ago, and her body was in the locker for a similar length of time. That'd make it the same night she came to see you.'

'Then that's what happened,' Jonah said. But he didn't like the way this felt.

'Good. So we can agree her body was in your garage for two days. The problem we've got then is that your landlord – who isn't a fan of yours, I have to say – insists your garage was intact when he was there a few hours earlier this evening. And when he was there yesterday as well, come to that. Grew quite indignant when we queried it. Said he'd have noticed one of his garages being sledgehammered open, and I'm inclined to believe him. It would've been sort of hard to miss.'

Jonah opened his mouth, but he didn't know what to say. Fletcher nodded.

'I know. Bit of a conundrum, isn't it? We know Daly's body was in there for two days, but the break-in only happened tonight. That sort of suggests whoever put it there must have had a key. Owen Stokes didn't have a key, did he?'

'Oh, for God's sake –'

'Did he have a key?'

'No, but –'

'Did anyone else have a key? Except you?'

Jonah searched for a way out. Couldn't find one. 'No.'

'No,' Fletcher echoed. 'Then you see the problem. If Daly's body was put there two days ago, but the garage was only broken into tonight and you're the only person with a key, then that narrows the list of suspects down, doesn't it? To . . . well, to you, actually.'

Jonah felt he was being boxed into a tighter and tighter corner. 'OK, then someone *else* must have broken in tonight. I thought at first it might be some local teenagers I've been having trouble with. It could have been them.'

'Teenagers? You should have said before! Little sods, you're probably right. Except . . .' Fletcher made a see-sawing gesture with his hand, 'except that leaves us with *two* break-ins to explain. I'll grant you, someone smashed their way in there tonight, no arguments there. But even if your landlord somehow didn't notice the first break-in, if someone – let's say Owen Stokes – had already bust in there two nights ago, these teenage rascals wouldn't have needed to smash the padlock off tonight, would they?'

'Look, *I didn't kill Corinne Daly*,' Jonah said, hearing the desperation in his own voice. 'You can't seriously believe I'd be stupid enough to hide her body in my own garage if I had?'

'Here's what I think. I think you lost your rag and killed her in your flat, waited till the middle of the night, then fetched your car and dragged her body down to the lift. You knew the CCTV cameras outside were broken – for all I know you could've smashed them yourself – so you didn't have to worry about that. You were limited by your knee, so you put her body in your garage while you decided what to do with it. But then you had bad luck. The garage got broken into, either by these teenagers you've only just remembered or someone else. They ransacked it, then ran off when they saw what was in the locker. And then when your landlord called to tell you, you knew you'd no choice but to report it and try and brazen it out.'

Fletcher crossed his arms, resting his case. Jonah could see the man wasn't playing devil's advocate this time. He actually *believed* it.

'For Christ's sake, this is what Stokes *wants*!'

'Here we go again,' Fletcher snorted. 'Give me one reason why Owen Stokes would go to all this trouble to kill a journalist he doesn't even know? Why would he want to set you up?'

'I don't *know!*' Jonah had to stop himself from yelling. 'I've no idea what goes through that sick bastard's mind! But he's on the run because of me! Jesus, he's even lost the money from the *bedsit* because of me! And why would *I* want to kill Corinne Daly anyway? Christ, I *liked* her!'

'That's very big of you. It probably made her job a lot easier.'

Jonah's anger was snuffed out. He'd thought the trap had been sprung: now he realised everything so far had only been the preliminary.

'She was writing another piece on you,' Fletcher said.

'I don't believe you,' Jonah said, but the denial was a reflex.

'Oh, it's true. According to her editor she'd been putting it together for a while,' Fletcher continued. 'He said she was certain there was more to the story. And she was right, wasn't she?'

'She turned her phone off, I saw her . . .'

But he was already thinking how Daly had made such a show of it. How quick she'd been to reassure him. *See? It's off, it's not recording.* And all those leading questions about Gavin . . .

Oh, Christ . . .

'And you're supposed to be a police officer,' Fletcher said, voice dripping contempt. 'DC Bennet, if you wouldn't mind.'

'We found Daly's bag shoved down the side of the locker,' she said, taking a small evidence bag from the box she'd brought in. 'Her phone wasn't in it, so whoever killed her obviously didn't want to risk it being traced. But there was this.'

Inside the evidence bag was a small, rectangular object. Jonah felt his stomach knot as he saw the digital recorder.

'Daly might have switched her phone off, but she still made a recording of her visit,' Fletcher said, taking over again. 'The quality isn't brilliant but it's good enough. We can hear you inviting her in, chatting away. All very cosy. And then we get to this.'

He pressed the play button through the plastic. Jonah heard Corinne Daly's voice followed by his own, tinny and remote but recognisable.

'. . . I've heard rumours about your friend. That he was in trouble. And he shouldn't even have been at that warehouse because he'd been suspended. Is that true?'

'Where'd you hear that?'

'It's OK, I don't expect you to confirm anything, but . . . Well, you can't deny it, can you?'

'Jesus Christ . . .'

'OK, I'm sorry, forget I said anything . . . Please don't –'

There was an inarticulate yell, then a confusion of noise. A loud thump and screech of furniture followed by a muffled clatter.

Then nothing.

Fletcher stopped the playback. In the accusing silence Jonah could feel his own heartbeat.

'The recording carries on, but you can't hear much after that except bumps and rustles,' the DI said, putting the evidence bag down. 'Still, I'd say there's more than enough, wouldn't you?'

Jonah felt in freefall, as though the ground had dropped away from under him. 'It's not how it sounds.'

'No? Because it *sounds* like you losing your temper and assaulting Corinne Daly.'

'No! Jesus, that's not what happened!' Jonah felt a clammy sweat that had nothing to do with the temperature in the interview room. 'OK, I was angry, but at myself for letting my guard down! I stood up, my knee gave out and I knocked the coffee table over as I fell! That's it, that's all! Daly's bag ended up on the floor, so the recorder must have got covered over.'

'And then what?' Fletcher asked.

'*Nothing*! That's it, that's all that happened. Gavin's wife called a few minutes later. You can check, it'll be logged on my phone. Daly left not long afterwards, and that was the last I saw of her. But I swear she was fine!'

'So you keep saying. Unfortunately, we've only your word for that.'

Jonah tried to think of something that could turn this around, make them realise he was innocent. He couldn't think of a single thing.

Fletcher looked at him, drumming the fingers of one hand on the Formica tabletop. 'Is the post-mortem going to find any of your DNA or semen on Corinne Daly?'

'What?' A shock ran through Jonah. 'No! You think I *raped* her?'

'We'll see, won't we?'

Fletcher rose to his feet and went out, leaving Bennet to pick up the evidence box and follow.

The interview room seemed to press in on Jonah after they'd left. He still had his watch, and each pass of the second hand seemed to take an age. Ten minutes crawled by, then twenty, then an hour. Then, as though time had restarted, the door opened and Fletcher and Bennet came back in.

Jonah tried to read their faces as they resumed their seats. The policewoman's was coldly unreadable but there was a calm about the DI now. An unnerving quietude Jonah hadn't seen in him before.

'Strictly speaking, this isn't my case so I shouldn't really be the one to do this,' Fletcher said. 'But in view of the connection, the SIO agreed.'

'I didn't kill Corinne Daly,' Jonah said. More to head off what was coming than with any hope it would do any good.

Fletcher regarded him.

'You know what, Colley? I'm getting tired of hearing you say that. You didn't kill Corinne Daly, you didn't kill McKinney, you didn't kill any of those poor bastards in the warehouse. And to start with I believed you. Not all of it – I knew something was off. But I honestly didn't tab you for a murderer. I still can't make up my mind if you're responsible for the others or not. Something still doesn't add up about that. But this . . .'

Suddenly there didn't seem to be enough air in the room.

'Jonah Colley,' Fletcher intoned. 'You are under arrest on suspicion of the murder of Corinne Daly.'

Chapter 26

He'd been arrested.

Arrested.

It didn't seem possible, even now. But the hard bunk underneath him was real enough. The small, windowless holding cell he was in stank of an astringent disinfectant that failed to hide an underlying odour of urine. A screened ceiling light shone on a lidless stainless-steel toilet and a small hand basin. Jonah had been allowed to keep his crutches but he'd had to surrender everything else. Watch, phone, wallet. His finger ends were smudged from having his fingerprints taken, and the back of his throat still felt scraped from the DNA swab. Even during the worst moments after the warehouse, he'd never considered this was a serious possibility. He'd remained anchored by the certainty that his innocence was a given, that his exoneration was never in doubt.

Now here he was.

Leaning forward on the edge of the bunk, Jonah put his head in his hands and pressed the heels of his palms into his eyes. Trying to blot out the image of Corinne Daly's body inside the locker. *His fault.* He might not have killed her himself, but it was because of him that she'd died. He'd underestimated Owen Stokes. Badly. He'd been so fixated on his own agenda, on trying to discover what bearing the carnage at the warehouse might have on what happened to Theo, that he'd overlooked what Stokes might do next.

And how desperate the man might be.

Thanks to Jonah, he was on the run and had lost the money from Gavin's bedsit. Because Jonah no longer had any doubt at all who he'd heard outside. It had seemed fanciful at the time, but he of all people should have realised what Stokes was capable of. He'd seen first-hand what he'd done to Nadine, to Daniel Kimani and that other poor bastard in the warehouse. Christ, he'd even watched him bundling up and dragging away Gavin's body.

Yet even after Stokes had brazenly broken into Marie's house, Jonah hadn't seen the danger. He'd naïvely assumed the man would compliantly accept the role of fugitive, too busy trying to avoid being caught to be an active threat. The idea that he might hold Jonah responsible for what had happened, that it might be personal for Stokes too, had never occurred to him.

And Corinne Daly had died because of it.

It seemed clear now that Stokes must have broken into the garage twice, the first time more subtle, to plant Corinne's body there, and the second to make the forced entry more visible when no one reported it. And the recording she'd made in the flat must have seemed like a gift, tying up Jonah's guilt in a neat bow.

He banged his hands against his head. *Oh, you fucking idiot! Stupid, stupid, stupid!*

But the outburst soon burned itself out. Self-recrimination wouldn't get him anywhere, not now. Taking a deep breath he sat up straight, trying to calm himself. To *think*. He didn't know why the journalist had been targeted. But Stokes was a killer, that much was obvious. Even leaving aside what may or may not have happened to Theo – and Jonah knew he couldn't afford to go down that rabbit hole now – he'd already murdered at least four people. He was unlikely to baulk at one more.

Perhaps Corinne had just been in the wrong place at the wrong time, tarnished by her association with Jonah and a convenient prop to frame him. The question of *why* Stokes would bother to do that still troubled him, but right now that was less important than what the twisted bastard might be planning to do next.

And what Jonah could do about it.

The duty solicitor was a woman in her forties called Farah. She had greying hair and tired eyes, and Jonah expected her to just go through the motions. But she seemed competent, and her questions were probing enough to make him feel the first flicker of hope since Fletcher had read him his rights.

'How long do you think they'll hold me?' he asked, even though he knew what she'd say.

'For something as serious as this I'll be surprised if they don't want to keep you in custody for the full ninety-six hours. Unless they charge you before.'

After that they would either have to charge him or let him go. If they charged him, then he'd be remanded in custody and kept locked up until the trial, for however many months that was. Funnelled into the British criminal justice system as that despised cliché, a police officer turned bad. Even worse than Gavin.

'I know you'll hear this a lot, but I didn't do it,' he told Farah.

Her smile gave nothing away. 'We'll go over things again tomorrow, OK?'

Back in the holding cell, Jonah lay with his arm over his eyes, shielding them from the bright overhead light. He tried to sleep but he might as well not have bothered. Each time he closed his eyes he was greeted by the sight of Corinne Daly's body, broken and twisted inside the locker like an obscene ventriloquist's dummy.

He drifted in and out of a thin, fitful sleep in which he never lost awareness of being in the cell. But at some point it must have given way to something deeper, because next he knew he was shocked awake by a metallic clatter. He sat up, with no idea of where he was. Then, as though he'd stepped through a trap door, memory came crashing back. *Oh, Christ.* He rubbed the fatigue from his eyes and swung his legs off the bunk as a hatch in the cell door opened and a tray was slid inside.

On it was a plate with two slices of anaemic toast smeared with a greasy butter substitute, and a mug of lukewarm tea. Breakfast. Jonah realised he was starving. He'd demolished the toast and was finishing the tea when there was another noise as the door was unlocked. Jonah felt his stomach tense as it swung open, expecting to be escorted back for more questioning.

But it was Bennet who appeared in the doorway, not a uniformed PC.

'You're free to go,' she said.

Jonah thought he must have misunderstood. 'What?'

'You're being released on bail.'

Bail? That wasn't usually granted for anything as serious as murder, so Jonah had never even considered it a possibility. And it didn't mean he'd been cleared. He could still be brought back in for questioning or charged at any time. But at least he'd be free until then.

'How come?' he asked, relief sweeping through him as he reached for his crutches.

'We've no further questions at this time.'

Pushing himself to his feet, Jonah stopped to look at her. Bennet's face was as closed as ever, but he thought there was a tension about her.

'You wouldn't be releasing me on bail without a good reason. What's happened?'

She held the door open. 'Do you want to go or not?'

He did, but now his relief was tempered by suspicion.

'Why am I being released now?' he asked, going out into the corridor.

'You'll have to ask DI Fletcher.'

She waited for him to go in front of her, but Jonah stayed where he was. She sighed.

'Now what?'

'Why won't you tell me what's going on?'

'Look, I don't have time to argue –'

'Then tell me why I'm being released.'

Bennet looked on the point of taking his head off, then some of the fight seemed to go from her. She looked away.

'There's new evidence.'

Jonah waited, but she didn't explain. 'What sort of evidence?'

Again, there was a pause.

'We've had a reported sighting of Owen Stokes at the house where McKinney had his bedsit. One of the residents saw someone matching his description running downstairs, the same afternoon you and McKinney's son were there. The witness described him as a tall man in a baseball cap, with what looked like either a birthmark or a tattoo on the back of his neck.'

So it *had* been Stokes at the bedsit. Jonah felt a bitter frustration to think how close he'd been, but that still didn't answer his question.

'That only proves Stokes knew about the bedsit,' he said,

setting off down the corridor. 'It doesn't have anything to do with Corinne Daly, so why are you letting me go?'

They'd come to a door. Bennet stopped to present her fob. 'Have you never heard what they say about mouths and gift horses?'

'Come on, there has to be something you're not telling me.'

Bennet wrenched on the door when it buzzed. She opened it and stood back for him to go through.

'The custody officer will return your things,' she said.

Jonah had lost all sense of time when he emerged from the police station. It had been night when he'd last passed through its doors, and once inside he'd been in a clockless limbo of artificial light. Walking out into broad daylight felt disorientating, as though he had emerged into a different world.

There was a fine mizzle in the air, cold and penetrating. He turned his face up to it as he stood on the wet pavement, relishing the clean feel. Relatively clean, anyway. His clothes were creased and grubby and there was a thick rasp of stubble on his face. With no clear idea of where he was going, he set off down the street. Joining the queue at a bus stop, he boarded the first bus that came without caring where it was going. Even that was a struggle on his crutches, but once he'd paid he found a window seat close to the doors. Taking it, he stretched his leg out as best he could and watched the streets slide by outside.

He felt as though his life had come untethered. The fact that he'd been arrested – for *murder* – was still too huge a concept to grasp. As the bus swayed and jolted through the traffic, he tried to think what to do. His mistake had been to regard this as a one-way contest, with himself the hunter and Stokes the quarry. He couldn't afford to do that anymore, not after Corinne Daly. Stokes had obviously been watching him. Stalking him, just as he had Gavin. If he was going to survive, Jonah had to adapt to a frightening new reality.

He was being hunted as well.

It took three changes of bus before he found a route that went close to where he lived. A fresh tension grew in him as he got off at a stop in his neighbourhood and began walking back to his flat. He scanned the street and doorways, alert for any sign of ambush. None came, and the forecourt in front of the flats was deserted except for a group of young kids slouching on bikes. There was no sign of Owen Stokes, or the teenagers who'd thrown the bottle at him, come to that. An elderly woman came out of the flats' entrance as he was going in. As he stood back to let her pass, she looked at his crutches.

'Lifts aren't working,' she told him.

By the time he'd hauled himself up to his floor, labouring one step at a time on his crutches, Jonah was out of breath and sweating. Unlocking his door, he let himself into his flat. Stripping off his clothes, he showered and then sat on the bed to pull on a clean T-shirt and jeans. His phone was next to him, and as he finished dressing there was the chime of an incoming text. It was from a number he didn't recognise, and a shock ran through him as he read the short message.

Slaughter Quay, 7 p.m. Come alone.

Chapter 27

'You've got a fucking nerve!'

Stan stood in the middle of his workshop, sleeves rolled up on his oil-stained overalls to display corded forearms and knotted fists. A radio played classical music in the background, while somewhere out of sight someone was whistling a completely different tune. A car was hoisted up at head-height on a ramp, and several others were nearby in various states of disassembly.

'I'm sorry –' Jonah began.

'Fuck sorry! I keep my nose clean, I run a good business. I don't want nothing more to do with you!'

'Come on, Stan. If I'd known what was in there, do you think I'd have let you see?'

'You think I liked being dragged off to some police station? Interrogated like *I'd* done something wrong!'

'Just hear me out. Please!' Jonah didn't think Stan would take a swing at him, but he'd never seen the old man this upset. 'You want your garage back, fine, I'll clear my things out as soon as I can. But I really need to hire a car. An automatic, I don't care what type.'

Jonah's own car had been seized by the police. He'd get it back eventually, but only after it had been forensically examined for any signs that Corinne Daly had been in it.

Stan's face was implacable. 'I don't care either, the answer's still no.'

'I wouldn't be asking if it wasn't important.'

'So what? Get a taxi!'

That would have been simpler. But Jonah had no idea what he was getting into. If he needed to get away from Slaughter Quay in a hurry he didn't want to have to call for a cab. And none of the car hire firms he'd tried would entertain the idea of renting to someone on crutches.

He tried again. 'If it's about the money, I'll pay whatever you want.'

'I don't want your money, I want you gone! Now!'

Jonah tried to think of something else he could say to persuade him, but came up blank. It was no use wasting any more time.

'OK,' he said heavily. 'I'm sorry you got dragged into this.'

He turned to make his way back through the obstacle course of oil cans and engine parts. Behind him, he heard the old man swear under his breath.

'What do you want it for?'

Jonah looked back. Stan was still glowering, but it had died to a smoulder.

'I've got to meet someone tonight. They might know who killed the woman in my garage.'

That was an understatement if the text came from who Jonah thought. But to find out he needed transport. He waited while Stan deliberated, shaking his head at some internal argument.

'You get me into any more trouble, you'll regret it,' the old man grumbled. 'It's round the back.'

The car was a beast. It was a huge Volvo estate, foul with stale cigarettes and boasting what smelled like an ancient dog blanket in the back. It looked as heavy as a tank, with manual locks and a faulty catch on the cavernous boot that made it prone to springing open. But on the plus side, there was more leg room than in the Saab.

Stan insisted on him filling out the proper paperwork, though that didn't prevent him from charging double the going rate.

'You bring it back in one piece or you're buying it, you hear?' he warned.

The Volvo's bulk gave a comforting sense of security as Jonah pulled into the rush-hour traffic. He headed straight for the quayside. He was early but he wanted time to scout the place out.

He'd need every advantage he could get.

There was no doubt in Jonah's mind that the text was from Owen Stokes. He'd no idea how the bastard had got hold of his phone number, but with the right know-how or contacts it wouldn't have posed too much of a problem. After he'd read the text Jonah had paced restlessly in the flat on his crutches, trying to decide what to do. Several times he'd been on the verge of phoning Fletcher. He'd missed one chance of catching Stokes at the bedsit: he couldn't let that happen again.

But Stokes wasn't stupid. He'd be watching for any sign that Jonah wasn't alone, and at the first hint of a police presence he'd be gone.

And with him, Jonah's chance of getting answers.

That was what ultimately decided him. He knew there was a good chance he'd be walking into a situation he wouldn't survive. In all likelihood, Stokes was intending to finish what he'd started at the warehouse. First he'd want to find out if Jonah had kept any of the money from the bedsit, then he'd kill him.

Yet if Jonah didn't go, he might never know what Stokes could tell him. Not only about the warehouse, but what had actually happened in the park ten years ago. If there was even the slightest chance Jonah could wring the truth from him, to find out if Theo really had drowned by accident or if Stokes had somehow played a part, then he had to take it.

Regardless of the risk.

It was after six when he pulled onto the waste ground. There was no other car there. Switching off the headlights, he climbed out of the Volvo and looked around. He gave a shiver. The air was cold and damp, but that wasn't the reason.

He was back at Slaughter Quay again.

The cloudy sky had cleared, and a full moon cast a monochrome light onto the Dickensian squalor. The moonlight was bright enough that he didn't need the Maglite to see, but that was only one reason he'd taken it anyway. The big torch also made a passable club. How much use it would be would depend on what Stokes had with him, but Jonah felt reassured by its metal heft.

Stokes hadn't said where to meet, but the warehouse was the obvious place. If he wasn't there, then Jonah would come back and wait in the car. The tang of bilges and rotting seaweed grew stronger as he cut down the cobbled lane by the old tannery. On the water, the moored barges undulated like floating caravans. *Or coffins.* The thought said a lot for Jonah's state of mind. The largest boat was still tethered slightly apart from its smaller cousins. The handwritten *For sale* sign still showed in one of its grimy windows, and as Jonah walked past a low growl came from the deck. The moonlight showed the feral cat was back in the boat's hatchway. It hissed and spat at him, hunching protectively over a chewed food wrapper until he'd gone past.

The quayside was an eerie place, lonely and bleak, and his unease grew as he approached the warehouse. Stopping by the gate, he shone the light through the wire-mesh fence. A new sign had been added since the last time he was there, a large board fixed to the chained gates that declared: *DANGER! UNSAFE STRUCTURE. DO NOT ENTER.*

Jonah stood listening for a moment, but the only sounds were the wind and the soft lap of the water. Switching on the torch, he fanned its beam across the building. There were only boarded-up windows and crumbling walls. If Stokes was there already, he was hiding.

He checked his watch. The glowing fingers showed half past six. There was no point in standing out there in the cold. His knee was aching and he might as well wait in the car until Stokes showed.

And then they'd finish this.

The walk seemed to take longer as he retraced his steps along the quayside. He felt more exposed, but told himself that was probably only his imagination. Even so, he was alert for any noises behind the click and scrape of his crutches, and as he walked he scanned the shadows outside the torch beam for any movement.

There was nothing, but his disquiet grew. By the time he reached the moored barges his nerves felt taut and frayed, ready to snap. When an angry *hiss* came off the water he spun around, gripping the Maglite, before he saw a pair of small eyes glinting on the boat and remembered the cat. Jonah sagged as the tension left him.

Jesus . . .

Cutting away from the water, he headed for the lane. He was keen to get back to the Volvo. Without meaning to, he started walking faster.

On the boat, the cat gave another low growl.

Jonah felt the hairs rise on the back of his neck. He didn't slow or look around, but now he heard the faint scuff of a footstep behind him, slightly out of sync with his own. He swore silently. He'd been assuming Stokes would drive there, but with everything that had happened he'd overlooked something obvious. Something he should have remembered from that night at the warehouse.

Stokes had a boat.

The footsteps were more audible now, but he didn't think they'd got any closer. The bastard was taunting him, trying to psych him out. He felt confident enough to play games, and the thought almost provoked Jonah into facing him there and then.

But galling as it was to admit, he knew he couldn't win a straight-out fight on crutches. He had to be cleverer than that. The boarded-up tannery was just ahead, an angular shadow on the corner of the lane. Once Jonah had turned down there he'd be out of sight for a few seconds. There was a doorway part way along, and if he could get to it before Stokes reached the corner then he could jump him as he went past. Approaching the entrance to the lane, he risked a quick glance back.

Backlit by the low moon, a bulky silhouette crossed through the shadows.

There was a bitter, coppery taste in Jonah's mouth as he turned away. Jesus, Stokes looked even bigger than he remembered. Suddenly, he felt terribly vulnerable on the crutches. What the hell had he been thinking, coming out here on his own? *Too late now. Just do it.* He started taking deep breaths, preparing to lunge for the doorway as soon as he was out of sight. *Get ready . . .* The footsteps behind him were louder, speeding up as Jonah turned the corner.

The lane in front of him was blocked by a dark SUV.

Jonah faltered as one of its doors cracked open, cutting off his path. It felt as though he were moving in slow motion as he started to turn around, desperate to get out of the trap.

As he did a tall figure appeared at the entrance to the lane. *Oh, fuck!* He shone the Maglite into the hulking figure's face, hoping to dazzle him long enough to swing the heavy torch. An arm was raised to ward off the light, but not before the beam had shown the immense size of the man and bland, childlike features in a boulder-like head.

It wasn't Owen Stokes.

Jonah heard someone climbing out of the car behind. Turning back to this new threat, he saw it was a woman. Then a massive hand clamped onto his forearm. The giant had moved silently and with shocking speed. Jonah tried to wrench free, hoping to jerk the man closer and ram a knee into his groin, but it was like trying to move a rock. The man squeezed harder, twisting Jonah's arm until he dropped the Maglite. Its beam stayed on after it hit the ground, sending shadows jumping as it rolled from side to side.

'It's all right, Stefan.'

The voice was low and slightly accented. The woman stepped closer, and Jonah stared as the light from the fallen torch lit her face.

Standing in front of him was the dead woman from the warehouse.

'Can we talk?' she said.

Chapter 28

She wore a long, smoke-coloured coat in what looked like cashmere. Her black hair was taken back, exposing the slender throat and accentuating the high cheekbones and almond-shaped eyes. The last time Jonah had seen that face it had been swaddled in filthy plastic, reddened and blistered from the quicklime powder.

Now the skin was unblemished.

'You can let him go, Stefan,' she told the giant. 'Sergeant Colley isn't going to cause any trouble.'

The giant released Jonah's wrist and stepped back. Rubbing it, Jonah flexed his fingers. Christ, the man was strong.

'What is this?' Jonah asked.

'I'll explain in the car. Please,' she added when he didn't move. 'I don't have long. I'm taking a risk just being here.'

Jonah hesitated. He began to stoop for the Maglite but the giant stepped forward and picked it up. Keeping hold of it, he moved back again, the small eyes watching Jonah with an utter lack of interest.

'Please,' the woman repeated, gesturing to the SUV.

No one objected when he went to the front and climbed into the driver's seat. Now he couldn't just be driven off, and the small act of defiance made his ego feel a little better. The woman slid gracefully into the front passenger seat as the giant held the door open for her. Jonah was relieved when he closed it behind her and went to stand guard on the corner.

'Thank you for agreeing to talk,' the woman said, turning to him.

Her perfume was a spiced musk, heady rather than over-powering. In the muted cabin light, her face was smooth and flawless, the olive skin only lightly touched with make-up. But the hair was straight rather than curled, while the features themselves were subtly altered. And although the young victim who'd called herself Nadine couldn't have been long out of her teens, the person in front of him was older, though perhaps not by much.

As she settled back in her seat her face was momentarily thrown into shadow. It deepened her eye sockets and cheek-bones, so that the skull seemed to press through the skin. Then she settled back into her seat and the illusion was gone.

Now she was the one who seemed nervous.

'Do you know who I am?'

He hesitated, but the resemblance was too strong to be accidental. And she was too young to be Nadine's mother.

'You look a lot like your sister,' he said.

She inclined her head in acknowledgement. 'Thank you, but that isn't what I meant. Do you know who I *am*?'

She was looking at him as though she expected him to, with an intentness that was discomfiting. He felt something start to shift in his subconscious, the first inkling of a bigger picture he hadn't even realised existed.

'My name's Eliana Salim.' She gave a small gesture with her hand. 'Or rather it was.'

It wasn't so much shock that silenced Jonah as a recalibra-tion. Wilkes had told him Salim had a younger sister, but he'd also said Gavin's informer had been murdered, her tongue cut out and her body dismembered. The ex-detective hadn't been lying, Jonah was certain of that. Yet he felt no doubt that the woman sitting next to him was telling the truth. This was Gavin's lover and one-time informer.

And Nadine's older sister.

'I was told you were dead.'

'Eliana Salim died. I didn't.'

'So what do you call yourself now?'

'That's unimportant. You were with Nadine when she died. I'd like you to tell me about it.'

Jonah was beginning to recover. 'If you wanted to talk, why didn't you say something when I saw you a few nights ago?'

'I was startled.' Salim looked down at where her hands lay entwined on her lap, elegant and perfectly manicured. She wore only one ring, an opal set in a plain gold band that looked like trapped moonlight. 'I come here sometimes, to be where my sister died. But I didn't expect to see you.'

The surprise was mutual, Jonah thought. 'Your sister hasn't been identified. How did you know she was one of the victims?'

Salim smoothed her coat over her lap, outwardly calm and composed. 'The news reports said the female victim was called Nadine, and that she matched my sister's description and was believed to be Middle Eastern. That wouldn't have been enough in itself, but I knew it had to be her when I saw that McKinney was involved.'

Jonah gave her a sharp look at that. 'Why?'

'It would have been too much of a coincidence for anything else.' The dark eyes were solemn and flecked with gold, like a cat's. 'Nadine was fifteen when I left Syria. She was living with our aunt and uncle in Aleppo but I hoped to earn enough money to bring her here. Legally, not like me. Unfortunately, because of my . . . circumstances, by the time I could try to contact her again our aunt and uncle had been killed in a bombing. I learned that Nadine had survived, but she was one refugee out of millions and I had no way of tracing her. I'd been trying to find her ever since. I'd no idea she was even in the country until I saw her name with McKinney's in the news reports. I couldn't believe he might know another Nadine, of the same age and description, so I knew then it was her. She must have come here to try and find me and somehow made contact with him, hoping he could help. What I don't understand is how she found him, or why she came to die in that place.'

That was the second time she'd referred to Gavin by his surname. There was a coldness to the way she said it, and Jonah hadn't missed how indifferent she seemed to her former lover's death. That didn't seem like the love affair Wilkes had made out. But then the fact that Salim was there in the car, alive and well, was proof the detective didn't know everything.

'I'm sorry,' Jonah said. 'I don't know that I can tell you much more than you'll already know.'

'You were with her.' The dark eyes were searching as she looked at him. 'Nadine was the only family I had. I know her death was slow and cruel, but I need to hear what happened. Please.'

She put her hand on his wrist, and suddenly Jonah was acutely conscious of her physical presence. He knew he was being manipulated, but Salim could hardly present herself to the police as next of kin when she was supposedly dead herself. And he could understand why she'd want to know how her sister had died.

So he told her. He limited his account to the basic facts, not dwelling on the more gruesome details but not shying away from them either. When he'd finished, she studied the opal ring, turning it slowly on her finger.

'Was she suffering very much when you found her?'

'She was very weak by then. But she still tried to warn me before I was attacked.'

'Do you think she could have survived at that point?'

'I don't know,' Jonah hedged, then felt that was dishonest. 'Perhaps.'

Salim brushed at her cheeks with the back of a long finger. 'Thank you. For telling me, and for trying to save her.'

'I'm sorry I couldn't do more.'

'So am I.'

It was said in sadness rather than reproach. Jonah hesitated, wondering how much he should say. But he had to ask.

'Does the name Daniel Kimani mean anything to you?'

'No.' Oddly, she didn't seem curious, but her next question drove it from his mind. 'Tell me about Owen Stokes.'

Jonah froze at the name. Details of her sister's death was one thing, but he'd been careful to avoid any mention of Stokes.

'Who told you about him?'

'I have . . . friends.' The gold-flecked eyes regarded him dispassionately. There was no trace of vulnerability about her now. 'They also told me this same man was a suspect in your son's disappearance.'

Jesus Christ, Jonah thought. Suddenly the whole atmosphere in the car had changed.

'What is this?' he demanded.

'What I said. I want to know how my sister came to be murdered. I know that this Stokes is believed to have killed her and McKinney as well as the other victims. I also know that you had good cause to suspect him even before this. That makes me question whether you're as innocent as you claim.'

The only way Salim could know about any of this was through someone with connections deep into the investigation.

Or access to police records. Either way, she might know about the rest of it as well. The money from the bedsit, even Corinne Daly's murder.

'If you know about that, then you'll know I've already been questioned,' he said. 'And if you're thinking your sister died because I was on some sort of vendetta against Stokes, you're wrong. Until recently, I'd no reason to think my son hadn't died accidentally. I didn't know anything about any of this until I walked into that warehouse, and I've been trying to understand it ever since.'

'And now?' she asked.

'What do you mean?'

'You said you believed your son's death was accidental "until recently". Do you think now that Owen Stokes was responsible?'

'I don't know,' he admitted. 'That's what I'd like to find out.'

'Then we have something in common.' She looked at him, the cat's eyes dark and contemplative. 'I heard that you and McKinney were good friends.'

It sounded like an accusation.

'We stopped being friends years ago, but I daresay you already know about that as well,' Jonah told her. 'And before you ask, I've no idea what Gavin was doing at the warehouse or what was going on between him and Owen Stokes. Until tonight I didn't even know that Nadine had a sister. So, now I've answered your questions, how about answering mine?'

'That depends what they are.'

'Let's start with you and Gavin McKinney. What was your relationship with him?'

Her face was cold as she turned away. 'There was no relationship. The police wanted to use me as an informer. He was my handler.'

'I heard it was more than that.'

'Then you heard wrong.' There was ice in her voice. 'We

had sex, but as I'm sure you're aware, that hardly put him in an exclusive club. McKinney wanted to use me, the same as everyone else. I gave him what he wanted.'

'Did he think it was more than that?'

'You think I *cared*?' she flashed. 'I asked for help and instead I was sent back to men who would have killed me if they'd found out! "Be patient," he'd say. *Patient*! Easy for him! When I saw all the stories about this "hero" after he'd died, I would have laughed if I hadn't been sickened! Because of him I lived in fear every day. *Every day*! Treated like I was just some worthless foreign whore! What did he do to stop that? Nothing, except fuck me as well!'

Outside the car, the bodyguard had noticed her agitation. He turned towards them, staring at Jonah with the emotionless intent of an attack dog. But Salim was composed once more.

'Do you have any more questions?' she asked, a sardonic lift to her mouth.

'Did he know you were still alive?'

'Of course not.'

'What about your sister?'

'Nadine knew nothing about any of it.'

'Then how could she have known about Gavin?'

A sigh escaped her. 'I told her.'

She looked down at her hands again, rotating the opal ring on her finger.

'I wrote her letters,' she said. 'Fantasies, about how wonderful my new life was. What else was I going to say to a fifteen-year-old schoolgirl? I used to keep them hidden until there was an opportunity to post them. Sometimes that could take weeks, so I didn't dare risk saying anything revealing in them in case they were found. It was easier once my . . . *employers* started trusting me enough to allow me out on my own. That's how

I was able to meet with McKinney. He let me try phoning and emailing Nadine, but there was never any response. So I continued with the letters, sending them to my aunt and uncle's address in the hope at least one would reach her and she'd know I was still alive. One of them must have.'

'You told her his name?'

'Of course not, I wasn't as stupid as that. I didn't even tell her his rank or where he worked. I just said I'd met someone. A police detective, tall and handsome. Another lie to make her happy. Like my lovely flat and job, and all my new friends.'

Her voice was heavy with bitterness and self-reproach.

'She'd need more to trace him than that,' Jonah said.

'That's all I told her. And she couldn't have gone to the police for help. There's no official documentation of her entering the country, so she can't have been here legally.'

Jonah didn't bother to ask how she knew. 'You think she was smuggled in?'

'Or somehow made her own way. Nadine was resourceful but also impatient. Official immigration channels would have been too slow. All I know is that, however she came here, it wasn't the same people who brought me. Thank God.'

'How can you be sure?'

Her eyes seemed to darken even more at whatever thoughts were behind them. 'I'd know.'

A muted vibration sounded, like a trapped bee in the car's quiet. Salim took a phone from her pocket. The light from its screen gave her face a cold, blue cast. She read whatever was on it without expression, then put it away.

'I have to go.'

'One more question,' Jonah said quickly. 'Everyone thought you'd been killed. How did you manage to get away?'

'Who says I did?'

'Then at least tell me whose body they found in the flat?'

A shadow seemed to cross her face. It was as though all the life and animation had drained out of her. She looked down at her lap, smoothing her coat over it.

'Someone who couldn't be saved.'

'What does that mean?'

'What does it matter now?' The atmosphere in the car crackled again as she turned on him. 'I had to survive for my sister. If it had been your son, what would *you* have done?'

Jonah was saved from answering by another buzz from her phone. This time Salim didn't check it, and after a few seconds it fell silent.

'I have to go,' she said again, signalling to the bodyguard.

'How can I get in touch with you?' Jonah asked, frustrated the conversation was over.

'Look in the glove compartment.' She gave a wry smile when he hesitated. 'Don't worry, it's not a trick.'

He had to reach across her. The glove compartment was empty except for a mobile phone.

'There's a number on it to contact me if you have information about Owen Stokes,' she told him as he took it out. 'You can only use it once. And I'm sure I needn't ask you not to tell anyone about this.'

Jonah slipped the phone into his jacket pocket. 'What would happen if I did?'

'You mustn't!' There was a new note in Salim's voice. She went on, calmer. 'It's better for everyone that you don't. Believe me.'

'Why? Who are you afraid of? If it's the gang who was holding you, I know people who can help.'

Her smile was coldly amused. 'I've been told that before. Don't worry, they aren't a threat anymore. But there are others who wouldn't be happy I'm here. And now you need to go.'

Jonah wanted to ask more, but cold air spilled into the car as the door beside him was opened. The bodyguard stood framed in the doorway, small eyes gazing down incuriously. Jonah had turned to get out when Salim spoke again.

'Anna Donari.'

He looked back, bewildered. 'What?'

'Just remember the name. Anna Donari.'

'Why, who is she?'

But a huge hand had clamped his arm as the bodyguard took hold of him. Jonah shrugged free but gave in to the inevitable and got out of the car. By the time he'd arranged himself on his crutches, Salim had already got into the back. She was invisible behind the tinted glass as the powerful engine grumbled to life. The glare from the headlights prevented him from seeing the number plate as the big Mercedes swiftly reversed out of the narrow lane and onto the waste ground. It executed a neat turn, headlights illuminating the weeds and rubble as they scythed across the blackness.

Then its rear lights were receding into the night, leaving Jonah alone in the darkness.

Chapter 29

Jonah parked on the same stretch of road near his flats. The Volvo's handbrake was stiff, an old-fashioned manual one, and he had to wrench on it several times before it caught. Switching off the engine, he sat in the stale, cigarette-and-dog atmosphere of the old car while he tried yet again to process what had happened at the quayside.

Even now, it was hard to adjust to the fact that Eliana Salim was alive. Wilkes had no reason to make up the story about her murder, and clearly believed the dismembered remains he'd identified were hers. But the ex-detective had also said the woman's body found in the flat could only be identified by its severed head, and had been partly eaten by rats. By his own admission, he'd never seen Salim up close, except in photographs. And with everyone already convinced she was the victim, the identification would have been little more than a formality.

Except everyone had been wrong.

Climbing wearily from the Volvo, Jonah locked it and set off down the dark street. A fine rain was falling, but he was oblivious. The weight of Salim's phone in his pocket felt like an accusation. He knew accepting it could have been a mistake, tying him to a woman who'd allowed another to die in her place, and whose 'friends' had access to confidential information from a murder enquiry. Jonah didn't need the bruises forming on his arm from her bodyguard's fingers to tell him that Salim was dangerous.

Yet she wanted Owen Stokes as badly as he did, and he'd instinctively felt he could trust her that far, at least. The discovery that Nadine was her sister threw a whole new light on what had happened at the warehouse. Including Gavin's reasons for being there. Whether Nadine had somehow traced him or fallen foul of Stokes on her own, he must have found out and tried to do for her what he'd failed to do for her sister. Save her.

This time it had cost both their lives.

Which left Jonah with an impossible choice. Fletcher needed to know who Nadine was, yet Salim's fear that Jonah might tell anyone about her had been real. If he betrayed her trust that would make him no better than Gavin.

So what did he do?

A wave of fatigue settled on him as the well-lit entrance to the flats came into view. Suddenly it was all he could do to put one foot – or crutch – in front of the other. In the past twenty-four hours he'd discovered Corinne Daly's body, been arrested and released on bail, and come face-to-face with a woman he'd thought was dead. It was a busy day, by any standards. Right now, he needed food and he needed sleep. Whatever decisions he had to make could wait till tomorrow, he decided.

That's when he saw the hooded figures across the street.

There were three of them, half hidden in the shadows of a shuttered shop doorway. Jonah didn't need to see their faces to know it was the same young thugs he'd had trouble with before. *Oh, come on. Not tonight.* He could feel them silently watching him but kept going, as though indifferent to their presence. The illuminated foyer of the flats wasn't much further. He listened for any footsteps behind him as he approached it. *Almost there.*

Then one of his crutches snagged the edge of a paving stone.

The stumble was only slight. He caught himself straight away, but it broke the steady rhythm he'd been keeping. As though they'd been waiting for it, he heard hurried footsteps on the street behind him.

'Hang on, mate.'

Jonah ignored them and kept going. He wouldn't make it to the foyer, but the forecourt in front of it was lit with security lights. At least there any attack could be seen, for all the good that would do.

'I'm talking to you, bastard!'

Jonah knew then he wasn't even going to make it as far as the forecourt. There was a wall at one side, though. Veering over to it, he stopped and turned round so it was at his back. The three youths halted in front of him. He recognised baseball cap and acne from the lift. The third he didn't know, but he had a wired look that said he was on something as well.

The acned one grinned. 'Got the time?'

Jonah said nothing. He shifted his weight on his crutches, bracing himself on his good leg.

'I like your crutches,' the third one said. 'Can I have a go?'

There were sniggers. Jonah glanced around, hoping to see someone passing who might phone for help if this kicked off. But the four of them were alone.

'I'm a police officer. You don't want to do this.'

'So where's your fucking uniform?'

'He's part of the cripple unit,' baseball cap said. 'His crutches have got sirens.'

There were guffaws.

'Come on, show us,' the third one said, grinning. 'Turn them on.'

The one wearing the baseball cap started making a siren noise.

'I said fucking turn them on!' the third one said, no longer grinning. 'Come on, bastard, do it!'

He kicked out, intending to take one of Jonah's crutches out from under him, but Jonah had been waiting for that. He snatched the crutch out of the way, hooking it under the youth's foot as it swung past. He was hoping to sweep it up so he'd fall, but the crutch didn't have the heft. The youth was caught off-balance, but before Jonah could follow up something slammed into him from the other side.

The air was driven from him as he smacked down onto the rain-wet tarmac. Pain lanced from his knee as he abandoned the crutches, curling himself into a tight ball. He knew what was coming next.

And then the kicking started.

'Bastard! Fucking Bastard!'

Jonah was buffeted as kicks and stamps rained down. He tried to keep his back wedged against the wall to protect his kidneys, ignoring the pain in his knee as he focused on covering his head and groin. A kick got through his forearms to glance off his jaw with a *thock*. Jonah snatched blindly at the foot and pulled. There was a shout and a heavy body crashed down on top of him, winding him again. But it gave a respite from the kicking, and before whoever had fallen had the chance to recover, Jonah grabbed hold of him. Twisting round so the fallen body was in front of him, he wrapped arms and legs around the thrashing limbs and clamped down.

'Fucker! Fucking get *off!'*

The voice was only inches away, loud and panicked. A sour, acrid smell of sweat and cheap deodorant filled Jonah's nose and mouth as his captive bucked and thrashed. Jonah kept his head tucked down and held on. With the wall at his back there was less of him to target now. That didn't stop them trying. Someone stamped on his shoulder, trying to force him to let go. Refusing to, Jonah twisted away and there was a yell as his human shield took the next blow.

'*Fuck*, that's me, you stupid fuck!'

Jonah felt his foot seized. He kicked out with his good leg, connecting with bone and prompting another cry.

'Fuck this!' a breathless voice panted from above him. 'Move, let me stab the fucker!'

Jonah's stomach coiled. He looked past his captive's shoulder, saw baseball cap reach into his pocket and pull something out.

And then he was dazzled by headlights.

'*Police! Drop the weapon!*'

The night was suddenly full of squealing tyres, flashing blue lights and slamming car doors. As more headlights converged on them, the two attackers still on their feet took off like sprinters. Relief flooded through Jonah, but the third youth was struggling even more frantically, bucking and thrashing as footsteps pounded towards them. Jonah tried to cling on, then a flailing foot struck his knee. Pain erupted from it, and as his hold loosened his captive wrenched free. Jonah grabbed at his legs as he scrambled away, only to catch another foot in the face. His head snapped back, teeth clicking together, and the next moment the youth had gone.

Jonah slumped onto the wet tarmac. Footsteps pounded past him but he was too exhausted to care. Closing his eyes, he rested his head on his forearm, laying in the grit and dirt as his chest heaved for breath.

'You OK?'

He recognised the voice. Raising his head, he looked up as Bennet knelt beside him. Behind her, police cars were skewed at angles by the concrete bollards blocking the road, their silently strobing lights turning the night blue. Christ, it looked like a full-scale op.

'Are you stabbed? Do you need an ambulance?' Bennet asked.

Jonah shook his head. He hurt all over and fresh aches were announcing themselves every second. His face felt weird and his mouth was filled with the coppery taste of blood, but it could have been worse. A lot worse. He began to struggle to sit up.

'Stay there,' Bennet said, putting a restraining hand on his shoulder.

'I'm all right.' But he didn't try to stand. Leaning back against the wall, he took in the swarming police uniforms and cars. 'What's going on?'

Bennet didn't answer, and the effort of sitting up had made Jonah feel light-headed. He closed his eyes and put his head back. Dimly, above the other sounds filtering through to him, he heard more footsteps approaching. Unhurried, this time.

They stopped in front of him. Jonah opened his eyes and looked up. Backlit by the police cars' lights, DI Fletcher stared down at him.

'Congratulations, Colley. You fucked up again.'

Wrapped in a towel, the bag of frozen peas looked like a giant poultice on his knee. It still throbbed but the ice was helping, and it didn't feel any more swollen than usual. Apart from cleaning the worst of the cuts and abrasions on his face and hands, Jonah hadn't had a chance to examine any of his injuries yet. But nothing seemed broken and he'd declined the offer of paramedics. Everything hurt, though, and he felt so tired his head swam. What he wanted to do was strip off his clothes, take a stinging-hot shower and then collapse into bed.

But that wasn't happening yet either.

'Are you rearresting me?' Jonah asked, for the third time.

He was in his living room, left leg propped up on the sofa with the frozen peas strapped to it. Blue lights flickered through the window from the street below, though not so many now. Fletcher stalked around the flat, eyes probing everywhere as though the flat hadn't already been searched.

'If I was arresting you, we'd be at the station instead of up here,' he said, picking up a paperback novel and riffling through its pages.

'Then are you going to tell me what's going on?'

'I'd have thought it was obvious. We saved you from getting your arse kicked by teenagers.' Fletcher tossed the book down onto a chair. 'I take it they were the gang you told us about before?'

'Three of them. They jumped me as I was coming home.'

'So I saw. Remind me what you did to upset them?'

'Refused to be mugged in a lift. After that, just breathing seemed to do it.'

'You have that effect on people.' Fletcher gave his parody of a smile. 'Could be they didn't like what they found in your garage.'

'Do you honestly think they'd come anywhere near me if they'd broken in and found Daly's body?'

'Rough justice, perhaps.'

'Right, because they're so civic-minded. Or perhaps they didn't know anything about it, because Stokes stage-managed the whole thing.'

Jonah expected Fletcher to sneer as he had before, but this time the DI let it pass. Going to a chair he sat down, hitching up his trouser knees before crossing his legs.

'Where were you earlier?'

'Why?'

'Because I'm asking.'

'If you've had me under surveillance you already know. You don't need me to tell you.'

It was the only reason Jonah could think of for the covert police presence outside the block of flats. He'd been released from custody on some pretext in order to see what he did and who he met. In which case Fletcher would know full well where he'd been. And who he'd seen.

But the DI gave no sign of that. 'If you'd been under surveillance, I wouldn't be asking,' he snapped. 'So you can either tell me here or back at the station.'

Either he was playing some game, or else he really didn't know. Jonah couldn't tell, but he didn't see that he had any choice.

'I went to Slaughter Quay.'

He had the satisfaction of seeing the DI silenced for a few seconds. 'OK, then I'm sure you can guess my next question. Why?'

'There's an old barge for sale. I was thinking of buying it.'

'Bollocks. Try again.'

Jonah felt himself on a knife edge. If he didn't tell Fletcher about Salim and her sister, he'd be withholding evidence, pure and simple. Yet if he did, he'd be setting in motion events he couldn't begin to predict. Salim clearly had access to the investigation through her 'friends', so he had to assume she'd find out if he told Fletcher about her. That in itself wouldn't have stopped him, but she'd seemed genuinely scared of anyone discovering they'd met. And she didn't seem the sort to scare easily. Jonah could take the decision to put his own life in danger, but not hers. Not after she'd trusted him.

That would make him no better than Gavin.

Fletcher was waiting. *Time to decide.*

'I thought Stokes might be there,' Jonah said.

There was no thunderclap, and the earth didn't split open. The DI studied him. 'And was he?'

'No.'

'There's a surprise.'

It was hard to read the scarred face, but if Fletcher was pretending then he'd missed a promising career on the stage. Jonah felt encouraged and guilty at the same time.

The sound of the front door opening came from the hallway. A moment later Bennet came into the living room.

'No sign of the attackers, but we found a knife in the gutter,' she told Fletcher.

The DI nodded. Turning to Jonah, he cupped a hand behind an ear.

'What's that, Colley? Thank you for saving my life?'

'I owe you one,' Jonah said flatly. 'So are you going to tell me what's going on?'

The DI tapped his hands in an alternating rhythm on the chair arm. 'We've come across CCTV footage from the night Corinne Daly disappeared,' he said at last. 'The street cameras immediately outside the flats had been deliberately knocked out, but she was picked up by an internal security camera in a shop as she walked past. We had to clean up the image, but it's her. She was heading in the direction of her car just before eleven o'clock.'

That explained why he'd been released on bail. He felt anger as well as relief. 'How long have you known?'

'None of your business. It doesn't prove you didn't still go after her, so don't get carried away,' Fletcher said. 'As far as I'm concerned, you're still a suspect.'

Jonah didn't bother to argue. It was no use, and he felt there was more to come. Radiating unhappiness, the DI scratched the angry skin of his neck.

'We also found this on the same security camera, taken a couple of minutes later. You might as well show him, Bennet.'

Taking out her phone, the policewoman tapped a few keys, then held out the screen for him to see. It looked like an enlargement from a bigger image taken through a shop window, with vague shadows that could have been shelves in the foreground. Framed walking past on the street outside was a tall, gangly figure, frozen mid-step. The image was grainy and the face was obscured by a baseball cap, but both cap and jacket were familiar from the other CCTV photographs Jonah had seen, showing Owen Stokes outside Gavin's flat, and later on the road where Marie lived.

Jonah's anger was growing. 'You *knew* Stokes had followed her? Jesus Christ, is that why you released me?'

'You were released because new evidence came to light.'

'Bullshit! You knew Stokes had been here, so you staked out the flats hoping he'd come back! You were using me as bait!'

'Good job we did, otherwise you'd be bleeding out in a gutter by now.' Fletcher's chin came up pugnaciously. 'We saw an opportunity to bring Stokes into custody so we took it. We just hadn't planned on you and your little friends royally fucking things up. After tonight's farce Stokes won't show his face again within a mile of here.'

'*I* didn't fuck anything up, I didn't know!' Jonah realised he was shouting. 'Why the hell didn't you tell me?'

'You don't get it, do you?' Fletcher snarled back. 'We're not on the same side, you're not part of the *team*. You're a suspect! You think we're going to run it by you first?'

That stopped Jonah in his tracks. He looked from Fletcher to Bennet. She at least had the decency to look away.

'Still? Even after this? You still think I might have killed Corinne Daly?'

'As far as I'm concerned, you're as dirty as McKinney until we prove otherwise.'

Giving Jonah a last glower, he stood up and headed for the door. As Bennet followed, Jonah felt his anger wither and sour. The DI's words were close enough to the mark to strike home. Not in the way he'd intended, but Jonah's conscience was far from clear right now.

'Wait.'

The two detectives paused. Jonah found it hard to meet their eyes as he picked his words.

'The past few days, I've been asking around. I heard . . . I heard Gavin was involved with a case that went bad. Five or six years ago, a police informer was killed. A Syrian woman.'

Fletcher looked at Bennet, then back at Jonah. 'What are you talking about?'

'The young woman from the warehouse. Nadine.' Jonah ploughed on. 'There might be a connection.'

'*Might* be a connection? With a dead informer from years ago?' Fletcher's stare was angry and penetrating. 'You know something, don't you?'

'I just think you need to look into it, that's all.'

'Bollocks.' Fletcher came back into the room, finger levelled at Jonah. 'Whatever you're holding back, now's the time to tell me, Colley. Because I will find out, and when I do, I promise I will hang you out to dry.'

Jonah almost told him. The words were in his mouth, but somehow he couldn't bring himself to say them. Fletcher stared at him, then gave a nod.

'Don't say I didn't warn you.'

He turned and went out. Bennet paused in the doorway to look back at Jonah. She shook her head.

'You really are a glutton for punishment.'

When he'd heard the front door close behind them, Jonah sagged back into the sofa. *Shit.* He hadn't wanted to compromise Eliana Salim but he'd had to say something. At least now they'd check back through Gavin's records, and one look at Salim's photograph would show the resemblance to her younger sister. They should be able to join the dots themselves from there.

He just hoped he'd done the right thing.

God, he hurt all over. Gingerly, he reached for his crutches. They were badly scuffed and one was slightly bent from the fight, but he was too tired to do anything about it. Too tired to do anything but take a hot shower and then go to bed.

He slept for eight straight hours, a record by his usual standards. When he woke he still felt sore and stiff, but not much more so than after a heavy training session. And his knee seemed none the worse for what had happened. The sun was shining through the flat window, and as he ate breakfast he felt his spirits lift. Things were starting to come together. Despite what Fletcher had said, the CCTV footage cleared him of Corinne Daly's murder. Without that hanging over him he could start to dig deeper himself. Maybe follow the same trail she had to Daniel Kimani's friends, and hear what they had to say himself.

He was still planning how to do that when his phone rang. It was Chrissie, but he couldn't understand what she was saying. She was hysterical.

'Slow down, I can't understand you,' he told her.

Then her words took shape, and all Jonah's plans fell apart.

Chapter 30

Rosa had been busy on Instagram, enjoying the early-morning sun. Although it was half-term, the park was quiet this early in the day, except for the bickering of the twins. They were sweet kids most of the time, except for the squabbling. Usually she ignored it, unless it became too loud or threatened to spill over into actual violence. Which it sometimes did, and God forbid she should take them home with so much as a scratch. The last time that happened she'd been lucky to keep her job, and losing it would be even more of a pain in the ass than putting up with their stuck-up bitch mother. She needed the references as well as the money.

Although she sometimes wondered if it was worth it.

The noise level was rising enough to be a nuisance. Rosa looked up from her phone. 'Harry, please leave your sister alone.'

The boy put on an expression of injured innocence. 'I was only explaining the rules.'

'Yes, but why do you get to make them?' his sister protested.

'Because that's one of the rules.'

'No, it *isn't*! That's not fair!'

Rosa sighed and lowered her phone. 'No arguing, please.'

The boy considered. 'Mum and Dad do.'

'They argue all the time,' his sister agreed, suddenly on his side. 'Dad always loses.'

'Well, that's . . .' Rosa tried to think of a convincing counter-argument, then abandoned the attempt. 'That's because they're grown-ups.'

The two children looked at each other, as though communing on some level that excluded anyone else.

'But why is it OK for them and not us?'

'Because they're your parents, OK? Do you want me to tell them you've been quarrelling again?'

They both considered, then gave near-identical grins. 'No.'

They'd inherited their looks from their mother, Rosa thought. But, lucky for them, not their natures. She felt a smile tug at her mouth.

'Well, it's time to go home anyway.'

There were moans but not heartfelt. The twins only dragged their feet a little as they gathered their things. Carrying her phone, Rosa ushered them towards the park gates. There were more joggers and cyclists on the paths than park users, so Rosa automatically walked on the outside of the twins. The volume of their argument made them hard to miss, but she didn't want to have to explain grazes or broken bones either, thank you.

The park was within easy walking distance of the house. When she'd started working there, Rosa had hoped that she'd be allowed to borrow the mother's Range Rover for outings. She'd tried hinting, telling the parents she had a clean licence and liked to drive. But the father seemed not to hear and the mother had looked at her and said, 'Better save up for a car, then.'

So, they walked.

They took the usual route home, on the quieter streets away from the main road. Her phone vibrated in her hand, alerting her to a notification. She had it permanently on silent, because it was better to miss a call than be lectured on socialising when she should be watching the twins. She glanced at them now, but they'd resumed their squabble and were too engrossed to care what she did. She swiped her phone screen, and a second later was smiling at an Instagram post.

She didn't notice the white van ahead of them.

It was parked under the low-hanging branches of a horse chestnut. As Rosa passed into its shade, the rear door of the van opened. Still preoccupied with her phone, she heard the squeal of its hinges as she drew level. Sight and air were suddenly cut off, choking her scream before it started. She felt herself lifted and spun, and then the cold metal floor of the van slammed into her. Stunned, she tried to wrestle whatever it was that covered her face, and then the air was knocked out of her again as something small and solid hit her. She could hear the twins wailing as they floundered on top of her, and there was a slam as the van doors were shut. Half suffocated, she was still trying to free herself from the sack or whatever was over her head when the engine growled to life. The next moment she was flung to one side as the van pulled out, tasting blood in her mouth as a small head caromed into hers. The twins were screaming and crying, and she was too, but then a gruff voice came from in front and above them.

'Shut the fuck up!'

The twins continued to howl.

'I said shut the fuck up!' the man's voice boomed. He had a strange accent, different to the London one she was used to hearing. 'You want something to fucking cry about?'

'No, please –' Rosa began, but then the van took a corner and sent the three of them sliding to the other side in a tangle of arms and legs.

A new cacophony joined theirs, and in her dazed state it took her a moment to realise it was music. Heavy metal, deafeningly loud. She felt a small body against her and instinctively pulled it close. Long hair: Abigail. Rosa couldn't feel Harry but she could hear him close by.

'It's all right, it's all right,' she shouted, knowing it wasn't. She was struggling to breathe, and with her free hand she tried to pull up the sack or hood from her face. As she got it part way the van swung around another corner, tumbling her and the twins over again.

And then she was thrown forward as the van came to an abrupt halt. Bruised and dazed, she was still trying to process what was happening when there was a grating screech as the doors were opened. She felt herself seized and dragged backwards.

'*No!*'

Daylight seeped underneath the sack as she was pulled out of the van. She thumped down onto a hard, gritty surface, banging her head and tearing her skin. Rough hands gripped the front of her jacket, lifting her. She felt warm breath through the cloth as the accented voice hissed in her ear.

'Tell the parents I want Colley to bring half a million to the warehouse at midnight. Alone. He knows the one. If they fuck around or tell the police, they'll get their kids back in pieces, all right?'

The next second she'd been pushed down onto the ground. She heard the van doors slam. The hood had ridden up and through the dazzling sunlight she recognised her surroundings. She was lying in the road outside the house where she worked.

The twins were nowhere to be seen.

'It's your fault! You did this. You fucking brought him here.'

Jonah stood mutely in the kitchen of the big house, making no attempt to defend himself as Chrissie flailed at him while her husband tried to pull her away. He felt simultaneously numb and raw, as though in shock from some injury too big to process. Two thoughts chased each other around in his head. One was disbelief that history could be repeating itself. The other was that Chrissie was right.

It was his fault.

He'd heard the story in more detail from the nanny. She'd been in the kitchen when he arrived, her face tear-stained and her knees grazed and bloody. She couldn't describe the man who'd bundled her and the twins into the van, but she'd had an impression of size and strength. Then there was the voice. Gruff, with a funny accent like she'd heard on TV. Liverpudlian.

'I don't want to get into trouble,' Rosa told Jonah, a fearful expression on her face.

'It's all right,' he told her. 'Why don't you go up to your room for now?'

Chrissie had stopped crying but her face was a clown's mask of smeared make-up. Her husband was slumped on a bar stool at the granite island, ashen and dazed as he gripped a tumbler of whisky like a lifeline. As the nanny went out they were both looking at him, hoping for answers he didn't have.

'Don't just *stand* there!' Chrissie burst out. 'For fuck sake, *say* something! What do we *do*?'

Jonah felt in freefall. But there was really only one thing to say.

'You've got to tell the police.'

They should have called them straight away. Each minute that passed diminished the probability of getting the twins back alive, though he didn't say so. Waverly had wanted to, as soon as they'd made sense of what the hysterical nanny had been telling them. It had been Chrissie who'd overruled him and called Jonah instead.

And now he had to convince them that had been a mistake.

'The *police*? Didn't you hear what he *told* her? He warned he'd send them back in *pieces*!' She ran her fingers through her hair, her face a mask of disbelief. 'Jesus, I can't believe this is happening again! It's him, isn't it? Owen *fucking* Stokes! I *asked* you if there was a risk, and what did you say? Don't *worry*, Chrissie, it'll be fine! Well, it's not fucking fine, is it? He's got my kids! My *kids*!'

Her husband stirred, looking like someone trying to surface from a nightmare. Jonah had never liked the man, even before he suspected him of sleeping with Chrissie, but he felt for him now.

He'd been through the same nightmare himself.

'Jonah's right,' Waverly said. 'We should call the police. They have specialist teams. Experts. They'll . . . they'll know what to do.'

'Like they did with Theo? I've lost one son, I can't . . .' Chrissie pressed her hands to her head. 'Jesus, this isn't happening! Not again! Why *us*? What does he *want*?'

Me. This time, he wants me. Jonah felt as though his heart was being cut out. 'Chrissie, I'm sorry but you don't have any choice.'

'Any *choice*? We do what he says, *that's* the choice! This sick bastard wouldn't even *know* about us if you hadn't led him here, so don't you *dare* tell me I don't have a choice!'

Jonah felt flayed by her words. He knew Stokes must have followed him to Chrissie's, and that guilt weighed on him heavily enough already. And this must be at least partly because – thanks to Jonah – the police had found the money hidden in the bedsit. Money Jonah was now certain Gavin had either stolen or somehow cheated Stokes of. How that had happened remained a mystery, but an unimportant one now. If the twins had any chance of survival, Jonah knew he couldn't afford to trust the man who'd kidnapped them. Chrissie didn't know what they were dealing with. She hadn't seen Stokes's handiwork in the warehouse at Slaughter Quay, didn't know what he'd done to Corinne Daly. Giving in to his demands wouldn't save the twins. It would only ensure he killed them.

If he hadn't already.

'I'd give myself up to him now if I thought it would do any good,' he told her. 'But it won't. That's not how he works. I know it's hard, but the best chance of getting the twins back is to let the police take over. Right now.'

'Why, so I can wait while they piss around and hold press conferences, and then be told "sorry, there's nothing more we can do"?' Chrissie gave a broken laugh. 'Been there, done that. I'm not playing that game again!'

'This is different –' Jonah began.

'Yes, because this time we *know* where they are! We *know* what's happened, the bastard's taken them! And we know what he wants, so for fuck's sake let's give it to him! I'm not losing my babies because you're too scared to put your own neck on the line!'

'You know that isn't –'

'*Then prove it!*' she shouted. 'Let's do what he wants! He can have the fucking money, and if you won't take it to him, I'll do it myself!'

'We don't have that sort of cash,' her husband began.

'So *find* it! I don't care if you have to steal it from the fucking practice, just –'

'For Christ's sake, *shut up!*' Waverly's hand slammed down on the granite island. 'You think this is helping? Just . . . let me *think!*'

Jonah expected an explosion, but instead Chrissie's face crumbled. She pulled away from her husband's hand when he reached for her, but then sagged against him as he folded her into a hug. Watching, Jonah felt the fear and pain of losing Theo again as fresh as when it happened.

Except he couldn't remember he and Chrissie ever comforting each other. When Theo had disappeared they'd turned *on* rather than *to* one another, tearing themselves apart in the process.

'I'm sorry, but you need to decide,' he told them. 'I'll go with whatever you say, but if you're going to involve the police it has to be now.'

Wiping his eyes, Waverly moved away from his wife, trying to compose himself.

'If we . . .' He cleared his throat and tried again. 'If we go to the police, what'll happen?'

'They'll put out a Child Rescue Alert for Abigail and Harry. It'll go out on email, text and social media as well as TV and radio stations. They'll release Stokes's name and description as well. They'll throw everything at it.'

Waverly was nodding as though he understood, but there was a dazed look in his eye. 'This Stokes . . . he was a suspect for your son as well.'

There was a low moan from Chrissie. Jonah felt a corresponding pain in his own chest.

'Yes.'

There would be a time to talk about what had happened in the past, but this wasn't it. Waverly had the sense to realise as much.

'Then this isn't the first time he's . . . I mean, he'll know what the police do in this sort of situation.'

'It's possible, yes.'

'And if an alert goes out on TV and radio, he'll hear it as well. He'll know that we've ignored his instructions.'

Jonah could see which way this was heading but he couldn't think of a way to prevent it.

'They'd use discretion. They wouldn't do anything to put a child at risk.'

'Perhaps not, but Stokes obviously planned this. I think we've got to assume he'll have anticipated the police response as well.' Waverly's confidence was returning now as he turned his lawyer's mind onto the problem. 'He'll cover his tracks and take the twins somewhere that won't be easy to find. He's given us till midnight for you to take the money, which gives us . . . OK, that's a little more than twelve hours. Can you guarantee the police will be able to find the twins by then?'

'No,' Jonah admitted. 'But there's no guarantee Stokes will keep his word even if he gets what he wants. I know it's not what you want to hear, but I don't think he's got any intention of doing what he says.'

Waverly looked as though he might be sick. 'Chrissie? What do you think?'

Her face was a ball of misery. 'I just want my babies, I don't care how. Please, just get them back.'

Waverly passed a hand over his hair, unconsciously smoothing it. 'I agree. We have to do what he wants.'

Even though logic said it was the wrong thing to do, Jonah couldn't blame the man or fault his reasoning. Faced with the same choice – the same *chance* – when Theo had disappeared, would he have ignored it?

'Can you get the money?' he asked.

'By tonight?' Waverly seemed to sag. 'Not that much. Nowhere near.'

Chrissie rounded on him. 'Then *try*! Jesus Christ, these are your *children* we're talking about!'

'You think I don't *know* that? I can't just snap my fingers and . . .' He ran out of steam. 'Even if I empty the firm's accounts it wouldn't be anywhere near enough. We don't have

284

access to that sort of money, not by tonight. If I call in a few favours I might be able to raise a hundred thousand or so, but that's all.'

Chrissie was looking at him, her desperation laid bare. 'If we can get the money, are you going to help us?'

If Jonah agreed, he'd be gambling his own life as well as Chrissie's young son's and daughter's. Stokes had unfinished business with him, that much was obvious. Wanting to meet again at the warehouse sent a clear message, and Jonah knew this time would be different. He'd had surprise and luck on his side before. Especially luck. But now Stokes would be ready for him.

Yet if Jonah didn't do as he'd demanded, he'd be condemning two children to death. Barring miracles, there was little chance the police could locate them before Stokes's deadline expired, and his faith in miracles had disappeared along with Theo. The twins might be dead already, he knew that. But Jonah had brought this down on Chrissie's family. If there was even a faint chance of saving them, he had to take it. That was an opportunity he'd never had with his own son, and he was going to do everything he could to grasp it now.

'I'll need some things,' he said.

Chapter 31

Wilkes looked even worse than usual. He wore a stained pair of sweatpants and a T-shirt that hung over his sagging gut. They were a similar grey, giving him the look of a bad-tempered toddler in a dirty romper suit. One with what looked like a fading love bite on his neck. Squinting in the daylight, the deep-set eyes glared at Jonah as though struggling to recognise him.

'Fuck do you want?' he demanded, his voice a thick croak.

Jonah had tried phoning him before driving over. He could have been out, but he'd gambled the big man might just be sleeping off another bender.

'Something's happened. Can I come in?'

Wilkes regarded him sourly, still barring the door. 'What happened to your face?'

Jonah's eye had blackened overnight and his jaw was swollen from where he'd been kicked.

'Nothing. Look, we need to talk. It's important.'

'I'm busy.'

'I'll pay you,' Jonah said before he could close the door. 'It's to do with Gavin.'

Wilkes stared out at him, eyes narrow and calculating. He absently scratched his crotch.

'What about Gavin?'

'Not out here. I'll tell you inside.'

The pouched eyes were no more friendly, but Jonah could almost see the cogs whirring behind them.

'I need a piss.'

Turning away, he went back into the house, leaving Jonah to follow. Wilkes disappeared into a door by the stairs.

'Do something useful and stick the kettle on.'

'We don't have –'

But the toilet door had already shut. As the sound of splashing came from inside, Jonah reluctantly went into the kitchen. The sight of unwashed dishes and an overflowing bin greeted him. Digging out two mugs that were reasonably clean, he hunted through cupboards for tea or coffee as he waited for the kettle to boil. He'd made two coffees and was pouring curdled-looking milk he'd found in the fridge into one when the flush sounded from the hallway. There was the sound of a tap running and Wilkes hacking something up, then he came into the kitchen, hitching up his sweatpants.

'I feel like my fucking head's been poached,' he announced, rubbing a hand over his face with a rasp of stubble. It was beaded from the water he'd splashed on it, and although his eyes were still red and puffy he didn't look as bad as before. 'I was up all night playing online poker. Waste of fucking time that was.'

'I tried calling earlier –'

'There any sugar in this?'

Wilkes picked up the white coffee, sampled it and grimaced. Jonah clenched his jaw as the big man added three heaped spoonfuls of sugar, then topped the mug up with more milk before taking it to the kitchen table. The wooden dining chair creaked under his weight as he sat down, knees splayed. He'd yet to look at Jonah.

'So what's this about Gavin?' he asked, taking a drink of coffee.

'I know who killed him. The same man kidnapped my ex-wife's twins this morning.'

At another time it might have been comical. Wilkes choked on the coffee, eyes widening. Coughing, he fumbled the mug onto the table, spilling more from it as he stared at Jonah.

'You *what*?'

Jonah lowered himself onto the only other chair at the table. 'His name's Owen Stokes. He killed Gavin and the other warehouse victims, as well as a journalist who was writing a story about the case. I think he was either responsible, or knows about what happened to my son as well.'

Wilkes's mouth hung open in shock. 'Are you taking the piss?'

'He wants us to have half a million pounds ready by midnight for me to deliver to him. If we involve the police, he says he'll kill them. They're six years old.'

'Jesus fucking Christ.' Wilkes seemed dazed. 'Is there an alert out?'

'No, the parents have decided to do what Stokes says.' Jonah shook his head, still hating this. 'I warned them against it, but they're terrified. I don't blame them.'

'They're going to pay it?'

'They don't feel they have any choice.'

'And he wants half a *million*? Jesus.' Wilkes blew out his cheeks. 'Can your ex raise that sort of money?'

'I don't think so, not so soon. They're going to get as much as they can and hope it's enough.'

'It better be. They're gambling with their kids' lives.' Wilkes finally seemed to be focusing. 'So you're taking the ransom yourself?'

'I don't have a choice either. That's why I'm here.'

It was as though a shutter came down in Wilkes's eyes. 'Meaning what?'

Jonah had considered asking the big man to go with him. He was in no shape to tackle Stokes on his own, even less so after the beating he'd taken the night before. But it would be asking a lot, and there was another way of evening the odds. He took a breath and said the words.

'I need a gun.'

'Are you fucking *mad*?' Wilkes yelped.

No, just desperate. Jonah knew it would be crossing a line from which there'd be no going back. But he couldn't see how he had a choice. Not when the alternative was going up against Stokes unarmed and on crutches. And not when it was Chrissie's children's lives at stake.

'Just hear me out,' he began.

'No! No fucking *way*! You're the firearms dickhead, get your own fucking gun!'

'That's what I'm trying to do. But I don't have those sorts of contacts, and there's not much time.'

'So go and ask one of your mates to sort you out! Jesus!'

'You know I can't do that.'

Not that he hadn't considered it. But police firearms were kept locked away under tight security, their whereabouts strictly logged and traced. Even if they weren't, Jonah wasn't stupid or desperate enough to approach any of his old team. He knew how that would go. If he had more time, he might have been able to come up with a better way of finding something.

But he hadn't.

Wilkes gave a strangled laugh. 'But it's OK to ask me? Fuck's sake, you think I just happen to have a fucking *gun* lying around?'

'No, but I thought you might know where I could get hold of one.'

'Oh, is that all? Jesus, what sort of fucking copper do you

think I was?'

Jonah didn't answer that. 'You were a detective for twenty-five years. Are you telling me in all that time you didn't know who was selling what? Or know somebody who did?'

'That's beside the point! You know what you're asking, don't you? Jesus Christ, if you use it, I'm looking at accessory to murder!'

'I hope I don't have to use it.' A gun would be a far stronger deterrent than Jonah turning up on his own and unarmed. The threat alone might be enough to convince Stokes to give up the twins. 'And I wouldn't say where I got it anyway.'

'Oh, yeah, I've heard that before! Fuck off!'

'I'm not asking you to do it for me. There're two six-year-olds –'

'Don't you fucking dare!' Wilkes stabbed a thick finger at Jonah. 'This isn't my fault. I didn't take them kids, so don't come all high and fucking mighty, wanting me to stick my neck out! This has fuck all to do with me.'

'I only want a name. If you don't have one, then say so because I don't have much time.'

'Fine, I'm fucking saying! Door's over there.'

Face burning, Jonah got to his feet. He couldn't blame Wilkes for being outraged. It had always been a long shot, yet he'd still hoped the man might come up with something.

'Wait. Just . . . wait.'

Jonah stopped at the kitchen door and looked back. Wilkes was gnawing at his lip, one foot bouncing agitatedly up and down as he sat in the chair.

'What will you do?' he asked.

'Don't worry about it. Like you say, it's nothing to do with you.'

'No, I know, but . . .' Wilkes passed a hand over his face. 'He might not hurt the kids. If you give him what he wants, he might let them go.'

'You mean like he did with the other victims? Sorry, I don't think hoping for the best is much of a strategy.'

'Jesus.' Wilkes blew out his cheeks. 'If you go to the wrong person asking for a gun, you're fucked. You know that, don't you?'

'If I don't have a gun, I'm fucked anyway.' Doubt and fatigue suddenly washed over Jonah. 'I don't know, maybe I'll talk to my ex-wife again. Try to persuade her to bring the police in.'

'It's too late for that,' Wilkes said. 'The parents are right. If you've only got till midnight, there's no way they'll be able to find them in time.'

'Then what do you suggest? Because I'm running out of ideas.'

Wilkes didn't answer. The florid features were pensive as he stared at the floor, gnawing at his lower lip. Jonah had enough sense to stay quiet, letting him battle it out on his own. Suddenly, he smacked a fist down onto the table.

'Fuck! *Fuck!*' Abruptly, he got to his feet. 'Stay here.'

Brushing past Jonah, he went out into the hallway, almost slamming the door behind him. Jonah heard his footsteps recede towards the living room. He hesitated, then went to the closed kitchen door to listen. He could just make out the murmur of Wilkes's voice on the phone, but the one-sided conversation was too low and indistinct to make out. At one point Wilkes's voice became raised, then there was a long silence as he listened to whoever was on the other end. When he spoke again his tone was brisker, as though winding up the call.

Jonah moved away from the door. A few seconds later it opened and Wilkes came back into the kitchen.

'OK, I might be able to help you.'

'You can get a gun?' Jonah wasn't sure if he was relieved or not.

'That's what you wanted, isn't it?' Wilkes's cockiness had

returned now he'd made the decision. 'But if you've changed your mind . . .'

'No.' Jonah closed down his doubts. 'Can they get a Glock 17?'

That was the handgun model he was most used to. Wilkes gave a sour laugh.

'Do you want to pick the colour as well? How about a nice red one?'

'Fine, I'll take whatever they can get.' Jonah couldn't believe he was really doing this. 'How many rounds?'

Wilkes gave a shrug. 'I don't know, whatever it comes with.'

Jonah didn't argue. He felt nauseous enough as it was. 'How much?'

The ex-detective's eyes darted away. Jonah could almost see him calculating his mark-up on top of the price.

'Call it a grand.'

That was more than Jonah had anticipated, but it didn't matter. He'd have to pay, regardless of how much it cost.

'Where do I need to go for it?'

Wilkes didn't answer. He was scowling down at the floor, as though still undecided about something.

'Where are you supposed to take the money?' he asked at last. He sounded angry, almost aggrieved.

'The warehouse at Slaughter Quay. Why?'

The big ex-detective shook his head, as though he couldn't believe it himself.

'Because I'm coming with you.'

Chapter 32

Jonah didn't dare risk going back to his flat after he'd left Wilkes. Now he'd pointed Fletcher towards Eliana Salim it was only a matter of time before her sister was identified, and when that happened he'd have awkward questions to answer. The DI would want to know how he knew about Gavin's old case, and this time he wouldn't be fobbed off. Jonah would have to provide answers at some point, but he couldn't afford to be tied up by a police interview today. However bad it looked, he needed to avoid Fletcher until this was over. After that . . .

After that, it didn't matter.

It left him with nowhere to go. Chrissie and her husband would phone him when they'd gathered the money together, or as much of it as they could, and Wilkes didn't want Jonah with him when he bought the gun. At his insistence, they'd agreed to meet at half past eleven that night on the waste ground at Slaughter Quay. Jonah would have preferred to pick Wilkes up first in the rented Volvo. Stokes had said he should deliver the money alone, so having two cars showing up was a risk.

But only if Stokes saw them. If he went to the quayside by boat like last time, then he wouldn't know. And even if he didn't, the chances were that by then he'd already be waiting for Jonah at the warehouse, Wilkes argued. He could follow behind Jonah, staying out of sight but ready to rush to help or call for back-up if it was needed.

Jonah didn't like it, but the ex-detective had been adamant. Apart from anything else, he couldn't say how long it would take him to get the gun. If the buy took longer than anticipated it was better for Jonah to be waiting at the quayside than sitting outside Wilkes's house.

'What if you can't make it there by twelve?' Jonah had asked.

'Then something's gone tits up and we're both fucked,' he'd answered.

Jonah hated waiting. He could feel the nervous energy running in him like an over-revved engine. It was the same before an op, when the adrenaline was pumping and the imagination was free to think of all the things that could go wrong.

He needed something to occupy his mind.

The last of the light was fading outside as he parked on a quiet street to wait for Chrissie's call. He'd bought a pre-packed sandwich and bottled water, and he took out his phone as he ate. A search for Daniel Kimani revealed notices on missing persons websites, which meant the police still hadn't publicly confirmed the identification. There was a photograph showing a plump and smiling young man, cropped to cut out the other people from it, and in addition to the official sites, a Facebook page had been set up by Kimani's friends and family. Jonah guessed that was how Daly had started the trail. He considered contacting them himself, but if they hadn't been informed that a formal identification had been made, he didn't want to be the one to break the news. Always assuming it had, he reminded himself. Neither Fletcher nor Bennet had confirmed it to him.

Regardless, chasing down information on Daniel Kimani would take more time and concentration than he could spare just then. Checking the time, he cleared the search from his phone and then typed in *Anna Donari*.

The spelling was a best guess, based on how Salim had pronounced the name. There were thousands of results, far too many to be of any use. Jonah added *UK* and tried again. That reduced the number of hits, but when nothing obvious jumped out he keyed in *London* as well. He didn't even know if that was where Donari was from, but he had to try something. Even so, he was still dispirited at the unpromising list of results that filled the screen.

Then one caught his eye. He almost skipped past it at first, because it was a variant of the name: *Ana*, not *Anna* and *Donauri* rather than *Donari*. The first thing that caught his attention was the date. The entry was from ten years ago.

A week after Theo vanished.

It was a report from a local newspaper. A woman's body found in an alley near Euston Station had been identified as Ana Donauri, a thirty-seven-year-old Georgian national. The cause of death wasn't given, but the report said the body's hands had both been cut off. Jonah frowned at that, but the piece didn't elaborate. Retyping the name with the new spelling, he searched again. That yielded an earlier report in the same newspaper, from when the body had been discovered. But there were no more details than the later piece. It ended with the stock phrase, '*Police are continuing with their enquiries.*'

That was all.

Jonah's knee was hurting, cramped from so long in the car. Flexing it, he took out the phone Salim had given him. He weighed it in his hand, tempted to call and ask if this was who she'd meant. But she'd made it clear it was for one-time use only, and he didn't want to waste the call. If she'd wanted to tell him more, she would have.

So why had she given him the name?

Putting Salim's phone away again, he jumped as his own rang. He snatched it up, expecting it would be Chrissie. Or even Wilkes, contacting him to say there was a problem.

But it was Fletcher's number on the screen. *Shit.* Jonah let it ring. If he answered Fletcher would ask him to go in or want to see him at his flat. Jonah couldn't do either, and he didn't want a lengthy conversation with an irate detective inspector when he was waiting for Chrissie to call. Still, avoiding the DI made him feel uncomfortably like a fugitive.

When the ringing stopped, even the silence felt accusing.

It was fully dark outside now, the streetlights casting a sickly light into the car. Jonah had been avoiding checking the time again, but he gave in now and saw it was half past seven. Only a few hours to go. The realisation brought an acid burn in his gut. *Come on, Chrissie, where are you?*

As though in response his phone rang again. This time it showed Chrissie's name on the screen. Her voice sounded cracked and broken when Jonah answered.

'We've got it,' she said.

There had been an accident on the dual carriageway. One lane had been closed and traffic was backed up, which meant it was almost nine o'clock when Jonah pulled up outside the white-painted Georgian terrace. Fretting at the delay, he limped up to the gate and pressed the intercom. There was no answer, only a click as the lock was released. The glossy front door opened before he reached it, and Jonah felt a shock when he saw Chrissie.

She seemed to have aged years since that morning. The emotional toll was etched on every feature, prematurely turning her into an older version of herself. Neither of them spoke as he followed her to the open-plan kitchen and dining room. It seemed that every light in the house was on, as though driving out the shadows might usher in an illusion of normal life. Waverly was at the table, smartly dressed as though he'd just got in from work. But the strain was visible on his face as well. His cheeks looked sunken, the flesh of his face even more pallid than it had been that morning. Bank statements and spreadsheets were set out in front of him, and there was a tumbler of what looked like whisky on a slate coaster to one side.

'Jonah, thanks for coming,' he said, straightening. It might have been a social visit, but Jonah could see the effort it was taking to keep himself together. 'Can we get you a drink?'

'No, thanks.'

'Tea or coffee, then?'

There was a strangled noise from Chrissie. 'Oh, for God's sake!'

Her husband looked blankly at her, his mouth working as though gears had slipped.

'Actually, a coffee would be great,' Jonah said.

Waverly seized on it. He nodded, as though something momentous had been decided. 'OK, then. Good.'

But neither he nor his wife moved. The atmosphere in the kitchen was suffocating. 'You managed to get the money?' Jonah prompted.

'Not all of it.' Waverly faltered. 'I managed to get a little over a hundred thousand.'

'Jesus,' Chrissie said, shaking her head.

'We've been through this. I told you, it's the best I could do.'

'The *best*? We're talking about your kids' *lives*!'

Her husband looked stricken. 'You think I don't know that?'

'Do you have it here?' Jonah asked, hoping to head off a row.

'Yes, of course.' Waverly picked up a leather laptop bag and put it on the table. He unzipped it, showing Jonah the bundles of notes inside as though for his approval. 'I didn't know what denominations he . . . Anyway, I got fifties. They take up less room, so . . . you know.'

'That's fine,' Jonah told him. Stokes hadn't specified, and he didn't think it would matter. If all went well it wouldn't make any difference anyway.

Waverly pushed the bag across the table towards Jonah. 'So what happens now?'

Jonah hesitated. He hadn't told them about the gun, and he still hadn't decided if that was something they needed to know or not. But Chrissie didn't give him a chance to answer.

'I want to tell the police.'

She was hugging herself, her face white. Her husband looked stunned.

'What? But you said –'

'I don't *care* what I said, this isn't right.' Chrissie was shaking her head repeatedly, as though trying to dislodge her thoughts. 'We need to tell them. Before it's too late!'

'Are you *serious*? It *is* too late, you can't change your mind now.'

'Yes, I can. We can explain! Tell them why we, why we . . .'

She was starting to shiver, like a broken machine shaking itself apart. Waverly went to her.

'Chrissie –'

'I can't do this! I *can't*, not again. Please!'

Her husband put an arm around her, gently steering her to the hallway. 'I know. Come on.'

She didn't resist as he led her out. Jonah heard Waverly murmuring softly to her as their footsteps sounded on the stairs. *God.* Suddenly drained, he eased himself onto one of the bar stools at the island, his bad leg held stiffly out to one side. There was a framed photograph of the twins. One dark-haired and grinning broadly, one blonde with a shy smile, both in private school uniforms. Seeing them, Jonah felt his own doubts threaten to overwhelm him. He thought about calling Bennet. He'd find it easier explaining to her than Fletcher, and for a moment the temptation to hand this over to someone else was almost too much.

But if the police were going to be brought in, it should have been that morning, when the twins were first snatched. Not with – he checked his watch, though he knew to the minute what the time was – under three hours left until he had to meet Owen Stokes. For better or worse, they were committed.

It was another twenty minutes before he heard someone coming back down the stairs. Waverly reappeared in the kitchen doorway, his eyes red.

'Is she OK?' Jonah asked.

'She's under the shower. I think that's her fifth today.' He went to the table, picked up his glass and drank it off. He gave a shudder and turned to Jonah. 'You sure you don't want one?'

More temptation, but Jonah shook his head. He needed to stay sharp. 'No thanks.'

Crossing to a low wooden sideboard, Waverly opened a door and took a bottle of single malt from inside. He poured himself a good measure, hesitated, then poured again before replacing the bottle.

'I don't think I've thanked you for doing this,' he said, taking one of the other bar stools.

'There's no need.' Jonah was beginning to wish he'd accepted the offer of a drink. 'Chrissie's right. If not for me, none of this would have happened.'

Waverly sighed. 'She didn't mean that. You couldn't have known what this . . . this sick *fucker* would do.'

He was slurring slightly, and Jonah wondered how many he'd had. Not that he blamed him. Waverly raised his glass again, then lowered it without taking a drink.

'Do you think the police got it wrong? You know, ten years ago?'

He didn't have to say what he meant. Jonah shook his head. He couldn't afford to let himself get into that, not now.

Waverly didn't take the hint. 'How did you stand it? I don't think I could . . . you know, if this . . .'

'You need to stop thinking like that.' It came out harsher than Jonah intended, but this wasn't helping either of them. 'And maybe ease up on the whisky, as well.'

'Yes, you're right.' Waverly nodded. He set his glass down again. 'I did try, you know. To get the rest of the money.'

'I'm sure you did.'

'Do you think it'll be enough?'

'It's a lot of money,' Jonah said, ducking the question.

Waverly nodded, as though trying to reassure himself. 'But what if it isn't? What will you do if he tries anything, or takes the money but doesn't . . . you know . . .'

Jonah did. 'Like I say, try not to think about that.'

'But have you got some sort of contingency plan if he doesn't make the exchange? God knows, I'm grateful you're doing this, but . . .' He gave Jonah's crutches a fearful, almost furtive look. 'Are you sure you're up to it?'

It was a little late for him to ask that, but Jonah could understand why. Until now Waverly had been focused on raising the ransom money, blocking out any thoughts beyond that. Now there was nothing to keep them at bay.

'I'm not going to lie to you about the risks,' Jonah told him.

'But I'm not stupid enough to just walk in there and hope for the best. Trust me.'

'I do, but . . . well, perhaps I should come with you?'

That was the last thing Jonah wanted. He'd been wondering how much to tell them. The less they knew the less trouble they'd be in afterwards, especially if things went wrong. But if the situations were reversed, Jonah knew he wouldn't want to be kept in the dark.

'I've arranged for someone to back me up,' he said. 'An ex-police officer who knows how to look after himself. He's going to stay in the background unless he's needed, but he'll be there if Stokes tries anything.'

'Right. Good, that's . . . that's . . .' Waverly nodded but his thoughts were still running ahead. 'Will that be enough, though? What if Stokes is armed?'

Jonah had hoped he wouldn't have to get into this. But they'd a right to know when it was their children's lives at stake. Even so, the admission weighed heavily on him.

'I'll be armed as well.'

He'd thought Waverly looked pale before. Now the other man's face turned bone white. His hand went to his mouth.

'You mean you're taking a *gun*? Oh, Jesus . . .'

'It's just a precaution. I probably won't need it.' Jonah spoke with a confidence he didn't feel.

'But a *gun!*' Waverly looked as though he might throw up. He shook his head. 'No, I can't . . . I mean, this isn't –'

'*Good!*'

Jonah hadn't heard Chrissie come back downstairs. She'd showered and was wearing a thick white bathrobe, her still-wet hair brushed straight back as she walked into the kitchen. Waverly had half risen to his feet, looking shell-shocked.

'Chrissie, we can't –'

'Shoot him,' she told Jonah, as though her husband wasn't there. She stopped in front of him, her eyes bright and hard. 'I don't care if he begs for his life, I want the bastard dead.'

'I'm not going to shoot anyone, if I can help it.'

'Why the fuck not? You think he won't do the same to you? Look what happened to Gavin!' Chrissie grabbed the front of Jonah's jacket in her fists. 'I *know* you, Jonah, I know what you're thinking! You want Stokes alive in case he knows something about Theo. But this isn't about him anymore. This is about Harry and Abigail, so the first chance you get I want you to put a bullet in that bastard's head! You hear me?'

Tears were rolling down her face. Jonah took hold of Chrissie's knotted hands, rubbing them before gently disengaging them from his jacket. Waverly had gone to her as well. He laid his hands on his wife's shoulders, trying to ease her away.

'He'll get them back,' he told her. 'Won't you, Jonah?'

'I will. I promise,' Jonah heard himself say.

It was only then he remembered how Gavin had once said the same thing to him.

The journey to the quayside felt unreal. The lights from the other cars seemed more dazzling than usual, the darkness more absolute. He'd put the laptop case in the passenger seat footwell, unwilling to have it out of his sight even while he drove. It was more money than he'd ever had in his life, and he found himself constantly glancing at it as he drove, reassuring a subliminal fear that it might somehow have vanished.

But he knew that was only a symptom of his tension, not its cause. The thought of where he was heading, what he was about to do, made his hands clammy on the steering wheel. In all his years as a firearms officer, Jonah had never shot anyone.

He'd hoped to keep it that way, and now here he was. On his way to collect an illegal weapon, with a good chance he'd need to use it in the next couple of hours.

Yet as he neared the quayside Jonah felt his nerves begin to quieten. The confrontation with Stokes was no longer something abstract, still hours in the future. It was happening *now*, and in accepting that a sense of clarity came over Jonah. He hadn't been able to save Theo, but history didn't have to repeat itself. Questions of morals and legality, all his doubts, fell away. It was simple, really.

He would either save Chrissie's twins or die trying.

As he pulled onto the waste ground at Slaughter Quay, a glance at the dashboard clock told him it was just after eleven. He was early. He couldn't see Wilkes's car at first, but after he'd switched off his headlights he made out the dark shape of an unlit vehicle at the far side. *Good.* If he had to look for it there was less chance of Stokes seeing it either.

Climbing out of his car, Jonah slung the laptop bag's strap over his shoulder and made his way over. It was slow-going on the uneven ground. The night was cloudy and he didn't want to switch on his torch, so he had to be careful where he put his crutches. It was only when he was a couple of metres away that he was able to recognise the ex-detective's old Vauxhall. There was no cabin light showing, and as he went to the passenger side Jonah hoped Wilkes had thought to switch it off so it wouldn't come on when the door was opened.

As he approached the dark car he could make out the bulky figure behind the wheel. With a last glance around the waste ground, Jonah gave a light rap on the window before opening the passenger door and climbing in.

'Did you get it?' he asked, keeping his voice down. 'What did you . . .?'

His voice failed. Wilkes was slumped in the driving seat. He might have been sleeping, except that there was something on his head. Under the transparent film of a plastic bag Jonah saw the blank eyes and gaping mouth, and then there was movement behind him. He twisted round, already starting to react as a pale, shaved head rose into view from the back seat. Then he caught sight of an impossible, familiar face and shock wiped all thought from his mind.

Something crashed into his head and the world turned black.

Chapter 33

His head hurt. That was his first awareness, but other pains and discomforts quickly made themselves known. He felt sick and ached all over. He was lying on something hard and bristly. Carpet, brown and tufted. Not his. It seemed to move under him with a queasy, rolling motion that made his nausea worse. His arms were twisted behind him, and when he tried to move something thin and hard cut into his wrists. His ankles were bound as well.

Nylon ties.

'Don't waste your time. They aren't meant to come undone like the last lot.'

Shock ran through Jonah at the voice. Then memory returned. Wilkes's car, the big man slumped dead. The face staring back at him from the back seat. *No. Not possible* . . . He turned his head.

The sickly light from a wall lamp showed a long, narrow room with a low ceiling. There was a sour, unwashed smell, an odour of mildew and damp. The wood-panelled walls sloped inwards, and as well as the floor's subtle movement he could hear a deep, hollow slopping of water. Not a room, he realised sluggishly. A cabin.

He was on a boat.

A broad-shouldered figure was watching him from a fitted seat a few feet away, leaning forward with elbows on knees. Through blurred vision, Jonah took in the shaved head and worn combat jacket he'd seen in the CCTV stills. At first glance it was Owen Stokes, but the features that stared back at him were all wrong. The stubbled face cracked in a lopsided smile.

'Hiya, Jonah,' Gavin said.

Jonah felt as if his thoughts were on ice, slipping without gaining traction. His mind insisted that this wasn't happening, that he was still dreaming. But the pain in his head and body, the discomfort from his bound wrists and ankles, told him it was real.

'I was starting to think I'd hit you too hard,' Gavin said. 'You've been out for ages.'

The face was older than he remembered, and without its dark curls the shaven head looked strangely alien. But it was unmistakably Gavin, the man who'd been his best friend and godfather to his son. The man whose body he'd found lying on the warehouse floor, head beaten to a bloodied pulp.

It took two attempts before Jonah could speak. 'You're dead.'

Gavin spread his hands. 'Not yet.'

'I found your body . . .'

'That was just someone I found on a dating website. Right sort of build and hair but not as good-looking. My blood, though.' He pulled back his sleeve, displaying a grubby white dressing on his forearm. 'Had to be for the DNA, but I got a bit carried away. Bled like a stuck pig.'

The shock of seeing Gavin had robbed Jonah of all other thoughts. Now the rest of it came flooding back. *Oh, Christ . . .*

'Where are the twins?' *Please let them be all right . . .*

'Asleep in one of the cabins. I put diazepam in their milk.'

'You *drugged* them?'

'Calm down, they're fine. It was only a low dose to put them out for a few hours.'

'You're going to let them go?'

'Of course I am! They're only kids, what do you think I'm going to do?' Gavin sounded offended. 'Don't worry, I didn't let them see my face.'

He had no reason to lie, and Jonah allowed himself to feel minimally reassured. Still groggy, he wriggled and heaved himself into a sitting position against the wall. It was awkward with his hands and feet tied, and the effort made his head and knee hurt even more. In the lamplight, the wood panelling and floral-pattern curtains covering the portholes gave the cabin an incongruously cosy look. It was a mess, with crushed beer cans and empty bottles scattered on the floor and dirty dishes heaped in a tiny sink. At the far end was a part-open door, through which Jonah could see a narrow passageway and steps, running up to the deck.

But between him and them was Gavin. The laptop case was on the floor at his feet, next to a half-full bottle of vodka. On top of it were both Jonah's phones, his own and the one from Eliana Salim. Then Jonah noticed something that sent a jolt of adrenaline through him. On the seat cushion by Gavin was a thick leather cosh.

Beside it was a roll of freezer bags and black gaffer tape.

Tearing his eyes from them, he looked back at Gavin. 'Where are we?'

'Moored about a quarter of a mile from Slaughter Quay. You like it?' He gestured ironically around the shabby cabin. 'I "liberated" it, let's say, from some former associates who used it for smuggling people across the Channel. Should get me back across there safely enough.'

'Jesus, Gavin . . .' The worst of the shock might have passed, but the enormity of the deception left Jonah winded. 'Marie and Dylan think you're dead! They held a *memorial* service for you!'

Gavin looked away. 'I didn't have a choice.'

'A *choice*? For Christ's sake, you murdered innocent people!'

'They weren't all innocent.' Reaching for the vodka, Gavin took a long pull before lowering it again. 'I needed to disappear. The only way I could do it without anything coming back on Marie and Dylan was if everyone thought I was dead. It had to be convincing.'

Anger was replacing Jonah's shock. Careful not to let Gavin see, he began testing the tie binding his wrists behind his back. '*Why*? Jesus, it can't just be because of the suspension! Was it the money?'

'You really think I'd put myself through all this crap over *money*?' Gavin gave a sour laugh. 'You really don't have a clue, do you?'

'No, I don't! I knew you didn't give a shit about anyone but yourself, but Jesus! What *happened* to you?'

A cold, set look had come over Gavin's face. 'You know, I'd forgotten what a self-righteous prick you are. Just remember I didn't have to let you wake up. Don't make me change my mind.'

Jonah's eyes went to the cosh on the seat cushion. It was a vicious little weapon, and he already knew how effective it was. Yet it was the everyday mundanity of the freezer bags and gaffer tape next to it that frightened him far more. Looking back at Gavin, he saw a tacit acknowledgement in his eyes.

They both knew how this was going to end.

'So why am I here?' Jonah asked, straining at the tie behind him. 'You could have killed me in the car, the same as Wilkes. I wouldn't have known anything about it, so why didn't you?'

'Maybe because I wanted you to know.' Gavin let that hang, then took another drink. 'Anyway, it wouldn't work if they found you with Wilkes.'

It took a moment for Jonah to understand. He was already under suspicion for Corinne Daly's murder. If his DNA and fingerprints were found with Wilkes's body in the car, it would look like he'd killed the ex-detective as well and then taken off with the money. There would still be unanswered questions, but they'd likely remain just that. Unanswered. For that to work it wasn't enough for him to be dead.

He had to disappear as well.

Jonah applied more pressure to the tie behind his back, feeling the thin plastic bite into the flesh of his wrists.

'Why me? I know we didn't exactly end on good terms, but I can't believe you're still pissed off over the fight?'

Gavin gave a laugh. 'You think this is because you caught me fucking Chrissie? Grow up.'

'*Why* then? Why go to all this trouble to set me up?'

'Why do you think?' Gavin's expression was almost lazy, watching to see how Jonah would react. 'Owen Stokes.'

For a moment Jonah thought he might have got it all wrong, that Gavin really had discovered something about Theo. But then reality intervened. Whatever was behind this, Gavin wasn't doing it for Jonah's son.

'I don't understand,' he said.

'I told you, I needed a way out. Stokes provided it, but everyone had to think something else was going on. That's where you came in. You're so fucking predictable, Jonah. I knew you wouldn't be able to see straight if you thought he was involved. And I was right, wasn't I?'

Jonah felt an ugly burn in his gut again. 'That's it? That's all? Stokes didn't . . .?'

'He didn't have anything to do with what happened to Theo, if that's what you're wondering. Not a thing. But he did make a fantastic decoy.'

Twisting in his seat, he turned to let Jonah see the back of his neck. Above the greasy collar was the black tracery of a spider-web tattoo.

'Only a felt-tip pen, but it does the job,' he said, turning round again. 'Enough to fool CCTV cameras, anyway.'

The strength seemed to drain from Jonah. He thought about the photographs Fletcher and Bennet had shown him. The 'sightings'. A man with a shaven head, baseball cap pulled low and head tucked down, making sure the identifying tattoo on the back of his neck could be seen. All that time and energy wasted, chasing a mirage. And with that realisation came a sharper pain.

That his last hope of finding answers about Theo had gone as well.

'Is Stokes dead?' he asked, already knowing the answer.

'Oh, yeah. I didn't kill him, though. That's on you. The poor bastard thought he was getting paid to shift stolen TVs, but you really fucked him up. I didn't think you had it in you. All I had to do was get rid of the body.'

A new wound opened in Jonah's soul when he heard that. 'Where?'

'At the bottom of the river, with my body double from the warehouse.' Gavin's eyes were fixed on him, soaking up every reaction. 'You'll be seeing him soon.'

Jonah almost gave up then. Jesus, it was too much. Then anger began to return, and with it a new determination. There was still something else going on here, something he didn't know about yet. Gavin might need him to disappear, but that didn't explain why he was still alive now.

310

He wants to talk. So let him.

Ignoring the pain from his torn wrists, Jonah began working harder at the tie. 'What about Corinne Daly? And *Wilkes?*'

Gavin reached for the vodka and took a swig. 'You're the one who dragged Jim into this. I was happy for him to carry on thinking I was dead until you started knocking on his door. After the journalist, I'd started getting twitchy about how much you knew. Jim never could keep his mouth shut after a drink, so I had to find out what the pair of you were talking about. Christ, he nearly shit himself when he saw me again.'

'He was your friend!'

'He was a gobshite who would have sold his own mother. Anyway, I wouldn't shed any tears over him. Who do you think he called about the gun?'

He grinned at the expression on Jonah's face.

'A Glock 17 you wanted, wasn't it? Nasty. Have to admit, I didn't see that coming. Poor old Jim was bricking himself. He didn't know about the twins and he was still getting over me being alive. I'd fed him some guff about being stitched up, but after that I had to promise to cut him in.' He shook his head. 'Stupid bastard. How much did he tell you the gun was going to cost?'

Jonah remembered listening to the one-sided conversation when Wilkes had left the room, trying to make out what was being said. He'd assumed he'd been calling some old contact. *Christ, how stupid could you get?*

'A thousand,' he said, disgusted at his own gullibility.

'Yeah?' Gavin gave a snort. 'Cheating fuck. He told me he'd said five hundred.'

Taking another drink, he settled back onto the seat. He was hitting the vodka hard now, as though he was building up to something. Jonah's wrists were slick with blood where the nylon tie had broken the skin, but it didn't feel any looser. He kept on working at it.

'Corinne Daly had a young daughter, did you know that? Maddie.'

Gavin grimaced. 'Don't start. I saw her talking to you at the memorial service —'

'You were there?' Jonah broke in.

'Parked further down the road. You don't think I'd have missed that, do you?' The bottle was raised again. 'You got your feet under that table pretty smartish, didn't you? Can't say I blame you, but she was a nosy bitch. She wasn't going to stop digging until she'd raked up all the shit about me. I couldn't let her do that.'

Jonah remembered the woman who he'd shared beer and pizza with, the life and animation in her face. Then he thought about that same face, still and lifeless inside a plastic bag, and wanted to throw himself at the man in front of him.

'So you murdered her and used her to frame me,' he said, twisting at the tie behind his back. He thought there might be a little more give in it, although with all the blood it was hard to tell.

'Well, you know. Two birds and one stone.'

'Jesus, can you *hear* yourself?' Jonah yelled. 'What about the people in the warehouse? What did they do to you?'

Gavin made a show of linking his hands over his head, stretching till his joints cracked. It meant he didn't have to look at Jonah as he answered.

'Nothing. They were just nobodies I picked up off the street. If it was going to work, everyone had to think Stokes was an evil bastard. I had to make him look like one. Why do you think I chose somewhere called Slaughter Quay?' He gave a scornful laugh. 'I mean, come on.'

Slowing his breathing to control his anger, Jonah continued to strain at the tie around his wrists.

'Was Daniel Kimani just a nobody as well?'

Gavin stopped mid-stretch. He lowered his arms, staring down at Jonah with a new watchfulness.

'Daly told you about him, did she? What else did she say?'

'That he was a PhD student, a human rights activist. You didn't pick him up off the street, did you?'

'Maybe I didn't know who he was.' Gavin sounded indifferent, but his eyes were wary. 'I didn't bother to check his CV.'

'But you knew who Nadine was, didn't you?'

The indifference vanished. 'What's that supposed to mean?'

'Nadine, remember her? You covered her in quicklime and left her to suffocate. She was in agony when I found her,' Jonah said, pressing his advantage. 'Did you know she was still alive?'

'I made a mistake. That's why I started using these.' Gavin picked up the roll of freezer bags from the seat next to him, holding it up to show Jonah. 'They're really good. You'll see for yourself soon.'

The threat sent a chill through Jonah but he didn't let himself be deflected. 'How come you only made the mistake with her? Was it because she reminded you of someone?'

Gavin went very still. 'What did you say?'

'You heard. What do you think Eliana would say if she knew you'd murdered her sister?'

Shock drained the blood from Gavin's face. In the light from the lamp he looked corpse-like.

'Who told you?'

Jonah knew he had to be careful. He only had one card to play. He couldn't afford to push Gavin too far.

'I can't remember. Maybe it was Wilkes. If you hadn't killed him you could ask him yourself.'

'Bullshit! Wilkes didn't even know her sister was in the country!' Gavin was poised on the edge of his seat, the cosh clenched in his fist. 'No one did. And there's no way anyone from the enquiry could have made the connection, so how the fuck did you?'

'Why'd you kill her?' Jonah asked, ignoring the question. 'How did Nadine even *find* you?'

'Tell me how you knew they were sisters, or I'll beat it out of you.'

'What were you scared of? That she'd find out you'd forced her sister back into prostitution? That's not enough to –'

Gavin lunged from the seat and lashed out with the cosh. Jonah tried to twist away as the lead-filled leather smacked into his thigh.

'Who told you?' Gavin yelled, swinging it again. 'Tell me, or I'll fucking –'

'*She did!*'

Silence. Gavin stood over him, chest rising and falling. His face was ashen.

'What are you talking about?

'She's not dead.' Jonah's breath came in gasps. 'It was someone else's body at the flat. Sound familiar?'

Pain exploded in his arm as Gavin swung the cosh again. And again. 'I fucking *warned* you!'

'I saw her yesterday!' Jonah yelled, trying to evade the blows. 'She's alive!'

The beating stopped. Cautiously, Jonah uncurled himself. Gavin still held the cosh raised, but now he lowered his arm as though he'd forgotten about it.

'You're lying,' he said, but it was a reflex.

'Then how did I know she looked like Nadine?'

Gavin took a step backwards. He half fell back onto the seat.

'She can't be. It's not possible, I saw . . .'

He trailed off. Jonah pushed himself upright, shaking from pain. He felt only a small compunction at telling Gavin about Salim. She'd told him not to tell anyone, but even she couldn't have foreseen this.

'It wasn't her body at the flat,' he went on, relentless now. 'You all assumed it must be her and Wilkes screwed up the identification. But she's alive. I know how to get in touch with her.'

The look Gavin gave him held a wild hope, but also fear. 'No. No, that's . . . How?'

Jonah kept his eyes away from the phone Eliana Salim had given him. 'Cut me loose and I'll tell you.'

Gavin gave a broken laugh. 'Do I look fucking stupid? Why shouldn't I just beat it out of you?'

'You can try, but then you won't know if I'm lying or not. And if you kill me, you'll never find out.'

Jonah could feel the rapid beat of his heart. He tried to stay outwardly calm as Gavin thought it through.

'I'm not going to let you go,' Gavin said at last. 'We both know that's not going to happen, but I'll make you a deal. I kept you alive because I was in two minds about something. So let's swap. You tell me what you know, and I'll tell you something in return.'

Jonah had always known it was a long shot. But this wasn't what he'd expected. Gavin's confidence had returned. There was something knowing, almost cruel about the way he was looking at Jonah.

He felt the first presentiment that this was about to get even worse.

'What?' he asked, afraid to hear.

Gavin's smile was a travesty.

'I know what happened to Theo.'

Chapter 34

The young woman crouched down by the pushchair, smiling as she tucked the blanket around its small occupant.

'Who's a beautiful little girl, then? Yes, you are! You're Mummy's little angel.'

Her English was good but slightly accented. She was attractive but underweight, with dark shadows under her eyes that told of sleepless nights. Although her clothes were clean they were cheap and worn, and while the pushchair looked passable from a distance, up close the wear and tear was obvious on that as well. It was serviceable but rusted, with one stiff wheel that tended to squeak and stick.

Still, it served its purpose.

There weren't many people in the park. A wino was drinking on a bench some distance away, lost in his bottle. Other than that, the only other users were the man and small boy in the playground. She watched them over the top of the pushchair, making yet another adjustment to the blankets and waggling the fluffy toy rabbit back and forth. They'd been there about half an hour, the father first pushing his son on the swings, then being led by him to the other playground equipment in succession. The little boy's laughter carried clearly in the cold air, and the warmth in his father's smile was infectious.

They were on the roundabout now. Or rather, the boy was. The father was on a nearby bench while the roundabout turned with a rhythmic creaking. The young woman's baby-talk trailed off as she saw the man's head droop and rise, droop and rise. Then it sank without rising, his chin tucked onto his chest. Her eyes narrowed.

Was he asleep?

Looking around, she saw that the other park bench was now empty. The wino who'd been there had gone. There was no one else nearby. Only the sleeping father, and the little boy on the slowing roundabout.

And her.

She stood up, scratching at the needle marks under her coat sleeve. She'd been told to just follow and observe, to report back. Nothing else. But this . . . surely this was an opportunity? It would be worth more than a report, maybe even earn her a night off from working the street.

The little boy had climbed off the now stationary roundabout and gone to the crawl-pipe. Further away from the sleeping father, on the edge of bushes. Twitchy from adrenaline and withdrawal, she looked down into the pushchair. The lifelike doll's dead eyes stared back at her.

She made up her mind.

'It was just bad luck.' Gavin was watching Jonah as you would an unpredictable animal. 'The people who sent her weren't interested in you. You won't remember, but back then I was part of a big joint op with NCA and Interpol, investigating illegal migrants found dead in a railway siding. We knew a gang of local traffickers was involved, but we thought they were just the facilitators for a much bigger organisation working out of the Balkans. We were right, but it turned out we weren't the only ones doing the investigating. These bastards had been keeping my whole fucking team under observation, looking for weak points. And not just us, friends and family as well. Like you.'

There was a rushing in Jonah's head. The lamplit cabin with its wood-panelled walls, the shaven-headed man sitting in front of him, had all taken on the hyperreal quality of a nightmare. It wasn't happening. It couldn't be.

'No,' he said. But he remembered the young mother. Remembered her smiling at him as she'd tucked the blanket into the pushchair. 'No, she couldn't have just taken him like that. Somebody would have seen . . .'

'Somebody did. CCTV picked her up leaving the park, but the cameras couldn't make out what was under the blankets. She'd already been picked up going in with the same push-chair, so what was there to suspect? It was just another young mother taking her baby to the park. And Owen Stokes made a much better suspect. Obviously, they tried to trace her, but only as a witness. When they couldn't find her, no one saw any need to follow it up.'

'I don't believe you!' Jonah felt the onset of panic. 'Theo would've have struggled or . . . or yelled! Or *something*! I'd have heard!'

'But you didn't, did you?' Gavin raised the bottle of vodka and took another sip. Slower this time, more measured now he was in control again. 'She grabbed him before he'd had a chance to make a noise. She was a junkie, you think a four-year-old was going to cause her any problems? As soon as she'd got him far enough away, she gave him a good crack to keep him quiet and pushed him straight out. There was a car parked not far away, and even if he *had* started to make a fuss, who was going to look twice at another harassed mother with a screaming kid?'

'No!' Jonah felt like he'd been kicked in the heart. 'His shoe was in the culvert . . .'

'It was *planted*, for fuck's sake. They loosened the cover afterwards so it'd look like he could have crawled in.'

No, no, no . . . 'You're lying! How can you know any of this?'

'Because the bastards were already blackmailing me. A few days before I'd got an anonymous email, with a video of me fucking a girl I'd picked up in a bar. Turned out it was a set-up. She was working for them, here illegally and underage as well. They gave me a choice. I could either have a retainer of five hundred a week, or they'd send the link to Marie, my chief and the press. Told me I had till the end of the week to decide.'

Gavin broke off to take another drink. Lowering the bottle, he shook his head.

'Honest to God, I still don't know what I'd have done, but I didn't get the chance to find out. I was still agonising over it when Theo disappeared. I'd no idea they'd anything to do with that, but then the next morning I got another email. It said they were bringing forward the deadline and gave me an hour to decide. There was a photograph of Theo with it.'

It was as though all the air had been sucked from the room.

'You *knew*?' Jonah managed. 'They sent *proof*, and you never fucking *said* anything?'

'How could I? What do you think they'd have done to me if I had? To *my* family?'

Jonah tried to fling himself at him, yelling as he thrashed and wrenched at the ties binding his ankles and wrists. Unhurriedly, Gavin got up and brought the cosh down on Jonah's knee. Something in it crunched, and a bolt of white-hot pain took his breath away.

'Are you going to behave or do you want another?' Gavin said, standing over him.

Jonah sucked air through gritted teeth, his eyes screwed shut. But the turmoil within him wouldn't have allowed him to speak even if he could. After a moment, Gavin returned to the seat and sat down.

'I was trying to keep him *alive*,' he said, as though the violence hadn't happened. 'I tried, I really fucking tried. If I thought it'd help get him back, I'd have told you there and then, but what good would that have done? They wouldn't have sent anything that could be traced, and if I'd said anything, they'd have killed him for sure. Jesus, you think I didn't *want* to? I did the only one thing I could. I told them I'd do what they wanted if they let him go.'

Even though the news was ten years old, even though Jonah knew what the outcome had to be, hearing it for the first time he still found himself clinging to an irrational hope that his son had somehow survived.

That made it even crueller.

'They didn't, though,' he said.

'No.' Gavin looked away. 'They sent someone to my house. My *house*. A woman, butter wouldn't have melted. Marie and Dylan were there, so I had to pretend it was work. She said she was an 'envoy', all very formal and polite. She apologised. Told me what happened in the park hadn't been authorised and the person responsible would be punished. But that it couldn't be undone.'

Jonah couldn't breathe. 'What's that supposed to mean, "*couldn't be undone*"?'

'What do you think it means?' Gavin made a helpless gesture, half shrug, half apology. 'If I could have done any more I –'

'What did they do to my *son*?' Tears were blinding Jonah, smearing his vision. 'Did they kill him?'

'They never told me exactly what –'

'*Did they kill him?*'

'*Of course they fucking killed him!*' Gavin yelled, slamming the cosh down on the seat arm with a heavy *thwock*. He paused, breathing heavily, then went on in a flat voice. 'He was a four-year-old kid, what else were they going to do? These fuckers buy and sell people like livestock. You think they'd care about a *child?*'

Jonah felt his heart stutter, as though it was trying to stop. He thought he'd been prepared. Thought he'd accepted long ago that Theo was dead. But he hadn't. The physical hurts were nothing compared to this ache of fresh loss. He sat immobile, stunned by it.

'They didn't say how, and I didn't ask. But they were never going to let him go, not once that stupid bitch had taken him. I could've spared myself a lot of grief if I'd realised that earlier.' Gavin took another drink, then raised the vodka bottle in a salute. 'Happy now? You wanted answers, you've got them.'

Jonah had thought he'd hated Owen Stokes, but that was nothing to what he felt as he stared at the stranger in front of him. He began working on the tie behind his back with a furious resolve.

'Ten years,' he said, emotion making his voice unsteady. 'You knew what happened to him for *ten years*, and you said nothing.'

'You think I *enjoyed* it? Having to live with something like that? Jesus, why do you think I fucked Chrissie? I *wanted* you to find out, because at least then I could stop pretending!'

'You fucking coward!'

'Oh, here we go! Because this is all *my* fault!' Gavin's grin was savage. 'You wanted to know why I dragged you into all of this? Well, this is why! It wasn't only *your* life you fucked up! You think we'd be sitting here now, on this shitty boat, if you'd not fallen asleep and let a crack whore walk off with your son? Thanks to you those bastards *owned* me! They said jump, I jumped!'

A cold anger was spreading through Jonah. 'You got well paid for it.'

'Oh, fuck off! I earned every penny in that bedsit! Every fucking penny! Jesus, some of the things I had to do . . . And you even fouled that up as well. Three quarters of a million gone, because you stuck your fucking nose in! Now look.' He gave the laptop bag a derisory kick. 'A lousy hundred grand. How far is that supposed to get me?'

A preternatural calm seemed to settle over Jonah. The pain from his torn wrists seemed distant and unimportant as he continued working at the tie.

'Tell me their names.'

'Why, what good's that going to do?' Gavin waved the bottle at where Jonah was bound on the cabin floor. 'It's not like you're going to do anything about it.'

'Then there's no reason not to tell me,' Jonah said. In that moment nothing else mattered. 'I want to know who killed my son.'

Gavin sat back, pretending to think. 'OK, well, let's see. The local boss was Lee Sissons, who ran things with his sons, Patrick and Jez. The order to have you followed would have come from one of them. Except – no, hang on. That's right, he disappeared not long afterwards. And his sons not long after that. In fact, pretty much everyone involved with them either died or disappeared. Inside six months all their operations had been taken over by their rivals. Funny that, isn't it?'

The vodka sloshed as Gavin swigged from the bottle. Lowering it, he looked at Jonah with contempt.

'When they said the people responsible would be punished, they didn't just mean the junkie who took Theo. Snatching a police officer's kid is bad for business. And that's what this is. The drugs, trafficking, prostitution or whatever, it's a business. *Big* business. The people behind it don't just own gangs, they own politicians and bankers as well. It's an international industry, a giant machine. And if someone throws grit in it, then it gets cleaned out. So if it's payback you're wanting, you're too late.'

Whatever had happened to them, it wasn't enough. Jonah felt no satisfaction, only a seething frustration that the people who'd murdered his son were out of reach. Except for this man.

'What about the woman who took Theo?' he said, unmindful of the blood dripping from his hands as he struggled with the tie. 'The one with the pushchair?'

'Oh, she was the first. They wanted to make an example of her, so they cut off her hands and dumped her body in an alleyway.'

Jonah stopped, the nylon tie momentarily forgotten. 'What was her name?'

'It won't mean anything to you –'

'Was it Ana Donauri?'

Gavin's surprise was confirmation enough. 'Who told you?'

Jonah didn't answer. He couldn't begin to guess how Eliana Salim could have known, but now there seemed an inevitability about it. Gavin leaned forward, gripping the cosh.

'I said who fucking told you?'

Jonah looked Gavin in the eye, wrenching at the tie again. *Come on, you bastard . . .*

'It was Eliana.'

'Don't piss me about. Even if you're telling the truth about her being alive, there's no way she'd know about that.'

'No?' Jonah managed a shrug. 'Well, she did. She told me to remember the name but wouldn't say why.'

'Fuck, this is – *fuck!*' Gavin looked as though he'd been punched. He jumped up and came to stand over Jonah, cosh held ready. 'Where did you speak to her?'

'I got a text telling me to go to Slaughter Quay last night. I didn't know who it was from until I went there and saw her.'

'So she just turned up, out of the blue?' Gavin's sneer was wafer-thin. 'Why would she want to meet you?'

'Why do you think? She wanted to hear how her sister had died.' Jonah shifted slightly, trying to position himself to kick out at Gavin's legs. If he could bring him down . . .

'She's come a long way from when you knew her. Expensive clothes, a big car. She told me about you and her. How you'd used her.'

The leather gloves made a small squeaking sound as Gavin's fist tightened on the cosh. 'You're lying. She didn't say that.'

'Yes, she did. She told me she lived in fear every day because of you. Why *did* you make her go back to those bastards? Were you on their payroll as well?' Jonah stared at him, incredulous. 'You were, weren't you?'

'I told you, it's a business,' Gavin said coldly. 'When a new crew take over, they get all the assets. I was one of them.'

No wonder Gavin had wanted Salim released so quickly, Jonah thought. He didn't want to risk her telling anyone about a pet detective on the gang's payroll. And that was why he'd wanted to be her handler, dropping Wilkes off at the pub so he could meet her on his own. That way he could control the information he fed back to his team.

Except he hadn't really been controlling anything.

'You really are a piece of shit,' Jonah said.

'Yeah, well, we don't all have your moral high ground.' Gavin had begun tapping the cosh against his leg, a rapid, agitated rhythm. 'I didn't just do it for myself, I was looking out for her as well. You think they can't get to people in prisons or detention centres?'

'Right, you did it all for her. She doesn't see it that way, though. She told me she felt sickened when people started calling you a hero. What do you think she'll say when she finds out you killed her sister?'

For a second Gavin seemed about to come at him again, then he snatched up the bottle and flung it across the cabin. It hit the wall but didn't break, spilling vodka as it fell to the floor with a discordant clatter. The cabin filled with the sharpness of raw alcohol. Gavin stood rigidly in its centre, his breathing ragged as though he were in pain.

'Why'd you do it?' Jonah asked.

Gavin glared at him, but even that seemed like too much effort. He went back to the padded seat and slumped down.

'I was tired. So fucking *tired*. All the lies, the fucking fear. Never knowing when it was all going to blow up in my face. There was no end to it, but after ten years you get so you don't care anymore. Or think you don't.' All the energy seemed to have left him. He passed a hand over his face. 'I'd been getting sloppy. Taking payments from other gangs, making promises I couldn't keep. And the DPS were already on my back. I knew it was only a matter of time before they put together a case against me, and then I'd be fucked. As long as I was useful I was fairly safe. Even the bastards pulling my strings would think twice about killing an active police officer. But one who'd been disgraced, who they thought might start *talking*, that was a different thing. I couldn't run and leave Marie and Dylan. I was getting desperate, and then, to cap it off, the sister showed up.'

'She had a name,' Jonah said. 'She was called Nadine.'

Gavin gave him a sour look. 'She was a *threat*. I thought the Armenians had killed Eliana because they'd found out she was an informer. But they didn't know about me and her. If they'd had any idea I'd been her fucking *handler* I'd have wound up with my throat cut, cop or not. If her sister knew about us, the last thing I needed was her mouthing off.'

'How did she find you?'

'She didn't.' A spasm seemed to cross Gavin's face. 'I found her.'

He'd learned that a missing persons report had been filed for Eliana Salim. Fortunately, he'd found out early, before it had raised any red flags. Salim's murder was an old case, left to gather dust beneath years of official embarrassment. There was nothing to say that the woman reported missing now was the same person whose dismembered body had been found years before. But Gavin had his own reasons for heading off any awkward questions. So he'd pulled the report to see who'd made it.

It was a Kenyan post-grad student called Daniel Kimani.

'The name didn't mean anything to me, so I went to talk to him,' Gavin said, slumped back in the seat. 'He lived in a shared house in Notting Hill. Typical student. Told me he'd filed the report on behalf of a friend but wouldn't say who. I was wondering how hard to lean on him when the door opened and Eliana's sister walked in.

Gavin closed his eyes at the memory. He shook his head.

'Jesus Christ, when I saw her I thought . . . Anyway, she must have known from my face, because she just looks at me and says, "You're him, aren't you?" Turned out Eliana had written to her about this detective she'd met.'

He gave Jonah a crooked smile.

'So that was it. I'd fucked myself. She was in the country illegally, so she'd had to get Kimani to file the report for her. But once I got them talking it was obvious they didn't know anything I needed to worry about. If I'd let it go, they'd never have got any further. Once they knew who I was, though, I had to do something.'

'So you killed them.' Jonah didn't try to keep the disgust from his voice.

'I told you, I needed a way out. And then when I saw Stokes, everything sort of fell into place.'

Fell into place. All those lives, Jonah thought, still pulling at the tie.

'What about the other man you murdered? Who was he?'

An oddly furtive expression crossed Gavin's face. 'Just a rough sleeper I found in an alley. Somebody no one would miss. If it was just the two of them it'd be too suspicious. I couldn't have that. It had to look like they were random victims.'

So he'd found one. Jonah had thought nothing else would shock him, but that did. He used it as a goad, clenching his jaw as the nylon tie bit deeper into his flesh. It had snagged in a flap of torn skin on the heel of his hand. If he could get it over that, he might be able to wrench free.

But Gavin was rising to his feet. He seemed calmer now as he went to retrieve the vodka, holding it up to see how much was left in the bottle.

'You know, I've thought about telling you for years,' he said, after taking a drink. 'I wondered how it'd feel to get it off my chest. That's why I let you wake up. I was still in two minds whether to or not, but it was now or never. And you know what? It makes fuck all difference.'

Draining the bottle, he set it down. The cosh hung from his hand as he came over.

'Tell me how to find Eliana.'

'Not until you –'

The cosh struck the meat of his thigh before Jonah could

move. He cried out, trying to kick Gavin's legs out from under him, but it was a futile effort. Easily evading it, Gavin laid into him with the cosh, the solid leather weight smacking into bone and muscle with deadening impacts.

'All *right!*' Jonah yelled. 'Her number's on the phone! The small one!'

Gavin stopped. He looked over to where both phones were lying on the laptop bag. There was an almost hunted look on his face when he turned back to Jonah.

'If this is a trick . . .'

Jonah let his head sag. 'It's not. There's only one number on it.'

He watched as Gavin went to the phone. *Go on, call her.* He couldn't see how Salim could help now, even if she wanted to. But Jonah would take a savage satisfaction from her knowing that Gavin was alive.

She'd be able to work the rest out for herself.

Gavin picked up the phone as though afraid of it. He looked uncertainly over at Jonah.

'How do I know −'

But before he could finish, there was a noise from the far side of the cabin. Looking past Gavin, Jonah felt his heart drop.

Chrissie's daughter stood in the doorway.

Her hair was tousled from sleep and her eyes were large and unfocused. 'Where's Mummy?' she mumbled.

Gavin was staring at the little girl, his face a picture of dismay. Then his shoulders sank.

'Ah, fuck.'

A coldness was spreading through Jonah. 'Gavin, no −'

'Where's *Mummy?*' the little girl repeated, rubbing her eyes.

'It's all right, sweetheart.' Gavin slipped the cosh and Salim's phone into his pockets as he went to her. 'You're just having a bad dream.'

'I want Mummy . . .'

'Shhh, it's OK. Let's get you a glass of milk and put you back to bed.'

'Don't, please!' Jonah said, as Gavin picked her up. The little girl was unresisting, cuddling sleepily into his shoulder. 'You don't have to do this! She won't remember anything.'

'You need to be quiet,' Gavin told him, picking up Jonah's phone as well. 'Don't make it any harder than it has to be.'

'Please! You can still let them go,' Jonah begged. Gavin ignored him, pausing by the sink to collect a container of milk. '*Wait . . .!*'

But Gavin was already carrying the little girl out, pulling the door shut behind them.

Chapter 35

Jonah wrenched at the nylon ties around his wrists and ankles as the sound of footfalls disappeared down the passageway. There was a creak of a door closing, then nothing. Silence, except for the low slap of water against the hull. Gavin would be setting Chrissie's daughter down in one of the other cabins, he guessed. And then what? More doped milk, a lethal dose this time? Suffocate them? Now the little girl had seen his face Gavin wouldn't let either her or her brother go.

Jonah couldn't let that happen.

He forced himself to slow his breathing, taking deep breaths to counter the rising panic. *Come on, don't just lie here!* He wouldn't have long before Gavin came back: he had to get out of the ties before then. He looked around the room for something to cut them. The vodka bottle was on the seat cushion a few feet away, but even if he was able to smash it Gavin would hear. But there must be a knife or scissors in the kitchen units by the sink. Jonah started to push himself across the floor to the far side of the cabin. He tried to use his good leg to propel himself across the carpet, but with his ankles fastened together it was impossible not to bend his bad knee as well. Each flex sent a fresh jolt of pain through the damaged joint, and his progress was agonisingly slow. At this rate Gavin would be back before he reached them. Even if he wasn't, Jonah would still have to lever himself upright to search in the drawers. Gritting his teeth, he continued anyway, pushing himself past the fitted seat with the empty beer cans littering the floor . . .

He stopped as he realised.

Idiot.

Shunting himself around, Jonah groped behind him for the nearest can. It was awkward with his hands tied and slippery with blood, but he managed to pick it up. Gavin had already crushed it almost flat. Gripping it tightly in both hands, Jonah began to twist.

The flimsy aluminium flexed and bent like paper, but stubbornly remained intact. Listening for any sound from the passageway, he twisted harder. *Come on, come on . . .!*

The can ripped.

The jagged edge sliced through Jonah's fingers and the meat of his palm, adding to the blood from his torn wrists. He didn't care: he wanted it to be sharp. It was difficult bending his hands enough to hack at the nylon strip, feeling it pluck like a guitar string. But he managed to keep hold of it, dragging the torn edge backwards and forwards across the tie. *Cut, you bastard! Why can't you just –*

The tie snapped.

As he reached down to cut the tie fastening his ankles, the sound of a door closing came from the passageway.

Shit.

The sharp metal sliced into his fingers as Jonah sawed furiously at the tie. It severed with a more-felt-than-heard *snap*. There was no sign of his crutches and no time to look. He started levering himself upright by the fitted seat, expecting the cabin door to open at any second.

Instead, the hollow sound of running water sounded through the wall.

Gavin had stopped to piss.

After being bound, even Jonah's good leg felt stiff and weak as he stood upright. The boat had a subtle, queasy motion, which further unbalanced him. Leaning on the back of the seat, he looked around for a weapon. There was a heavy glass ashtray nearby on a shelf. Ash and old cigarette stubs cascaded onto the carpet as Jonah grabbed it and half hopped, half lunged for the cabin door. He couldn't put any weight on his bad knee, but it only had to support him for one swing. If he connected it wouldn't matter. If he didn't . . .

Then it wouldn't matter anyway.

He heard movement in the boat's passageway as he reached the door. Flattening himself to the wall behind it, he raised the ashtray.

The sounds stopped outside.

For a second nothing happened. Then Jonah's breath was forced from him as the cabin door smashed into him, pinning him against the wall. As it was wrenched away again, he threw all his weight against it, and was rewarded by an oath from the other side. While Gavin was still off-balance, Jonah yanked the door aside and swung the ashtray. It caught him a glancing blow on the jaw, but that was enough to stagger him. *Yes!* Feeling a fierce exultation, Jonah raised the ashtray as he stepped forward to end it.

And his knee gave way.

He collapsed against the door, dropping the ashtray as Gavin barrelled into him. They fell to the floor, and as Jonah tried to push himself away something heavy crashed onto his head. The room seemed to blur and tilt, and then a second impact took the use from his limbs. He felt weightless and detached, only dimly aware of being flipped over onto his front. He breathed in grit and crumbs from the bristly carpet.

'Nice try, but I heard you moving.' Gavin's voice seemed to come from a long way away. Jonah felt his arms jerked roughly behind him. 'That fucking hurt, though, so I don't think we'll take any more chances.'

Jonah could do nothing as his wrists were fastened again. Then he was rolled over onto his back so he was lying on his arms. From the corner of his vision he saw Gavin walk away and bend to pick something up. There was a soft tearing noise, then he came back.

In his hand was a plastic freezer bag.

A translucent film descended over his vision as the bag slid over his eyes, blurring Gavin and the ceiling above him into a blue-tinged nightmare. It was pulled down over Jonah's nose and mouth, the plastic instantly fogging and inflating as he breathed out.

And then he breathed in, and the blue film sucked tight.

NO! He scrabbled and kicked, fighting for breath. That only drew the plastic tighter over his face. His lungs heaved and burned. He thrashed as he felt the bag being twisted around his neck, sound suddenly developing an underwater, seashell quality as his head was enclosed. From a long way off, he heard the rip of gaffer tape being unwound, then Gavin's indistinct shape bent over him again.

Abruptly, it stopped. Through the misted plastic he saw Gavin turn towards the doorway. Then he felt it as well. The boat dipped at one side, as though pressed down.

'The fuck . . .?'

Letting go of him, Gavin stood up. Ducking his chin, Jonah frantically tried to loosen the bag from around his throat. As he tried to work his mouth free, he heard an exclamation from the passageway.

'Who the fuck are –?'

Gavin's voice was cut off. There was the sound of scuffling outside the cabin, and the boat began to rock as the thump of heavy bodies set up a deep, hollow slosh of water against it. Jonah heard a gasp and a bone-jarring thud.

Then silence.

The slopping of water quietened as the boat's motion slowed. Jonah lay immobile, head cocked to listen. Although the bag had loosened, the plastic amplified his ragged breathing, drowning out other sounds. As it fogged and cleared, he felt rather than heard someone come into the cabin. He could make out a blurred figure through the plastic. There was the impression of a dark coat, darker than the jacket Gavin had been wearing. The newcomer made hardly any noise on the carpet, but Jonah could feel the boat tip and sway under the stranger's weight.

'There are two children in another cabin that need help,' he gasped, his voice raw. 'At least make sure they're all right. Please!'

The floor creaked as the newcomer came to stand over him. Through the misted plastic, Jonah had the impression of size and bulk. A faint sound filtered down, like whispered tapping. He said nothing now, hardly daring to breathe.

Then the figure moved silently away. Jonah strained to listen over his ragged breathing and the pounding of his heart. The newcomer had gone into the passageway, and suddenly Jonah desperately didn't want whoever this was going into the twins' cabin. *There's nothing there for you. Please, just go.*

He didn't hear a cabin door opening, as he had when Gavin had taken the little girl back to bed. Instead, there were indistinct sounds from the passageway. A quiet rustling and a soft thump. The boat began to rock again, less violently this time, and Jonah heard the sound of someone climbing

334

steps. A moment later he felt a waft of cold, damp-smelling air, followed by the muted *click* of a door being closed.

And silence.

He lay there for a second, making sure, then started wriggling his head against the carpet to drag the bag off. He lost hair and gained friction burns, but soon his face emerged into air. Clammy with sweat and condensation from the plastic, he gulped for breath as he rolled over to look through the open doorway.

There was no sign of Gavin.

Jonah's hands were still bound but his ankles were free. Pushing himself across the floor to the wall, he used it to lean against as he struggled to his feet. Intent on finding the twins, he almost didn't notice the small object on the seat cushion.

His phone.

He'd seen Gavin put it in his pocket. Whoever had come on board must have left it there, but Jonah didn't care. The torn can he'd used to cut the ties was still on the floor, shining and bloodstained. His knee throbbed unmercifully, and his head felt like it was splitting as he lurched over to retrieve it. When he picked up the can his hands were shaking so much he could barely hold it. Gripping it as firmly as he could, he hacked blindly at the nylon band.

It seemed to take longer this time, but then his hands were free. They felt dead and unresponsive, his fingers slippery with blood as he grabbed for the phone and called emergency. Switching to speaker phone, he pushed himself to his feet and was already hobbling for the door as it began to ring. Identifying himself as a Metropolitan police officer, he gave as many details as he could as he limped into the passageway. He had to lean against the wall for support, and something in his knee grated with every laborious step. He couldn't give the boat's exact location, only that Gavin had said they were moored about a quarter of a mile from Slaughter Quay.

But the need to find the twins crowded out every other concern. Jonah's hands left a bloody trail on the walls as he continued down the passageway. Part way along, the wood panelling had been damaged. There was an indentation at head-height, the splintered wood glistening wetly as though something had struck it. Hard. Seeing it, Jonah remembered the scuffle he'd heard, and the dull thud that ended it.

He moved on. Jesus, it was hard to stay upright. The boat was larger than he'd thought, with a dogleg in the passageway at the far end. He opened doors as he came to them, pushing them open to reveal storage cupboards, a tiny toilet and an empty cabin. The operator was still speaking, saying something about him going up on deck to check for landmarks.

'What . . .?' he said, struggling to make sense of it.

But it was hard to concentrate on the tinny voice. Hard to focus at all. His head was hurting and the rocking motion of the boat seemed to be getting worse. Then he pushed open another door and forgot about the voice altogether.

The cabin was in darkness. There was a stale smell of unwashed sheets. The curtains were drawn, but the light from the passageway showed two still forms on a bunk inside. Jonah stopped in the doorway, afraid to go in. He realised he was holding his own breath as he listened for sounds of breathing. But the darkened cabin was silent.

The tinny voice was growing insistent, so he put the phone in his pocket to quieten it. Better. Lurching inside, he groped for a light switch. Brightness flooded the cabin, hurting his head and eyes.

Lying on the bunk were Chrissie's young son and daughter.

They looked tiny. Both lay on their backs, unmoving. Their eyes were closed, and in the overhead light their faces were unnaturally still and pale. The empty carton of milk stood on a small cabinet next to two grubby mugs. No, Jonah thought, through the loud buzzing in his head. *No, no, no . . .*

All the pain and loss for Theo seemed to condense and crystallise. *Oh, Jesus, please don't do this, not again . . .* Jonah stumbled over with some vague idea of checking for a pulse. But his hands were so bloodied he didn't like to touch the still forms. He knew there was something he should be doing, something more, but he couldn't –

The little girl grumbled and rolled over onto her side.

Jonah had to support himself on the edge of the bunk. Through blurred eyes he saw a beat in the boy's throat as well, strong and regular. A laugh that was more like a sob escaped him as the abscess of grief was suddenly lanced. He wanted to sink down onto the floor as relief surged through him, but he couldn't do that. Through the pain and buzzing in his head he became aware of a muted voice, small but urgent. At first he couldn't place it, then it came to him.

Oh, yeah, that's right . . . His movements were clumsy and uncoordinated as he took the phone from his pocket. The voice became louder, asking what was happening and urging him to go on deck. With a last look at the sleeping forms, unaware of either the tears running down his face or the grin on it, Jonah turned and began laboriously making his way along the passageway to the steps.

'Give me a minute,' he told the voice.

Chapter 36

The cat had gone, although a few torn scraps of food wrapper remained. There was also a small, well-chewed object that was harder to identify. Some sort of animal head, by the look of it. Probably a rat.

Nice.

Standing on the edge of the quay, Jonah squinted against the winter sunlight that flickered off the water's surface. The barge nudged against the smaller vessels, the weed-draped tyres on its sides making protesting squeals at each rubber contact. Looking at his watch, Jonah saw he still had a half-hour to kill. Turning away from the swaying boats, he limped along the cobbled quayside. The aluminium walking stick was an improvement on the crutches, but he'd be glad to be rid of it. Although the physios wanted him to use it for a few more weeks, he'd already started trying to manage without it. Only for short stints, but he hadn't fallen over yet.

Progress, of sorts.

His knee was still painful, and he'd been warned it wouldn't regain its full strength or mobility. But the last operation had gone better than expected. The cosh had shattered the still-healing bone, sending fragments into the already traumatised soft tissue. There had been no option but to have a replacement kneecap fitted, and while there was still considerable damage to tendons and ligaments, time and exercise would help with those. He might not be running again any time soon – as in ever – and he'd likely always walk with a limp. But he could live with that.

He was learning to live with a lot of things.

A lot had changed in the weeks since the twins' kidnapping. For the first time in his adult life, Jonah was no longer a police officer. He'd woken one morning with the realisation that a stage in his life was over, and he'd submitted his resignation that same day. He'd chosen to commute his pension to a lump sum payment, and together with injury compensation and the insurance he was due, he was in a better position financially than he'd been his entire life.

Now he just had to work out what to do with it.

One of the first things was to find a new place to live. Since the night their ambush had been interrupted by a full-scale police operation, he hadn't had any more problems with the teenage thugs. But Jonah had begun to feel a prickling sense of being watched when he came and left the flats. It could have been paranoia, but he'd grown tired of looking over his shoulder. It was no way to live.

He'd discussed it with Miles before reaching a decision. They'd met at the small meeting hall in Hammersmith, during the last week before its lease ran out. Given her illness, Penny and Miles had decided to end the support group.

'It's sad, but it's fulfilled its purpose,' Miles had said, pouring tea into mugs. 'Nothing lasts forever. We enjoy it while it does and then move on. That's the nature of life.'

The eyes behind the glasses had been shrewd as he handed Jonah a mug. 'You seem better these past weeks.'

'The knee's improving, and I don't get as many headaches.'

'That wasn't what I meant.' The eyes crinkled. 'It's surprising what can make us turn a corner, isn't it?'

Jonah had looked down at his tea. 'I don't . . .'

Miles raised his eyebrows. 'Don't believe you have the right to feel better? Don't want to let Theo down?'

Jonah nodded. Cleared his throat. 'I suppose so.'

'I've never been a believer in hair shirts. And learning to accept isn't the same as ignoring. Or forgetting.' The smile was warm and understanding. 'As long as we're on this earth, we have a duty to go on living. That's why I'm pleased you're moving out of the flat. It's a sign that you're ready for change. You should embrace it.'

'I don't know . . .' Jonah was still undecided. 'It's as good a place as any.'

'That's not good enough.' Miles snapped a biscuit in half. A custard cream, naturally. 'Give me for and against.'

Against were lifts that didn't work, a location that was no longer convenient, noisy neighbours and the chance of being attacked when he stepped outside his front door.

'And for?' Miles prompted.

Try as he might, Jonah couldn't think of anything.

He'd reached the fencing outside the old warehouse. There were signs of life inside. The whole of the building was now covered with scaffolding, encasing it in a giant cage. Intact polythene had replaced the tattered sheets, the plastic billowing in slow motion as it caught the faint breeze. The sight caused a momentary tightening in Jonah's chest, as though something had taken his breath. But it was quickly gone.

A new sign had gone up, showing an architect's optimistic imagining of 'a landmark new project' of retail outlets, bars and restaurants. The development was now being called

Lugger's Quay, but changing the name wouldn't erase what had happened there. The murder enquiry remained open, despite the events on the boat. Or perhaps because of it. Unsurprisingly, Fletcher had been incredulous when he'd heard Jonah's story.

'So now you're saying it was McKinney rather than Owen Stokes. Slaughter Quay, Corinne Daly, the abduction of your ex's twins – McKinney engineered all of it.'

'That's right,' Jonah had told him.

Lying there in the hospital bed, with his knee mangled and his head freshly shaved and stitched, he'd had an uncomfortable sense of déjà vu. The DI mopped at a running eye with a tissue.

'And then, just as he was about to kill you as well, someone came onto the boat, calm as you like. Killed or disabled McKinney, and then magically disappeared along with him. Leaving you, the kids and a hundred grand in ransom money behind. But you don't know why, and you didn't see who it was.'

Jonah agreed once more.

'Are you taking the piss?'

It was hard to say which offended Fletcher the most, the idea that Jonah could have made something like that up or the possibility that it might be true. As the DI had pointed out – loudly, and at length – this was the second time Gavin's body had disappeared, with Jonah as the sole witness.

But even the DI couldn't dispute the evidence. Although there had been no further sign of Gavin, the scene on the boat told a clear story. When Jonah had hauled himself outside onto the deck that night, he'd found they were moored at a concrete jetty outside a strip of unused industrial units. He'd described landmarks to the emergency operator as best he could, but by then they'd already located his mobile phone. Within a few minutes he'd heard the chop of a police helicopter overhead, the bright shaft of its searchlight stabbing down. Soon afterwards there was a marine unit boat moored alongside and police cars swarming the area. The twins had been taken away in an ambulance, still drowsy, but the paramedics had said their vital signs were good. Either Gavin had decided to wait till later before committing an act even he must have baulked at, or he'd had a change of heart.

Jonah hoped it was the latter.

This time there was more evidence of Gavin's presence than the blood he'd left at the warehouse. The indentation in the panelling that Jonah had seen in the passageway was consistent with a skull being rammed into it. Skin and blood from that had yielded Gavin's DNA, which was also found with his fingerprints all over the boat. There was clear evidence that he'd been living on board, navigating the river mainly at night and holed up in out-of-the way moorings.

His fingerprints and DNA were also found in the Transit van that had been used to abduct the twins. That was parked by the jetty, next to Jonah's hired Volvo. Gavin had driven him to the boat in that while Jonah was unconscious, leaving Wilkes's body to be found in his own car at Slaughter Quay.

Even so, without Gavin's body, Fletcher might have argued that there still wasn't enough to support Jonah's story. But a police raid had recovered the laptop that Dylan had sold to his dealer. Its hard drive was intact, and on its search history was the dating website where Gavin had found the lookalike whose body Jonah had seen at the warehouse. The man was a thirty-eight-year-old estate agent called Neill Davison, who had gone missing after telling friends he was going on a date with someone he'd met online. The resemblance to Gavin was superficial – similar age, height and build, both with dark curly hair. But face down in the dark warehouse, covered in Gavin's blood and wearing his clothes, watch and wedding ring, it was enough.

That didn't stop Fletcher from quibbling. 'Doesn't say much for your powers of observation. I thought he was supposed to be a friend of yours?'

'I'm not the one who confirmed his DNA,' Jonah shot back. Call that one a draw.

If there was one aspect of Jonah's story the DI was most suspicious of, it was his claim not to know who had come onto the boat and saved his life. Fletcher had returned to that time and again, worrying at it to try and prise open a chink in Jonah's story.

'So you didn't get a good look at him?'

'I had a plastic bag on my head. I was busy trying not to suffocate.'

'And he didn't say anything? Nothing to indicate who he was or why he was there?'

'No, but Gavin had upset some dangerous people. They must have caught up with him.'

Fletcher studied him as though searching for a lie. 'Then why didn't he take the ransom money? Why leave a hundred grand behind?'

'I don't know. Maybe he didn't realise it was there.'

'So it was just a happy coincidence this individual showed up when he did? Saved your neck and then left, just like that?'

'It must have been. All I can tell you is I didn't invite him,' Jonah said.

Technically, that was true. Jonah didn't *know* the intruder's identity, not for certain. Yet he could remember the way the boat had tipped when it was boarded, the heavy thump from the deck. There had been an impression of size and bulk as the figure had prowled around the cabin, and it would have taken frightening strength to overpower Gavin so quickly. Jonah could recall the feeling he'd had as he lay helpless on the floor, the certainty that his life hung in the balance. And he could remember the soft tapping as the blurred figure stood over him. While he'd been fighting for breath at his feet, the intruder had been calmly sending a text. Jonah could only think of one reason for that.

To ask instructions.

He couldn't say for sure how Eliana Salim's bodyguard had found him, or why he'd chosen that moment to intervene. But it would have been simple enough to install a location tracking app on the phone she'd given him. That had disappeared along with Gavin, but Jonah guessed it wouldn't have been too difficult to set up the phone's microphone to eavesdrop remotely. Salim could have heard everything Gavin said and told her bodyguard when to step in. Just as she'd told him to leave Jonah's phone behind, so he could call for help for the twins. He didn't know if Gavin was already dead when the bodyguard carried him from the boat, but after meeting Salim he didn't think so. She'd want her sister's killer taken alive.

Especially when she discovered who it was.

It still bothered him that he'd withheld any mention of Eliana Salim or her bodyguard. But each time he'd been tempted to tell Fletcher about them, he'd come up against the same objections. He'd no proof, either that Salim was alive or that any of what she'd told him was true. He didn't even know what name she was using. And even if he was believed, Jonah couldn't see what use the information would be.

Balanced against that was the knowledge that he owed his life and those of the twins to her intervention. Betraying her trust would be a shoddy repayment, especially if it put her in danger from whatever faceless people she'd been scared of. Jonah didn't know how or why, but instinctively he knew that telling anyone about Salim would be a bad mistake. So would crossing her.

Just ask Gavin.

Standing outside the warehouse fence, Jonah shivered. The plastic sheets covering the scaffolding billowed and snapped, as though the building underneath were breathing. Below it a section of the façade had been sandblasted, clearing away centuries of grime to reveal pale stone underneath. A literal airbrushing of the past. But it didn't matter how the developers rebranded this place, Jonah thought, turning away. It would always be Slaughter Quay to him.

As he retraced his steps to where the barges were moored, a now-familiar heaviness weighed on him. There were unanswered questions over more than Gavin's fate. The third warehouse victim remained unidentified, and was likely to stay that way. Gavin had said the man had been a rough sleeper, a random victim killed for no other reason than to muddy the waters over Nadine Salim's and Daniel Kimani's murders. A still-young man, probably Eastern European, though even that was uncertain. No one had come forward to claim him, and Gavin's callous dismissal had proved all too accurate. *Somebody no one would miss.*

It was a sad epitaph.

But it was another, unlikely victim who weighed heaviest on Jonah's conscience. Owen Stokes's body still hadn't been found, and Jonah didn't think it ever would be. Gavin had said it was weighted down at the bottom of the river, and there was no reason to doubt that he'd been telling the truth. About that, or the way Stokes had died. No matter that Gavin had orchestrated it, or that Jonah believed he'd been fighting for his own life and that of Nadine Salim, the cold fact remained.

He'd killed an innocent man.

He'd been told there wouldn't be any charges. There was no actual evidence that Owen Stokes was dead, and even if there was, the intent and the crime had been Gavin's, not his. Even Fletcher didn't hold him to account over Stokes's death. But that didn't change what had happened, or how Jonah felt. Duped or not, he'd blood on his hands.

That was something else he'd have to learn to live with.

He was back at the tethered barges. They bobbed sluggishly on the oily water, a flock of squat ugly ducklings with the dirty swan of the larger barge riding behind. Jonah went to sit on a low wall nearby, where he could see its faded name: *The Oracle*.

Picking a piece of crumbling mortar from the wall, he flicked it into the water. The thought of Gavin's betrayal was still raw. That a man he'd trusted, once called his best friend, could have known what had happened to Theo and yet said nothing, remained unfathomable.

The case was being reassessed in the light of the new information, but Jonah didn't hold out much hope. Even if it was reopened, too much time had passed. The CCTV footage from the park that morning, which might have confirmed that the woman with the pram was Ana Donauri, had been wiped years before. Without that, or any other proof, all they had to go on was hearsay. Gavin's word, and how ironic was that?

The Theo-shaped hole that had opened that morning at the park was still as dark and empty as ever. It sat at Jonah's centre, a void that would never be filled. He would tell himself that at least now he was closer to the truth. But then Gavin's words would come back to him and take the pain to a whole new level.

Of course they fucking killed him.

He'd known that there was no chance his son could still be alive, not after all this time. But hearing Gavin so casually confirm it left a wound too deep to heal. And festering in it was still the awful canker of not knowing. Not knowing if Theo had suffered before he'd died, of what had been done to him. Of how scared his tiny scrap of a boy must have been.

Yet regardless of whether or not the case was reopened, for the first time Jonah felt in his heart there was at least the possibility of answers. The people who had actually abducted Theo might be dead themselves, but there were still the ones above them. The faceless power brokers, whose decisions had sealed fates and ended lives. Including his son's. Jonah didn't know how he could find them, but if Eliana Salim had given him Ana Donauri's name, then she must know others. Finding Salim again wouldn't be easy, but it was a place to start.

If nothing else, it gave him a sense of purpose he hadn't felt in a long time. And behind it was something else, something so fragile he was afraid to consider it. Because despite everything Gavin had told him, despite everything logic said, there was still no proof that Theo had been killed. Jonah had spent the last ten years wrongly believing his son had drowned, based on nothing more than a shoe found in a culvert. This time there wasn't even that. Only the assertion that what had happened 'couldn't be undone'. Jonah knew how dangerous self-deception could be, but this didn't feel like denial. It wasn't even hope, just the barest sliver of possibility.

That was enough.

'You Jonah Colley?'

He turned, rising to his feet as a stocky man with barrel legs approached. He wore a grubby plaid lumberjack jacket, unfastened despite the cold. A gold chain glinted around his neck.

'That's me,' Jonah said, retrieving the walking stick.

'You're early.' The man had bushy eyebrows from which longer hairs protruded, like the legs of dead spiders. He eyed Jonah's walking stick doubtfully. 'You going to be OK getting on board?'

347

'I'll manage.'

'Up to you.' He took a bunch of keys from his jacket pocket, attached to a cork float. 'So, you a fan of tjalks?'

'Of what?'

He gave Jonah an odd look. 'Tjalks. That's what this is, a Dutch sailing barge. Don't you even know what you're buying?'

'I might not be buying it yet.'

After what had happened on Gavin's cabin cruiser, Jonah knew it was perverse for him to be even considering it. But the idea had been at the back of his mind since before then, and he hadn't been able to shake it. It was time for a fresh start, and no matter what associations this place might hold for him, from the moment Jonah had set eyes on the old barge he'd been drawn to it.

It just felt . . . right.

'It needs a lot of work, I'll warn you,' the man told him. 'My brother was in a nursing home for the last two years, and wasn't in any state to look after it much before then.'

'That's OK.'

'You know you won't be able to keep it moored here?' the man said, looking around the quayside. 'They're clearing out the whole place. Redeveloping the entire thing. Not before time, if you ask me.'

'I wouldn't want to stay here anyway,' Jonah told him.

'Don't blame you. Wait there.'

Surprisingly nimble, the man climbed over the handrail of the smaller barge moored alongside the pontoon. Waddling to its stern, he swung his legs one at a time over onto the larger deck of the tjalk. Bending out of sight, he lifted a battered gangplank and slid it over the water until the other end rested on the quayside.

'So if you're not an enthusiast, how come you're interested in a pile of junk like this?' the man asked, making sure the gangplank was secure.

Jonah paused before stepping onto it. From where he stood, a car tyre used as a fender obscured part of the name painted on the boat's bow. Only the first four letters of *The Oracle* were visible, just as they'd been the first time he saw it.

Theo.

'I liked the look of it,' he said, crossing over the water.

Acknowledgements

When I was starting out as a writer, I laboriously wrote everything on an old-fashioned typewriter, promising myself I would buy a computer once I was published. 'If you buy one now you might get published sooner,' was my Mom's comment. Annoyingly, she was right. She and my late Dad were an unfailing a source of encouragement, never losing faith even when the prospect of my becoming a writer seemed an unrealistic fantasy. She died in August 2021, so neither of them got to see *The Lost* in print. But, even though it's my twelfth novel, I know how pleased they'd be.

I was helped in its writing by people who generously gave up their time to answer questions. Thanks to Tony Cook, Head of Operations at the National Crime Agency's CEOP, whose *Senior Investigating Officer's Handbook* as ever provided a valuable resource; Mark Williams, Chief Executive Officer of the Police Firearms Officers Association; and the Press Bureau of the Metropolitan Police Service. Any errors are mine, not theirs.

Thanks also to my agents Gordon Wise and Sarah Harvey at Curtis Brown, editors Sam Eades and Rachel Neely and the team for welcoming Jonah Colley and myself to Orion; Ulrike Beck, Friederike Ney and all at my German publishing house Rowohlt; and to Ben Steiner and SCF for reading and commenting on the manuscript.

As ever, the biggest thank you goes to my wife Hilary for her support, ideas and patience, and for sharing the highs and lows.

Simon Beckett, April 2021

Credits

Orion Fiction would like to thank everyone at Orion who worked on the publication of *The Lost*.

Agent
Gordon Wise

Editor
Sam Eades
Rachel Neely

Copy editor
Marian Reid

Proofreader
Jenny Page

Editorial Management
Rosie Pearce
Charlie Panayiotou
Jane Hughes
Claire Boyle

Audio
Paul Stark

Contracts
Anne Goddard
Jake Alderson

Design
Joanna Ridley
Nick May
Clare Sivell
Helen Ewing

Finance
Jasdip Nandra
Rabale Mustafa
Elizabeth Beaumont
Sue Baker
Tom Costello

Marketing
Folayemi Adebayo

Production
Claire Keep
Fiona McIntosh

Publicity
Alex Layt

Sales
Jennifer Wilson
Victoria Laws
Esther Waters
Frances Doyle
Ben Goddard
Georgina Cutler
Jack Hallam
Ellie Kyrke-Smith
Inês Figuiera
Barbara Ronan
Andrew Hally
Dominic Smith
Deborah Deyong
Lauren Buck
Maggy Park

Linda McGregor
Sinead White
Jemimah James
Rachel Jones
Jack Dennison
Nigel Andrews
Ian Williamson
Julia Benson
Declan Kyle
Robert Mackenzie
Imogen Clarke
Megan Smith
Charlotte Clay
Rebecca Cobbold

Operations
Jo Jacobs
Sharon Willis

Rights
Susan Howe
Krystyna Kujawinska
Jessica Purdue
Louise Henderson

About the Author

Simon Beckett is the no.1 internationally bestselling author of the David Hunter series. His books have been translated into twenty-nine languages, appeared in the *Sunday Times* Top 10 bestseller lists and sold over 10 million copies worldwide. A former freelance journalist, he has written for *The Times, Daily Telegraph, Independent on Sunday* and *Observer*.

Simon was co-winner of the European Crime Fiction Star Award 2018/19 (also known as the 'Ripper'), the largest European crime prize. He has also won the Raymond Chandler Society's 'Marlowe' Award and been shortlisted for the CWA Gold Dagger, CWA Dagger in the Library and Theakston's Crime Novel of the Year.

The Lost is the first in Simon's new Jonah Colley series, and his twelfth novel.

Help us make the next generation of readers

We – both author and publisher – hope you enjoyed this book. We believe that you can become a reader at any time in your life, but we'd love your help to give the next generation a head start.

Did you know that 9 per cent of children don't have a book of their own in their home, rising to 13 per cent in disadvantaged families*? We'd like to try to change that by asking you to consider the role you could play in helping to build readers of the future.

We'd love you to think of sharing, borrowing, reading, buying or talking about a book with a child in your life and spreading the love of reading. We want to make sure the next generation continue to have access to books, wherever they come from.

And if you would like to consider donating to charities that help fund literacy projects, find out more at **www.literacytrust.org.uk** and **www.booktrust.org.uk**.

THANK YOU

*As reported by the National Literacy Trust